Chris —
Thank you very much for your help in spreading the message of this book.

BROKEN

A STORY OF REDEMPTION

Endorsements

Jane Daly has a flair for creating compelling stories around tough topics, and you'll find yourself rooting for several characters in her latest novel, *Broken*. Janice, a widow, finds herself in a multi-layered challenge where her patience, compassion, and faith are stretched to the limits. As we peer over the shoulders of Janice, Jinxi, and Dean, we see how brokenness doesn't come in one package, but God is always for us, working in events around us, drawing us to himself. With its snappy dialogue and descriptions, this book will keep you riveted from beginning to end.
—**Jan Kern**, author of *Scars That Wound, Scars That Heal: A Journey Out of Self Injury*, and cofounder of Voice of Courage

Broken is simultaneously gut-wrenching and hopeful. From the first chapter, I found myself rooting for the ever-likable Jinxi, cheering her on in one scene and then whispering "no, Jinxi, don't do it" in the next. As the plot unfolds, author Jane Daly guides the reader through an authentic look at the ebbs and flows present in a person's faith journey. In addition, she tells an entertaining story, injecting enough love, compassion, and humor to keep the reader hopeful and entertained. Most importantly, the book addresses two critical questions—"Who is my neighbor?" and "What is the cost of a person's soul?" *Broken*'s answers to these questions has me wondering about my own life. Do I possess the faith and grace shown by the characters surrounding Jinxi? As an introspective reader, I love a good look in the mirror.
—**Steven Rogers**, author of *Into the Room*

What makes a life valuable? What makes a person worthy? Who deserves kindness, care, and sympathy? *Broken* explores these issues in an emotion-packed contemporary novel exploring real problems in today's broken world.

Officer Dean Rafferty was raised with all the privileges a middle-class kid could enjoy and is now working his dream job. Not that life is perfect. After his father's accidental death, Dean steps in to help care for his mother but can no longer share her faith in the God who had let him down.

Janice Rafferty has been drifting since her husband died. Despite being financially stable, having a close circle of friends, and knowing that her son is nearby in his apartment over the garage, every day, Janice prays that God will give her life meaning.

Jinxi Lansing has never experienced a loving home or a peaceful existence. As a result, she colors every human interaction with suspicion. After being charged with solicitation, Jinxi spends a rough night in jail. The following day isn't much better when, as she's leaving the courthouse, a cop bumps into her, almost knocking her over. Then out of the blue, he asks her to breakfast. And that's when the lives of three people begin to change.

Broken is a novel worth reading.

—**Marbeth Skwarczynski**, author of *The Rose Collection*

Enter the forbidden and misunderstood world of a cutter. Jinxi's strong voice and realistic choices foster clarity and compassion for this underrepresented population. An engaging story of imperfect choices and the marvelous, redeeming grace of our Lord toward every broken vessel.

—**Sharon Hughson**, author of *Reflections: A Pondering Heart*

For readers who enjoy fiction with layers of turns and trouble, *Broken* will not disappoint. If you're looking for a great read full of biblical truth carefully braided into the plot, *Broken* is for you. Fans of a love story with just enough tension to be a page-turner because the "need to know" part of the brain won't rest? Well, *Broken* is your go-to.

What about the avid booklover who is always searching for the next favorite mix of all of the above? *Broken*.

Best of all, Jane Daly has painted a word picture for us that beautifully depicts the forever truth of God's redemptive love.

—**Shelley Pierce**, author of *Sweet Moments* and *The Crumberry Chronicles*

BROKEN

A STORY OF REDEMPTION

JANE DALY

Cover and Interior Design:

Editor(s): Mary W. Johnson, Cristel Phelps, Deb Haggerty

Author Represented By: Credo Communications LLC

PUBLISHED BY: Elk Lake Publishing, Inc., 35 Dogwood Drive, Plymouth, MA 02360, 2022

Library Cataloging Data

Names: Daly, Jane (Jane Daly)

Broken / Jane Daly

406 p. 23cm × 15cm (9in × 6 in.)

ISBN-13: 978-1-64949-613-3 (paperback) | 978-1-64949-614-0 (trade paperback) | 978-1-64949-615-7 (e-book)

Key Words: Redemption, Self-mutilation, Cutting, Police Drama, Adoption, Unplanned Pregnancy, Mother-Daughter Relationships

Library of Congress Control Number: 2022941472 Fiction

DEDICATION

For Mike
Don't ever stop making me laugh every day.

ACKNOWLEDGMENTS

I first pitched the idea for this book at a writer's conference. The workshop leader that year told me my idea was "boring" and it had "been done before." Needless to say, I was crushed. Ten years later, I can now say "I told you so" to my good friend, James L. Rubart. You were right, James L. That first novel *was* boring. But you helped make it better.

My original critique group helped me work through all the ghastly mistakes a newbie writer makes. Mary Allen, Lori Sinclair, and Michelle Jenae—you ladies are my besties in the writing world. Now you get to read the entire book.

Ten (or is it twelve?) years ago, my hubby became my champion. He won't let me quit writing. And as any writer knows, wanting to quit happens monthly. Sometimes weekly. Mike, I still only want to play with my sister.

Elk Lake Publishing, you are my family! Thanks to my cover designer, Derinda Babcock. I love your artistry. Mary Johnson, I'm amazed by your eye for detail without changing my voice. Thank you for all your hard work on this manuscript. Last but not least, Deb H. Your leadership is unparalleled.

Dear reader, if you've made it this far in reading these acknowledgements, a huge THANK YOU for spreading the word about my books. You can connect with me on my website www.JaneSdaly.com and of course, on practically all social media.

Watch for *Broken Silence*, the sequel to *Broken*. We will answer the burning question, "Will Jinxi and Dean ever get together?"

And just to get you started, Chapter One of *Broken Silence* is included at the back of this book. Enjoy!

CHAPTER 1

Worst. Night. Ever. She stank like the inside of a porta potty—human misery baked to perfection in ninety-degree heat. Spending a night in jail will do that.

Jinxi Lansing shoved open the door to the Sacramento City Courthouse and squinted in the August morning. She gingerly crossed the concrete porch, careful of the stiletto-grabbing cracks in the pavement. No wonder they were called ankle-breakers.

She heaved a deep sigh as a group of women in heavy makeup crowded through the door. Everyone wanted outta there. Including her.

A couple of the women bumped her off balance.

"Geez, am I invisible?" Jinxi muttered with a curse. She tugged the hot-pink mini skirt to cover what needed to be covered, at least in broad daylight.

Plan A. She'd collect her backpack from the bus station locker, change out of these ridiculous clothes, and grab a shower at the YWCA.

Plan B. If the Y was full, she'd—

Bam!

A cop with his head down, texting, nearly bowled her over. Stupid jerk.

"My bad. Didn't see you." He held out a hand as she lost her balance and regained it.

He looked her up and down, but not in a creepy way. Weird, considering how she was dressed.

"What're you looking at?" Jinxi demanded, hand on her hip.

"Sorry."

She flicked her fingers at him. "Move along. Nothing to see here." Maybe he wouldn't bust her for telling a cop to get lost.

When he didn't move, she gave him a full dose of the stink eye. What the—why was he still staring? He didn't look creepy. More like some guy on a TV cop show. Dark buzzed hair, the shadow of a beard—all clean-cut and American. His cop stare still creeped her out.

He spoke at last. "You hungry?"

"Why do you care?" He was trying to trap her like the cop last night.

"I'm heading up the street to grab some breakfast. You look like you could use something to eat after ... you know." He waved an arm in the general direction of the jail.

Jinxi narrowed her eyes. "And you get what, exactly, for buying me breakfast?" Had to be a catch. There always was.

The cop shrugged. "Nothing. Hey, it's no biggie to me. Eat or don't eat. Your choice." He turned toward I Street and started walking.

Jinxi's stomach growled. Dang, she *was* hungry. Maybe it wouldn't hurt to let him buy breakfast. If this *was* another setup, at least she'd have food in her.

"Hey, wait up." Jinxi tripped, struggling to catch up. Stupid shoes. Why had she ever listened to Shana? An easy way to make money, she'd said. Yeah, right. Hard to tell who was lamer— Shana or Jinxi for believing her. At least the cop had the decency to slow down until she reached him.

"How far is it?" she huffed.

"Couple of blocks."

"Hold up. Let me take these off." Jinxi slipped off the shoes, wincing.

They walked the two blocks in silence. Jinxi's bare feet slammed onto the hot concrete as she scrambled to keep up with his longer strides. At the diner's entrance, she shoved her aching toes back into the shoes.

Delicious aromas wafted out. Coffee. Bacon. Her stomach took that moment to growl again. Loud.

The cop grinned at her. "See? I knew you looked hungry."

He held the door to let her enter first before heading toward a booth in the back. He took the bench on the side facing the front. Jinxi hesitated. Could this be another in a string of bad decisions? With a sigh, she tossed her purse on the cracked plastic-covered bench. As soon as she was seated, the waitress dropped two mugs on the table and sloshed coffee into each.

"Mornin', Dean. Who's your friend?" She motioned to Jinxi with the pot.

Before Jinxi could protest that they weren't friends, the cop answered, "Well, Mindy, I'm about to find out." He smiled at the older woman. Mindy chuckled as she strolled to the next booth.

So his name was Dean. Figured. It suited him. All muscular and jock-like. Not much older than her. But seriously, what kind of a guy was a regular at a dump diner like this?

"If I'm going to buy your breakfast, I guess I should know your name."

Jinxi watched him ruin his coffee by adding two creamers and three sugars. Disgusting. She looked up to find him staring at her.

"Huh?"

"Name." He pointed his spoon at himself. "Dean." At her. "You?"

"Oh, uh, Jinxi." She picked at the black nail polish on her thumb.

Wait for it, wait for it.

"Is that a nickname?"

Bam. This guy was right on point. "Yup."

She took a swig of pure, unadulterated coffee, waiting for the caffeine to kick in. She'd need it if this guy was a talker.

"What's your real name?"

Yeah, he was a talker. She grimaced as she said her full name. Did she *look* like a Jeanette? Hard no. "Jeanette Xaviera Lansing."

"I'm Dean Rafferty. Nice to meet you."

She shifted on the bench. Her skirt stuck to the Naugahyde, trapping her legs in a pink sheath.

"Could it get any hotter?" asked the waitress as she sidled up to their table. She had a pencil tucked behind her ear, apparently forgotten as she dug around in her apron pocket, order pad in one hand.

"Makes me glad I work nights," the cop answered.

Jinxi grimaced. Yeah, she tried to work nights, too. That didn't always go so well.

"What'll it be today?" All business, once the missing pencil was located.

Jinxi scanned the one-page laminated menu, searching for the plate with the most food.

"Ladies first," the cop said.

"I'll have the Big Breakfast."

"Same for me," the cop said.

"Bacon or sausage."

"Bacon," they answered in unison.

"Pancakes or French toast."

"Pancakes." Again, they answered at the same time.

"All righty, I'll be back to warm up your coffees."

Not soon enough. Jinxi took another swig from the thick mug as Dean stared at the thin scars crisscrossing her arms.

Color darkened his face.

"What's the matter? Never seen a cutter before?"

He rubbed the back of his neck with one hand. "Uh, yeah."

Jinxi put her hands in her lap. "Lucky you. Now you got to see it up close and personal." She should never have agreed to breakfast. Her thoughts turned to the knife in her backpack, and to how long it would be until she could get out of here, locate the bus station, and find release.

At least he'd stopped talking for, like, ten seconds.

"I was watching this cool video on YouTube the other day," he said, "about how these guys train their dogs."

What the ... where did that train of thought come from? This guy was too much.

"They put a dog biscuit on the dog's nose. The dogs are trained to stay still until the owner says, 'go,' or something. The dogs throw the treat up off their nose and grab it in midair."

Despite herself, she answered, "Sounds mean, making the dogs wait. Like animal abuse."

"Hmm. I never thought of it that way. I guess if someone told me to put a Twinkie on my nose and not eat it until they said to, I'd have a hard time with that."

"A Twinkie, no. That wouldn't do it for me. But a Taco Bell Burrito Supreme, yeah, that'd be tough."

Go figure. She was having a conversation with a cop.

Dean laughed. "Oh, yeah. Definitely couldn't wait for a Burrito Supreme."

"Looks like you've known lots of Burrito Supremes." Oh, great. Did she tell this cop he looked fat? That *had* to be against the law.

Jinxi looked up to see his face as red as if he'd been sissy slapped. He was blushing.

"It's the Kevlar vest," he said. "It adds twenty pounds."

Wow. The cop was embarrassed about his weight. Priceless. Jinxi took a sip of coffee to keep from grinning.

The cop mowed through his breakfast as if he hadn't eaten in a week. His masculinity filled the small booth, suffocating her. The guy was massive, intimidating. Appetite gone, she shoved her plate away.

After he'd sopped up every bit of syrup and eaten every piece of egg, he drained his coffee cup. He leaned back and rubbed his stomach.

"You done?" He indicated her half-eaten breakfast with a wave of his hand. Before she could answer, he reached across the table and grabbed a piece of bacon off her plate.

Yup, done now.

Jinxi followed him to the register while he paid. Outside the diner, the sky had turned a dirty gray while they'd been inside.

Dean sniffed. "Smells like a fire somewhere."

A fire. Jinxi's hand flew to her mouth. Images of a house in flames threatened to make her hurl. She needed to get away. Ripping off the shoes, she strode back the way they'd come.

"Thanks for breakfast," she called over her shoulder. But the cop was right behind her. She startled, dropping her shoes. "Dude. Are you trying to give me a heart attack? What do you want?"

"Do you need a ride somewhere?"

So that's what this was all about. *Here's where the guy gets you into his car and expects payment for breakfast.* She clicked the lip stud back and forth against her teeth and shrugged. Might as well get it over with. If she said no, he'd probably find a way to arrest her. Ten minutes. She could put up with anything for ten minutes. Maybe he'd drop her at the bus station after.

"Sure. Whatever. Drop me at Greyhound."

"All right. My truck is parked at the police station." He turned and started back toward the jail as she doubled-stepped alongside.

Dean's truck's cab was as clean as a new penny and smelled like the furniture polish they used at the Girls' Ranch. Yuck.

Dean swung around to the driver's side. Jumping in, he shoved the key into the ignition and pulled out of the parking spot with a jerk. They bounced over the curb and into the street as he gunned the accelerator.

"Geez, what's the rush?" Was he that desperate? Jinxi gripped the armrest, wondering where he would take her. "Mind if I smoke?" A cigarette would calm her jangling nerves.

"As a matter of fact, I do."

Figured. Jinxi pulled down the sun visor and flipped open the mirror. And gasped. "Why didn't you tell me I had black stuff smeared around my eyes?" The streaks of mascara created a macabre mask.

Dean shrugged. "I thought it was all part of the, you know, Goth thing."

Jinxi muttered a curse. "You got a tissue or anything in here?" She pulled open the glove box and found some crumpled fast-food napkins. She licked one to moisten it and went to work on the mess.

Satisfied she'd gotten the worst of it, she finger-combed her hair.

"That your natural color?" Dean asked.

Are you always this nosy?

"Nope." He didn't need to know she dyed her hair black to cover up the white-blonde mane she'd been cursed with, making her look even younger than her twenty-one years.

Maybe if she faced the passenger window, he'd shut up. They turned onto a residential street in the downtown area. Seemed every other house was under construction. Prominent Victorians with wraparound porches and square pillars were sandwiched between smaller homes, vying for position. She pictured families eating breakfast together, children getting ready for school, cozy and happy. A foreign country. A secret language with no translation.

"What are you thinking about?"

Geez, this guy was relentless. Jinxi glared at him. "I was thinking you could give me fifty bucks for a hotel room."

"What?" His head rotated between her and the windshield. Twice.

"Fifty bucks. Hotel room. Isn't that where we're going? So you can get paid back for breakfast? You get a little something extra, and I get something extra." The words rolled out from a dark place. A place where everything had its price, and nobody expected something for nothing.

Dean maneuvered the truck around a slow-moving cab.

"All right. I see how it is. How 'bout I offer you something better than fifty bucks and a hotel room?"

This situation was getting weirder by the minute. Maybe the cop *was* a perv. Jinxi reached into her backpack and wrapped her hand around the cold canister of pepper spray. The cop was going down. He just didn't know it yet.

CHAPTER 2

After a brutal night shift at the jail, Dean's goal was to have a hearty breakfast, inhale some coffee, and, after a long shower, fall into bed. Why had he let a pair of blue eyes pull him into extending a breakfast invitation? Never mind those eyes had shot daggers at him. She was a hot mess, all right, and now he was taking her to his mother's house. He'd always had a soft spot for strays. But seriously, taking this girl to his mom's. What was he thinking? His hero complex always came back to bite him in the backside.

"We're going *where?*" The daggers had come back and were pointed in his direction.

Dean turned his gaze back to the road. "To my mom's. She'll let you get cleaned up, catch some z's." Maybe. Unless Mom killed him. Jinxi wasn't some high school friend kicked out of the house for smoking.

Jinxi shook her head. "Right. How do I know your mom will be cool? I mean, what are you going to say?" She put her hands on her hips and mimicked an air-head college coed. "'Hey Mom, like, look who I brought home. This person got busted last night and wondered if you might, you know, let her use the bathroom and crash for a while.' Do you *really* think she's going to go for that?"

He didn't know. Mom never protested when he brought home one of his friends who needed a temporary place to stay—couch surfers, friends who fought with the parents, typical high school stuff. This situation was a bit different. No, this was a *lot* different. Maybe some of that Jesus stuff his mom always talked about would come in handy now. Like how God spoke to prostitutes and sinners. The stuff he used to believe in.

"Huh?" He'd spaced out for a moment.

"I said, what if your mom kicks me to the curb?" She pulled the lip stud against her teeth, clicking it back and forth.

Dean spoke through clenched teeth. "She won't." He hoped. "Anyway, you should be thinking about your arraignment." Good job changing the subject.

"Arraignment?"

"Yeah. The courts have been moving these Clean Sweep arrests through the system pretty fast. You're probably scheduled for Tuesday."

Jinxi dug through her backpack and pulled out a stack of papers. "It's probably in that paperwork."

Dean slowed and coasted to a stop at a red light. His stomach tightened. Only a few more blocks to his mom's house. And his. All his friends teased him about living with his mom. Though technically, he had his own place above the detached garage.

"Still living with Mommy?" they'd ask.

If they knew he wanted to keep an eye on his mom, they'd probably give him even more grief. Since his dad's death, Mom was a sucker for anyone coming to the door selling something. Plus, their neighborhood had declined in the past few years. But that wasn't information he'd share with Jinxi. Best drop her at Mom's and let her deal with it.

Jinxi swore and threw the papers on the dash. "How'm I supposed to figure all this stuff out?"

Oh, yeah. Drop her and run in the other direction.

A train barred their way, so Dean punched the button for the radio. J. Cole's voice boomed from the speakers. Jinxi winced.

"What, you don't like hip-hop?"

He glanced over to find Jinxi staring at him with a look of disgust.

"You're kidding, right?" she asked. "You actually listen to this stuff?"

Dean's face and neck grew warm. He should've taken off the Kevlar vest. That's what was making him sweat. That and the ninety-degree heat outside. It had nothing to do with the pretty little Goth girl staring at him as if he was some bug to be smashed. Although in her case, she might pin the bug to her earlobe or something.

Dean jabbed the search button. "Let's find something more to your taste. What is it, grunge? Heavy metal? Dystopian, maybe." The stations rotated through. "I know," he said, snapping his fingers. "Español." Her body language spoke volumes. She was royally ticked off. Good. The search ended at a country station. Her shoulders relaxed a bit.

"I never would have pegged you for a country music fan."

Her head swiveled to face him. "H-how ..."

Dean held up two fingers to his eyes and then turned them toward her. "I see everything."

Jinxi scowled and pressed her lips together. Dean laughed. She was cute, despite the streaked mascara and dyed black hair.

He braked on the street in front of his mother's house.

"Here, give me those." Dean held out his hand for the messy stack of papers she'd gotten from the jail. Her black nail polish stood in stark contrast to the paleness of her fingers as she grabbed the sheets and shoved them toward him.

"These are about community service," he commented, scanning two pages of information.

"Community service?"

"Yeah, you know, in lieu of jail time."

She snorted. "Nice to have a choice."

Dean ignored her and read through the last few paragraphs. "Here," he leaned over and pointed to a date in bold print. "Says your court date is Tuesday, August 14 at 1:00."

"Peachy."

"Your sarcasm underwhelms me."

Jinxi rolled her eyes. "Whatever." She rested her elbow on the windowsill, rubbing her hand across her cheek.

"Don't miss your court date," Dean warned. "Otherwise, they'll put out a warrant for your arrest."

"Things keep getting better and better."

Dean resisted the urge to make another comment and returned to the papers. "You have a choice of community service options. Let's see, working with homeless kids. Probably not a good choice for you. I think they have rules about eating children."

"You are so freaking funny."

"Here's a good one. Cleaning bathrooms at McKinley Park. Bet that would be fun."

Jinxi stuck her finger in her mouth and made a gagging sound.

"Last one. Serving meals at the food bank. Can't go wrong there. I'm sure they'll keep any sharp objects out of your reach."

Without waiting for her response, he swung the driver-side door open. "We're here. This is my mom's house."

Jinxi opened her door. "Better get this little family reunion over with."

Dean walked around the back of his truck, pausing to close the door after Jinxi slid out. In her bare feet, she barely reached his shoulder. He glanced at his mom's house, wondering what Jinxi saw. Did she notice the concrete steps with the peeling paint? Or the expansive wraparound porch? Why should it matter? Maybe her attention was distracted by the lace curtain falling back into place as they ascended the steps.

He pulled open the screen, holding it with one hand while turning the knob on the front door with the other.

Pushing the door open, he let Jinxi go in first. He bumped into her when she halted over the threshold. She turned, but instead of shooting daggers, this time, her eyes were filled with fear. Interesting.

"Hey, Mom. How ya doin'?" Dean stepped around Jinxi to give his mother a peck on the cheek. He caught a whiff of her usual citrus scent. Mom's skirt covered her legs past her knees, unlike Jinxi's, whose constant tugging barely left hers G-rated.

"Hello, Son."

"Mom, I'd like you to meet Jinxi. Jinxi, this is my mom, Janice."

Jinxi mumbled something, but he couldn't hear it. He hoped it wasn't a swear word.

"Nice to meet you, Jinxi. What an unusual name. But pretty."

Mom looked toward him. Dean could practically see the question mark on her face.

"Uh, Mom, Jinxi needs a place to, you know, get cleaned up. Maybe take a nap." He hated the way his voice sounded. As if he was in seventh grade, asking if he could spend the night at a friend's house on a school night. "She's kind of between places right now."

His mom fingered the cross around her neck as an ancient grandfather clock chimed the half-hour. "I'd love to have you stay. Welcome to my home."

Dean let out a breath. Maybe his mom really was serious about all that talk about loving people. Something about showing hospitality to strangers, in case they were angels. Fat chance Jinxi was an angel, though. More likely from the other place.

"Great," he said, clapping his hands together. "I'll go home now. It's been a long night, and I'm whipped." Dean hesitated. "Are you sure you'll be okay?" Was he addressing Mom or Jinxi?

Mom answered, keeping him from figuring it out. "We're fine. Go ahead and get some sleep."

"If you're sure. I'm across the yard if you need me." A subtle reminder for Jinxi that she'd better not try anything.

Dean turned and strode toward the door. Before crossing the threshold, he looked back, making eye contact with Jinxi. She was back to shooting daggers. Good. Easier to make a run for it.

CHAPTER 3

How dare he leave her? Dumped off like a stray cat. With his *mom*. How was she supposed to make nice with a taller version of Betty White? And this house—had an antique store thrown up in it? Lace was everywhere, from the window coverings to the white things on the tables to the backs of the sofas and chairs.

Jinxi brought her gaze around to find the woman staring. She resisted the urge to tug her skirt down. She needed to take a shower and bounce. Like, now.

"So, Dean said you wanted to get cleaned up." Betty White rubbed her hands together.

She's probably never been this close to someone like me.

"Yeah. If that's okay." Jinxi narrowed her eyes and searched the woman's face. Was she going to change her mind?

"Of course. Come this way." The woman led her toward the dining room and opened a door to reveal a set of stairs. To the left of the door, Jinxi could see into the kitchen. Not a dish or a pan sat on the Formica counters. Only a wooden knife rack.

Betty indicated the stairs with an outstretched arm. "Go on up. The bathroom is to the right at the top of the stairs. There should be clean towels in there. If not, the linen closet is in the hall. The bedroom is on the right, next to the bathroom, if you want to take a nap."

"Uh, thanks." Jinxi slung her backpack over her shoulder and started up the narrow wooden stairs. At the landing, she looked back to find Betty White watching her with a smile. Creepy.

"I forgot to tell you," the woman said. "It's hot up there, so turn on the portable air conditioner."

"Okay."

Jinxi clomped down the hall toward the bedroom at one end. A puffy pink bedspread covered the double-sized bed. The picture above the bed was of an angel watching over a sleeping child. The caption said, "Now I lay me down to sleep …."

Give me a freakin' break. She definitely wasn't in Bakersfield anymore.

Jinxi quietly slid open every drawer in the dresser and the nightstands. All empty. The closet held a few wire hangers and books on the shelf above the rod. Dolls sat haphazardly next to the books. She closed the closet door and headed into the bathroom.

Now, standing in a stranger's bathroom, the panic she'd felt downstairs pressed against her chest. Heart pounding, the shame of the past twelve hours burned inside. Jinxi scrambled through her backpack until her fingers closed on a pouch.

The knife slid out like it knew what to do. Jinxi clicked it open and shut, remembering how the cop had stared at the scars on her arms. She ran her fingers over the marks which covered her from wrist to shoulder. With one swift movement, she shoved the knife into her backpack before she could change her mind.

In her bedroom, Janice picked up the phone and dialed a number from memory.

"Emma. It's me," Janice said in a low voice.

"Jan, dear. What a pleasant surprise. I was praying for you." Emma's voice rustled like old parchment.

Janice sank onto the bed. "Good. I need prayer. You'll never believe what happened today." She began with recounting her own quiet time that morning. "I was feeling so useless. You know what I mean? Like Halloween decorations at Christmas. Not ten minutes after I asked God to use me, Dean showed up at the house with a young woman in tow." Janice glanced toward her bedroom door and lowered her voice. "She's not any normal girl, Emma."

"Go on," her friend urged.

"She has ... tattoos, and this rod stuck in her bottom lip. She kept clicking it against her teeth until I thought I'd lose my mind."

Emma laughed. "Why did Dean bring her to your house? Certainly not to make you lose your mind."

"He wanted to let her shower and take a nap here." Janice kept her voice low, even though she could hear water running from the upstairs shower.

"What's wrong with that, honey? Remember how your boy used to bring home all the neighborhood strays?"

"Yes, but this one is dressed like a—you know, one of *those* women." Janice didn't voice the question niggling at her mind. Why was Dean hanging around that kind of girl in the first place?

"Jan, dear, sounds like God answered your prayer, but in a way you didn't expect."

"Certainly not!" Janice exclaimed and immediately regretted it. Lowering her voice, she repeated, "Certainly not."

"I'll spend some time in prayer about your situation, and it sounds as if you should, too."

"You're right. I'll pray about it," Janice promised. *Later*, she added to herself. "I should go now. I'll talk to you soon." She disconnected and looked toward the ceiling.

Why today, when she was committed to the after-school Bible group with the third graders? Could she leave that girl alone here?

Her fingers hovered over the numbers on the phone. Should she call Dean and ask him what he was thinking? Jinxi—and what a strange name *that* was. She was nothing like the friends Dean had brought home before. She and Tom had always been willing to help out when it was convenient. Housing traveling missionaries, providing meals for friends who were ill, driving someone to a doctor's appointment, all situations involving regular people.

People like Tom and me.

This girl with the pierced lip and eyebrow, black eye makeup, and tattoos was far beyond anything she'd done before. How could this be God's will?

Nothing like a hot shower to feel human again. Jinxi returned to her backpack on the bed and pulled out a T-shirt. She hadn't intended to nap here. But now she was clean, the bed called to her.

Turning to the bedroom door, she intended to flip the lock. But there was none. Pulling the stud against her front teeth, she glanced around the room. The dresser looked solid and too heavy to move, but the nightstand slid easily in front of the door. It would have to do.

The sheets were cool against her bare legs. She slid down and eyed the door. If the cop wanted to, he'd be able to shove open the door. *Dang.* She reached for her backpack and pulled out the pepper spray. With her arms wrapped around her gear and the pepper spray firmly in her hand, she fell into a restless sleep.

Two hours later, her stomach grumbled. Rubbing the sleep from her eyes, Jinxi sat up and looked around. The nightstand was unmoved, the door still shut. She padded to the window and looked down. The red car was gone from the driveway. Good. Maybe she could grab some food and some money while Betty White was gone. *If* she was gone.

Jinxi tiptoed to the bottom of the stairs, poised like a deer. Her sense of danger, honed through the years, told her she was alone. Still, her pulse quickened as she turned left into the living room, appraising the room in a glance. To the right of the hall sat a piano covered with framed pictures. A flat-screen television was mounted to the wall above a dark wooden cabinet. The living room opened up to the dining room on her right, bright with afternoon sun. A worn sofa and two end chairs completed the circle. A leather book sat on the seat of one of the chairs. Except for the TV, the house was in a time warp. Nothing here worth stealing. So why the chain-link fence surrounding the property?

Two bedrooms were at the end of the short hall leading from the living room. One was Betty White's bedroom. Yuck. More lace. The other room held a desk with a computer and a long table with photos and colored paper. Scrapbooking stuff was piled on one corner, spilling over onto the floor.

Jinxi ignored the messy room and made her way down a short, dark hall to the kitchen. The worn linoleum and Formica countertops reminded her of her childhood home, where her mom still lived. All that was missing was the pile of dirty dishes in the sink and an overflowing trash can. And the stench of rotting garbage.

Something sat on the small wooden table. Jinxi sidled closer to have a look. A sandwich, wrapped in plastic wrap, sat on a plate. A yellow Post-it read, *Hope you like turkey.*

Jinxi reached toward it. Yanked her hand back. Was the food for her? No way. Who makes food for a total stranger? Peeking into the living room, she double-checked that the red car was gone. After a moment's indecision, she bounded up the stairs to retrieve her cell phone. She returned to the kitchen with her phone in hand, grabbed the sandwich, and headed out the back door. No way she'd eat in the house as if she belonged there.

She sank onto a rocking bench sitting beneath a towering oak tree and pulled the plastic off the plate. The oak tree offered some respite from the relentless heat, like at home, except this backyard bore no resemblance to her mom's house. The lawn was green and slightly overgrown. A child's swing set sat directly across from the bench. The detached garage had wooden stairs leading up to a second story.

What would it have been like to grow up here? Would she have climbed this tree? Played outside? What if she'd had a mom ...

Don't go there.

She pulled herself out of a fantasy back into the stark reality of the present. Best to eat this sandwich and leave.

Powering up the phone, she saw seven missed calls from Skeeter. Even more texts, each one more threatening. A missed call from Savannah. Hitting the call button, she chewed and waited to see if her friend would pick up.

"Jinxi, where in the world are you? You disappeared, girlfriend."

"I'm in Sacramento."

Savannah's voice took on an urgent tone. "Skeeter's asking about you."

Jinxi's stomach tightened.

"Don't tell him where I am, Savvy." What a hot mess if her boyfriend showed up now. The bruises on her upper arm had faded to green. "I thought he got arrested. How'd he get out?"

Savvy laughed. "You know Skeeter. He's greased lightning. Nothing sticks to his behind. What's in Sac-town, anyway?"

Jinxi swallowed the last of the sandwich. "You'll never believe me when I tell you."

She started with the ride from Bakersfield to Sacramento in a long-haul truck, driven by a girl Jinxi swore was on meth. Sleeping in the park, trying to make some money, getting busted, and ending up with a cop and his mom.

"No freakin' way," Savvy exclaimed.

By the time she finished, Jinxi's head pounded, and the sandwich threatened to explode from her stomach. "I gotta go, Sav. Please don't tell Skeeter where I am, K?"

As she disconnected, Jinxi heard a door close. The cop appeared, bounding down the outside wooden stairs of the garage, striding toward her. Why had she thought he was fat? He looked smaller without his uniform, but muscles bulged in his T-shirt. Her head throbbed as she watched him getting closer.

Perfect. A killer headache, a psycho boyfriend, and a cop. Could this day get any worse?

CHAPTER 4

Dean awakened slowly, stretched, and turned on his side. Three hours of sleep wasn't enough. Maybe he should try to catch a few more z's before his next graveyard shift. His mind drifted to what he might encounter that night at the jail.

Dang. Dean remembered he'd left that girl—scratch that—woman at his mom's. With a sick feeling, he shot up and rolled off the futon. He strode toward the window overlooking the backyard while pulling a T-shirt over his head. Jinxi was sitting under the big oak tree in his mom's rocker, talking on a cell phone. Probably plotting to rob them blind. His mom's Prius was gone. How could Mom leave her alone in the house? Those third graders could get along without his mom's Bible stuff for one afternoon.

Dean took two steps into the apartment kitchen and pulled a Gatorade from the refrigerator. He guzzled half of it before putting it back into the fridge. Without bothering to put shoes on, he opened the door and headed down the worn wooden stairs.

Striding across the yard, he rehearsed what he'd say. Was "Time for you to leave" too blunt? He mentally kicked himself for that morning's events. No more breakfasts for scared-looking women. Even if they did have unusual dark blue eyes. And a snarky wit.

Jinxi looked up from her cell phone as he approached.

"What?" she demanded as he plowed to a stop.

"You still here?"

"Yes, Captain Obvious. Still here. Leaving now."

Jinxi swayed as she stood. Her T-shirt rose above the waistband of her shorts as she grabbed for the arm of the swing. Dean's gaze locked on a mosaic of scars on her stomach.

Jinxi's face turned gray shading to green. She looked ready to hurl.

"Hey, you okay?" Still reeling from what he'd seen, Dean reached out to steady her. She flinched away.

"Yeah. Fine. Need some water."

Dean watched as she weaved her way toward his mom's back door. Was she on drugs? Or drunk? He followed as Jinxi climbed the concrete steps leading up to the house. Once inside, he grabbed a bottle of water from the fridge and handed it to her. After drinking half of it, she rolled the bottle across her forehead. With her fair skin, no doubt the heat had affected her.

"It's pretty hot out there," he commented. No sarcastic response. Dean watched her stumble toward the door. He'd stick around until she left, just in case.

Once again, his impulsiveness had caused a significant inconvenience for his mom and him.

His cell rang. He dug the phone out of the pocket of his shorts and checked the display. It was his best friend.

"Li'l D," he exclaimed.

"Big D," came the usual response.

Dean pictured his smaller buddy Damaris pacing back and forth in his apartment. "What's up?"

"I'm heading over to Folsom Lake with the jet skis. You down for that? I can be at your house in ten."

Dean listened for sounds of Jinxi moving around upstairs. "Uh, probably not. I've got something I gotta take care of at my mom's."

"You sure? Folsom's calling your name, bro."

He rubbed his hand across the back of his neck. Jumping into the refreshing waters of the lake sounded awesome.

"My mom has this, uh, person staying at her house, and my mom's not here. I kinda need to stay here till she leaves."

Damaris laughed. "What, some eighty-year-old's gonna steal your mom's silver?"

"Something like that." Dean hated the heat rising up his neck. Damaris knew what buttons to push. "She's kind of—"

"Hot?" His buddy laughed at his own joke. "You should come. Friends of Sommer will be there, too. You know, girls. Women. Persons of the opposite sex."

That didn't matter. None of Sommer's friends would want to go out with him. With his plain face, he was destined to be a lifelong bachelor.

"Look, I gotta go," Dean said with a sigh as he disconnected. Jet skiing sounded a lot more fun than staying at his mom's until Jinxi left.

Dean spied his mom pulling into the driveway and went to open the door. Mom swept in from the carport, bringing with her a gust of hot air.

"Hi, Son. Didn't expect to see you here." She hung her purse over the back of a dining room chair and laid her keys on the table.

Dean kept his voice low.

"Mom, she's still here," he said, pointing toward the ceiling.

Janice's hand flew to her chest. "Oh, my. I thought she'd be gone by now." She walked past him into the kitchen. "I shouldn't have left her here alone. But my children rely on me for their Bible reading circle."

Dean followed. "You're right. You should have let me know you were leaving. I could have slept on the couch." He rubbed the back of his neck with a sigh. "I'm staying here till she leaves." He pulled a package of Oreos from the pantry. His mom reached into the refrigerator for the milk and poured both of them a glass.

"Don't eat all those," she warned. "You'll get a stomachache."

"Yeah, if I was five." Mom never let him forget that one time.

They sat at the small kitchen table, dunking their cookies in the milk.

"I'm sorry, Mom," Dean said, his mouth full. "I should never have brought her here. I didn't think before I opened my mouth." He took a sip of milk. "Not the first time, huh?"

His mom reached across the table, laying her hand on his arm. "And most likely not the last. You have your father's soft heart."

Dean winced. This wasn't the time to be reminded of his dad. Mom needed him to be strong. "I'll get rid of her. I promise."

Her face wrinkled into a frown. "I feel sorry for her. Mercy, can you imagine not having any place to stay?"

Now it was Dean's turn to frown. "You're not thinking—"

"Heavens, no."

"Good." Dean slapped his hands on his thighs and stood. "Time I took care of our problem."

Jinxi set the bottle of water on the nightstand. Chills wracked her body as she turned off the air conditioner. Her teeth chattered as she dug through her backpack for a sweatshirt, buried at the bottom. Did Betty White poison her sandwich? Would she find herself in a bathtub full of ice, missing a kidney? Maybe if she lay down for a minute, she'd feel better. Just until the nausea passed.

Dean sprinted up the stairs, bare feet soundless on the worn steps. At the top, he looked left toward his and his brother's old bedroom. Nostalgia hit him, reminding him of the times he and Brian played together. Back when they were close.

No sound came from his sister's old bedroom. Was Jinxi waiting for him, knife poised to stab him in the neck? Adrenaline surged as he crept toward the open door. He spied her on the bed, unmoving.

"Hey, wake up," he called, stepping into the room.

Jinxi raised her hand, mumbled something, and waved him away.

She was drunk. Or high. Dean grabbed her shoulder, surprised by the heat radiating off her. And the bones he felt even through the thick sweatshirt. He brushed her black spiky locks away and laid a hand on her forehead.

Dean turned and hustled down the stairs to where his mom waited at the bottom.

"What's wrong?" she asked.

"I think she's sick or something."

"Goodness. What should we do?"

"Nothing for now. Jinxi isn't going anywhere in her condition."

"Should I take her some water and an aspirin?"

"Couldn't hurt." Dean wasn't sure how much to share. If she was strung out, the aspirin wouldn't do much good. On the other hand, if she was drunk, both would help.

Mom hurried into the kitchen. Dean hadn't detected the smell of alcohol when he touched Jinxi's forehead. If she'd passed out from drinking, the odor would be coming out her pores. Plus he hadn't seen any evidence of bottles or cans. He wracked his brain to remember which drugs put a person to sleep. *And* caused a fever. Coming up empty, he concluded she might really be sick. *Dang.*

Now he'd have to leave her at his mom's, at least for a day or two. This wasn't good. What madness had prompted him to start this disastrous chain of events? Like a boulder rolling down a hill, gathering speed, his spontaneous offer had turned into something scary. As soon as Jinxi awakened, he'd talk his mom into shaking her loose. Mom was in no position to have Jinxi living here. No matter how sorry he felt for her.

CHAPTER 5

The phone rang as Janice glanced through the morning paper. There'd been no movement from upstairs. Yet.

"Good morning, Jan, dear."

"Oh, Emma, so good to hear your voice."

"I was reading the Bible this morning, and I believe I have something for you from the Lord."

Janice's heart quickened. More often than not, Janice needed Emma's spiritual maturity based on their twenty-year age difference. Janice hoped it was the same verse that had flitted through her mind all morning. Something about keeping oneself unspotted from the world. That young woman sleeping upstairs certainly represented the world. As soon as Jinxi was well ....

Emma's voice cut into her musings. "Are you familiar with the passage in Luke 10?"

Janice's head drooped.

"The Good Samaritan."

"Yes, that's the story."

Janice didn't want to think about being any kind of Samaritan, good or otherwise. She wanted her nice, uncomplicated life.

Or did she?

Her eldest, Brian, rarely called. He and his wife Courtney usually arrived late and left early at the monthly family pizza night. Her daughter, Robin, only called when she needed a babysitter for Hannah for her prenatal doctor's appointments. Then there was Dean. With his late-night work schedule, he only had time for a quick hello as he checked on her on his way to work.

With Tom gone, what was left to give her life meaning? Sure, the after-school Bible Club kids loved her. And the weekly ladies' coffee and prayer group was a welcome distraction from the monotony. There was enough money from Tom's life insurance and the accident settlement to keep her provided for, so why this unsettled feeling in her spirit?

It must be the young woman upstairs in Robin's old bedroom.

"Jan, are you listening?" Emma's voice was sharp with reproof.

"Of course. The Good Samaritan." Her stomach knotted with what she knew was coming.

"Jesus asks the question of his disciples, 'Who is my neighbor?' I believe the Lord has something for you that pertains to that girl."

"Jinxi." Janice couldn't help the stiffness in her response. "What are you saying? That I should ... let her stay here?" Her voice rose at the audacity of Emma's suggestion.

Emma sighed into the phone. "I'm sorry you're upset. Take some time to listen to God before your chance to obey him passes you by."

Janice disconnected with a feeling of heaviness as she shuffled to her favorite chair in the living room. She sank into the well-worn fabric. The leather-covered Bible settled easily into her hands, comfortable as an old friend. Turning to Luke 10, she reread Jesus's story. She stood and paced the room, lips moving in silent prayer.

Why would you ask this of me, God? She's not the sort of person I've ever had in my home. Even the Good Samaritan didn't take the person to his house. He paid for a room. Couldn't I do that instead?

Janice's feet took her to the bedroom, where she dug around in her sock drawer until she found what she was looking for. This time, touching the cash hidden inside didn't give the usual comfort.

I have so much to lose, God. I don't want to do this. What if this girl steals from me?

The world would say, 'everything happens for a reason.' Janice knew there were no coincidences, no surprises in God's economy. But what could she offer to Jinxi? Even more, what did she herself have to lose? Everything they had built over the years. The paid-off house, retirement and savings, and enough money to live comfortably. Three kids, two of them happily married. A niggle of doubt pushed its way in. Could she offer it all up?

Tom should be here to help her figure out what to do. Letting a stranger stay for a night or two was one thing. Asking her to stay longer was far out of her comfort zone. Anyway, why would she do that? Janice was sure the girl was as anxious to leave as Janice was to see her go.

The grandfather clock in the hall chimed three-quarters of an hour before she finished her prayer. By the time thuds from upstairs indicated Jinxi was moving around, Janice had made her decision.

Jinxi's head throbbed like she'd stabbed herself in the temple. She'd awakened from a nightmare of being back at the Girls' Ranch, which didn't resemble a ranch in any way. Built to punish girls who'd broken the law, the sand-colored concrete walls blended into the surrounding desert. In her dream, she'd been in the infirmary courtyard, outside in the hot sun.

Where was she now?

Bright sunlight and heat pressed against the glass, searching for an opportunity to invade the room. Lace curtains brought her back to the present. This was Betty White's house, mother of that jail cop.

The light over the bathroom vanity revealed dark circles under her sunken eyes. Death warmed over. Coffee would rid her mouth of sludge.

After a long, hot shower, she headed toward the stairs. Pausing at the top, she listened. All was quiet. Maybe she was alone in the house again. An excellent opportunity to search for some money before she packed up. Didn't all old people hide cash somewhere?

When she reached the bottom of the stairs, Jinxi startled at the sound of Betty White's voice from the living room.

"Good morning. You must be feeling better."

"Yeah."

Snap.

Now she'd have to leave without a chance to case the old lady's house.

"Are you hungry?" the woman asked.

What was her name again?

"Um, yeah."

Betty White was already heading into the kitchen, speaking over her shoulder. "I'm glad you're feeling better. You had the flu or something. You've been down over a day."

"Can I have some coffee?" Jinxi gestured toward the pot.

"Of course. Cups are in the cupboard overhead."

Jinxi hesitated before moving toward the cupboard. Watching warily from the corner of her eye, she stood on tiptoes and pulled down a mug, filling it to the top. She almost groaned with pleasure from the first sip.

Her gaze fell on some envelopes lying on the small table. She sauntered over, stealthy, looking for some clue to this woman's name. She couldn't keep calling her Betty White. Ah, a cable bill addressed to Janice Rafferty.

Janice whirled around. "Oh, I thought you'd disappeared. You're so quiet."

"No, I, um, I wanted to sit down. I'm kinda tired." Did Janice see her eyeing the bills on the table?

"Of course you are. Sit, drink your coffee, and let me make you some eggs and toast." Janice flitted around the kitchen, pushing bread down in the toaster, pulling things from the refrigerator. "How do you like your eggs?"

Really. This woman was going to cook breakfast for her. Unreal. No one had ever cooked her breakfast, except in a restaurant. When she was growing up, her first meal of the day was either cold cereal or nothing at all, depending on Mom's state of sobriety. With Skeeter, they never woke up before noon. Breakfast didn't exist.

The smell of toast tickled her nose. She could get used to this. Maybe a change of plans was in order.

Plan A. Stay here and let someone take care of her.

Yeah, right. Like that's going to happen.

Betty—or rather, Janice—probably thought she couldn't in good conscience kick her out on an empty stomach.

Plan B. Fake being sick again to stay a little longer until she could figure things out. If Skeeter found out where she was, she could kiss any kind of new life goodbye. He'd show up here in a hot minute, and—

"Is scrambled okay?"

"Oh, sure. Fine." Whatever. Who cared as long as she didn't have to fend for herself. She pulled the lip stud back and forth across her teeth. Savannah would only hold out for so long as it worked to her advantage. She'd rat her out to Skeeter, and he'd show up and drag her back to Bakersfield.

If she stayed in Sacramento, there was the little matter of the arraignment. If she left, there'd be a bench warrant out for her. Too many choices, all of them bad. Stay and endure community service, plus find a place to live, or go back and be protected but have to face Skeeter's quick temper. Her head ached with the effort of thinking.

Why did it seem like she was always searching for something that didn't exist? Jinxi was so done with Skeeter,

Savannah, and the rest of the group, along with the nomad life. She'd had a home growing up, such as it was. At least she'd had her own bedroom. Though her mom wouldn't win 'Mother of the Year,' at least Jinxi had a safe place to return to, most of the time. With her mom's new boyfriend, that option was off the table. Besides, it was the first place Skeeter would go to find her. Best to be three hundred miles away.

Jinxi sighed. Where did she belong? Back in Bakersfield, hanging with her friends? Here with strangers and a very masculine cop? He was kinda funny—in a scary kind of way. Nice too.

The smell of scrambled eggs wafted through the kitchen, pulling Jinxi's attention away from her train of thought. Janice plunked a plate down in front of her.

"Here you go." Her cheery voice set Jinxi's nerves on edge. No one should be that ecstatic about cooking for someone else. Janice handed her a fork and a glass of orange juice and sat across the table, a mug of coffee gripped between her hands. Creepy having someone watch her eat. Jinxi shrugged and dug into the food.

"Everything all right?" Janice cleared her throat, jumped up, grabbed the frying pan, and headed to the sink. "Are the eggs cooked okay?"

Geez, like mother, like son. Did these people never stop talking?

"Fine," Jinxi answered, mouth full.

"I was wondering," Janice said as she squirted soap onto a sponge. Words tumbled out as she attacked the egg remnants in the frying pan. "What are your plans when you leave here?

Jinxi froze, hand halfway to her mouth. "Huh?"

Janice's gaze darted around the room, looking everywhere but at Jinxi. "Dean mentioned, and I hope he didn't betray a confidence, that you might have come into some hard times lately."

Jinxi was still back at 'betray a confidence.' Who talked like that?

Stabbing pain behind Jinxi's left eye traveled across the top of her head.

"Could I go lay down?" Jinxi whispered. She stood, gripping the table for support before wobbling out of the kitchen toward the stairs.

Behind her, Janice's voice sounded as if it drifted to her through a tunnel. "Think about it, all right?"

Think about *what*?

CHAPTER 6

Jinxi lay on the bed, legs crossed, looking at her phone. More texts from Skeeter, each one more threatening than the last.

SKEETER: If u think u can leave me ur wrong. I will find you

Mouth dry, she sent a quick text to Savannah.

JINXI: Can u talk

A moment later, the phone buzzed as Savvy's face filled the screen.

"Oh my gosh, Jinxi, Skeeter's so mad. You better come back."

Jinxi's stomach tightened. "I don't think I can."

"Can't? Or won't?"

"You didn't tell him where I am, did you?" Jinxi held a breath until her friend answered.

"No way. But he's pressuring me. What should I say?"

Jinxi's hand started to sweat, and she nearly dropped the phone.

"Remember I said I was at some lady's house. I got sick for a couple of days, and I'm still here. I kinda want to stay." Saying the words made her realize she'd finally found someplace safe.

"What the *what*? With the mom of that cop? Are you gonna? Stay, that is?"

"I don't know. Maybe. Probably not. Too weird."

"For sure." Savvy lowered her voice. "Look, I gotta go. Everyone is heading out for some food."

"Okay. Talk later."

Where were they going? To one of their favorite hangouts, or someplace new? She missed being part of a group, dysfunctional as it was. It was almost like having a family. Someone to watch her back. What she didn't miss was the petty fighting and jockeying for position in the loose hierarchy of the group.

Skeeter usually made the decisions—where they'd move when things got hot, who got picked for the next drug delivery, who made the next beer run. Her boyfriend didn't allow anyone to challenge his authority. She'd worn enough bruises to prove it.

What did she need to do to stay here? And for how long?

Maybe as long as it took to get some money from the old lady and either start over somewhere, or take the cash down to Bakersfield as a bribe to get back into Skeeter's good graces.

What about the cop? He seemed nice enough, but that was probably a front. Cops weren't nice. Their sole joy in life was to toss you into the back of a patrol car with your hands firmly fastened in plastic zip ties or handcuffs.

Something in one of the many books she'd read while at the Girls' Ranch came to mind. *Better the devil you know than the devil you don't.*

Or was it better? Or was *he* better?

If only there was someone to help figure out what to do. Savannah's friendship couldn't be relied on, especially if betraying Jinxi gave Savannah an advantage.

The sound of a car door slamming brought Jinxi to the window. The red Prius backed out of the driveway and headed away from the house.

Great time to search for some cash.

Heart pounding, Jinxi crept down the hall to Betty White's bedroom. Nothing hidden under the mattress. The top drawer to the dresser held a mishmash of scarves and more crocheted doilies. Socks and underwear filled the second drawer. One pair of socks bulged with something hard.

Score.

Jinxi's pulse quickened as she unrolled the socks, pulling out a wad of money. Adrenaline raced through her like a series of electric shocks. Over four hundred dollars. Not much compared to the rolls of cash she and her group carried. How much could she safely take? A car roared by the house, music thumping. Jinxi jumped, fumbled the money, dropped some bills on the floor. She picked up a couple of twenties and shoved the rest back.

Janice drove away from the coffee meeting with her friends, intending to go straight home. She startled when a car behind her honked as she'd sat too long at a green light. Flustered, she took several wrong turns, ending up in an unfamiliar neighborhood before pulling over in front of a weather-beaten house.

Tears filled her eyes as the warnings from her friends rolled through her head.

"How could your son bring some ragamuffin into your home? Isn't their motto 'To Serve and Protect'? How is that protecting you, his own mother?"

"You're asking for trouble."

"You don't know who this person is or what she's done."

"Elder abuse."

Janice shook her head to clear the voices. She needed to get home and figure things out.

Today was the first time she'd gotten confused while driving. Probably due to the stress of the past few days. With a shaking hand, she put her home address in the Prius's GPS.

A few minutes later, Janice pulled into the driveway and jerked to a stop. Sweaty hands gripped the steering wheel. Her old house still looked the same, unaffected by the strange girl she'd invited in, unaffected by her current storm of emotions. Meeting with her friends was supposed to make her feel better. Now she was more confused than ever.

As the car warmed in the afternoon heat, a pang of longing shocked her with its intensity. She hadn't missed Tom this much in months. If he were here, everything would be better. Tom would know how to handle this situation. He'd protect her. He always had.

"I don't want my life disrupted," she said aloud. Tears filled her eyes and threatened to spill over as she faced the truth—she was afraid to go into her own house. The minutes lengthened.

The insistent ring of the car's cell connection jarred her from her downward spiral.

"My goodness," she muttered, punching the button on the screen to answer. "Hello."

"I hope I caught you at a good time."

"Oh, Emma, your voice is what I need to hear."

"I thought you might need some cheering up. I would have called earlier, but there was a bit of a ruckus at the nursing home, and I couldn't get into my room right away."

Janice pulled at the neck of her blouse, using it to fan her damp skin. "I'm sitting outside the house in my car," she admitted. "I'm frightened." She choked on a sob.

"I'm glad I called. Remember, God hasn't given us a spirit of fear. But of love, power, and a sound mind."

"I know that in my head, but I'm—"

"Let's pray," Emma interrupted. Janice knew that voice. When Dean took that tone, it meant no arguing.

"Amen," Janice said when Emma finished. "Thank you, friend. I'll keep you posted."

Taking a deep breath, Janice climbed out of the car and shuffled to the side door. Inside the house, cool air freshened Janice's spirits.

You can do this.

She spied Jinxi, standing on the bottom step of the stairs, dressed in jeans and a T-shirt, a bulging backpack by her side.

"Hello," Janice greeted her. "You look better." The word "better" was a stretch. Dark eyeliner and black lipstick accentuated the girl's pallor.

"Yeah, I think I'm okay." Jinxi stood, staggering as she threw the pack over one shoulder. "Thanks for letting me stay."

"Wait." Janice held out a hand, stopping Jinxi's forward momentum. "This morning, when we were in the kitchen ..." Janice rubbed her hands together. How could she put this?

Jinxi let the backpack drop with a thud onto the floor, keeping one hand on the stair rail.

Janice exhaled. "What I'm trying to say is, you can stay here. For a few days. Or weeks. Or however long you want. But only a while. So you can get back on your feet." She was helpless to stop babbling.

God, help me out here.

Jinxi raised her mouth in a ghost of a smile.

"Okay." She picked up the backpack, turned, and headed up the stairs.

Flummoxed by the response, Janice froze for several seconds before marching down the hall to her bedroom. After closing the door firmly, she collapsed on the bed.

Really, God?

This was what God wanted her to do. Where was the thanks, the gratitude? Why hadn't she asked any questions? "What are your house rules? Can I help with housework or cooking?" Janice took a mental step back.

Perhaps it was too much to ask of a person like Jinxi. What had she suffered in her young life to present such a hard shell? Janice's mothering heart soften. How could she ignore God's leading and send this young woman back out onto the streets?

Janice stopped as another thought hit her. What would Dean say? He would throw a fit when he found out. The bigger question was, *what had she gotten herself into?*

CHAPTER 7

Dean had been spat on, vomited on, punched, cursed, and kicked during his shift at the jail. Just another day at work. Head down, he shuffled toward the office to clock out.

"Hey, Dean." His friend Patrice greeted him with a weary smile. "Still saving the world, one perp at a time?"

He shrugged and grinned, indicating the smears on his uniform pants. "I had a hurler tonight."

Patrice laughed out loud. "I hate when that happens. Say, we missed you at the lake the other day."

"Yeah, I had, you know, stuff to do for my mom."

Patrice nodded and snapped her fingers. "Hey, did you hear?"

"You mean there's new gossip? What a surprise."

"This is better than gossip. Sac PD got a grant. They'll be putting a few more uniforms out on the streets." Patrice glanced at him with a smile as she adjusted her belt. "Maybe you'll get that patrol gig you've been wanting."

Dean grinned. Way cool. How many cops would be moved to patrol? He did a quick mental inventory of guys who were at his same level. Maybe it was his turn to move from rookie jail monitor to actual police work.

Dean jumped when his sergeant barked, "Hey, Romeo. When you're done flirting, I'd like a word with you."

"Huh?" Dean whirled around, aware of the snickers from the other cops in the room. "I mean, yes, Sarge."

Sarge's bulky frame nearly filled the doorway to his office. "My office," he demanded.

Dean's stomach clenched. Hope he wasn't getting chewed out for something.

He stood in front of his sergeant's desk, like a kid in the principal's office. Sarge's chocolate-brown face wore a perpetual frown. The joke behind his back was he probably hadn't even smiled when his kids were born.

Sarge removed his reading glasses and gave Dean a hard stare. "I've been watching you, Rafferty," he growled.

Dean gulped and nodded.

Sarge continued, "I see the way you handle yourself. You keep a cool head. That's important when you're out on patrol."

Dean swallowed, his throat dry as dust. "Yes, sir. Thank you, sir."

"That's what you want, isn't it? To be on patrol?" Sarge scowled.

Was this a trick question?

"A simple yes or no will suffice."

"Yes. That's what I want, sir."

Sarge nodded. "Good." He replaced his glasses, picked up some papers, and began to read. Dismissed, Dean turned and double-stepped out of the office.

The closer he got to the parking lot and his truck, the lighter his steps. The sergeant's words buzzed in his head; the compliment repeated and repeated. *Patrol, here I come.* He hopped in the truck, exhaustion forgotten.

It wasn't until he pulled up at his apartment and glanced at his mother's house that he remembered. He'd worked overtime the past two days and hadn't had a chance to check on his mom. Maybe the problem would be solved, and Jinxi would be gone.

He found himself surprised at being disappointed at the thought. Was it her quick wit that intrigued him? He'd like to get to know her better. Of course, there was the little situation of her arrest. He winced. He couldn't afford to let anything interfere with his chance to finally be on patrol.

Nope. He'd have to talk some sense into his mom before something bad went down.

Jinxi dropped her backpack and sat on the edge of the bed. Exhaustion pulled her into a prone position. She'd decided to stay. What a relief to stay somewhere, even if for a few weeks. How many times had she and Skeeter moved in the past two years? More than a dozen. Maybe even more than two dozen. Always staying one step ahead of the cops, landlords, and rival drug dealers. A dangerous lifestyle, but what else could she expect? Women like her couldn't have a typical home and family like the one she'd landed in. Maybe after a few weeks Skeeter would move on.

If only.

In the meantime, something to eat would help satisfy the monster growling in her stomach. Jinxi headed down the short hall to the stairs leading down. Her foot froze on the top step, recognizing the cop's explosion of words.

"You did *what*?"

Janice shushed him. "She's right upstairs. Lower your voice."

"I don't care if she's in this room. Have you lost your mind?"

"Don't be insulting."

Jinxi sat on the second stair, easing herself down a few steps, to better hear the blowup. She was used to this kind of drama.

"Mom, you can't ask a total stranger into your home."

"If my memory serves me correctly, *you're* the one who asked a total stranger into *my* home."

Jinxi smiled to herself. Go Betty White.

"That was different. I said she needed a shower and a rest, not a permanent housing situation. Good grief, Mom. How am I supposed to keep an eye on you *and* her?"

"I wasn't aware I needed an eye kept on me."

There was silence for a few moments. Had they suspected she was listening? Jinxi scooted to the top of the stairs. *Shoot.* If only she could see what was going on.

"Mom, please, give this some more consideration." The cop's voice was begging. "You haven't been yourself lately. Besides, have you seen her arms? She's a cutter."

"I have to be obedient to God."

Jinxi jumped at the smack of what sounded like a hand hitting a counter. "Seriously, Mom. *God* told you to do this?"

"I know you don't understand—"

"You're right. I don't. Why would God tell you to ask her to live with you?"

Ouch. That was hurtful. Jinxi winced, remembering the forty dollars she'd stuffed in the bottom of her backpack. The cop was right. She wasn't somebody anyone should want in their house. Jinxi braced herself for the rejection she knew was coming. The cop would convince his mom to say 'buh-bye.'

Jinxi scooted back up the stairs and tiptoed to the bedroom. It was all she could do not to grimace every time the room's pinkness assaulted her. If this were her room ...

No sense going down that path. Jinxi sat cross-legged on the bed, stomach in knots.

Plan A. Get Betty on her side before the cop got to her. Shouldn't be too hard.

Dean was finally gone, headed home to sleep. Janice sighed her relief and walked into the living room to sink onto her favorite chair. She'd heard of self-mutilation. What drove a young woman to cut herself? Janice could only imagine the emotional pain that would cause a person to do such a thing.

What if Tom were still alive—what would he do? Would Tom show this girl the door and tell her to have a nice life? Would he drive her to the bus station and buy her a ticket somewhere else?

What kind of monster had she let into her home? How would she protect herself? The girl needed to go—*now.* Janice's hands shook as she opened her Bible to find some comfort. She frantically thumbed through the pages until she landed on a highlighted verse. Matthew 25:40: *And the King will answer and say to them, "Truly I say to you, to the extent that you did it to one of these brothers of Mine, even the least of them, you did it to Me."*

Janice rested her chin in her hands and exhaled. "I don't want to do this," she said aloud. The words bounced off the ceiling.

I'm frightened.

What if the girl was violent and attacked Janice in her sleep? She must have a knife, if she was able to cut herself. Or if she broke things or even set fire to the house, would Dean be able to get there fast enough to save her?

Janice's mind spun as she got up and headed into her office and booted up the computer to do a Google search on self-injury. Thousands of sites popped up. Janice chose one written by a Doctor of Psychology, fighting down nausea as she read. The photos sent a shiver down her back.

She finished reading the article and sat back, releasing a breath. Cutting was an indication a person, usually a girl, didn't feel she deserved to be loved, the article said. Or the cutter wasn't capable of expressing or feeling emotion because of deep psychological hurts. Cutting became a punishment or a release. It was possible to be cured with counseling and showing the person she was worthy of love.

Was this what God was asking her to do?

Was she capable of that kind of love?

No. But I AM.

Janice covered her face with her hands and grieved for the broken young woman who now resided—if only temporarily—in her daughter's childhood bedroom.

CHAPTER 8

Jinxi sat on the edge of the bed, backpack clutched to her chest, stalling the long walk downstairs and out the door to the courthouse. She should never have let the cop talk her into riding with him to the arraignment. She could manage on her own. He'd been at his most persuasive last night, making it sound as if going downtown from where they lived was like crossing the Donner Summit in the dead of winter. He would probably ditch her once they got downtown, despite what Betty White said.

She slid off the bed and scrambled through her backpack, searching through clothes, a few faded photographs, a stuffed bunny with an eye missing, a child's heart-shaped necklace. The sum total of her existence. Everything else had either been lost, stolen, or left behind.

Her fingers found the knife. She brought it out, testing its heaviness in her palm before opening the blade.

The first cut brought release. The second was punishment for getting herself into such a hot mess. Tears pooled in the corners of her eyes, but she refused to let them fall. She dropped the knife into the backpack and pulled her sleeve down to absorb the blood.

Gritting her teeth, Jinxi stood, slinging the heavy pack over one bony shoulder. She clomped down the stairs and turned the corner to the living room. Betty White and the cop swung their heads toward her at the same time. Had they been talking about her? Probably. Minus the uniform, the cop didn't look as menacing today. Nor as big. Even sort of cute, in a Captain America kind of way. His nose sat slightly off-kilter, like he'd had it broken more than once. Clean-shaven cheeks showed the pitted evidence of past teenage acne. He wore a pair of dark slacks and a golf shirt with a logo she didn't recognize.

Dean swept his gaze from her black-lined eyes to the heavy Doc Marten boots. "Could you have maybe toned down the costume today? You are going to court, after all."

Costume. Really? Dean was dressed like some preppy wannabe. "As if I didn't know."

Dean exhaled. "Fine. Let's go." He gave his mom a quick peck on the cheek before they left out the back door and across the yard.

As they got into the truck, Dean asked, "Do you have your ID with you?"

"Duh."

"Good. You'll need it. Also, they'll check your backpack at the door to the courthouse. Anything in there I should know about?"

"You mean, like a gun?" As if she would be that stupid.

"Exactly."

"Yeah. I'll be sure to leave it in your truck." She stared straight ahead, concentrating on keeping the hornets in her stomach at bay.

Dean punched the button for the radio, skipping through the stations until landing on a country station. Dang, he actually remembered what kind of music she liked.

He pulled the truck into the public lot across the street at the courthouse, got out, and, without saying a word, entered the building through the main door. Jinxi followed, hurrying to keep up. Two police officers inside the entrance took turns searching the bags of those entering. One of them greeted Dean while the other went through Jinxi's pack, taking particular interest in her pepper spray and knife.

Sweat tickled her armpits as he examined them. When he finished, he put everything back in the pack except for those two items.

"You can pick these up on the way out," the officer said and motioned for them to pass through the metal detector. Jinxi's face burned as she bit back a curse. She should have left them in Dean's truck.

The cacophony of noise inside the courtroom assaulted Jinxi's senses. The bailiff called names in groups of five while the judge spoke to one of the court reporters. Public defenders whispered conversations to their clients seated in the holding area. The unmistakable smell of fear burned her nostrils and caused her stomach to churn. Juvy court was nothing like this.

Jinxi clicked her lip stud against her teeth and fiddled with the hoops in her ears. She could do this. The court thing would be over in a few minutes. She crossed one leg over the other and let her foot bounce up and down in a silent cadence. As always, endure for a few minutes.

"Sit tight until the bailiff calls your name," Dean told her, leaning close to her ear. His breath was a mixture of coffee and peppermints. Nice. "Go up to where he tells you and wait for your turn in front of the judge."

She twisted away from him, concentrating on the half dozen tired-looking women in heavy makeup, several drunken men, and at least ten young guys with tattoos on their arms and necks, some with heads shaved, looking tough and street-smart. Kind of like her boyfriend Skeeter. Except he was still in Bakersfield. Or Los Angeles. In jail.

She hoped.

Jinxi picked at a loose thread in her jeans. What if she had to go back to jail? For longer than one night. How much worse than Juvy would it be?

Oh, snap. She was going to barf. She clenched her teeth and swallowed hard.

What seemed like hours later, the bailiff called her name along with several other women. Jinxi followed him to where a harried public defender met with them as a group to discuss their options. The too-young lawyer made it obvious they were expected to plead guilty. He told them if they pled any other way and went to trial, the sentence would be harsher.

When it was all over—paperwork signed, filed, and stamped—they pushed through the courtroom doors and into the sunlight. This was where the cop would ditch her.

"So—"

"You—" They both spoke at the same time.

"Ladies first," Dean said with a grin.

"You know you're going to dump me as soon as you can." She glared at him, daring him to argue.

"No way." A smirk played at the corner of Dean's mouth. "Not that I don't want to. But my mom would kill me if I didn't bring you back safe and sound."

Figured as much.

The cop couldn't wait to kick her to the curb. At least she had Betty on her side. Plan A was working, at least for now. Jinxi plastered a sweet smile on her face.

"I guess you better take me *home*." She pulled a cigarette out of the crumpled pack and lit it before he could protest.

Dean muttered something under his breath. She didn't quite catch it, but Jinxi was pretty sure there was a swear word involved somewhere in there. *He's not quite as clean-cut as he looks. Interesting.*

Waves of heat radiated off the hood of Dean's truck. She stubbed out the half-smoked cigarette on the sole of her boot and replaced the stub in the pack. They settled in, and Dean cranked up the air conditioning.

Jinxi closed her eyes and drummed her fingers on her thigh. What if she jumped out at the next light and stuck out her thumb? Forget she was ever in Sacramento?

As if reading her mind, Dean said, "Don't even think about bailing. If you get picked up anywhere for anything, you'll find yourself in jail quicker than you can blink. The legal system doesn't tolerate runaways."

His cop voice jumped onto her last nerve.

"Why should you care."

He turned in his seat to face her. "You got any idea how dangerous it is to work the streets? Do you know what happens to sweet young things like you who sell their bodies to strangers?"

Jinxi glared at him, quietly daring him to continue.

"They end up raped, cut up, or even killed. The lucky ones get adopted by a pimp, which is about the same as being a slave. That what you want?"

She cringed. All she wanted to do was leave the madness of Skeeter's lifestyle and go someplace where she could start over. She had planned to get to San Francisco, but when Interstate 5 split to Sacramento or San Francisco, the trucker she had hitched a ride with took the Sacramento exit. At the time, she had thought nothing of it. Sacramento, San Francisco, wherever. Someplace to start again, away from a drunken mother and an abusive boyfriend. Someplace to settle. Find a home. Maybe even love.

If that existed.

CHAPTER 9

The cop dumped her at his mom's and roared off in his white pickup.

Spotting the swing under the oak tree, Jinxi threw herself down on the seat and swung wildly. She dug through the backpack, searching for the crumpled pack of cigarettes and her lighter. Only two cigarettes left. She'd have to do something about that soon. Maybe use some of the money she'd taken from the sock drawer.

Jinxi lit up and took a long drag.

Eighty hours of community service. They'd trapped her. Not part of the plan. She inhaled again and let the smoke fill her lungs. At least she had a place to stay, *if* Betty White hadn't changed her mind.

Would she? Jinxi frowned and sucked her cigarette down to the filter. If Betty *did* kick her out, where would she go?

After stubbing out the cigarette, she grabbed her backpack and stalked across the lawn toward the house. Janice was pouring a glass of juice in the kitchen as Jinxi came through the door.

"Would you like something cool to drink? It's hot out there." She held out the glass.

"No." Jinxi hitched her bag back up over her shoulder. She looked around the kitchen, her gaze settling on a point over Janice's right shoulder.

"I got eighty hours of community service." Eighty hours of torture was more like it.

Janice beckoned her with a wave. "Come into the front room for a minute. I want to talk to you about something."

Jinxi followed her through the door, past the dining room, and into the living room. Janice sat in one of the upholstered chairs and motioned for Jinxi to sit on the sofa.

Jinxi sat on the edge of the sofa cushion and jiggled her leg. *Click, click*. Back and forth went the lip stud. Had Janice changed her mind about wanting her to stay? Her mind spun with possibilities. What should she say to convince the woman? Maybe if she cried. Think about something sad. Think about the fire. That always worked.

Tears sprang to her eyes.

Janice smiled softly. "I think court must have been stressful this morning."

Jinxi sniffled. "Uh-huh."

"I know this is awkward for you, staying with someone you hardly know." Janice took a deep breath. "You've had a hard time lately, but I wanted you to know ..." Janice twisted her hands together. "I meant it when I said you could stay here."

Jinxi stared down at her feet, hiding a smile. She sniffed again and wiped her eyes with her fingers, smearing the heavy black eyeliner.

"That would be great." She wiped her hands on her jeans and looked as earnestly as she could muster into Janice's eyes. "I can't thank you enough."

Jinxi retreated upstairs, closed the bedroom door, and slung her backpack on the bed. She clicked on the air conditioner and tapped her foot as she waited for the machine to rumble to life. Could this room get any hotter? She paced around until a stream of cool air reluctantly trickled out.

Eighty hours of community service for one tiny mistake. For trying to survive. Jinxi swore silently, pulling her backpack across the bed. On the other hand, there was Dean. He'd been nice to take her to court. Even acting like a big brother, warning her of the dangers on the street. As if she didn't know. Maybe hanging around here wouldn't be so bad. He didn't seem to mind their verbal sparring.

But first, time for some reconnaissance.

Jinxi crept down the stairs, pausing at the bottom. She turned to enter the kitchen and jumped back a step when she came face-to-face with Janice.

"Sorry. Didn't mean to startle you. I forgot my wallet. I'm heading to Walmart. Do you need anything?"

Jinxi shook her head. "Could I get your wi-fi password? Please?"

"Sure." Janice smiled as she tucked her wallet into her purse. "It's tacked on the bulletin board over my desk. I'll show you."

Janice slipped her purse over her shoulder and headed down the hall. She stopped by the office door and motioned with one hand. "It's a bit of a mess. I do my scrapbooking in here."

"Uh, thanks." Jinxi's fingers tapped the password into her phone.

"Okay. I'll see you later."

After the wi-fi connected, a text from Savannah popped up.

SAVANNAH: Skeeter is freaking out wanting to know where u r. I don't know if I can keep quiet.

Jinxi clicked the stud back and forth against her front teeth while hammering out a quick response.

JINXI: I'm stuck in this hole until I do 80 hrs of community service. I'll be back after. J

Maybe that would hold him off for a while.

Jinxi set the phone down and went to work searching through every drawer in the office. One of the desk drawers held a box of blank checks. She filed that information away for the future. Stapler, pens, loose keys—the drawers held the accumulated junk that ends up in a home office.

The skinny center drawer didn't open all the way. She stuck her hand in and moved it to the back, closing in on an envelope. She pulled it out with two fingers. *Score.* Block letters spelled out the word, PASSWORDS. The envelope held a folded piece of paper with a list of bank and investment accounts, credit cards, and email addresses. Neatly written next to each was the username and password. One long look, and she'd memorized the list.

The words 'investment account' tickled at the edge of her brain. What might she find?

CHAPTER 10

"Good morning," Janice chirped when Jinxi stumbled into the kitchen.

Give me coffee. After that, you may speak.

"Mnhm." Jinxi reached for the mug with the gold star on one side. The one she'd begun to think of as her own. In her haste to pour, some of the scalding liquid splashed onto her hand.

She shrieked out a four-letter word and wiped her hand on her T-shirt. Janice's smile froze.

"Sorry," Jinxi mumbled. Her face grew warm as she sank onto a chair.

The older woman busied herself around the small room, wiping the counters, putting dishes in the cupboard.

"Tonight is our monthly family pizza night. Everyone comes. My son Brian and his wife, Courtney. My daughter, Robin, and her husband, Carlos. My granddaughter, Hannah. And, of course, Dean. You're welcome to join us."

A shiver started at Jinxi's toes and worked its way up to her stomach. So many eyes, boring into her, measuring, judging. She'd rather stab herself in the head.

"There's always plenty." Janice hung the dishtowel on the oven door. "Well, I'm off to church." She turned and headed down the dark hall toward her room.

Jinxi took a slow sip from her mug. How long till Janice would leave? Five minutes? Ten?

Janice's family arrived in a flood of noise. Jinxi hovered at the top of the stairs, out of sight but not out of earshot. Unwilling to go downstairs, yet powerless to stay in her room.

"It's so hot out, my Kevlar feels like it weighs a hundred pounds."

"You think that's bad? The air conditioning in my car broke."

Two male voices vied for worst off. Must be the cop and his brother.

"You guys are wimps." Had to be the cop's sister. "I had yard duty at Hannah's preschool last week. At noon. Outside. With no shade. Imagine twenty preschoolers all whining. Now *that's* hot."

"Mommy, I'm hungry." A child's voice halted the friendly banter.

Jinxi strained to see down the stairs without being noticed. Longing pulled her closer. This was what a normal family sounded like. Tears prickled the corners of her eyes as she retreated.

The fragrance of pizza sauce drifted to the bedroom.

Janice's voice drifted up the stairs, "Jinxi, we're getting ready to eat. Come on down if you want some pizza."

The lip stud clicked back forth against her teeth as she weighed her options. Sit up here like a prisoner, or go downstairs, face all those strangers, and get something to eat.

Jinxi's stomach growled as she thumbed through the pages of a book she'd found on a shelf in the closet. Some novel that was supposed to be inspirational. The family loved each other and faced their difficulties with God's help. Definitely a fantasy.

Words swam in front of her eyes. Jinxi set the book down and gave in to her hunger. She crept down the stairs, heart pounding against her ribs. Janice noticed her first and motioned toward the open pizza boxes on the table.

"Help yourself, honey," she said with a smile. "There's plenty."

Conversation around the table trickled to a stop as the family turned to stare.

Janice eased the moment by saying, "Let me introduce you to everyone. You know Dean, of course." She continued around the table. "This is Robin and her husband, Carlos." Janice's look turned soft. "And this is their daughter, Hannah." She indicated a child sitting between Carlos and Dean. "Brian and his wife, Courtney."

Robin frowned and quickly looked away, her red hair swinging against her shoulders. Her husband seemed nice enough, all dark and Latino. Dean's brother looked a little creepy as he eyed her from across the table. His wife stood and reached across the table, her hand extended.

"Nice to meet you. I'm Courtney."

Jinxi's hand brushed against Dean's shoulder as she grasped Courtney's hand. His eyes flicked toward her, an amused question showing in them. Jinxi took the opportunity to snag a piece of pizza, turning toward the stairs.

"There's room at the table," Janice said, scooting her chair over.

Not yet. There were too many of them.

"I'm good," Jinxi said, retracing her steps. As she mounted the stairs, the conversation gradually resumed. She parked herself on the top step and strained to listen.

"So, when are *you* going to settle down, Dean?"

"C'mon, man. You think because you and my sister have found everlasting bliss, the entire world should do the same. Although equating Robin with bliss does seem like an oxymoron."

"Hey, watch it. I don't want to have to ask Carlos to beat you up."

"Could you please not involve me in any of your battles, *mi amor*? I'm not sure I could take him down."

"To settle down, as you put it ..." The other male voice. The cop's brother. "Dean has to start with dating, right?" Pause. "When was the last time you went on a date?"

Yeah, Captain America, when *was* the last time you went on a date?

"Yeah. When *was* your last date, baby brother?"

Right on, sister.

"I date."

Jinxi imagined the cop rubbing the back of his neck. Or blushing.

"Sure you do. But you're not answering."

The brother's voice again. "Dean, in order to date, you have to go at least where there are women. From what I see, you go to work, come home, work out, and go back to work. Am I right?"

The sister took up where the cop's brother left off.

"Yeah, bro, you don't go to church, you don't go to a gym, you aren't involved in any clubs, and you work mainly around men—at a jail. Seriously, Dean. What kind of women could you possibly meet at the jail? I can only imagine—" There was a simultaneous *shush* from Janice and someone else.

"Time to change the subject."

That's right, Janice. Let's not talk about the criminal living upstairs.

Jinxi stomped to the bedroom and retrieved her crumpled cigarette pack and lighter. She was down the stairs through the kitchen, grabbing a soda from the counter as she passed. She was out the back door in a flash.

The swing rocked crazily as she threw herself into its seat. She lit a cigarette with shaking hands. The first draw didn't have its usual calming effect, and angry tears filled her eyes at the hurt and humiliation. What was she doing here? These people didn't care about her. Staying in Janice's good graces would be impossible with that red-headed witch daughter staring at her with suspicious eyes. They were probably plotting how to get rid of her.

Janice had been kind enough to let her stay here, but the family would have the last word, and Jinxi'd be kicked to the curb. She saw it in her mind's eye—Janice standing there, her face wrinkled in sympathy. "I've changed my mind," she would say. Dean would be standing behind his mom, watching to be sure Jinxi left. He'd have on his cop face, brown eyes hard as granite.

As she smoked, her heart hardened. She wouldn't let them kick her out. There had to be a way.

The back door opened, and a little girl descended the steps. What was her name?

Hannah.

The girl crossed the overgrown lawn and stopped.

"Are they still talking about me?" Jinxi asked.

Hannah shook her head. "My mommy says smoking is bad."

Jinxi dropped the end of her cigarette into the soda can she'd been using as an ashtray. "Your mommy is probably right. What else does your mommy say?"

"I'm going to have a brother or sister soon."

Dark curly hair cascaded down the kid's back. Her skin was the color of a pumpkin spice latte. Her green eyes stared unblinkingly.

"How old are you?" Jinxi asked.

Hannah held up three fingers. "I'm three. I mean, I'm four." She slowly released her pinkie and held up the correct number of fingers. "Can I sit with you?"

Without waiting for an answer, Hannah pulled herself up on the bench. She leaned into Jinxi's side, resting her hand on Jinxi's bare leg below her shorts.

Jinxi froze. She'd never been around little kids. Now this one snuggled up to her like it was the most natural thing in the world. A hundred butterfly wings gently touched her where Hannah's hand rested. She closed her eyes and smelled the sweet fragrance of baby shampoo. The hurt from the conversation indoors was forgotten, and she and the child were all that existed. Jinxi used the toe of one foot to move the swing gently back and forth.

Hannah sat up, and the spell was broken. She looked Jinxi in the eye and asked, "Will you push me on the swings?"

Hannah jumped up and ran to the swing set. Jinxi slowly got to her feet, feeling like she wore a pair of shoes that didn't fit.

Hannah waited in front of one of the seats, patiently holding on to the chains. Would she be able to touch the kid without hurting her?

CHAPTER 11

Dean watched Jinxi slip through the kitchen. The outburst he expected from his family came as soon as the back door slammed.

First, his sister Robin. "Mom, we need to talk. What are you *doing?*"

Brian said, "Yeah, Mom, this isn't some stray animal you can bring home and expect everything to turn out okay."

"Look, kids, I know you're concerned—"

Robin's voice rose. "Concerned? Concerned isn't the word for it. I'm appalled you have that girl in the house. I mean, *look* at her."

Brian kept his voice level and began his argument logically, as was his habit.

"First of all, you don't know who this girl is or where she's from. For all you know, she could have a record of robbery or even elder abuse."

Dean cut in, an uncomfortable twitch in his gut. "I work at Sac PD, remember. She didn't have any priors before this week." Why did he feel the need to defend her?

"This is all *your* fault, anyway," Robin said, glaring at him. She stood up and stalked to the window, yanking back the lace curtain. Over her shoulder, Dean saw Jinxi pushing Hannah on the swing. Robin dropped the curtain and paced back and forth from the window to the table. "Mom, you've never done anything like this before."

"Maybe it's time I start. And I don't appreciate you kids treating me as if I have dementia or something. I'm not even sixty-five years old, and I won't have you acting as if I've lost my ability to make decisions." Robin started to open her mouth, but Janice cut her off without missing a beat. "Robin, sit down and let me talk."

"Fine." Robin sank into her seat and propped her elbows on the table.

"I have prayed about this and sought the Lord's guidance. I believe he's telling me to show mercy and compassion to this girl. She's obviously hurting, and she needs God as much as anybody."

Brian leaned back in his chair. "Someone could be looking for her, maybe even missing her."

"Maybe so," Janice said. "But until she's ready to share that information with me, she's a welcome guest in this house, and I expect all of you"—she looked meaningfully around the table—"to treat her as such." She continued more calmly, "If you're all so worried, why don't you pray for Jinxi and me as well? God knows she needs it."

Dean sighed. This situation was a train wreck, all right. "Relax, people. I've been checking on Mom every day, twice a day since she got here."

Brian nodded. "Good idea."

Janice turned to her daughter. "Robin?"

His sister hated to lose an argument.

"Fine, Mom. I'll be praying."

Later, the family gathered in the front room to play a game of Guesstures. While they broke into teams, Dean offered to go outside to check on Hannah and Jinxi. Bounding down the back steps, he saw them kicking a ball back and forth. Occasionally the ball went sideways, and Hannah would run after it, giggling.

Dean grinned. "Looks like you two are having a ball."

Jinxi rolled her eyes at his attempt to be funny.

"Look, Unca Dean," Hannah shrieked. "Jinxi teached me to kick backward." She lined up the ball behind her heel, threw her leg out in front of her, and pulled her leg back. The ball went flying out behind her. "See? Jinxi's a good soccer player."

"Is she, now?" Dean stooped to ruffle the child's hair. He looked at Jinxi as he said it, but she avoided his eyes. "Maybe she's a professional soccer player."

Hannah's eyes got as big as dinner plates. She swung her gaze over to Jinxi. "*Are* you, Jinxi? Are you a prof, profesh ..." She glanced up at Dean. "What's that word?"

"Professional."

Jinxi got down on Hannah's level to hand her the ball. "No, I'm not a professional soccer player. Your Uncle Dean is telling you a lie."

"A lie?" Hannah looked up at him with serious eyes. "A lie is bad, Unca Dean. Mommy says you have to get a time out if you tell a lie."

Dean felt his face flush. He didn't want to have to explain to his niece he was kidding. He frowned at Jinxi's attempt to hide a smile.

Hannah began jumping up and down. "I hafta go potty. I hafta go potty."

Dean put out a hand. "C'mon, I'll take you."

"Nooooo," Hannah wailed. She threw herself against Jinxi and hugged her waist. "I want you to take me."

Dean looked at Jinxi and shrugged. "I guess that settles it." He grinned at her look of panic. Payback.

Jinxi struggled toward the house, Hannah clinging to her legs.

"Nooooo. I want to go to Unca Dean's house." Hannah turned and pointed toward the upstairs apartment. "I hafta go nowwwwwwww."

Dean took a deep breath. He was accustomed to his little niece's strong will. It was only a matter of moments before there would be a full-scale meltdown.

"Hurry up. Let's go." He started for the garage.

Hannah released Jinxi's legs and grabbed her hand, dragging her across the lawn. They scurried up the stairs,

Hannah still clenching Jinxi's hand, bouncing from one foot to the other while Dean unlocked the door. Once inside, he pointed to the bathroom. Hannah tugged at Jinxi with one hand and tried to pull her shorts down with the other.

Jinxi paused with her hand on the bathroom door handle and took a deep breath. After a moment, she turned the knob and pushed the door open. Dean lowered the Sunday comics when Jinxi exited the bathroom. Glancing around the single room, she took in the tiny kitchen and the table and two chairs shoved into the corner under a window. A futon along the opposite wall doubled as a bed and a sofa. A closet, its doors hanging open, was set into the wall next to the bathroom. She spied his police uniform hanging on a wooden hanger. The leather belt and gun holster sat on a shelf above the clothing. Ugh. He was definitely armed and dangerous, especially with his brown-eyed cop stare.

The one he was leveling at her right now.

Jinxi pointed toward the comics. "Getting a little intellectual stimulation?"

Dean put down the paper with a snap. "Wow. Did you make a joke?"

Jinxi pinched her lips together and let her eyes wander around the apartment again.

"Let me mark this moment down in time." He pretended to write something in the air with his finger.

"Whatever."

Hannah ran to the front door. "C'mon, let's go back outside."

Jinxi had no choice but to follow the kid as Hannah opened the door and skipped down the stairs.

When they reached the bottom, Dean laid a gentle hand on Hannah's shoulder. Some tough cop he was. Maybe his toughness was all a put-on.

"Listen. Did you hear that?" He stooped toward the kid and held a finger to his lips.

"Hear what, Unca Dean?" Hannah asked in a whisper.

"Shh. You can see the leaves move a little bit. There's a breeze blowing, and you can hear the leaves rustling." He blew in her ear, and Hannah giggled.

"Come on, munchkin. Let's get you back to your mom." He straightened, using his hand to propel the kid toward the house. "You coming?" he asked over his shoulder.

"Maybe in a minute." Jinxi needed some space. His tenderness toward the kid had hit a nerve.

Dean stopped before going up the concrete steps to the house. "By the way, I'm taking you to the food bank tomorrow, so you'll know where it's located. After that, you can take the bus. I'll show you the route and everything."

Jinxi opened her mouth to argue, but he'd already turned his back.

"C'mon, baby girl. It's time to go inside."

"Okay, Unca Dean." Hannah took his hand, then dropped it and ran back to Jinxi, throwing her arms around her. "I love you, Jinxi."

Hannah's embrace had nearly knocked her off her feet, physically and emotionally. Why would a child say *I love you*, especially to her?

When they got to the back door, Hannah turned and waved. "Bye, Jinxi. See you later."

Jinxi raised a hand to wave back. She walked toward the swing set and collapsed on one of the seats, gripping the chains. Head down, she used her feet to turn herself around and around until the chains wound tight. She lifted her feet and let the swing spin until she was dizzy.

Dizzy and disoriented. That summed up her existence. How had her life gotten into such a twisted mess?

You can't do anything right. You should never have been born.

The words roared through her brain like a wildfire. Like the fire that raced through that house, destroying everything.

Was the fire the turning point? That's when the downhill spiral began. She imagined the newspaper headlines in her mind's eye: ARSON SUSPECTED IN SERIES OF BRUSH FIRES. What had started as a prank had turned into something she could never have predicted.

Or was she doomed from birth, as her mother said? Unwanted, unworthy of love.

But Hannah, with her unabashed affection, had knocked her off her game. Jinxi bit her lip hard enough to draw blood. Hannah was too young to know Jinxi was a monster.

CHAPTER 12

Dean lay in bed a moment before opening his eyes. He sucked in a deep breath and exhaled in a long, slow stream. His first decent night's sleep in a week. Finally. He rubbed his eyes and pictured the time when he'd be able to work a day shift.

His cell phone sprang to life. Dean snatched it off the nightstand.

Damaris's voice greeted him. "Big D. 'S up?"

"Little D."

Damaris continued, "A bunch of us are getting together to play pool later. You in?"

Dean thought about his commitment to take Jinxi to her community service at the food bank and pick her up when she was done. "Well, I ... I have something I gotta do."

"Like what?"

"I ... um ... have to take someone somewhere." Dean rubbed a hand across the back of his neck.

Damaris laughed, then whistled. "Someone as in a female-type someone?"

Perspiration prickled on his forehead. No way did he want to explain about Jinxi. The gossip mill at Sac PD was worse than a high school locker room.

"It's a friend of my mom's."

Damaris chuckled. "Well, why didn't you say so? Here I was, picturing our Forty-Year-Old Virgin out on a date with some hottie."

Dean gritted his teeth at one of the many nicknames from the PD. If they only knew.

"Well, what time you gonna be done?"

Dean shrugged and answered, "I dunno. Maybe five, five-thirty?"

"Right on. We're meeting at seven. Blue Cue. Oh, and—" Damaris' voice went up an octave, "—bring your mom's friend." He disconnected before Dean could respond.

Dean laughed humorlessly at what the group would say if he *did* show up with Jinxi.

He walked the four steps to his kitchen and poured a bowl of cereal while waiting for the coffee to brew. As he looked out his window toward his mom's house, he remembered the argument over pizza the night before, and his sister's vehement objection to having Jinxi stay with their mother. He was worried, too. Jinxi's lifestyle was a polar opposite from his mother's. Mom was ill-equipped to handle Jinxi. How could she possibly relate? Did Mom think she could change Jinxi into some clean-cut church girl? He'd seen far too many girls like Jinxi do unspeakable things to survive on the streets.

Dean shook his head as he poured a cup of coffee. His mom constantly talked about how God always worked things out, but Dean had his doubts. How could God protect her if Jinxi managed to steal from her, or even worse, earn his mom's trust so that she signed things over to the girl? People went to jail for similar crimes. Older people who were lonely often allowed someone to live with them, and somehow they always ended up being fleeced.

He wouldn't allow that to happen. *My mom may have God, but she also has me.* He wasn't too confident about God's ability to protect, especially since he'd done a poor job with his dad, but Dean was confident in his own ability. He could keep a close eye on the girl and his mom to make sure nothing weird transpired.

For the hundredth time, he regretted the impulse that had made him offer breakfast to the lost-looking waif outside the jail. What was it about her that had grabbed him? Jinxi was different from the women he was used to being around. His friends included the girlfriends of his college buddies and a couple of female police officers. The dates his friends set him up with had no visible tattoos, and from what he could tell, weren't into cutting.

Dean took a sip of coffee and smiled when he remembered her joke about reading the Sunday comics. Yes, he was attracted to her feistiness. His smile dimmed. She'd made it clear she didn't like him. *What's not to like? I'm fun.* Must be the cop thing. *Shouldn't even go down that road.*

He shifted the coffee mug from one hand to the other.

Date Jinxi?

He allowed himself one moment to head down that path before yanking his thoughts back to the present. Nope. Too much drama there. Besides, he had his mom to consider.

"Eat."

Jinxi looked up into Janice's too-hopeful face. She tried to force a smile—a real feat this early in the morning. "I'm not hungry.

"You need to keep up your strength after being sick." Janice pushed a plate with scrambled eggs and buttered toast toward her.

Jinxi bit back a growl. "Really, I'm fine."

"But dear, you have a full day ahead—"

"I'm not hungry, okay?" Jinxi was almost surprised by the harsh bark of her voice.

Janice's face fell. "Sorry."

Remorse washed over her, but she clamped her mouth shut. Janice nodded and headed down the hall toward her bedroom.

Awesome. *Nice move, genius.*

Jinxi stared blankly at the newspaper in front of her. She needed to stay on Janice's good side. And she'd completely bitten the lady's head off. Grave tactical error.

The cop breezed through the back door and into the kitchen, dressed in snug jeans and a chocolate-brown T-shirt that stretched tight across his chest. The color matched his eyes.

"Ready?" Dean asked, eyeing her backpack on the floor next to her chair.

Jinxi nodded.

"C'mon."

They climbed in Dean's pickup. He rolled down the windows to let in the cool morning air. Jinxi huddled into her oversized sweatshirt and crossed her arms.

As they drove, the cop showed her where she could catch the bus the next day. A couple of guys in wife-beaters sat on the bench at the bus stop. She made a mental note to have her pepper spray handy. They crossed under a railroad overpass and wound down by the river.

"This isn't a good section of town," the cop said. "Make sure you don't get off the bus here by mistake."

Homeless camps made of cardboard boxes leaned at drunken angles under the trees near the riverbank, landscaped with litter. A couple of rusted-out cars served as more upscale residences for some.

Moments later they ascended onto a busy road. Along each side were businesses advertising everything from X-rated movies to discount furniture. Several derelict men and women gathered in front of a Goodwill store. On either side, people walked with their heads down. Some led mangy dogs on leashes or carried them under their arms. Others pushed grocery carts loaded down with blankets and garbage bags full of questionable contents. Where were they going? She should have chosen another place for community service. This neighborhood was like South Central Los Angeles. Maybe worse.

Jinxi let out a breath as they passed through the area and emerged into downtown.

"Sacramento is laid out like a grid," Dean explained. "Numbered streets go one way, letters the other. You'll be at Fourteenth and D Streets. The bus stop is across from the food bank. I can pick you up today if you want, or you can try it on your own. I don't go back to work until Tuesday night."

"Okay."

"Okay, what? I'm picking you up, or you'll try it on your own?"

Jinxi grabbed the neck of her sweatshirt and pulled it up around her chin. "You can pick me up." Nice to have a choice. Ride with the cop or take the bus and get off at the wrong stop.

Dean pulled into a parking spot a block down from the food bank.

"We're here. Come on," Dean muttered over his shoulder as he climbed out of the pickup. Jinxi took her time climbing down. She grabbed onto the door to keep herself from falling as her legs buckled. Would they like her or reject her? Would she have some nasty job, like cleaning bathrooms? Her fingers gripped the strap of her backpack.

Please let them like me.

"Come on," Dean encouraged. He walked around the truck and held out a hand. "I'll introduce you to the director before I take off."

"Anxious to cut me loose?" She shot him a sidelong glance, ignoring his outstretched hand.

Dean snorted. "Maybe."

The building looked a hundred years old. Some of the bricks had crumbled, leaving holes like a gap-toothed smile. As she entered the front door, Jinxi's nostrils burned with the smells of food cooking, unwashed bodies, and disinfectant.

The entry led into a large cafeteria. Dean tapped twice on a door on the left side of the entrance, opened it, and ushered Jinxi into an office.

Two desks, several file cabinets, and a copier jammed the room. Stacks of papers lay on every surface. A tall, dark-skinned man jumped up from one of the desks and smiled broadly. He wore a crisp checkered shirt tucked into a pair of khaki slacks. His black hair was parted on one side.

"Welcome, Dean." He extended his hand and moved in to embrace him. "It's been way too long, my friend." The man had a melodious way of talking. "How is your wonderful mother?"

"She's fine, Padish. Just fine."

The man turned his attention to Jinxi. "And who is your friend?" he asked, still smiling. Jinxi stared at the contrast of white teeth against his brown face.

"Padish, this is Jinxi. She's going to be doing some community service here."

Padish nodded. "Ah, yes. I remember now." He extended his hand to shake Jinxi's. "Our new slave!"

Her stomach lurched as she yanked her hand back.

"Kidding."

"Jinxi, this is Padish Singh. He's the director here."

Padish had not stopped smiling. "So nice to meet you. You will like it here, yes? Come," Padish gestured toward the door. "I will show you around, yes? And introduce you to the others."

"I'm outta here," Dean said. "I'll pick you up this afternoon."

As she nodded, Padish spoke. "Around three o'clock, yes?"

Dean raised a hand in assent as he turned toward the door.

Padish showed her where she could leave her backpack in a cubby on one side of the office. As they exited, he explained the history of the food bank, but his voice barely registered over the throbbing in her temples. *Don't leave me*, she silently implored as she watched Dean's retreating back.

CHAPTER 13

Padish led Jinxi into a cafeteria off the front entry hall. "This is where we serve lunch, five days a week."

An African American man, thin as the broom in his hand, looked up as they entered the room.

"You will meet Hank, yes?" Padish motioned toward the man. "Hank is our lead custodian, correct?" He addressed the tall man, who nodded vigorously.

"Th-that's r-r-r-right, M-Mr. Singh." He smiled at Jinxi, revealing a gap between his two front teeth. He extended a giant hand, engulfing hers.

"Hank, this is Jinxi, who will be working with us for a few weeks."

"N-nice to meet you," Hank said. "You're awful small."

Thanks for reminding me, Bubba.

"Nice to meet you, too," she mumbled, tugging her hand back. These people were way too touchy.

"Next, we go to the kitchen. Yes?" Padish pointed toward the left. The commercially equipped kitchen took up most of the room. Metal roll-down windows covered the serving area. The smell of cooking permeated the cafeteria. A diminutive woman stirred something in a deep stockpot, while another peeled potatoes in a double aluminum sink.

"Ladies, this is our new friend, Jinxi. She will be working here for a few weeks. Jinxi, this is Consuela, or Connie." He indicated the woman at the stove, then gestured toward the other woman. "And this is Norma."

Norma glared sideways at Jinxi. A white hairnet held her hair back, but a few dreadlocks hung over her right cheek. She raised a shoulder to push them out of her face.

"Nice to meet you," the shorter woman said. She had a thick accent, which sounded like "joo" when she said *you*. "You speak Spanish?" she asked, looking hopeful.

Jinxi shook her head.

"*Que lastima*. Too bad," Connie answered. "I no spick Eengleesh berry well. I think you maybe can help me."

Padish put a hand on Connie's shoulder. "Your English is fine. Keep practicing." He clapped his hands and said, "Come. I show you where you will work."

His smile had to be fake. No one could be that happy.

Padish took her into a back storeroom. A double door at the back opened onto a loading dock. Shelves filled with food lined the room.

"This is our main storeroom, yes? We keep all the food for the kitchen in here. Through there"—he pointed toward a set of doors on one side of the room—"we have another storeroom with items for the food closet. We fill boxes with donated food and give the boxes to families who apply for help through our office."

He paused. "You understand so far? Your job is to unpack these boxes, yes?" He indicated a van parked with its rear doors open, filled with cardboard boxes. "I will have Hank unload them. You are too small to carry them." He laughed and held his hand out with the palm facing down. Moving his hand down, he indicated her small stature. "They must weigh as much as you."

Yeah, yeah. She was short. Thanks for the reminder.

As if he had heard his name mentioned, Hank entered through the outside door. "I'll unload the van, M-Mr. Singh."

"Very good." Padish clapped his hands again and turned to Jinxi. "I will get a box cutter for you."

Hank hoisted the cardboard cases from the van and carried them over to where Jinxi stood. Padish appeared a few moments later and handed her a box cutter.

"Here you go."

The box cutter lay comfortably in her hand. She glanced at Hank moving things around in the van. While he was occupied, she shoved up her sleeve.

"M-Miss J-Jinxi."

"What?" she snapped, tugging down her sleeve. Hank stood right next to her. Why hadn't she heard him approach?

"You ok-kay?"

"Fine." Had he seen? Would he say something to the boss?

Shoulders hunched, she bent down to cut the tape on the first box. Inside were industrial-sized cans of peaches. She unloaded four cans before Padish burst through the door.

"I forgot to tell you," he exclaimed with a smile. "You must rotate the food. If there is food on the shelf, move it to the front and put the new cans in the back. You understand?"

Jinxi nodded. *Oh, snap.* Why hadn't he told her the first time? She muttered curses while shoving the cans of peaches aside and trying to remember which ones were old and which were new. She bit her lip and hoped that no one would notice she'd blown it as she hurried to rearrange the cans.

Hank unloaded all the boxes from the van and disappeared. Sweat formed beads on Jinxi's forehead as the heat outside pressed in through the open doors. The van started up and drove away. Hank appeared a few moments later and closed the outer doors. Jinxi heaved a sigh of relief.

"You okay, M-Miss J-Jinxi?"

"Water?" she asked.

Hank nodded his head vigorously and held up a finger. He disappeared through the doors leading into the cafeteria and returned with a red plastic cup filled with icy water. He handed it to her with both hands.

"Thanks," she said, taking huge gulps. She set the cup down on a shelf next to her discarded sweatshirt and returned to work. Hank stood for a few minutes in her periphery, watching. Raising her head, she glared.

Instead of breaking eye contact, he smiled. "M-more?"

"No. Thanks."

Bobbing his head, he disappeared again.

This community service must be some kind of purgatory. She'd never be able to finish eighty hours of this torture. No wonder that girl in the kitchen—Norma—was surly. Maybe she was stuck doing community service too.

This bites big time.

She'd be better off heading back down to Bakersfield and being Skeeter's delivery girl.

Or would she?

Jinxi's stomach clenched as she slid yet another can onto a shelf, remembering life with Skeeter. Money in, money out, always on the move. Without thinking, she rubbed her forearm. Their last fight had gotten physical. Again. The bruises had faded, but the pain hadn't.

How long had she been unloading these stupid boxes? Her cell phone was in the backpack in the office, so she had no idea what time it was. If she made it until tomorrow, she'd have to remember to tuck the phone in her back pocket.

The cans of fruit and the oversized bags of beans and rice became as heavy as bricks. Her stomach rumbled as she reached for the last box and pulled it toward an empty shelf.

Padish pushed through the double door and surveyed her progress.

"Very good," he exclaimed. "When you finish that last box, you will come and eat some lunch, yes?"

About time. At least they wouldn't starve her to death in this slave den.

Jinxi unloaded a box of spaghetti sauce and piled the empty box on top of the others in a corner. After dusting off her hands on the legs of her jeans, she opened the door leading into the cafeteria and peered in.

The surly kitchen lady and the other woman spooned enchiladas and salad onto plates as people lined up along the serving bar. Women with small children, grizzled old men, and everyone in between waited to be served. Padish walked between the rows of tables, greeting someone here and touching another there. He seemed to know everyone in the room and even leaned down to listen to a child whisper something in his ear.

The Spanish-speaking lady motioned to her to come.

"*Ven aqui,*" she said. "Come here." She smiled and nodded as Jinxi entered the kitchen. Norma continued serving, ignoring her. "Here is a plate," Connie said, filling one for her. "You can eat here, or sit at a table." Jinxi nodded her thanks and took her plate into the cafeteria. Better to keep away from that meth head Norma and her negative vibes.

Jinxi sat down next to a woman with stringy gray hair and black, uneven fingernails. The woman scooted over, leaving a three-foot space between them, as if Jinxi was the grungy one. She looked down at her own hands and realized they were brown with dirt from the work she had done in the storeroom. The sleeves of her T-shirt held evidence that she had used them to wipe her face more than once.

Dirty white girl.

The words sprang to mind from her childhood. Inwardly cringing, she remembered the bullying taunts from some older girls at her elementary school. It wasn't her fault. Sometimes she had to wear dirty clothes because those were all she had.

Jinxi left her untouched plate of food and made her way to the restroom. Her reflection in the mirror showed she was as grimy as some of the people receiving free food. She had a smudge of dirt on one cheek and sweat had smudged her eyeliner. She washed quickly, hoping no one had taken her plate away while she was in the restroom.

Back at the table, she reached for a fork and began to eat. The enchiladas were different from any she'd ever had. Spicy meat and chunks of potato filled the tortillas. Not her standard fast-food fare.

If this was a typical food bank meal, maybe this gig wouldn't be that bad. It sure beat the scrounging she'd had to do the last couple of weeks. Or rather the last couple of weeks before she met the cop and his mom. Digging through garbage cans for other people's leftovers reminded her too much of her childhood. She'd left that behind when she and Skeeter hooked up. He always had money. Too bad he was such a jerk.

When Jinxi finished her meal, Padish made his way to her table and sat down across from her. "You will go into the office now, yes? There is paperwork to be filled out, and you will see Aneesa, who will help you."

He laid his hand lightly on her arm. She looked up to see Padish peering at her intently. "You are doing fine," he said, his smile firmly in place. "I believe God has a plan for you. Do not doubt that."

Yeah, right. Like God even knows my name.

He stood up, seemingly oblivious to her discomfort. "Go into the office now. Paperwork." He clapped his hands and strode toward the kitchen, calling, "Connie. Great lunch. Norma, good work."

Jinxi got up from the table, carried her plate into the kitchen, and helped herself to a glass of water. As she wandered from the kitchen to the cafeteria, she observed the people who ate there. Most wore the familiar look of hopelessness. Some of the children wore clothes that were too small, and their bare feet were filthy. A depressing group. Too reminiscent of monthly trips to the Bakersfield food closet.

Jinxi made her way toward the office and opened the door to be blasted by pandemonium. A radio somewhere in the mess blared music at an ear-piercing level, while a dark-skinned woman exclaimed into the phone tucked between her ear and her shoulder. As she talked, the woman paced between piles of paper. Her hands flew around like winged birds. The woman looked up from her conversation and gestured toward Jinxi.

"Come in," she mouthed, going back to her conversation. "Yeah, yeah," she said, "I know it's here, Duane. I'll find it. I swear, sometimes Padish files things according to the Hindi alphabet. When he comes back into the office later today, I'll ask him to look for it." She took hold of the phone with one hand and switched ears, all the while nodding enthusiastically to the other end of the conversation.

"Right. Right. I'll call you tomorrow morning. Okay. Great. Thanks." With a sigh, she hung up and turned her attention to Jinxi.

"Don't just stand there, child, come on in." The palpable energy around the woman shimmered in the air. Her hair, pulled back by a wide band, seemed to quiver with electricity. "I've got your paperwork right here. Have a seat." She moved a pile of papers off a wooden chair, motioned for Jinxi to sit, and reached behind her to turn down the volume on the radio.

"Padish wanted me to make sure you understood everything before you sign it." She stuck out her hand. "I'm Aneesa. Every day when you get here, you check in with me. I'll record your time on this card. When you leave, same thing. You're not required to be here for any specific time each day, but you must complete eighty hours. Padish wants you here from ten o'clock to two or three. That's our busiest time. Are you with me so far?"

Jinxi nodded. Yeah, yeah. Whatever.

"If you feel this place isn't working out, call this number" —she pointed to a telephone number on the timecard— "and you can request to go someplace else." Aneesa shook a finger in Jinxi's direction. "If you say the work is too hard here, or you're not able to get along with someone, there may be an investigation before you're allowed to switch."

Jinxi crossed her arms, resisting the urge to roll her eyes. Aneesa took another ten minutes to explain all the reporting requirements and what to do if Jinxi was sick and couldn't come in one day or got hurt while working there. Jinxi's head spun, not only from all the information, but because the woman talked fast and barely paused to take a breath.

Aneesa finally wound down. "You have to think of this like a job. You have a time that you have to start, and you work until it's time to go. People here will be relying on you, so it isn't fair if you decide not to show up one day. Everyone's contribution is important. You'll be able to eat lunch here every day, so that's a plus. And you'll find that Connie is about the best cook anywhere." She smiled and rubbed her ample stomach. "Don't be surprised if you gain a few pounds."

The phone rang, and as she picked it up, she waved her hand and said, "After you sign the paperwork, go see if anyone needs help. I'm done with you."

Jinxi sucked in her bottom lip, clicking the stud against her teeth. She watched the woman for a few moments before she silently slipped out. Think of this as a job? More like indentured servitude. She was as imprisoned as if she'd been thrown back in jail. This was way more physical than any work she'd had to do at the Girls' Ranch. At least here, no one tried to undermine her work. Yet. That Norma chick in the kitchen reminded her too much of her former fellow inmates. She'd have to watch her own back here, too.

CHAPTER 14

Janice stood at her bedroom window and watched Dean drive away with Jinxi in the passenger seat. As she turned around, she caught sight of the smiling photo of her and Tom on their wedding day. Grief ambushed her again. Why had Tom died? He should be here, guiding her and comforting her. He would have encouraged her and told her she was doing the right thing. Or had she made a colossal mistake by defying her children and letting Jinxi into her home?

Her thoughts turned to last night's confrontation with her kids. She'd strongly defended her decision, but watching Dean drive away flooded her with doubt. Tom's death had left her vulnerable. He had been her rock, her foundation.

The house phone rang. Caller ID showed Robin's name. Janice braced for another confrontation.

Robin's strident voice ripped the fragile peace Janice struggled to maintain. Although she loved her daughter, she sometimes struggled to like her.

"Mom. I need to talk to you. Hannah woke up this morning with her hand swollen. Do you think I should take her to the doctor?"

Janice immediately shifted into grandma mode.

"Did she sleep on it wrong?"

"No, I don't think so."

"Does it look like she got bit by something? A spider, maybe."

"I thought that, but she says she doesn't remember any bugs being near her. And you know how she hates bugs."

"Well, can you see anything that looks like a bite?"

"I checked, but I don't see anything. It's mainly the first two knuckles on her left hand."

"Hmm." Janice couldn't remember anything similar her three kids had experienced growing up. "Does it hurt?"

"She says it doesn't, but she's favoring it." Robin took a deep breath. "Mom, do you think Jinxi—"

"Robin, no," Janice said. She struggled to regain her composure, balancing grandmotherly worry with concern Robin might be unjustly accusing Jinxi of something. "Let me talk to Hannah."

Hannah's response was clear. "Don't want to talk right now."

Heavy breathing into the mouthpiece indicated Hannah had come on—or had been put on—the phone anyway.

"Hi, princess. Grammy wants to ask you something, okay?"

"Okay."

"Remember yesterday when you were at Grammy's house?"

"Uh-huh."

"Do you remember playing outside with Jinxi?"

"Uh-huh."

"What did you two do?"

There was silence for a moment. "We went potty at Unca Dean's house."

Janice took a moment to digest this. "Did Jinxi take you into the bathroom?"

Hannah giggled. "Yes, silly." She giggled again.

"Did she touch you?"

"She helped me wash my hands," Hannah offered.

"Did anything else happen?"

Hannah began to giggle in earnest. "Unca Dean was reading the cartoons." She laughed as if it was the funniest thing she had ever seen. "Grammy, next time I come to your house, can we play that funny game again?"

"Sure, princess, that sounds fun."

"Do you want to talk to my mom?" Before Janice could answer, Robin spoke.

"Well, that wasn't terribly enlightening," Robin commented.

"If anything had happened to her hand, she'd surely remember. Maybe you'd better put some ice on it and call the doctor. Let me know what she says."

"Okay, Mom. But I still want to talk to you some more about Jinxi." Robin's voice held a warning.

"I'll talk to you, sweetie, but only if you want to talk about God's redemptive plan for *all* his children."

Janice hung up the phone and chewed her bottom lip. The tiny tendril of doubt grew into a huge vine. Maybe this wasn't such a good idea, having a stranger stay with her. Maybe this would bring harm to her family, to her only grandchild. She would never forgive herself if that happened. How could she bring the love of God to someone who desperately needed him while still protecting her family?

Perhaps she'd check out Robin's old room. Taking the steps one at a time, she willed her arthritic knees to cooperate. Heart pounding, Janice approached the closed bedroom door. The knob turned smoothly in her hand. She took a deep breath and pushed open the door, stunned by what she observed.

Jinxi had made the bed, but there was no indication anyone had been in the room. No personal items sat on the dresser, and no clothing dropped on the floor. Same thing in the bathroom. Nothing to show Jinxi had been there.

Janice wasn't sure what she expected. Perhaps a bloody knife lying on the counter. She pushed a shaky hand through her hair before dropping it to her side. The girl must take all her things with her in that backpack.

But why?

Jinxi dropped her last cigarette and crushed it under her boot as Dean's truck pulled to the curb. She clambered in, too tired to pull down the straps of her backpack. Naturally, the cop started talking the minute he pulled into the street. She let his words wash over her, a welcome distraction. As he complained about having to fax a canceled check to the insurance company and all the hassles that happened along the way, she clicked her lip stud back and forth against her teeth. Could she do this community service? Show up every day, at the same time. Having others rely on her. Jinxi bit down hard on her lip.

"And what's with the backpack, anyway?"

"Huh?"

"I said, what's with the backpack? You look like a turtle carrying that thing around. It must weigh more than you do."

She shrugged. At least he remained quiet the rest of the drive.

Jinxi hurried into the house, intent upon reaching the solitude of the bedroom upstairs. Her arms and shoulders ached from unloading all the boxes. Even the familiar weight of the backpack chafed. Dust covered her like a second skin.

A child's voice greeted her with a shriek as she came around the corner from the kitchen.

"Jinxi!"

Hannah hurled herself at Jinxi and threw her arms around her. "I wanted to see you."

Janice and Robin stood in the living room. Their heads swiveled toward her. That witch was probably trying to convince her mom to dump her.

"Hi," Janice said, her smile reaching her eyes. Robin said nothing.

"I'm going upstairs," Jinxi said, attempting to untangle herself from Hannah.

"I want to go upstairs with you." Both Robin and Janice reached for the child, but she dodged their hands. "I want to go upstairs with Jinxi!"

Janice's voice soothed, "Perhaps she doesn't want you to go with her."

"That's right." Robin's voice was harsh. "Jinxi's busy. And she probably wants to take a shower." Robin's sharp eyes traveled over Jinxi's grubby clothing.

Hannah's chin began to quiver. She appeared to be on the verge of a meltdown.

"It's all right, I guess." Jinxi didn't mind taking Hannah upstairs if it meant ticking Robin off.

Hannah didn't wait for Janice or Robin to agree. She grabbed Jinxi's hand and pulled her toward the stairs. "C'mon, let's go. You hold my hand." As they ascended, Hannah kept up a steady stream of chatter.

"Are you sleeping in the pink room? You should, because that's the girls' room. The blue room is for boys. You hafta sleep in the pink room. That's where I sleep when I stay at Grammy's. Well, I'll sleep there when I'm bigger. Did you know my mommy has some dolls in the closet? Sometimes Grammy lets me play with them, but I have to be very, very careful."

When they got to the bedroom, Hannah jumped up on the bed.

"Where's all your stuff? Do you have a suitcase? I have a suitcase for when I spend the night here. It's pink. Is yours pink? Do you have a toothbrush? I have a Barbie toothbrush in the bathroom. Want to see it?" Without waiting for an answer, Hannah jumped down off the bed and scurried into the bathroom. Jinxi heard her rooting around in one of the drawers.

Jinxi's head spun. She had no idea kids talked so much.

"Hannah. Three minutes." Robin's voice echoed up the stairwell.

Hannah appeared a moment later with her toothbrush in her mouth. "See? Mine's Barbie." She took it out of her mouth long enough to display the handle to Jinxi.

Jinxi smiled. "Did you hear your mom? She said three minutes."

Hannah nodded. "I hafta rinse it now. Do you want a drink?" She disappeared into the bathroom again and came back with a Dixie cup filled with water. She carefully carried it over to Jinxi. "Here. This is for you."

Jinxi took the cup of water and drank it.

"You hafta say thank you. It's polite."

"Thank you," Jinxi said, biting her lip to keep from laughing.

Hannah answered solemnly, "You're welcome." She climbed back up on the bed and sat next to Jinxi. "You have lots of earrings," she said, looking up at Jinxi's ears. "I can count them." She touched each ring as she counted. She skipped the number seven and went from six to eight. "You have eight earrings." Her eyes went wide. "Does your mommy know that you drawed on your neck?" She pointed to the tattoo on Jinxi's neck. Without waiting for an answer, Hannah leaned into her and said, "I'm so glad you're staying with Grammy."

"Why?"

Maybe this child got her talkativeness from her Uncle Dean. They sure had that in common.

"Because you're nice," Hannah said. "And because Grammy needs someone to keep her company. She gets lonely here since Grampa went to be with Jesus."

"How do you know he's with Jesus?"

Hannah turned and looked up at her. "Because the Bible says." As if everyone should know. She giggled. "And because Mommy says, too."

Hannah jumped off the bed when Robin yelled up the stairs again. “Hannah. Time to go.”

“Bye, Jinxi. See you tomorrow.” Hannah took off running down the hall toward the stairs, her tiny flip-flops making a smacking noise on the wood floor. She turned around and ran back into the bedroom, throwing her arms around Jinxi. “I love you.” Without waiting for an answer, she took off down the hall again and down the stairs.

Jinxi lay back on the bed, dangling her legs over the side.

I love you.

When was the last time she had heard those words? She had a vague memory of her dad hugging her as he said goodbye. *Be a good girl for your mommy, okay. I love you, Jinxi-girl.”* She must have been three or four years old. Was that when her heart began to break?

Or when it began to harden?

CHAPTER 15

Jinxi crept into the kitchen, searching for food. All the stuff in the pantry begged to be taken. So weird to have a fully stocked fridge. If she weren't careful, she'd balloon out of her size zero skinny jeans. Her stash of food in the bedroom dresser drawer grew bit by bit. Best to be prepared if she had to escape in a flash.

She jerked when Janice approached up the short hall from her bedroom into the kitchen.

"I'm going out for the evening to a ladies' Bible study." Janice shrugged into a flowered sweater. "I'll leave you a key in case you want to go anywhere."

Where would she go? Not like she had any friends here.

"Also, here's my cell phone number, and Dean's." Janice handed her a piece of paper with two numbers written on it. "Help yourself to whatever you can find in the fridge. All I ask is if you use the last of something, write it down on the notepad that's over the phone on the bulletin board."

"Okay." Jinxi took the slip of paper and memorized the numbers with one glance.

Janice gathered up her purse and headed toward the door. Her summer dress swirled around her legs as she turned. Janice wore low-heeled sandals, grandma-style. She was wearing lipstick. Was that allowed with the Jesus crowd?

The door closed behind Janice. Jinxi surveyed the contents of the refrigerator. So many choices. Some green leafy stuff. Raw hamburger. Onions. She didn't know what to do with all this stuff.

She settled for a PB and J. The one thing she knew how to cook.

Wow, another quiet evening with nothing to do. Super fun. What she wouldn't give for a six-pack of beer and a pack of cigarettes.

Jinxi ate the sandwich as she sauntered down the hall toward the office. She stood in the doorway for a moment, surveying the room. Looking over her shoulder, she settled into the desk chair and pulled out her phone. Another text from Skeeter.

SKEETER: Savvy told me where your at. I'll be up there to get you.

"Blast it, Savvy! Why'd you tell Skeeter where I was?" If Skeeter showed up, there'd be trouble.

He didn't give a specific date or time. So like him. What if he arrived while she was at the food bank? And what if he showed up when the cop was around? That would be worse than awkward. Jinxi rubbed a hand across her mouth, remembering the feel of his backhanded slap.

Should she stay here in this soft prison or jump on the back of his motorcycle and return to the world of sharp corners and jagged edges? Neither choice put her in control. Life was *so* wonderful.

Skeeter's arrest for possession had been her chance to escape. She could begin making her own choices, determining her own destiny. What a dismal failure.

With a sigh, she stood and crept into the living room. She double-checked to make sure the red car wasn't outside before returning to the computer. Time to do a little more digging. Jinxi pulled the list of passwords out of her memory and began an online search into Janice's accounts.

On Tuesday, Janice received another frantic call from her daughter. "Mom, it's me. Something strange is going on."

"What now?"

"It's Hannah."

A swish of alarm. "What about her?"

"Remember how yesterday her left hand was swollen? Well, today, her right hand is swollen."

"What about the left one?"

"That one is fine. But I'm worried. Hannah says it doesn't hurt, but I'm concerned. The thing is—" Robin turned away from the phone. "Not now, Hannah. I'll get you some juice when I'm off the phone." She continued, "Sunday, she was with Jinxi alone, and Monday, her hand is swollen. Yesterday, she was alone with her, and today her other hand is swollen. Doesn't that seem strange to you?"

"You think Jinxi is doing something to hurt Hannah?" Janice ran a hand through her hair, sinking into the easy chair in the living room.

"I don't know, Mom. All I'm saying is it's awfully weird. There's something about that girl I don't like. She's creepy. I know you want her to get saved and all, but this is your granddaughter we're talking about."

"I think you should take her to the doctor. Hannah adores Jinxi, and I'd think Hannah would say something if Jinxi was hurting her. Be sure to call me if you end up taking her to the doctor. I'm anxious to know what she says."

Janice leaned back in her favorite chair and pulled her Bible onto her lap. The conviction she had felt while talking to Robin burned to ashes. Fear battled with faith. Which would be the victor?

Jinxi slid the backpack off her shoulder and let it tumble onto the bed. She followed with a weary sigh, shaking her arms to relieve the ache from the physical labor at the food bank. Maybe lugging her stuff back and forth every day wasn't a great idea. The stud in her lip clicked across her teeth as an idea formed.

Jinxi reached for the zipper on the pack and slowly pulled it open. She chewed on a fingernail, staring up at the picture of the angel before reaching for the clothes jammed into the backpack. A T-shirt, pair of shorts, and jeans all went into a pile. She dug around until her fingers landed on the stuffed bunny. She hugged him to her chest for a moment before sitting him up against the pillows. Next came the photographs. Thumbing through them, she lingered on the one of her mom and dad on their wedding day. She walked over to the dresser and propped the photo up against the lamp.

Her breath quickened. What was she doing? She didn't belong here. What made her think she could put down roots? If she had to leave in a hurry, she might have to leave her stuff. She reached for the photo. Picked it up again. Set it back down. What if Skeeter came and took her away from all this?

She'd been eighteen the first time she'd seen him at a party at a friend's home. His name was Steven, but everyone called him Skeeter. He'd been diagnosed with ADHD at an early age, and his mom had nicknamed him Skeeter because, she said, he buzzed around like a mosquito.

He'd sprawled on the sofa, drinking a beer, cigarette dangling from his fingertips. His eyes had skipped over Jinxi, seeming to take a greater interest in one of her more voluptuous friends. Later, when the weed was passed around, he'd planted himself beside her on the floor.

"What middle school do you go to?" he'd asked sarcastically. When Jinxi bristled and told him how old she was, he'd laughed. Skeeter took to driving by her house on his motorcycle, revving the engine until she came out. They'd moved in together when she graduated. He'd made good money dealing drugs, enough to buy his Harley for cash. Enough to buy the latest gadgets, and buy them again when they had to leave a place in a hurry.

The closest she'd ever come to normal was when they'd rented a bungalow in a rural area. For three months, she'd been able to pretend they were a regular couple. She'd bought a few knickknacks and throw pillows to make the place homey. Skeeter had teased her, said she was becoming a suburban housewife. She'd even let herself think they might start a family—in spite of the physical stuff. She'd learned to live with a few bruises. Small price for a place to stay.

The dream shattered when Skeeter roared to the house one afternoon and shouted at her to gather up her stuff and get on the bike.

"Someone tipped off the cops. They'll be here any minute."

Jinxi didn't waste time packing anything other than her few childhood possessions and some clothes. Skeeter dropped her off at a friend's and took off down the freeway. That was the last time she'd seen him. Savvy told her he'd been arrested at the Mexican border on a bench warrant.

The only thing waiting for her back in Bakersfield was a boyfriend who barely stayed one step away from the police and a lifestyle that grew more tiresome with every move. Better to be someplace safe. Someplace where she could survive. And maybe come out ahead financially.

Janice's checking and savings accounts held a grip load of money. But the amount in the investment account was staggering.

No one should have that much money.

The question was, how could she get at it without arousing Janice's suspicion? She'd notice a withdrawal from her regular bank account. But maybe one of the investment accounts ... Jinxi chewed on the stud in her lip. There had to be a way, but she hadn't thought of it yet.

CHAPTER 16

"I hope you like Chinese," Janice said, waving white sacks with red lettering. "We can eat while we watch TV." Janice opened up the containers and set them out on the dining room table. "I can't see sitting at the table all by myself."

Jinxi stood at the bottom of the stairs, stomach growling, perpetually hungry. Anything sounded good. This must be what it was like to live a normal life. A safe place to sleep, a clean house, and someone to feed her. Right on.

Janice beckoned. "C'mon. You don't have to stay in your room all the time, you know."

As if. Let Janice think that.

Janice retrieved two plates from the dish rack on the kitchen counter and brought them out along with utensils and glasses of ice water. After they filled their plates, they sat in silence, watching the local news.

"Have you called your folks?" Janice asked, spearing a shrimp.

"My folks?" Jinxi looked at her sideways. "You mean my mom?" The question came out of left field. Where was this going?

Janice shrugged. "I wondered if anyone at home was worried about you."

Jinxi's laugh was harsh. "I doubt it."

Janice pushed some food around on her plate. "If you were one of my kids, I'd want to know where you were."

"She's probably relieved."

"How do you know, unless you call her?" Janice pressed.

"It doesn't matter."

Her mother probably hadn't even noticed she was gone.

"Look, I know it's none of my business, but if you change your mind, I have free long distance on the landline." Jinxi stared at her plate, as Janice continued. "Think about it, okay?"

You're right. It's none of your business. Even as Jinxi nodded on the outside, her mind rebelled. Call her mother? Not a chance.

On the next commercial, Janice asked, "When you were with Hannah, did anything unusual happen?"

Jinxi pulled her attention away from the television. "What do you mean?"

"Well, it's just that Hannah's hands have been swollen, first the left one and now the right. I wondered if maybe she fell or something when you were with her." Janice touched her lips with her napkin before reaching over to place it on her empty plate, avoiding eye contact.

"You think I had something to do with it?" What was going on here? One moment we're eating some Chinese take-out, next, there's accusations of hurting a kid. Her mind closed around images she'd buried. Pictures of an out-of-control fire and the screams of a mother for her trapped child.

Jinxi threw her plate onto the coffee table and sprang to her feet.

"I don't know what to think," Janice admitted. She looked down at her hands, face red. "I mean—"

"Do you really think I'd do something to hurt a little kid?" Tears sprang to Jinxi's eyes, and she bit the inside of her cheek to keep them in check. "I'm not a monster."

Monster. The word the mother had shouted, even as she was held back by the firemen trying to douse the flames.

Janice rubbed her hands together. "I'm sorry. You're right. I don't think you did anything to hurt her. I shouldn't have said anything."

Jinxi didn't answer as she bolted for the stairs. Forcing down the hurt, she hurried toward the one thing that would relieve the pain.

She'd never escape her past.

The next day, Jinxi arrived at the food bank with a minute to spare. Aneesa looked her up and down, her gaze lingering on the long sleeves despite the heat outside.

"Wait here for a minute. Padish wants to talk to you."

Jinxi's stomach turned to stone. What had she done wrong? Maybe he found out she hadn't rotated the cans of peaches. She did a mental inventory of everything that had happened from then until now. Norma probably said something, told a lie about her. Maybe they had decided she couldn't do community service and had to return to jail. She rubbed the scars on her arms, wishing she hadn't had the second cup of coffee.

A few minutes later, Padish strolled through the door, all sunshine and rainbows. He smiled and clapped his hands together. "Ah, yes. Miss Jinxi. I need to talk to you."

His smile did nothing to offer comfort. He motioned Jinxi to sit and took his chair behind the cluttered desk, hands folded.

"You know our friend, Norma, yes?"

Here it comes. *Wait for it.*

"She took a fall last night and broke her ankle. She is unable to work for six weeks."

Jinxi knew she'd get blamed for something.

"We require someone to work in the kitchen. Connie has spoken of what a help you have been for her. I am saying this—do you want to work in Norma's place until she comes back? We will pay you."

Jinxi's brain reeled. A job. With pay.

"But what about the community service? Will they let you pay me for that?"

Padish laughed. "Oh, no. Not at all. You will work four hours for pay and four hours for the lovely City of Sacramento."

She'd never had a real job before. Did she even *want* to work here?

"When do I start?" Jinxi asked, surprising herself.

"Right now." He turned to the office manager. "Aneesa, will you get the paperwork for Miss Jinxi?"

"When we're done," Aneesa told Jinxi, "go see Connie. She's anxious for some assistance this morning. This thing with Norma has her an hour behind."

After agreeing she would report every morning at eight and work until four-thirty, Jinxi hurried into the kitchen to find Connie rushing around like a druggie on a three-day crack bender.

"Yinxi. I am glad to see you." Connie shoved a hairnet at her and pushed her toward the sink. "Always wash first. After that, we cook."

After Jinxi washed her hands, Connie showed her several heads of cabbage.

"Chop this more small and put in here." Connie pointed to the commercial-sized food processor sitting on the counter. "Today, we eat hot dogs and coleslaw," she said with a disapproving turn of her mouth. "Is easy because that one not come in today."

"You mean Norma." The cranky one.

"*Sí,*" answered Connie with a vigorous nod of her head. "I no like hot dogs. I going to make chili, but no time today because that one not here."

Jinxi fed several wedges of cabbage through the processor and transferred the result to a steel bowl. "So, Norma, is she always in a bad mood?"

Connie clicked her tongue as she moved to the oven to remove some cookies. "She a bad one. Mean, not nice. She tell *el jefe* I not nice to her." Connie shook her head in disbelief. "Me? Not nice? No is possible." She seemed at a loss for the English words and huffed out a breath full of indignation. "Some people not nice."

Jinxi mulled this over as she mindlessly shredded the slaw. Like the Girls' Ranch. Some seemed to relish picking on smaller girls. She'd had her share of being bullied because of her size. She'd had to learn to either fight dirty or stay out of their way.

Jinxi finished shredding the cabbage and turned to Connie for direction.

"Now you make the salsa. I mean the dressing." She showed her how to mix the mayonnaise and milk and the amount of vinegar needed.

"You taste to see how much spice to add." She showed Jinxi the seasonings set out earlier and indicated how to measure them in her palm. "Not too much at first."

Connie showed Jinxi how to crush the spices with the opposite hand's thumb to bring out the flavors. "First you mix, then you taste." Connie had several wooden stir sticks and dipped one end in to taste the concoction. She had Jinxi do the same.

"How will I know when it's right?"

"You will know," Connie answered with a smile.

Jinxi narrowed her eyes. Was she making fun of her?

Connie waved her arm. "You try. Don't worry yourself. When you think it is right, I will taste, okay?"

Jinxi chewed the stud in her bottom lip and shrugged. She experimented a little, tasted, added some salt and pepper.

"Very good," Connie observed. "Now try."

Jinxi tasted the dressing. Connie dipped her stick in, closed her eyes, and let the dressing roll around in her mouth for a moment. "*Excelente*." she proclaimed. "Now mix it in with the cabbage."

With a shimmer of pride, Jinxi stirred the bowl of coleslaw and put it into the refrigerator as directed.

"Tomorrow we make spaghetti," Connie declared. "I teach you to make the sauce."

The rest of the week flew by, with Connie teaching her rudimentary cooking techniques before sending Jinxi to work in the stock room. Jinxi dragged herself onto the bus each day, exhausted but with a strange new feeling of contentment.

The bus smelled old, like most of the riders. Jinxi could count on one hand the number of men and women dressed in business attire. Everyone else sat, head down, looking as worn out as she felt. Jinxi plopped on a seat and slung down her backpack.

Padish's lavish praise filled her with a warm glow. She'd devoured his words. She had to admit she and Connie worked together like they'd been at it forever. Maybe this community service thing wasn't so bad. She'd have a full stomach, a place to go, and with Janice's money, a way to start over.

The bus jerked to a halt at her stop. Jinxi alighted and began the block-and-a-half walk to the Rafferty home. As she drew closer to the house, she spotted a familiar jean-clad figure leaning up against a dangerous-looking motorcycle, smoking a cigarette in front of Janice's chain-link fence.

Jinxi skidded to a stop.

The boulder of reality crushed the warm glow from the day. Why did she think she could escape? Before she could turn and run, he spotted her and dropped his cigarette.

"Hey, baby."

"Hi, Skeeter."

CHAPTER 17

He'd taken off his helmet, shaggy brown hair pressed down with the imprint, looking as dangerous as his bike. A snake tattoo curled up one arm, and several Chinese alphabet symbols decorated the other. He had a devil character with a pitchfork and tail on the side of his neck under one ear. A peace sign dangled from the other lobe.

Skeeter dragged Jinxi to him as she approached. Crushed against his chest, her heart hammered against her ribs. He slapped his hands against her bottom and locked his lips on hers.

When he released her, he pushed his hair back and started that annoying foot-tapping habit of his.

"What made you think I wouldn't come after you?" He jingled his keys and fiddled with his earring. "Get your stuff and let's bounce."

Same story, different geography.

"Where are we going?"

"I'm taking you back to B-town. No one leaves me unless I say it's okay." His weight shifted from one leg to the other.

Used to be his fidgeting was endearing. Now it's getting on my last nerve. He totally owned his mom's nickname for him. "Like a mosquito, he is," she'd said.

"What are you waiting for?" Skeeter's voice took on a threatening tone. "Get your stuff and let's go."

Jinxi started toward the gate leading up to Janice's house. Why did she lose her identity when Skeeter was around? What consequences would there be when he got her alone? He'd want to show everyone not to question his authority.

Jinxi couldn't go back. She had a plan. One that didn't include Skeeter. She'd make her own way, get her own money. Stop the abuse.

"I can't go." There. She'd said it.

"Why not?" He grabbed her arms and shook her.

"It's that, I, um, I have a job now."

Jinxi winced as he squeezed her arms tighter. "You don't need some stupid job."

She forced herself to meet his eyes. "It's a real job where people depend on me."

How could she explain that it felt good to be needed?

"Don't tell me you've gone all *Modern Family* on me. Next thing you know, you'll be telling me you've decided to start going to church." He shook her harder. "Come on. You don't belong here."

Jinxi shifted from one foot to the other, eyes darting around. She'd enjoyed going places with Skeeter because she *had* felt like she belonged. She was someone's girlfriend. But it was peaceful here at Janice's. There was a purpose for getting up each day. *And maybe people might miss me if I was gone.* She thought of Hannah and her exuberant "I love you."

And all Janice's money.

"I'm not going," Jinxi said, voice quavering.

Skeeter dropped her arms, a dangerous look on his face. "You know what this means, don't you?"

She cringed, waiting for the blow.

"If I leave without you, don't expect me to come back. Ever. We're done." He crossed his arms and leaned against his bike. "Well? What're you going to do?"

Her stomach hurt, but she held her ground. "I'm not going."

Skeeter shrugged and jumped on his bike. He pulled on his helmet and shook his head.

"Don't think you can dump me that easy. You wait." He gunned his engine and rocketed away.

Jinxi shuddered despite the ninety-degree heat. She picked up her backpack and trudged up the front stairs to the porch. What just happened? She'd stood up to Skeeter. A feeling of power engulfed her, followed by a wave of doubt. Should she have gone with him? She chewed a fingernail, staring in the direction Skeeter had gone. Abandoned again.

She should be used to that by now. First her dad. Then her mom—a slow leaving through alcohol and men. It was probably better this way. If people knew who she was, what she was, they'd run from her as fast as they could. She was a broken toy, tossed aside. Worthless.

The inside of the house echoed with the sound of her boots. The photos of Janice, Dean, and the rest of the family stared back from their perch on the piano. Was this what a typical family looked like? A family without secrets, without shame. Or was Janice's family the odd one, the exception?

Jinxi crossed the room, pulled out her cell, and slumped on the sofa. She touched the 'favorites' icon.

After a few rings, her mom picked up. "Hullo?"

"Mom, it's me."

A pause. "Jinxi? Baby? That you?"

"Yeah, Mom, it's me." She pictured her mom sitting at the kitchen table, overflowing ashtray at her elbow. And a lukewarm cup of coffee. She'd be wearing faded jeans and a shapeless T-shirt over her skinny frame. So different from Janice's coordinated outfits.

Her mom's voice rasped from a lifetime of smoking cigarettes. "Where are you, baby? I've been so worried—"

Jinxi's heart jumped. Her mom missed her.

"—about Ron. He lost his job at the car place."

And as quickly, Jinxi's heart sank into her stomach. She bent over to ease the pain.

Her mom's voice droned on. "I don't know what we're going to do. The dealership is closing, and they laid off all the mechanics. He hasn't been able to find any work, and he's depressed."

"Mom. About me."

"Oh, baby, it's probably good you're not here. Ron would be so worried about how he was going to feed someone else."

Jinxi snorted. Ron had never given her anything but grief and stress.

"Jinxi, honey, don't be like that. You know he loves you."

Jinxi inhaled, ready to retort, but her mom continued. "I know he'll find something soon, but all he does is sit in front of the TV, drinking beer and moping. He's so depressed."

A scream crawled up Jinxi's throat. Some things never changed. Her finger stabbed the off button. *What a mistake.* She should never have called.

The house pulsed around her, filled with echoes of family life and laughter. Now the photos on the piano mocked her. She jumped up and ran for the front door, tripping onto the porch.

The convenience store a few blocks down beckoned her with the promise of something that might bring comfort. As she neared the door, she caught a glimpse of Janice's car, heading down the street toward the house. She ducked her head in case Janice spotted her.

There was no one at the counter. A voice called from somewhere in the back. "I'll be right there."

It appeared the clerk had been unpacking boxes of cigarettes into the locked cabinet behind the counter. She hadn't quite finished, and a few packs lay loose. Jinxi grabbed a pack off the counter and took off out the door. She sprinted across the street, dodging a car that was turning, and tore down the road toward Janice's. When she was within a block, she slowed down to catch her breath. What had she done? She scurried to her room and stashed the cigarettes in the bottom drawer of the bureau. Sitting on the edge of the bed, gasping while her heart slowed.

A shot of adrenaline hit her like a Taser when the doorbell rang downstairs. What if it was the woman from the store? What if someone followed her and knew what she had done?

"Jinxi," Janice called from the bottom of the stairs. "Someone's here to see you."

She was so busted. Now she really was going to jail. All because of a pack of cigarettes. Another lousy decision with worse consequences.

"You up there?" Janice called again.

"Be right down," she answered, heading to the window. How far down was the drop? Could she jump without breaking her legs? Probably not. She looked around the room, folded her arms across her chest, and headed for the stairs, dying more with each step.

CHAPTER 18

Dean sat on one of the barstools in his apartment and removed his black police-issue shoes. They dropped with a *thunk* on the wood floor. His socks followed, landing like deflated balloons. He stood, unbuttoned his uniform shirt, and let it flop to the floor, followed by his pants. He walked the four steps to his futon and fell face down with a grunt.

He had drifted off to sleep when he remembered to set his alarm. Four hours should do it.

The insistent bleating of the alarm woke him from a dreamless sleep. He smacked his hand on the clock to silence the noise and sat up, rubbing his face. He padded into the kitchen and started the coffee pot, letting it brew while he showered.

Two awesome days off in a row. And on the weekend, too. Pool with the guys tonight, barbeque tomorrow at Patrice and Sanjay's house, and Folsom Lake on Sunday. Wakeboarding, jet skis, awesomeness squared.

The first cup of coffee cleared the cobwebs from his brain. The second accompanied a bowl of cereal and a glance at the news on his tablet.

LOCAL COUPLE FOUND GUILTY OF ELDER ABUSE.

His hands gripped the edges of the iPad. The story told how a caregiver moved in with an older woman. She and her husband gradually manipulated the woman into signing over her property.

Dean shoved the tablet away, coffee sour in his stomach. His mom was so *vulnerable*. His dad should be here. Dean let his head drop onto the counter. Pressure built behind his eyes, forcing tears.

He still grieved for his dad after this long, and he hated it. Hated he had lost his best friend and idol.

I hate God. The words sprang unbidden to his mind, followed by remorse. *God will strike me dead. Like my dad.*

Dean knew all about the judgment of God. He'd learned every Old Testament Bible story about God's wrath toward the sinner. That's why God had taken his dad. God must be angry because of what Dean had done to that girl in college. Dean had to atone for his sin.

His dad was dead because of him.

They called it an accident. A thousand pounds of steel, crushing the life from his father. Had he suffered? What had been his last thought as the heavy steel hit his body?

Dean groaned, plagued by the questions that had no answers.

He sprang to his feet to head over to his mom's house and see what Jinxi was up to. Maybe he'd ask her to go with him and his friends to the lake. That way he could keep an eye on her.

Yeah, keep an eye on her. It had nothing to do with attraction. It was about protecting his mother.

He jogged across the yard, bounded up the steps, and entered the back door into the kitchen. Sounds of laughter and voices came from the living room. What man was visiting with his mom? He froze in the doorway leading from the kitchen into the dining room. Maybe the question should be, what man was visiting Jinxi?

Without pausing to think, he charged through the kitchen and into the dining room.

"Oof!" Jinxi exclaimed with a curse.

He'd barreled into her as she reached the bottom of the staircase.

"What's going on?" His mom appeared around the corner, Padish Singh on her heels.

Jinxi rubbed her shoulder. "You stupid jerk. You nearly killed me."

Dean's face grew hot.

His mom looked like she didn't know whether to be embarrassed by Jinxi's outburst or concerned she might be hurt.

"Sorry," Dean mumbled. "I was, you know, coming over to say hi. To my mom." Dean put his hands in his shorts pockets and rocked back on his heels.

Jinxi's eyes were twin lasers, ready to incinerate him into a pile of ash.

"Everyone come into the living room." Mom took control, turning everyone's attention away. Finally.

"Padish dropped by to see you, Jinxi," Mom said as they piled into the living room.

Jinxi looked down and clicked her lip stud against her teeth. Why was she nervous?

"You forgot something at work today," Padish said. "Every Friday is payday, and you did not take your check." He waved an envelope at her. Jinxi reached out a shaky hand to take it.

Dean's eyes narrowed.

"Wasn't that nice of him to stop by and bring it to you?" Janice asked.

Jinxi's shoulders slumped as she exhaled. He knew guilt when he saw it. But why?

Smile firmly in place, Padish said to Janice, "Ah, but it gave me a chance to see you again, Mrs. Rafferty. It has been too long."

Mom shrugged. "I know, I know. It's amazing how quickly my days fill up. I'll get over soon to help you in the office again."

"Not to worry yourself. Whenever you can, we will welcome you." With a bow, he turned to go.

"See you Monday," he called to Jinxi as he went through the door.

Mom closed the front door and turned toward Dean. "So, what's on your agenda for the evening, son?"

He ran a hand over his unshaven chin. "Uh, stopped in to say hi. I'm heading out to the Blue Cue with the guys."

"Lovely. Have fun."

Jinxi remained frozen in the same spot.

"So, Jinxi, you okay?"

Her head snapped up. "Uh, yeah. Fine." She pushed past him and headed up the stairs.

He and his mom locked eyes, shrugging in unison.

Jinxi threw herself on the bed, envelope in hand. There was a window on one side, showing her name. She ran her finger over the waxy surface. She'd never had a paycheck before.

The envelope wasn't sealed. Jinxi slid the check out, breathing hard.

"Pay To The Order Of Jeanette Lansing." The amount was $54.39. Big whoop.

She'd worked her tail off, and all she had to show was a measly fifty-four dollars? Things had better change and fast. She and Skeeter had made a thousand times that much in a day.

Her cell phone beeped. Savannah had sent a text and a selfie. The picture was of her with Skeeter wrapped around her neck. It figured her best friend would hook up with Jinxi's boyfriend.

SAVANNAH: Where r u girlfriend? U shd b here.

Looking at the photo caused Jinxi to rethink her decision to tell Skeeter she wouldn't go with him. Would it have been better to hop on Skeeter's bike and head back to Southern California? If only she had someone to talk to.

What about Dean?

The thought came unbidden to mind. There was no way to shake him loose, since he practically lived with his mom. Was Dean someone she could trust? Probably. He seemed open and honest, the character traits required of a cop. Her polar opposite. Cringing, Jinxi remembered the stolen pack of cigarettes. And the forty bucks she'd taken from Janice's stash.

The question was, did she want to trust him?

CHAPTER 19

A breeze tickled the lace curtains on the windows in Jinxi's room. She shivered and snuggled under the blanket. One eye opened to look at the clock. Eight a.m. Rolling over, she savored the additional moments in bed. All of a sudden, she remembered. Today, she could cash her check.

Springing out of bed like a kid on Christmas morning, she skipped to the bathroom to get ready. Forgoing the black makeup, she hurried through her morning routine, hoping to catch Janice before she left. It'd be nice not to have to walk to Walmart.

With the paycheck tucked into her purse, she rushed down the stairs and into the kitchen. Janice entered carrying a cup of coffee, dressed in a sleeveless cotton top and a pair of shorts that skimmed above her knees. Whoa. Betty White in something other than a dress.

Janice caught her eye and looked down at her outfit. "I'm babysitting Hannah, remember? I've got to be dressed for anything around *that* child."

And that was why Jinxi would never have kids.

"You're up early today," Janice commented as she rinsed her mug in the sink.

"Um, yeah. I thought you could, you know, drop me at Walmart?" Geez, was she begging? This was so messed up.

Janice's smile lit up her face. "Of course. I'll be ready to go in about ten minutes. Will that work for you?"

"Sure."

Janice set her cup in the dish drainer and retreated down the hall to her bedroom. Jinxi poured herself a cup of coffee, savoring the first sip of the day. After getting her cash and doing a little shopping, she'd do some snooping in those investment accounts. With Janice at her darling granddaughter's house, she'd have lots of time to herself.

Ten minutes later, they were in the car, heading down Del Paso Boulevard. Janice drove the few blocks to a strip mall with several shops and a Super Walmart.

"Here you go," Janice said. "The bus stop is right across the street, or you could probably walk back, depending on the heat. I won't be home until around ten or eleven tonight."

All the better to see what she had hidden.

Jinxi thanked her and climbed out of the car. The bank branch was easy to locate at the front of the store.

Plan A. Cash the check.

Plan B. Retail therapy.

First, the necessities. Work T-shirts, preferably long-sleeved, and underwear. Nail polish remover and more nail polish. Wandering around the store, Jinxi enjoyed the freedom of being able to look at everything without hurry. She settled on some clothing on the clearance rack and was happy to see that she had spent less than twenty dollars of her pay. The money she'd taken from Janice was folded into a corner of her wallet.

From the checkout line, she spied a booth next to the bank.

"Send and Receive Money Here," said the advertisement.

Plan C. Research.

After purchasing her items, she wandered to the booth.

"May I help you?"

"Yeah, uh, could someone transfer money to me here?"

The lady behind the counter nodded. "Yes. Where is the money coming from?"

"I'm expecting some money from my aunt," she lied. "She's transferring it from her investment account."

The clerk pulled out a brochure. "The instructions are in here. There is a charge for the transfer, a percentage of the amount of money. You understand?"

Jinxi understood perfectly. She smiled. "Thanks for your help."

"Any time."

Jinxi's heart beat with anticipation. It couldn't get much easier than that. Janice would be gone the rest of the day. Time enough to implement Plan D.

"How long does it take to get the money?"

"It takes three to five business days. You can call to see if it's arrived once your aunt initiates the transfer."

Perfect.

But first, a detour for some Mickey D's. Fast food she didn't have to dumpster-dive for.

As she munched on her burger and fries, a familiar voice called her.

"Yinxi. Yinxi. Is that you?" Connie waddled toward her, trailed by a boy and a girl, as short and as dark as she was.

Snap! Now she'd be forced to make nice to her food bank coworker.

"*Hola, amiga,*" Connie said, stopping in front of Jinxi's table. "I did not know you live near here." She was all smiles as if seeing Jinxi was the best thing that had happened to her today. Before Jinxi could answer, Connie pushed her children forward. "These are my children. This is Rosa and Miguel." She spoke in Spanish to the children, and they gave Jinxi shy smiles. Each of them carried a bag from the Goodwill store. Connie pulled a wire basket on two wheels, overflowing with food. She indicated Jinxi's bag. "You have shopped, *sí*?"

"*Sí*. I mean yes."

"We are going home now. What do you do today?"

I'm planning to "borrow" some money from Betty White.

Jinxi shrugged. "Nothing, I guess."

Connie beamed. "You come with us. I teach you to make tamales. *Delicioso* tamales."

Jinxi hesitated. What about Plan D? She chewed her lip, working the stud back and forth. Looking into Connie's friendly face, she surprised herself. "Okay."

The money would still be there when she got back to Janice's.

CHAPTER 20

Jinxi caught Connie's kids staring at the uneaten pile of French fries. She was about to gather them up to toss them but slid them toward the kids instead.

"Want these?"

The kids were on the fries as if they hadn't eaten in a week.

"I am sorry. The *papas fritas* are a treat." Connie shrugged and smiled.

"No problem." The fries disappeared in less than a minute.

"Come, *mijos*, is time to go home."

They exited the store, followed by the two kids.

"Where's your car?" Jinxi asked, scanning the parking lot.

Connie laughed good-naturedly. "I take the bus. No car."

Well, shoot. Another stinky bus ride. Jinxi shouldn't have agreed to go. She could be at Janice's by now, already digging into what might be waiting in the depths of Janice's computer.

Jinxi's steps lagged.

"*Vamos*," Connie urged as the bus screeched to a halt.

She was trapped now. They boarded the bus for the ride to Connie's house. The bus belched to a stop a short time later and they traveled deeper into the 'hood.

Connie lived in an apartment complex flanked by other identical units, painted drab-green with a splash of white trim around the doors and windows. A six-foot iron fence topped with sharp spikes surrounded the property. The buildings had the air of decay, as if they were once a thriving neighborhood but had given up because it was too much effort.

As they walked through the parking area, several young men sitting on the hoods of low-riding cars appraised Jinxi. She ignored them and shifted her bag from one hand to the other. Connie seemed oblivious, but the children huddled close to her. They passed by an open hallway where an Asian man wearing baggy khakis and open-toed rubber sandals swept the sidewalk. Connie greeted him with a smile.

"*Hola, Señor* Yee."

He turned and regarded her without smiling. "Good afternoon, Mrs. Reyes."

"I have rent today."

"Monday is fine," he answered, returning to his sweeping.

Connie opened the apartment door, speaking to Jinxi over her shoulder. "*Señor* Yee is the manager of this place."

Jinxi looked around at the sparsely furnished living room. A sofa stood against the wall, a scarred coffee table in front of it, and not much else. An older television sat on a TV tray in the corner, flanked by two bean bag chairs.

"*Mami*, can we go ride our bikes?" Miguel inquired.

"*Sí, mijo*," she said. "Be careful." She added something in Spanish, and all Jinxi caught was 'Rosa.'"

The kids retrieved their bikes from a bedroom down a short hall. They were out the door in a flash.

"Must have music." Connie shuffled into the living room. An ancient stereo sat on a small table. No iPod in sight. She switched it on, and mariachi music filled the room.

"First, we have some coffee," Connie said, filling a carafe with water from the tap. "I must rest my feet. Sit yourself."

At least the woman had her priorities straight. Coffee first before everything else.

Jinxi watched from the wooden table as Connie moved around the tiny kitchen. The spotless counters were dull from age, and the Formica had worn down in places. Connie used a stool to reach into the upper cupboards. She should get herself one of those for Janice's kitchen.

Soon the fragrance of fresh coffee filled the apartment. Connie cut two hunks of cake from a plastic plate.

She brought the cake and coffee to the table. Jinxi wrinkled her nose when Connie poured liberal amounts of cream and sugar into her cup. Why even bother putting any coffee in the cup?

"Black for me."

Connie shrugged and sat.

Jinxi cut a chunk of cake with her fork. She popped the bite in her mouth and savored the chocolate. This woman was a good cook. All those lunches at the food bank, and still she had time to make a cake. Jinxi tried to remember the last time she'd had homemade chocolate cake. Probably never.

"You like?"

Jinxi nodded, unable to speak. What she wouldn't give to be able to make this. She forced herself to eat the cake slowly as Connie talked.

"My husband, he is a good man. Hard worker. He work in a food cannery until one day ..." Connie paused with a pained expression. "One day, there was a, how you say ..."

"Accident?"

"No, no *accidente*. It was where the *policía* come and take all the workers without the green card."

"A raid?"

Connie nodded vigorously. "*Sí*, a raid. My husband, he no have the green card. The *policía* take him away and send him back to Mexico. His friend have a cell phone, and he call me and tell me. Otherwise, I not know." She shook her head. "It is six months. I still am trying to get the papers to bring him back."

"You mean INS took him away? No notice, no phone call, nothing?"

"Yes, that is it."

"Is there anything you can do? Will he be coming back?" Why should she care? This wasn't her problem. But she was still angry.

"I have an attorney who helps me. And the Immigration Office helps me too. But it takes time, and I have to go to work." Connie shrugged, lifting her open palms. "It will happen in God's time." She crossed herself and kissed her thumbnail. "How many years do you have?"

"What?"

Connie smacked herself on the forehead. "I mean, how old you are?"

"I'm twenty-one. How old are you?"

"I have twenty-nine years." She puffed out her chest. "I have lived in this country for six years."

"Are you a citizen?"

Connie nodded and smiled. "*Sí*. But my English is still not so good. You help me." she exclaimed, rocking back in her seat.

Jinxi shook her head. "I don't know about that. I barely remember the Spanish I took in high school."

"It is not important. You correct me when I say a mistake."

Jinxi took a sip of coffee. "I don't know." That sounded too much like a commitment.

"Is okay. I not mind."

Perhaps she could steer Connie in a different direction. "What about your kids? Can't they help you?"

"No, we talk in Spanish in the home. I don't want them to forget. I need a person who can tell me when I say a mistake. Is very important to me." Connie laid her hand on Jinxi's arm, face serious. "Please. I ask you."

Jinxi resisted the urge to yank her arm back. "I guess so." What had she committed herself to? She didn't need a BFF. As soon as she finished community service, she'd be gone. Maybe.

"*Excelente*. Now we make tamales." Connie stood and drained her cup, indicating Jinxi should wash her hands. She tied a long apron around Jinxi's waist and put its twin on herself.

Both women were about the same height, but Jinxi couldn't help noticing how pale her arms looked next to Connie's dark ones. Connie wore her long brown hair pulled back into a braid at the base of her neck. Her hair dangled down her back, touching her waist. Connie's face was devoid of makeup, and she wore tiny silver hoops in her ears. Jinxi tucked her hair behind her ears, hoping the tattoo on her neck wasn't too visible.

"The meat has cooked all day. We will shred it first."

Connie removed the lid from a large pot, and Jinxi nearly swooned from the spicy fragrance. Connie showed her how to shred the meat using two forks. While Connie retrieved some ingredients from a cupboard, Jinxi couldn't help sneaking a few bites. This stuff was amazing. If she could cook like this, she'd never be hungry again.

Connie beat the *masa* and shortening, explaining what she was doing the whole time. The kids came in asking for a snack and went back outside to play.

When they'd shredded the meat, and the *masa* mixture was finished, Connie retrieved the corn husks from where they'd been soaking.

"Why do you have to soak them in water?" Jinxi asked.

"It must be wet so it will go around the meat more easier. See, I show you."

Connie spread a spoonful of the *masa* mixture on the husk, added the meat, folding the whole thing up like a burrito. Looked easy enough.

"Come. Now you try." Connie's fingers were strong and sure, but Jinxi's first attempts were clumsy, and the mixture dribbled out of the sides.

"Geez, I'll never get it." Why bother? One more thing she couldn't do.

"*Sí, tú puedes*. Watch me." Connie was a patient teacher, and after a few more mistakes, Jinxi made a perfect one.

"Look. I did it!" She grinned.

Connie grinned back. "You are beautiful when you smile."

Jinxi's smile faded. Beautiful? Doubtful.

"*Bien hecho*. Well done."

Connie was wrong. She wasn't beautiful. But she could now wrap a tamale better than any *gringa* she knew.

What would it have been like to learn to cook when she still lived at home? Jinxi tried to picture her mother patiently teaching her some basic recipes. Connie's shoulder brushed hers, and the thought flew out the window. Be present. That's what the counselor at the Girls' Ranch continually preached. Stay in the moment.

They worked companionably for over an hour, spreading, stuffing, and folding over fifty tamales. When they finished, Connie set several aside and showed Jinxi how to steam them to eat right away.

"Go sit yourself," Connie said, bustling around the kitchen. "I will make a meal for us." She brought several of the tamales over to the table along with a roll of aluminum foil and showed Jinxi how to wrap each one individually. "These are gifts for people," she explained. "Everyone loves my tamales." She smiled with a glint of pride in her eyes. "Now they will know that you make the good tamales too."

Jinxi's phone vibrated in her back pocket. Another text from Savvy.

SAVANNAH: Whatever ur doing stop. Get up here to Reno. This street party is off the hook. Skeeter hooked up with some skank. U shd b here.

Her stomach clenched. Savvy was right. What was she doing here, playing house with this Mexican woman and her kids?

Dirty white girl.

The Mexican gang-bangers at the Girls' Ranch bullied her mercilessly. Always out of range from the guards, of course. They'd made her three years of incarceration a living hell. Why was Connie so nice to her? Was she waiting for an opportunity to make her feel stupid?

While Connie occupied herself in the kitchen, Jinxi reached for her backpack. She dug around until she found the knife.

"Can I use your bathroom?"

Connie turned away from the stove. "Of course." She pointed to a door.

Jinxi double-stepped into the bathroom and locked the door behind her, breathing in and out with a steady rhythm.

Dirty white girl.

The words cut like the knife in her backpack.

CHAPTER 21

Jinxi hunched over her coffee cup, vaguely aware of the sounds coming from Janice's bedroom. How could she get the woman out of the house? Time for Plan D. Money transfer.

She jumped when Janice's voice pierced her concentration. "Do you want to go to church with me?"

Jinxi glanced up at Janice's expectant expression. Hiding the hint of a smile, Jinxi shook her head. "Maybe next time."

"All right. See you later." Janice swept the strap of her bag over her shoulder and strode toward the door. Her low-heeled sandals made a *slub* sound on the wood floor. She wore a short-sleeved blue cotton shift with a leather belt around her waist. The silver ornamental buckle had pieces of turquoise, and she wore a turquoise and silver necklace.

Someone at Janice's church should call the fashion police.

As soon as the door closed, Jinxi sprang to her feet. She watched the Prius pull out of the driveway and head down the street before racing into the office to boot up the computer.

Come on, come on.

Anxiety was an icy hand around her throat. She gnawed on her fingers until the computer lumbered to life.

After logging on to the internet, she pulled up Janice's investment account, using the password she'd memorized.

Jinxi wiped her hands on her shorts and clicked the Transfer Funds tab.

Amount to transfer. Jinxi pulled her lip stud back and forth, considering. *One thousand dollars,* she typed in.

Transfer to. She rolled her shoulders back to ease the tension, typed *Jeanette Lansing.* Swallowing hard, she scrolled down to the boxes that asked where the money was going.

Snap! She'd left the brochure from Walmart upstairs. She'd hidden the information under her work T-shirts. She pulled it out and slapped it against her palm. Should she go through with it? A thousand bucks was a lot of money. Before an attack of conscience could talk her out of it, she turned and dashed back downstairs to the office.

Please verify information. Jinxi compared what she had typed with the brochure. Her hand hovered over the mouse. With a deep inhale, she pressed SEND.

Jinxi shook her hands to relieve the sudden blood pulsing through them. It didn't help. She had set something in motion that couldn't be reversed.

Janice would never miss such a small amount. *She doesn't need it. I do.* It was about survival. No one else would take care of her. She had to look out for herself.

Shaky after the adrenaline rush, Jinxi stood and twisted her neck back and forth. Wandering into the living room, she dropped into the big chair Janice favored and ran her hands up and down the wooden arms. The rocker creaked as it tilted back and forth. Jinxi halted the chair with both feet when she spied Janice's Bible. Jinxi looked out the window at the empty driveway. How long did church last, anyway? Jinxi picked up the Bible, running her hands along the worn leather. The thin parchment pages fell open at random to Psalm 139.

"O Lord you have searched me and you know me. You know when I sit and when I rise; you perceive my thoughts from afar. You discern my going out and my lying down; you

are familiar with all my ways. Before a word is on my tongue you know it completely, O Lord."

Jinxi skipped down further in the chapter.

"You created my inmost being; you knit me together in my mother's womb. My frame was not hidden from you when I was made in the secret place. When I was woven together in the depths of the earth, your eyes saw my unformed body."

So engrossed in reading, Jinxi barely registered the back door opening and someone entering the house. She slammed the Bible shut and threw the book on the table. It landed with a dull thud as Dean came into the room.

"What are you doing?" His eyes held her hostage.

"Nothing." She was certain he could see the pulse throbbing in her temple.

He settled his cop stare on her for ten long seconds. Heat crept up her neck. Did he suspect anything? What if he searched the browser history on Janice's computer? *Snap*. She should have remembered to erase the investment account site.

"Do you have a swimsuit?"

"Huh?"

"Wanna get out of the house?" Dean asked with a sudden grin. "Grab some shorts and put on some flip-flops. We're going to the lake."

Spend a whole day with a cop? Hardly tempting. But neither was sitting around the house. She got up from the chair and brushed past him to head up the stairs.

"Grab some of the striped beach towels from the linen closet, too," he told her.

Jinxi found the towels, quickly changed into shorts and a long-sleeved T-shirt, and hurried back downstairs. Dean wasn't in the house, but she spied him outside by his truck, loading an ice chest into the back. His tank shirt was snug across his chest. Jinxi took a moment to admire the muscles in his arms. Not exactly eye candy, but easy on the eyes.

After locking the side door behind her, she held the towels to one side to see her way down the concrete stairs. Being short was such a pain.

She threw the towels into the cab of the truck and climbed in after them. Dean secured the ice chest and jumped into the cab. He turned on the radio. Pop music blared out of the speakers.

"Whoa," he exclaimed, turning down the volume. "My bad. Let me put on some of that cowboy crap you love."

Carrie Underwood's voice crooned from the speakers, singing about church bells and wife beaters.

"What's with this music, anyway? It's all achy-breaky, my dog died, and my wife left me."

Jinxi shot him a hard look. "Maybe your jock brain has been bashed too much to understand the deeper meaning."

Dean snorted. He put the truck in drive and looked over at her. "You ready?"

"I guess." She'd jump out at the next stop if he made any more comments about her choice of music genre.

"Cool. Let's go." He put the truck in motion and took off from the curb with a squeal of the tires. Laughing, he said, "This is gonna be fun."

Fun, yeah. As much fun as going to church with Betty White.

He tossed his phone across the seat to her. "Send a text to my mom. Let her know we're headed to the lake."

So tempting to make him say *please*. "What's your mom's cell number?"

He leaned toward her, gesturing to the phone. "It's in my favorites."

Under 'Mommy'? She clamped her lips shut to keep the snark at bay. He might change his mind and drop her off at the next corner.

Dean explained that they were going to Folsom Lake, which was about thirty miles east. "It's not a huge lake, smaller than Lake Tahoe, but it's close, and we can boat and wakeboard there."

"Uh, aren't you forgetting something?" Jinxi asked, looking behind the truck and back at him.

"Like what?"

"Like a boat?" *Duh.*

"We're meeting some friends. Two of them have boats. One has a jet ski, so we'll have plenty to keep us busy today. And cool," he added, since the air conditioning in the truck wasn't keeping the heat outside at bay.

Fan-freaking-tastic. She'd agreed to spend an entire day with friends of a cop. Jumping out at the next stop sounded better by the minute.

They spent most of the ride in silence except when Dean pointed out landmarks along the way. He turned off at a sign pointing to Brown's Ravine Marina and drove around to the parking lot by the picnic area.

Jinxi hugged the towels to her chest. She should have brought her backpack. Without it, she wouldn't have any way to release the tension of facing a bunch of strangers.

Dean hefted the ice chest from the truck bed. "Hurry up."

She gritted her teeth and slid out of the pickup. Using his chin, Dean pointed to the path to the beach. His friends were already there, their boats and jet ski pulled up to the shore.

"Rafferty," one of the guys yelled, "It's about time."

"What took you so long, anyway? Did you have to work out first?" His friends laughed and joked with him while he good-naturedly returned the teasing.

They looked harmless enough, although all of them had short hair like Dean's. Most had tattoos on their shoulders or on the backs of their legs. *My people*. Maybe this would be okay.

"Hey, everybody, this is Jinxi. Jinxi, this is everybody. Don't worry about learning their names because they're totally forgettable."

Two of the guys jumped up from where they'd been sitting and dragged him toward the water. As they chased each other around for a moment, one of the women approached Jinxi.

"Come on over here and put the towels down," the brown-haired woman said. Her green eyes were friendly. "I'm Tara. Ignore those goons. They need to get rid of some of that testosterone. They'll be calmer once they get out on the water."

"Are you all cops?" Oh, gee. This would be fun.

Tara laughed. "Oh, no. No way." She indicated the group milling around the picnic table. "James is the one with the dark wavy hair. His wife is Patrice, and she's a cop, works with Dean." A blonde-haired woman waved. "Jason and Cora are friends of Dean's from way back, maybe even grade school. Damaris or 'D" is on the force with Dean. Sommer is a teacher." Cora's hair was short, and she was almost as fair as Jinxi. The girl named Sommer looked like a mix of two races. "My guy is the one who's dragging Dean into the lake. His name is Sanjay, and he's studying for his CPA test."

Holy cow. How would she remember all the names? Jinxi bit her lip, clicking the stud back and forth.

"I know," Tara said as if reading her mind. "There're a lot of people to remember. But don't worry too much. Come on over and get a sandwich before they're all gone." She turned toward the picnic table, every spot covered with sandwiches, chips, pickles, cookies, and an assortment of cupcakes.

"Glad you finally got here, Rafferty," the dark-skinned guy said.

"We had to wait for the drinks," Sanjay said to Jinxi. "Dean's not good for anything except bringing the liquid libations, being single and all."

Dean escaped the grasp of two guys, and they all gathered around the table, standing up while eating sandwiches and chips, as they bragged to each other about how long they would be able to stay up on the wakeboard. A couple of the girls pulled up webbed lawn chairs.

"Let the guys be animals," Tara said. "I prefer to eat like a human." The other girls sat in a loose circle, chatting easily.

Jinxi was as out of place as a nun at a rave.

She dumped the towels on the bench, reached for a plate, and piled a sandwich and some chips on it. Might as well eat while she could.

"You were smart to wear long sleeves," one of the girls commented. "With your fair skin, I bet you burn pretty fast."

Sure. Whatever. Jinxi mumbled what she hoped sounded like a yes.

"Patrice has sunscreen," Tara said. "You'll need it on your legs once we go out on the boat. Right, Patrice?"

Patrice nodded. "Sure thing." Jinxi looked over to find Patrice's eyes fixed on her.

"So, are you and Dean dating?"

CHAPTER 22

Jinxi choked on a sip of soda and coughed. Waving her hands and trying to control the spasm, she shook her head.

"Gosh, Patrice, be subtle, why don't you," Sommer asked.

After Jinxi regained control, Sommer locked eyes with her. "*Are* you two dating?"

The other women laughed.

"No."

"Did you grow up around here?"

"Where did you meet Dean?"

"If you're not dating, are you thinking about dating?"

"Are you related to him?"

The questions hit like bullets. Jinxi's head swung from one woman to the next.

"Quit interrogating her, ladies," Dean admonished, approaching the circle.

"But, Dean," Sommer said, with a sly smile, "you never bring anyone with you to the lake. We're curious, that's all." Her voice was all honey.

"Nice try, Sugar," he said, resting a hand on her shoulder. "Leave Jinxi alone. She's a friend, okay? End of story."

"Hey," Sommer exclaimed. "You're hurting me." She slapped his hand away and pretended to smack him. Jinxi watched the interplay in silence. So different from the cruel put-down humor of Skeeter and their friends.

"Sugar? I thought your name was Sommer." Jinxi took a bite of her sandwich.

"I know. It's a nickname I can't shake. My mama is white, and my daddy is black. When I was born, my mama said I was the color of brown sugar. The nickname stuck. *Some* people—" She looked up at Dean accusingly. "—won't let it go."

Jinxi pasted on a thin smile. She stared down at her sandwich and listened to the other's banter. She would have preferred to be alone with Dean, which surprised her. He never took offense at her sarcasm. Instead, her words slipped off him like water. She was more comfortable sniping at him than she ever was with Skeeter. With Skeeter, she never knew if her comments would get her a laugh or a slap.

She remembered watching Skeeter roar away from Janice's house. What had he said? Something about not being able to dump him. Maybe he wouldn't come back. Perhaps she could hang out here and be a part of a normal group.

Right. That's as likely as me turning into a girl church mouse.

After they'd eaten, they loaded the drinks and wakeboards into the boats. The jet ski towed an enormous inner tube. They all pushed off from the shore. Jinxi and Tara sat in the front of one of the boats, and Dean and Sanjay sat in the back while James drove. Four of the others were in another boat, and one of the guys drove the jet ski. Once out of the cove, the boats' speeds picked up. Jinxi gripped the edge of the seat as the boat bounced across the water.

They headed toward the middle of the lake and stopped, arguing good-naturedly about who would wakeboard first. The guys settled on "rock-paper-scissors" to decide. Dean won the round and whooped exuberantly. He quickly stripped off his shirt. Jinxi barely had time to appreciate his six-pack before he bundled into a life vest and jumped in the water.

The second boat took the inner tube from the jet ski, and the arguing started again, this time between the women.

Tara called out, "I think we need to let Jinxi go first since she's new."

Jinxi shook her head vigorously. "No way. I'm not, like, a water person."

"It's fun," Tara said. "Perfectly safe. They'll go slow for you."

Jinxi continued to shake her head. She wouldn't. Couldn't.

"I'll show you how it's done," Tara said as she pulled on a life jacket and climbed over the side of the boat into the other. The boats took off in opposite directions, the jet ski following one of them with Damaris and Sommer on board.

Jinxi watched as Tara climbed into the tube.

"See?" she yelled to Jinxi. "You'll hardly get wet." Tara adjusted her life vest and gripped the side handles of the tube as the boat slowly moved forward, and the towing rope became taut. When the rope was fully extended, the boat picked up speed, and the tube bounced across the water. Tara whooped as the inner tube skimmed the surface of the lake. Jinxi lost sight of her as their boat took off with Dean in tow on the wakeboard. She turned to watch as he got his balance and jumped the wake. Back and forth, he turned the board to jump from side to side. *Nice legs.*

He signaled he was ready to stop. The boat turned in a sharp circle and whipped him around until he was even with the boat before he began to sink. He untangled himself from the foot straps and hauled the board one-armed to the back of the boat.

"Who's next?" he asked, panting as he pulled himself up over the side. He grinned at Jinxi. "Want to try?"

"No." She leaned back against the seat, arms crossed. She was not getting into the water.

Sanjay pulled on a life vest and jumped into the lake. Dean stood up in the boat and shook his head, droplets of water shooting everywhere.

"Hey!" James squawked. "That's cold."

"Should feel good, bro.'" Dean found a towel and dried off.

Jinxi couldn't help notice the way Dean's muscles rippled as he leaned over to dry his legs. She'd been wrong to think he was thickly built. His police uniform and bullet-proof vest hid a nice physique. Solid. Dependable. She shook her head. Why was she even looking at him? Still, her gaze returned to watch as he pulled on his T-shirt. So what if his eyebrows were too heavy and his nose uneven. With the sun on his face, he might be okay.

They started again, and Dean asked, "Hey, Jinxi, come back here and help me spot." He waved her to the back of the boat. She got up, gripping the seats as she tottered to the back, and plopped down. Dean handed her a flag, one she'd seen earlier in the day.

"This is called a 'man down' flag," he shouted over the roar of the engine. "When someone falls, we hold the flag up so other boats know to watch for someone in the water."

Jinxi nodded and turned to watch Sanjay.

"He's a beginner, so he may fall a few times," Dean commented.

Jinxi nodded again. Over on the other boat, Patrice screamed as she flew by, bouncing up and down. The boat took a sharp turn, and the tube went up the wake. It turned sideways, dumping Patrice into the lake. A moment later, her head bobbed to the surface.

Patrice laughed as she gasped for breath. "Awesome. Did you see that?"

Jinxi saw, and questioned the sanity of letting oneself be flipped over in an inner tube going thirty miles per hour into a body of water. Willingly.

A few hours later, everyone except Jinxi had turns on either the wakeboard or tube and the whole party returned to shore for more food.

"C'mon, let's take a turn on the jet ski," Dean said, handing her a life vest.

Jinxi shuffled to the edge of the water, life vest dangling from one limp hand, insides quivering like Jell-O. What if she fell off into the dark green water? What if the life vest didn't keep her afloat? Her mind ran through several disastrous scenarios.

She'd been scared the first time she'd climbed on Skeeter's motorcycle. He'd been angry and abusive at her reticence, threatening to leave her stranded.

Would Dean get mad if she refused to go? Would his friends turn ugly and call her names? What if they bullied Dean because he'd brought her?

Jinxi took a deep breath. "I can't swim."

"What?" Dean asked. He turned from fiddling with the jet ski.

"I. Can't. Swim." She gritted her teeth, furious at having to admit her inadequacy.

"You don't need to know how to swim. First, you'll be wearing a life jacket. Second, I won't go very fast." He held out his hand. "C'mon. I'll take care of you."

Jinxi hesitated before taking his hand. It was big and warm, offering comfort and safety. This man wouldn't let her drown.

They waded through the shallow water, donned life vests, and climbed on. She squeezed her eyes shut. The others onshore shouted encouragement.

"Go on. It's fun."

"Perfectly safe, especially with Dean driving."

"He's an old man. He never goes very fast."

Dean waved them off. "Thanks a lot. Thought you were my friends."

His bulk closed the gap between them on the narrow seat. The jet ski was a little like riding a motorcycle. Jinxi had no choice but to wrap her arms around Dean's waist. At least the two life vests separated them, so she wouldn't have to press her body up against his. That would be way too weird.

After Dean backed out slowly, he put on a little speed. The jet ski jerked as he accelerated. He laughed as Jinxi gasped and tightened her grip.

"Scared? I won't dump us, don't worry." He carefully accelerated past the warning buoys, and they were out on the lake itself. He kept the speed at an acceptable level as he fiddled with the controls. Jinxi's hair blew all around her head, and her eyes watered from the wind. Dean accelerated and circled the jet ski into some lazy figure eights. Jinxi learned to shift her weight with him as he turned, similar to riding behind Skeeter on his bike.

A smile worked its way up from her belly. *I'm flying*. This was much better than riding on a motorcycle. The vibration from the jet ski and the undulation from plowing over the water lulled her. She relaxed for the first time since she had left Janice's house.

Dean turned part-way around. "You okay?"

She nodded.

"Hey," he exclaimed. "Are you smiling?"

Her smile faded.

"Don't stop."

"Stop looking at me," she retorted.

Dean turned back around and hit the accelerator. They were skipping across the water. Was he angry because she snapped at him? Would this ride end in her being tossed into the lake? She hung on for dear life. After a few minutes, he decelerated as they approached the picnic area again. When they got to the buoys, he slowed.

Without turning around, Dean said, "You should smile more often. You're pretty when you smile."

Pretty? No one had ever used that word to describe her.

Tara called out, "What'd you think? Fun, huh?"

"Yeah. Fun. If you have a death wish."

Dean laughed. "Don't even. You were enjoying yourself."

"Was not."

"You smiled." His gaze caught hers.

Heat jumped into Jinxi's cheeks. She looked away. "Whatever."

"Well, gang," James said. "I'm sorry to break up this party, but this boy has to get home. Who's gonna help me with the boat?"

There was a general acknowledgment the day was over, so everyone worked together to get the boats cleaned out and loaded on the trailers. The men carried the jet ski to the back of Jason's pickup. After much back-slapping and general ribbing among the guys, the women hugged and said goodbye. Jinxi stood with her arms across her chest. They'd better not hug her.

Sommer sidled up to her. "I *really* hope we see you again. With Dean," she added, under her breath.

"Sugar, would you *please* stop trying to get me hooked up with someone?" Dean clasped his hands together in entreaty.

"Now, honey, you know it's my sole purpose in life," she responded. "I have nothing better to do."

The other women said goodbye to Jinxi, saying they were glad to have her along.

When they were alone in Dean's truck, he rolled the windows down. The breeze cooled her hot, sticky skin. She couldn't wait to shower the sunscreen off her face and legs. Her stomach rumbled. Loud.

Dean quirked an eyebrow at her. "Do you want to stop and get something to eat?" he asked. "Or would you, maybe, possibly, be willing to share a couple of those tamales with me? The ones I saw in the fridge before we left?" He looked at her with sad puppy eyes.

"Fine." Her heart fluttered at the idea of him enjoying her food. He'd probably scarf all of them, leaving none for her. She mulled over the question of whether he was a pain in the backside or if she romantically hated him.

A few minutes later, Dean said, "Sorry about my friends. And the whole Sugar thing."

"'S'okay." She'd bet her last five bucks those girls were already gossiping about her. The guys were probably betting on whether she and Dean had hooked up yet.

"They liked you."

"Whatever." As if it mattered. She didn't need any more friends.

Or did she? Her mind jumped to the selfie of Savvy and Skeeter.

What would it be like to hang out with people who did fun stuff, like going to the lake? The girls had talked about playing pool and going shopping. Maybe that would be cool.

They liked you. The words warmed a cold place inside.

"So maybe we could, you know, do this again?" Dean sounded hesitant, not at all his normal cop voice.

A smile tugged at the corners of her mouth. "Sure."

They pulled up to Dean's garage apartment. Jinxi gathered the wet towels and slid from the cab. She spoke over her shoulder.

"Thanks for today."

Dean's voice called to her from the truck. "I'll shower and be over to grab some tamales."

Jinxi pushed through the gate and started walking across the backyard.

The roar of a motorcycle froze her in place. She caught a glimpse of a familiar figure zooming up the street by Dean's apartment. The bike turned in front of Janice's. The towels slipped from her nerveless hands.

CHAPTER 23

Dean stayed in the truck as Jinxi slid out, wet towels hugged against her chest. Had he asked her to go out to the lake again? And did she say yes? His smile turned to a grimace. Patrice and D would try to suck details out of him. He could hear them already.

Are you and she hanging out?

Have you hooked up yet?

Where did you meet her?

Yeah, right. Try answering that one.

He jumped out of the truck, reluctantly pulling his gaze away from watching Jinxi stride toward his mom's. He dragged the ice chest across the bed of his pickup. A Harley drove by, engine revving.

Nice bike. The rider made the turn in front of his mom's house before it roared up her street toward the Walmart shopping center. Maybe he should get a bike. He imagined himself decked out in leathers and a cool black helmet. Jinxi could ride behind him, and ...

The sound of his mom's back door slamming shook him out of his squirrel trail. Why had Jinxi dropped the towels on the grass? Did it have something to do with the bike? Her ex-boyfriend rode a motorcycle. His brain shifted into gear. What was going on?

He hefted the ice chest and closed the tailgate with his knee. He set the chest at the bottom of his steps to be dealt with later. Every muscle in his body complained. He'd had some good rides today. Jason was amazing behind the wheel of his boat.

Dean's phone buzzed from his pocket as he mounted the stairs to his apartment.

"Li'l D." *Wait for it.*

"Give it up, Big D. Who's the squeeze?"

"Ya couldn't wait, could ya?" Dean fumbled with the keys, dropping them in front of the door. He groaned as he reached to pick them up.

"Heck no, bro. You never, and I repeat, never, bring someone of the female persuasion to the lake. Or anywhere for that matter."

Dean found the key, shoved it into the lock, and pushed open the door. "What do you want me to say?"

"You're killing me. Give me the deets."

Dean sank onto the futon and put his feet on the coffee table. "You're worse than a girl."

"And you're dodging the question."

Dean rubbed the back of his neck. "Okay, dude. Grab a pencil and paper, and I'll give you all the deets."

"Ready?" he asked when Damaris came back on.

"Shoot."

"She's a friend of my mom's."

Damaris's voice broke the ten-second silence. "Nice try. Let's go over it again, son. Who is the tatted hottie you brought to the lake?"

"I told you. Jinxi is a friend of my mom's. She's staying there for a while. I thought she might want to get out of the house since she doesn't have any friends here." All technically true. As long as no one pressed him for more information.

He could practically hear the wheels turning in D's head.

"Tell you what, broseph," Damaris said. "You sleep on that answer, and I'll get back to you tomorrow."

One thing for sure. Damaris would make a fine detective someday.

A surge of adrenaline propelled Jinxi toward Janice's back door. She bounded up the concrete steps, grasping frantically for the knob. She slipped in the door, locked it, and leaned against it, gasping.

"Jinxi? Is that you?" Janice's voice cut through the darkened kitchen.

Jinxi willed her heart to return to normal and walked down the hall toward Janice's bedroom. Janice lay on the bed, blinds down, the room dark.

"Yeah," she answered, standing in the doorway. "Sorry I woke you." A slash of guilt hit her like a knife wound. Had Janice found out about the money transfer already? Was she lying there in the dark, waiting to ambush her?

"Don't be sorry. I wasn't asleep." Janice raised her head off the pillow to look at Jinxi. "Can you do something for me?"

"Sure." Like return the money? *No.*

Janice laid her head back down and used her arm to cover her eyes. "There's some headache medicine in the bathroom. Can you bring it to me? I think I'm getting a migraine."

Jinxi stepped into the room. The air, heavy and stale, reminded her of the smell of her mother's bedroom. Minus the booze fumes.

Janice's voice had none of its usual briskness. "It's on the top shelf of the medicine cabinet."

Jinxi found the prescription where Janice had said. Jinxi shook the bottle, rattling the pills against the side. "How many do you need?"

"One."

Jinxi poured a capsule into her hand and took it to Janice's side.

"Sorry to ask, but can you get me a drink of water too?" Janice hadn't removed her arm from over her face.

Jinxi brought a cup of water from the bathroom. "Here you go."

Janice struggled to a half-sitting position. She took the pill, swallowing with a small amount of water. "Thank you." She lay back down and gave Jinxi a weak smile. "I came home from babysitting Hannah with a headache." She closed her eyes again. "How was your day?"

"Fine." *Stole some money from you. Spent the day with your baby son. All in all, not bad.* When Janice didn't respond, Jinxi tiptoed into the living room.

The lace curtains hanging in the living room windows cast eerie shadows on the wood floor. Jinxi crept ninja-like toward the window closest to the front door. Without pulling aside the lace, she peered out onto the street that was turning to dusk. No Ghost Rider lurking outside. She could have been wrong. Maybe it wasn't Skeeter who'd ridden by on his bike. Must have been her imagination. Paranoia on steroids.

Jinxi shrugged off her anxiety and walked to the kitchen. Time to find something to eat. She pulled open the refrigerator and spied the bag of tamales. Nope. Save those for Dean. He said he'd be over later to snag some. She yawned and reached for the peanut butter and jelly. She'd probably be asleep by the time he'd unloaded the truck and showered. The sun and water has sapped every bit of her energy. She made herself a sandwich and carried it to the bedroom, wondering why she cared if there were any tamales left for him or not.

After showering, Jinxi crawled into bed. As soon as she fell asleep, the dream came hard and fast. Flames licked at her feet as she ran down a hall that stretched before her like an unending highway, following the sound of a crying child. Dodging falling pieces of ceiling, she peered into every room. Smoke and ash stung her eyes and burned her throat. Desperate to find the child, her pace quickened. She tripped over fallen timber and fell to her knees.

The dream changed, and she stood across from the house, watching it burn. A fireman carried someone out of the house, but it wasn't a child.

It was Janice, draped across his arms like a rag doll.

CHAPTER 24

The phone rang, jarring Janice from an uneasy sleep. She glanced at the clock as she reached to silence the noise. Eight-thirty. She sat up quickly and rubbed her eyes.

"Mom. It's me." Robin's voice was breathless, worried.

"What is it, honey?" Janice struggled to shake the remnants of sleep from her aching head.

"It's Hannah. She's got a high fever. I'm calling the doctor when the office opens at nine. I want you to go with me."

"Of course. I'll hop in the shower and be right over. What's her temp?" Janice slung her legs off to the side of the bed, feet searching for slippers.

"It's one-oh-three. She's been awake off and on all night. I'd ask Carlos to go with me, but he has some big meeting at the firm today, and he can't get out of it."

"Sure, honey, not a problem. I'll be there in an hour." Janice headed for the bathroom, making a mental list of what she needed to do before leaving the house. How had she slept through Jinxi getting ready for work? It must have been the migraine medicine.

Forty minutes later, she pulled up in front of Robin and Carlos's home and let herself in. Robin had the phone between her ear and her shoulder, supporting a limp Hannah on her hip. Robin's tank top stretched over the pregnancy bump. Janice took Hannah from her and sat in the rocking chair, smoothing back the hair from Hannah's forehead.

Robin straightened, nodded. "Sure, I'll bring her right in. Thanks." She ended the call and turned to Janice. "I'll go get my purse. The nurse said to bring her in."

They secured a whimpering Hannah into her car seat and drove the few miles to the doctor's office. After they signed in, a nurse ushered them to an exam room, where another nurse took the child's temperature and asked some questions. A few minutes later, the doctor entered.

Dr. Anita Bell, tall and dark-haired, wore a traditional white lab coat over a gray linen sheath dress. Janice's eyes immediately dropped to the doctor's shoes—bright red with fancy bows on the toes and heels.

The doctor saw her glance and blushed. "Shoes are my weakness. These are my feel-good shoes. I had a sneaking suspicion today was going to be busy, so I wore my favorites." She chuckled before becoming all business. "Talk to me about Hannah."

Robin went over the past week, reminding the doctor they'd been in because of Hannah's swollen hands. She'd seemed a little more tired than usual, and Robin thought she might have been in a growth spurt. But now she had this high fever.

"Well, let's take a look. You keep holding her. I'll pull up her shirt and listen to her lungs and heart."

Dr. Bell was quick and thorough in her exam, and after entering the information into the computer sitting on a table in the corner, she tapped her pen against her lips.

"I'm thinking," Dr. Bell said, eyes unfocused. "I've seen these symptoms once before." She turned to face Robin. "I want her to have a blood test to rule out some things. I want a urine test too. I want you to have the tests done as soon as possible—you can take her to the lab in the next building and get them done there. Have you given her anything for the fever?"

Robin shook her head.

"Try to keep her hydrated. I should have the lab results by this afternoon, tomorrow at the latest. I'll call you."

Robin's face wore a mask of worry. "What do you think it is, Dr. Bell?"

"I'll have a better idea once we get the test results. In the meantime, if Hannah's fever gets any higher, call the office. I'm on call tonight, so I'll be able to get back to you quickly."

When they returned home, Robin measured out the correct dose of fever reducer and squeezed the medicine into Hannah's mouth with a dropper. She coaxed her to drink a little juice. A few drops dribbled down Hannah's chin, and Robin wiped them off with her hand. She gently laid her on the couch and covered her with a light throw.

Robin went into the kitchen and poured two tall glasses of iced tea. She and Janice sat at the bar to talk.

"I'm scared, Mom. She's never had a fever this high." Robin's voice quivered. "What if there's something wrong? I mean, really bad?"

Janice put her hand over her daughter's. "Sometimes children can carry a higher fever than adults. How about we pray?" They closed their eyes as Janice began the prayer.

"Thanks, Mom," Robin said when Janice finished. She dabbed her eyes with a tissue. They both turned as Hannah whimpered in her sleep.

"You go up and try to get some rest, honey. I'll stay here and keep an eye on her."

Robin nodded gratefully, eyes dark-rimmed with exhaustion and worry. Before going upstairs to her bedroom, she leaned down one more time and put a hand on Hannah's forehead. "She feels cooler now."

"Don't worry, I'm sure she'll be fine," Janice said, urging her up the stairs. Janice sat at the end of the sofa and gently patted Hannah's feet as her daughter left.

Within the space of a few days, everything in her well-ordered world had changed. What was God doing? A few weeks ago, she could predict her life for the next few months. Robin and Carlos would have a healthy little boy. Brian and Courtney would get pregnant. Dean would realize his desire to be on a patrol shift and meet someone special.

Why did it seem Jinxi was the catalyst for all the changes? Or was it Janice's prayer on the day that Jinxi arrived on her doorstep?

Lord, help me see your goodness and your purpose for me.

Was her purpose to watch helplessly as her only grandchild, loved and spoiled, became seriously ill? Was her purpose to see her youngest son become enamored with a pierced and tattooed woman?

She wanted to beg God to move time back three weeks before any of this happened. Her hands balled into fists as she struggled to hold back tears. Why couldn't Tom still be alive? He had always been her rock. He would have held her close and told her no matter what, they would be able to handle anything life brought, because they had each other. Now she was alone, adrift on a flimsy raft on an ocean of uncertainty.

Dean glanced at his watch as he buzzed himself into the back door of the jail. Right on time for his graveyard shift. What would tonight bring? Same zoo, different monkeys.

He strode to the breakroom, intent on getting a cup of the sludge they called coffee before it was gone. The smell of burned toast assaulted him as he stepped through the door. Someone should replace the ancient toaster. Typical sounds of laughter and backslapping, along with crude jokes, filled the small room. Dean poured hot coffee into a Styrofoam cup and sniffed it before taking a tentative sip.

"Who's the new squeeze?"

"What?" Dean whipped around to see who had addressed him. The question came from one of Dean's fellow officers, who had joined the group gathered in the break room.

"You know, the little Goth girl you took to the lake." The stocky cop looked around to see if he had an audience before continuing. "Heard she looks like jail bait."

Dean's stomach dropped to his feet. Was he about to get outed for dating someone from jail?

A tall cop chimed in. "Yeah, someone said she was fourteen. You hooking up with minors?"

Dean threw a threatening look at Patrice, who raised her hands in mock surrender.

"Hey, don't look at me. You guys are worse gossips than women." She gestured toward Damaris with a shake of her thumb.

"Lil' D, you're killing me."

"Dude. You show up with a new girl, no explanation, no warning. What are we supposed to do?"

"You're supposed to mind your own business." Dean felt a rush of blood creeping up his neck.

"Look, guys," Damaris said. "He's blushing."

"What are you blushing about, Mr. Clean Dean?"

"Don't forget, he's the forty-year-old virgin."

Dean ducked his head in embarrassment. "Sheesh. She's a friend. She's staying at my mom's."

"How convenient," someone commented.

"She was bored, okay?" Dean rolled his shoulders and turned away.

One of the other officers leered, "So you thought you'd show her a little action, huh?"

Patrice took pity on him. "Lay off, guys. Back off." She good-naturedly shoved them away. "Don't make me hurt you."

After a few more comments, they drifted off to take their seats. Patrice put her hand on Dean's arm. "Ignore them."

Dean shrugged and grimaced.

"But you have to know. We're all curious. I mean, you never date, and—*bam*—you show up at the lake with this woman." With a lopsided grin, Patrice moved away to find a place to sit.

If Dean's friends knew he'd processed Jinxi's arrest papers a few weeks ago, he'd never hear the end of it.

Besides, he'd only invited Jinxi out to the lake so he could keep an eye on her. He nodded to himself. Yup, that was why.

His thoughts drifted to when he had first gone into the house. Jinxi wore a furtive look when she first glanced up.

But why? What was she up to? He'd better check with his mom to see if she'd noticed anything fishy going on.

CHAPTER 25

Jinxi let her backpack slip off her shoulder as she mounted the front steps to Janice's house. Sweat dripped down the back of her neck, soaking her T-shirt. When she was rich, she'd find a place to live by the ocean. Cool, salty breezes, the rolling crash of the waves. Jinxi could almost taste them. She pushed open the door and stepped into the living room.

Janice's voice and a fragment of a sentence came from the kitchen. "— is Hannah? ..."

Jinxi paused at the bottom of the stairs, foot poised to ascend.

"What's her temp now?" Janice's voice was a question, and then it paused before resuming.

She's on the phone.

"Uh-huh, okay. Has she had anything to eat? All right. How is she acting?"

Jinxi held her breath.

"Her fever is down. Great. Call me later if anything changes, okay?"

She peeked her head around the corner as Janice hung up. "Is everything okay?"

Janice stood motionless in the kitchen with the phone clutched in her hand. She looked at Jinxi as if she was seeing her for the first time. Exactly like her mom, every day of her childhood.

"Oh," she said, waving the phone. "Yes, fine. I mean, no. I don't know what I mean." Janice slumped on one of the wooden chairs and rubbed her forehead. "Hannah is sick. She's got a fever, and the doctor doesn't know what's wrong. They took blood from her. Do you know what it's like to watch a four-year-old get stuck with a needle?" She looked up at Jinxi with tortured eyes. "I think it's something serious the doctor isn't telling us." Janice's eyes welled with tears.

Jinxi's eyes did the same. She backed up, turned, and made a mad dash up the stairs.

Her backpack flew from her hand and hit the wall with a thud. She cursed, threw herself down on the bed, and buried her face in a pillow.

Jinxi remembered how Hannah had sat beside her, chattering like a bird about her Barbie toothbrush. Hot tears filled her eyes.

Janice tossed and turned in her bed. She alternated between praying and worrying, falling into a troubled sleep, and dreaming she was back in school with the bell ringing for class. She stumbled down an unfamiliar corridor but couldn't find her classroom.

She woke to the sound of the telephone. Sleep fogged her brain as she snatched the phone off her nightstand and answered. "Hello."

"Mom. We're taking Hannah to the hospital."

"Why? What's happened?" Janice struggled to sit up.

"Her fever went down for a few hours and then spiked again. It's one-oh-four now. I called Dr. Bell, and she's meeting us there. She's worried about dehydration."

"Do you want me to come?"

"No. I'll call you later. I thought you'd want to know."

"Okay, honey, thanks. I'll keep praying."

Janice got out of bed and slipped on a light robe. She went out to the front room, sat in her favorite chair, and picked up the worn Bible, turning to Psalms.

In the morning, Jinxi found Janice on the couch.

"I couldn't sleep," Janice said. "Robin called sometime after midnight to tell me they were taking Hannah to the hospital."

A knot formed in Jinxi's stomach.

"Her fever went up, and the doctor was worried about dehydration. I'm going to wait for Robin to call this morning before I go to the hospital."

"Do you know which one?" Jinxi chewed on her lip stud, willing her stomach to relax. It shouldn't make any difference to her if Hannah was sick. But it did.

"Probably Sierra Mercy Children's." Janice roused herself from the couch. "I'll make some coffee. My goodness, do I ever need it."

Jinxi followed her to the kitchen. Questions buzzed in her head. What was wrong with Hannah? Was she going to die? A crack had opened in her heart, the size of a child's finger.

When Jinxi arrived at the food bank, Connie greeted her with a smile that faded as soon as she saw Jinxi's face.

"What has happened, *chica*? You look very sad today."

"It's Hannah."

"The *chiquita*?"

"Yes. She's in the hospital."

"That is, how you say, a shame."

That was an understatement. "The doctors don't know what's wrong with her. She has, like, a bad fever or something."

Connie lifted the cross she wore around her neck and pressed it to her lips. "I will say a prayer." She crossed herself and kissed her thumb.

Jinxi shrugged. "If you say so." Hannah needed more than a prayer to some dead guy on a cross.

"What hospital is she in?"

"I think Janice said Sierra Mercy Children's. Do you know where it is?"

"*Sí*," nodded Connie. "It is in the downtown."

"Can I get there by bus?" Another stinky bus ride.

"Sí, I will show you."

A plan formed in Jinxi's mind as the two women walked back to the entry hallway. Tacked to the wall hung a map showing all the bus routes in the city. They kept it there to show the homeless and transients where the shelters were. Jinxi took a piece of scratch paper and made notes while Connie dictated.

"First, you ride the bus to the light rail. From there you take the train to the hospital. *Comprendes?*"

She comprendoed all right. Now how to escape without being seen by her boss and eagle-eyed Aneesa.

Too late.

Aneesa entered the hall from the bathroom at the same time Padish pushed through the front door.

Aneesa put both hands on her hips. "If you two cooks are in here, who's minding the kitchen?"

Connie's eyes widened, and she slapped her forehead. "*Madre de Dios!* The sauce!" With a swish of her skirt, she scooted toward the kitchen. Jinxi stared at her feet. A flush worked its way up her neck.

"What is happening?" Padish asked.

"Nothing," Jinxi mumbled, chewing the stud in her lip. "I'm going back to work."

"Stop." Aneesa held out her hand toward the note in Jinxi's hand. "What is that?"

Jinxi shrugged. "Directions." She slapped the paper into Aneesa's outstretched hand. Sheesh, she couldn't get even a tiny fraction of privacy.

"These are directions to the hospital."

Good guess, Sherlock.

"You are sick?" Padish asked, smile fading into a frown.

Jinxi shook her head. "Not me. A little girl."

"The granddaughter of Mrs. Rafferty?"

Jinxi nodded.

"She is in the hospital?"

Another nod.

"Of course you must go. Go now." He nodded vigorously, motioning her toward the door.

"But—but what about—"

"You don't worry about anything. Someone will help Connie. You go see the granddaughter."

"Well, if you're sure?" She looked from Padish to Aneesa.

Aneesa didn't look happy about this change of plans.

Jinxi hesitated, thinking about the money she'd lose by not working. Oh, well. Without another word, she turned and bolted.

Thirty minutes later, she stood in front of the hospital, staring up at the windows. Which room was Hannah in? Could Hannah look down from her bed and see her? She took a deep breath and squared her shoulders. What if they didn't let her in? They *had* to let her in.

The automatic door swooshed as it opened, releasing the noxious smell of sickness covered up with cleanser. Jinxi reminded herself to breathe through her mouth.

A registration area took up nearly one whole side of the room,s and a waiting area opened out on the other. The television played the morning news, and several people sat, eyes glued, as if trying to forget where they were. An information counter stood against the far wall, staffed by white-haired volunteers. Their eyes traveled up and down, taking in her appearance as she approached.

"Can I help you?"

Jinxi froze. She didn't know Hannah's last name. Her mouth went dry.

"Um—I'm looking for the children's wing," she said, realizing too late this was a *children's* hospital. They were never going to let her in.

"Of course, dear," one of the women said. "What is the name of the patient?"

One of the other volunteers looked over. "Aren't you from the youth group that volunteered to read to the three and four-year-olds?"

Youth group? It wasn't the first time people took her for a kid. This time she didn't mind. It would be her ticket in.

"Yes. Youth group."

"You're late. They've already gone up. Fifth floor."

Jinxi's legs sagged with relief. She'd gotten in.

She turned and sprinted toward the elevators, afraid they'd find her out. Inside the elevator, she pushed the button for the fifth floor and exhaled the breath she'd been holding. She'd have to wander around the different wings until she found the right room. But at least she'd made it past the gatekeepers.

The elevator doors opened soundlessly, and she exited into a foyer with a waiting area. Should she go left or right? She stood in the hall, chewing her lip. She glanced toward the nurses' station to the right. *Snap*. Was that Robin? Her red hair was a beacon as she talked with one of the nurses.

The last thing Jinxi wanted was a confrontation with Hannah's mom. She ducked into the restroom and locked the door, waited a few minutes before peeking out. The coast was clear.

Jinxi tiptoed toward the nurses' station. Without making eye contact, she turned abruptly to the left and paused in front of each door to glance in. At the third door, she saw a familiar little figure, dwarfed by the huge hospital bed. She entered the room silently, moving on tiptoe. Hannah was asleep, one arm under the covers, one hand curled up by her chin. She had an IV line taped to the back of her hand. The smell of disinfectant hung heavy in the room.

Jinxi couldn't help herself. She reached out and touched Hannah's cheek, marveling at its smoothness. Hannah's mouth opened and closed with a smacking sound. She stirred and opened her eyes.

"I was dreaming about you," she said, eyes droopy.

"You were?" Jinxi whispered.

"Umhmmm. I dreamed you came to see me." Hannah smiled.

The finger-sized crack in Jinxi's heart opened wider. Hannah took her hand and squeezed.

"I'm glad you came to see me. Want to play a game?"

"Sure. What game do you want to play?"

Hannah closed her eyes. Had she fallen asleep again? Jinxi started to pull her hand away.

"I want to go home," Hannah said, eyes closed. She opened her eyes. "I want to go home." Louder.

"I know you do."

Tears welled up in Hannah's eyes. "I want to go hoooome," she wailed, tears spilling over and coursing down her cheeks. Dark, wet circles formed on the thin hospital gown. Jinxi stood up and looked around. What should she do?

And what if Hannah's mom showed up? A noise from the doorway confirmed her worst nightmare.

Too late.

CHAPTER 26

Robin rushed into the room and skidded to a stop.

"What are *you* doing here?"

Jinxi was like a hiker who had gotten between a mama bear and her cub. "I was—"

"Mommy." Hannah's voice rose to a howl.

"Yes, baby," Robin cooed, hurrying toward the bed. She turned toward Jinxi, jaw clenched. "I don't want you here." Robin turned her back on Jinxi and gathered Hannah in her arms.

Robin was right. Jinxi didn't belong here. Despite Hannah's exclamation of love toward her, nothing had changed. She'd always be on the outside.

Jinxi hustled out of the room and into the hall, slamming into what felt like a steel post. Except this post had two arms and wore a uniform.

"Whoa," Dean said. "What's your hurry?" He grasped her arms and held her away from him.

Jinxi burst into tears. Dean let go of her arms and pulled her close.

"It's okay. Calm down. Everything will be okay."

He rested his chin on the top of her head. Hot tears of humiliation poured onto his shirt front. She wanted to crawl into a hole and pull a rock over herself. Why was it so important to see Hannah? She hadn't stopped to think Robin wouldn't want her there. What an idiot. Robin probably thought she was even more of a monster, what with Hannah's crying making it look like Jinxi's fault.

When her tears slowed, she jerked away. "Sorry," she mumbled, sniffling. Dean reached over to grab a box of tissues from the nurses' station and stuffed several in her hand.

His brow wrinkled with concern. "Is Hannah worse?"

Jinxi blew her nose and shook her head. "No, I don't think so. We were talking, and she started to cry. Robin came in and kicked me out." Her voice turned plaintive. "I didn't make her cry. Honest." She looked over to see a few of the scrubs-clad nurses were staring. Great.

Make a scene, why don't you.

Dean led her to a chair in a nearby waiting area. "Sit here, and I'll go get the lowdown."

Jinxi admired his broad back as he strode down the hall to Hannah's room. What a hot mess. Maybe if she sat here long enough, she'd spontaneously combust. Since that wasn't an option, she'd better figure out something quick.

Plan A. Get the heck out of there.

Plan B. Never, ever cry in front of Dean again.

Plan C. Never, ever hug him or be hugged by him again. He'd crush her like a bug if he knew she'd stolen money from his mom. Still, being in his arms felt nice.

Stop.

Plan D. Get away from this nice, middle-class family as soon as she could. A couple more withdrawals should do it. Unless Dean's witch sister convinced Janice to dump her. That could be problematic. Somehow she needed to get between Robin and Janice.

First, she'd put Plan A in motion and bounce. Jinxi dragged herself to her feet. She took a couple of steps, stopped. Dean strode down the hall toward her, his thick-soled shoes squeaking on the linoleum floor.

"Hannah's fever is gone, but she has a rash on her arms and legs. The doctor is running some more tests and hopefully should know something by this evening."

Jinxi didn't realize she'd been holding her breath. "I'm outta here." She turned to pick up her backpack.

"C'mon. I'll drive you back to work," Dean said, "unless you'd rather go home."

Funny how he used the word "home." A jolt of panic shot through her. Janice's house had started to feel more like home than the place where she'd grown up. Was it the family pictures scattered around? Maybe the piano in the front room. She couldn't put her finger on it, but with a burst of clarity, she knew it had little to do with the furnishings. Perhaps it was the lack of chaos, of drama.

"Back to work," Jinxi said.

For once, Dean didn't talk as they descended the elevator and passed through the hospital lobby. Jinxi needed time to process her tangled thoughts.

They drove out of the hospital parking lot and were soon out of the better part of downtown Sacramento. Block by block, the neighborhoods changed from well-kept homes and flower beds to derelict houses. Business signs went from advertising mom-and-pop restaurants and dry cleaners to video porn stores and pawn shops.

They pulled up to the food bank, but before she could jump out, Dean tugged at her arm.

"It'll be okay," he said softly. Jinxi stared into his brown eyes, wanting to believe.

The front office was empty, but clamor from the cafeteria echoed in the open entry. Maybe she had enough time to sneak into the restroom before reporting back to work. Holding her backpack like a shield, she tiptoed down the hall toward the ladies' bathroom. Safe so far. A toilet flushed as she eased the door open. Jinxi held her breath and rushed toward the other stall. Before she could get there, the stall door opened.

"Oh, child. You scared the livin' daylights out of me," Aneesa said, hand over her heart. "Why are you sneaking in here?"

"N-no reason," Jinxi stammered.

"Don't think I don't know what you're doing." Without warning, Aneesa grabbed Jinxi's arm and dragged her out of the bathroom, pulling her to the office, closing the door with a snap. Aneesa leaned up against the front of her desk, arms crossed.

"You were going in there to cut, weren't you." It was a statement, not a question. When Jinxi shook her head, Aneesa continued. "Don't deny it. It's all over you." Aneesa motioned toward Jinxi's clothes. "Who wears long-sleeved shirts in the middle of summer?" She didn't wait for an answer. "What happened at the hospital?"

Jinxi crossed her arms and shot Aneesa a defiant look. "I was going to the bathroom. Besides, what business is it of yours what I do?"

"Oh, child, it isn't any of my business. But let me tell you something—"

"You have no right to drag me in here and lock the door. I'm not even clocked in."

Aneesa gave her a hard stare before slowly pushing up the sleeves of her shirt, first one and the other.

Jinxi gaped. Scars like white, crisscrossed herringbones covered the other woman's dark skin.

"Don't tell me you were going to the bathroom," Aneesa said. "I know all about it. Something happens you can't deal with, and you cut. Someone hurts you, and you cut. You feel some emotion, and you cut."

Jinxi fixed her eyes on the toes of her boots as Aneesa's voice hit like hammer blows.

"Maybe your daddy abused you. Maybe your mama abandoned you, and your brother or uncle or cousin messed with you instead of watching over you."

"It wasn't like that," Jinxi spat out.

"Sure it was. It's always something. Anger, shame, whatever." Aneesa paused. "There's a way to stop."

Jinxi looked up and sneered. "What if I don't want to?"

Aneesa smiled. Smug. "Oh, you do. You can pretend you like it, but you wonder if someday you'll have to cut all the way through your arm to make it stop hurting." Aneesa pushed herself off the edge of the desk and walked to the door to unlock it.

"When you're ready to stop, come see me."

Sure. When hell freezes over.

CHAPTER 27

Dean drove up to his apartment and jerked the truck to a stop. Too weary to move after nine-plus hours of work, his hand rested on the keys, still in the ignition. The Friday night shift was similar to the zombie apocalypse. Relentless heat brought out the craziest of the crazies. For once, he'd like to come home to a typical Saturday.

Throughout his childhood, Saturday mornings meant a trip to the donut store with his dad. They'd pick up donuts for the rest of the family and sit and talk. His dad always had the plain cake. "Easier to dunk in my coffee," he'd say. Dean would eat his Frisbee-sized cinnamon roll and drink a carton of milk. After they'd solved the world's problems, they'd head back home. Now Saturday was like any other day. Dean mostly slept through until the evening, when he had to go back to work.

The familiar bitterness rose in his throat. Tired or not, he'd better get to his workout. Punching the boxing speed bag would be better than heading down this path. Again.

Maybe he'd check on his mom first and get to see Jinxi. He brightened at the thought. They hadn't had a chance to talk since the hospital. He'd head over to Mom's and get a cup of coffee. Maybe hang out until Jinxi came downstairs. He smiled, remembering the feel of her in his arms.

Dean stepped through the back door. "Hey, Mom."

She looked up from the sink with tired eyes. Soap bubbles clung to her forearms.

"You okay?"

"Goodness, yes. A little tired. I'm waiting to hear from Robin."

Dean headed for the coffee pot and poured himself a cup. He rummaged around in the fridge until he found the milk, adding a liberal amount to the brew. He sat at the table and reached for the sugar bowl.

"How's Hannah doing? She's been in the hospital, what—a week?" Working nights, Dean lost track of time.

"They're releasing her today. Dr. Bell is meeting with Robin and Carlos now."

Dean filed that information in a separate compartment.

"Where's Jinxi?"

"I don't know. Probably still sleeping." His mom's voice was tight.

Dean frowned. "You okay, Mom?"

She turned toward him. Her smile didn't quite reach her eyes. "I'm fine. A little tired, that's all. I didn't sleep well last night."

"Another migraine?"

Janice threaded the dishtowel through her hands. "No." She turned back to the sink, plunging her hands into the soapy water. "Why do you want to know where Jinxi is?"

Dean rubbed the back of his neck. "I, uh, wondered where she was."

His mom sent him a look over her shoulder. Dean felt his face grow warm.

"Okay, so I'm a little interested in her." He shrugged.

Janice turned back around, drying her hands again. "Dean, you don't know what you're getting yourself into."

Dean raised his eyebrows. "Sheesh, Mom, I only said I was a little interested. Don't go ordering wedding invitations." He watched as his mom set the dishtowel on the counter and carefully folded it, smoothing it over and over. "Is there something going on that I should know about?"

Janice inhaled deeply, exhaling in a sigh. "God is doing something, Dean, and I don't want you in the middle of it."

"In the middle of *what*?"

Janice turned back to the sink. "Be careful, that's all."

Dean frowned at her back. What was he missing?

He drained the rest of his coffee in two large gulps. Best not to wait for Jinxi under the circumstances. He took his mug to the sink and kissed his mom on the cheek. "Let me know about Hannah. I'm going to catch a few hours of sleep."

He exited the back door, wondering at his mother's words. What had they been about? A cryptic warning about Jinxi. Something was up, and he aimed to find out what it was.

Janice attacked the dirty frying pan with more vigor than was necessary. Merciful heavens, what should she do? Remorse overcame her. She'd lied to her youngest child. *Lied.*

Perhaps a look at her investments would bring the peace she craved. Janice logged on to the investment account to see how well it was performing. She'd always gotten a feeling of peace from looking at that large dollar amount. Tom had left her financially secure.

Hesitant to touch any of the money, yet unable to ignore the sad state of her kitchen, she'd considered remodeling.

She'd clicked on the account statement, hit PRINT.

"Interest credited: $1,332."

"Withdrawals: $1,000."

A thousand-dollar withdrawal. That couldn't be right.

Janice turned back to the computer. She clicked on the option to view the details of the withdrawal.

Nausea rose to her throat as she read. She fell back in her chair in disbelief. *I trusted her*. Tears sprang to Janice's eyes. She blinked them away as she stared at the computer screen. The information didn't change. Jinxi had stolen a thousand dollars from her.

As she reached for the phone to call Dean, a small voice whispered, *Wait*.

No, she wouldn't wait. She'd deal with this right now. She logged off the computer with clumsy fingers. She'd call Dean and wait for Jinxi to wake up. Janice picked up the statement and shook it, imagining herself shaking it in Jinxi's face. She'd get the truth from her, wait for Jinxi to pack her bags, see her to the door. *After* Janice got the money back.

Righteous indignation spurred her to action. Janice strode across the hall to her bedroom and yanked open the sock drawer. Her fingers closed over the money-filled sock. Feeling its comfortable fullness calmed her.

She sank on the bed, Jinxi's betrayal a stab to her heart.

Wait.

"God, what am I waiting for?" her voice cried to the heavens.

The phone rang, jarring her already-frayed nerves. She reached for the phone, removing it from the cradle. "Hello."

"Jan, dear, it's Emma."

"Oh, Emma," Janice's throat closed. Unable to speak, she squeezed her eyes shut.

"What is it?" Emma's voice exuded concern.

Janice gave a muffled sob. "I—I think Jinxi stole from me."

There was silence on Emma's end for ten seconds. "Jan, I was praying for you today, and I have something I believe is from the Lord."

Janice nodded while tears leaked out of her closed eyes. "Okay," she choked out.

"The Lord led me to read the book of Hosea. Remember the story of Hosea redeeming his wife Gomer after she had returned to prostitution. The theme of the book is how merciful God is toward the people of Israel, despite their sins."

Janice stood and reached for a tissue from her nightstand before dropping back down on the bed.

Emma continued, "I believe God is telling you to love Jinxi unconditionally."

"But, *Emma*. It's a thousand *dollars*."

Emma's voice softened as she spoke.

"What is the cost of a person's soul?"

CHAPTER 28

Now that Jinxi was working, Saturdays were for sleeping in. She took a leisurely shower, letting the warm water pummel her sore muscles. While dabbing the black eyeliner, she made her plans.

First, a stop at the Walmart money kiosk. After that, to Connie's apartment for more cooking lessons.

When she finished, Jinxi grabbed her backpack and tiptoed down the stairs. How would she be able to look Janice in the eye? Janice's bedroom door was closed. Good. Maybe she'd slept in, too. Jinxi already felt terrible for her, worrying about Hannah. With a deep sigh, she turned around and headed out the door to the bus stop.

The bus spit her out on the dirty sidewalk in front of the superstore. Jinxi hiked across the parking lot, intent on her errand.

Inside the store, she headed toward the money booth. The clerk finished pushing up the metal gate.

"I'll be right with you," she said over her shoulder.

Jinxi drummed her fingers on the counter while the plus-sized clerk shuffled behind the counter, wheezing with each breath.

The stool at the counter creaked as the clerk settled herself at the window. "How can I help you?"

Nerves tingled in Jinxi's head. "I, uh, I'm here to pick up some money. My aunt wired it to me."

"Name."

"Mine or my aunt's?"

"Yours." The clerk didn't raise her eyes from the computer.

Here it goes. "Jeanette Lansing."

The clerk's brightly painted fingernails clicked on the keys. Would there be some hidden warning that she'd stolen the money from Janice? Would the police storm Walmart and drag her out in handcuffs? She turned to look over her shoulder.

"ID."

"Huh?" Jinxi's head snapped around.

"I need to see your ID," the clerk said.

Jinxi fumbled for her license and handed it across the counter with a shaky hand.

A few seconds later, a printer spewed out some paper.

"Sign here," the clerk said, pointing with one red talon.

Jinxi signed her name. Two minutes later, she strode from the store, nine one-hundred-dollar bills and some smaller, safely tucked into the outer pocket of her backpack.

A familiar voice cut off her exit.

"Whatcha got there?"

A hand grabbed her arm and pulled her toward the motorcycle parked nearby.

"Let me go, Skeeter." Jinxi dug in her heels, but her flip-flops weren't made for heel-digging.

Janice paced from her bedroom to the living room to the kitchen. She picked up the phone, listening for a dial tone. She rechecked her cell.

Still no call from Robin.

The landline rang. Janice jumped.

"Hello."

"Hey, Sis. Long time, no talk to."

Janice sank onto the sofa. "Oh, Debbie, it's good to hear your voice. It's been a month of Sundays since we've talked."

"You're not busy, are you?"

Janice spoke through stiff lips. "I'm waiting for a call from Robin. Hannah's been in the hospital."

"What's going on?"

Janice pulled out her cell phone, watching for Robin's call as she unloaded on her sister, telling her everything, including Jinxi's theft.

"To top it all off, I think Dean has a little crush on her."

"You've got a mess on your hands. My boys would call it a hot mess."

"That's certainly true. I don't understand why God is allowing all this to happen. I need Tom here. He'd sort it all out."

Her sister chuckled. "Perhaps God wants you to rely on him, not on Tom."

Janice sat up, cut to the heart. "I can't believe you'd say such a thing. I've always relied on God." How could Debbie suggest she didn't rely on God? She'd always depended on the Lord.

Hadn't she?

"Let me *go*." Jinxi squirmed in his grasp. Skeeter held her with one hand, grabbed her pack with the other. He shoved her away and went right for the outer pocket where she'd zipped the money.

He grinned. "Where'd you get the stash?"

Jinxi sniffed. "None of your business."

He counted it, whistled. "Nice score."

"Give it back or I'll scream."

Skeeter laughed. "Go ahead. Maybe when your cop boyfriend shows up, you can explain where this came from." He waved the bills in her face.

Jinxi's heart dropped into her stomach. How did he know about Dean? Had he been stalking her?

Her voice quavered. "Give it."

"What's it worth to you?"

Several thoughts raced through her head. Could she get to her pepper spray before he rode off with her money? Should she let him go and be done with him? Would she *ever* be done with him?

She narrowed her eyes and glared. "You can have half." She held out her hand.

Skeeter took his time, counting out the five hundred dollar bills one at a time. When he finished, Jinxi shoved the money in her backpack before he could snatch it back.

"Thanks for stopping by," he said, mounting his bike. He grinned as he pulled on his helmet. The bike started with a roar.

Jinxi's nerves shredded to threads when he peeled out of the parking lot.

She cursed him, his mother, his friends, even his bike. She cursed her bad luck as she trudged toward the bus stop, head down.

Mariachi music pounded through Connie's apartment door. After Jinxi knocked, the volume decreased and the door opened, Little Rosa standing on the other side.

"Hi." Rosa smiled as Jinxi entered.

"Hi." Jinxi set her backpack down inside the door.

"Welcome, *mi amiga*." Connie greeted her with a hug and a kiss on the cheek. Jinxi kept her arms at her sides.

"Come in. I am working in the kitchen."

Jinxi stood for a moment surveying the scene. Miguel mixed a salad while Rosa set the table. Connie rotated between the stove and the counter, directing her children. They moved in a dance of duties they'd done many times before. She realized with a pang that she was an outsider. Again. A familiar wave of loneliness washed over her. She'd always be an outsider, standing on the fringes, wanting but never having. At Janice's, she was nothing more than a guest. When Janice found out about the money, she'd be mad. Janice would show her the door.

"Come," Connie said. "We prepare the lunch. You can help me." She handed Jinxi a spoon. "Taste this. What is missing?"

Jinxi rolled the flavors around in her mouth and opened her eyes. "A little salt, I think."

Connie smiled and nodded approval. "Very good. That is correct." She reached for the salt and handed it to her. "You see. You are good at learning the cooking. You will be fine next week by yourself."

"Next week?" By herself?

"*Sí*. Did not Mr. Padish tell you?"

"No." More surprises.

"He will tell you on the Monday. I am not at work on the Tuesday."

Okay. No big deal. She'd help Aneesa. They'd be fine.

"Come, now. Let us eat together before we cook."

They gathered at the table. Connie grasped her hand, Miguel took the other. Three dark heads bowed as Connie prayed in Spanish.

Would it be wrong to ask God to get her five hundred dollars back from Skeeter?

As if God would.

At the close of the prayer, the children filled their plates with enthusiasm. With a word in Spanish from their mother, both children stopped, eyes down, and waited for Connie to pass the food to Jinxi. Once Jinxi filled her plate, the children were allowed to eat.

"I am very nervous," Connie said. She took a bite of salad.

"What's up?"

"I have a, how you say, meeting. On Tuesday. It is with the *abogado*."

"Attorney," Miguel translated.

"*Sí*. Attorney. We meet with the Department of Immigration about my husband."

"Will he be able to come back to the US?"

"I am hopeful that it is so. He works here legally, but in the raid, no one ask if he is legal. They only want to see the green card."

Rosa piped up. "I miss my daddy."

Connie put her hand on the child's head and murmured something in Spanish.

After lunch, Connie made coffee while the children did the dishes. The women sat on the couch and watched television until the kids finished.

"I am working on the menu for you. I think something easy, maybe spaghetti, for you to cook. We could prepare the sauce the day before, and you can cook the meat in the morning. What do you think?"

Jinxi gripped the coffee cup with white-knuckled hands. "What are you talking about? I can't cook a whole meal."

"Of course you can. It will be easy. How you say, easy peasy." Connie laughed at her joke. She went on, ignoring Jinxi's angst. "I will tell you everything you need to know."

Connie picked up a sheet of paper from the coffee table. "Here. You write down the recipe."

Jinxi wrote while Connie dictated. When they finished, Jinxi committed it to memory, folded the paper, and stuffed it in her backpack.

"This is going to be a disaster." Jinxi clicked the lip stud back and forth against her teeth. Whose brilliant idea was it to put her in charge of something?

The closest she had come to that kind of responsibility was during her three years in Juvenile Hall. Her caseworker, fresh out of college, had something to prove. She'd given Jinxi the task of ensuring the younger girls did their homework. The caseworker checked the homework weekly. Never mind that some of the girls resented Jinxi's attempt to tutor them. In the end, Jinxi faced the punishment, assigned to cleaning duty for not doing what she was supposed to do.

This situation would probably end in the same way. Something would go wrong, and she'd be to blame.

Connie grasped Jinxi's arm. "It is in God's hands." She made the sign of the cross, kissed her thumbnail, and smiled.

God's hands? Well, he'd better show up, or she was toast.

CHAPTER 29

They worked together on a menu for the next month at the food bank, and before Jinxi knew it, it was dinnertime.

"I will fix us something to eat," Connie told her.

Jinxi pushed back her chair and stood, stretching the kinks from her back. "I should probably go."

"Of course you must stay," Connie said.

Jinxi thought of how Janice's bedroom door had been closed that morning. "Okay." If Janice had any suspicion of what Jinxi had done, she'd rather avoid Janice for as long as possible.

They spent the evening playing a game called *Aggravation*, which Miguel said was stupid, but only because he kept losing.

When it was time for bed, after Rosa and Miguel brushed their teeth and put on their pajamas, Connie went into the bedroom to kiss them goodnight. Jinxi sat on the couch and remembered her childhood bedtime routine. If her mom had someone spend the night, Jinxi would hurry into her room and change into her pajamas as quickly as possible. She'd turn out the light and pull the covers up over her head, hoping no one knocked on the door. She couldn't remember how old she was when she started pushing the dresser in front of the door.

Connie returned to the living room. "The children are asking for you."

Jinxi looked up, eyes wide. "Why?"

"They want to say goodnight to you."

Jinxi rose and walked down the hall. There was only one bedroom in the apartment. Where did Connie sleep? On the sofa?

The children slept in twin beds. The lamp on the nightstand cast a soft light. Each child exhibited their personality on their side of the room. Rosa had dozens of stuffed animals on a low shelf at the end of her bed, while Miguel's side had posters of rock bands on the wall. Jinxi stood between the two beds.

"Well, goodnight."

Rosa held out her arms, asking for a hug. Jinxi leaned down, and the little girl wrapped her arms around Jinxi's neck and kissed her on the cheek as her mother had done.

"Goodnight, Jinxi. Thank you for coming to our house," she said.

"'Night," said Miguel. He had already pulled the blankets up around him and lay curled on his side.

Jinxi turned the lamp off and said, "Goodnight."

As she turned to leave the room, Miguel said, "Next time, I won't let you beat me at *Aggravation*."

She smiled to herself. Little boys grew up to become little boys in men's bodies. Dean's face came to mind. Jinxi mentally shook herself. She needed to stay far away from that guy, even in her thoughts.

The porch light gleamed an invitation as Jinxi mounted the steps to the house. The windows were dark. Good. Janice must be in bed.

Jinxi let herself in and tiptoed into the kitchen. The pantry door opened with a quiet squeak. She hurriedly grabbed a jar of peanut butter and a sleeve of crackers and crept up the stairs.

After changing into her boxers and T-shirt, she opened the windows. A sudden gust puffed the curtains like a mischievous ghost. She sank into the bed, hoping for the oblivion of sleep. A heaviness settled over her. Who was she to think she could cook a meal? A meal where everyone would depend on her?

This was the real world, where real people would go hungry if she messed up. She should quit now. Find a way to leave, take Janice's money, and disappear. No one would care. They'd be relieved she was gone once her community service was complete.

It was only a matter of time before Janice discovered the missing money. Jinxi would have to be long gone before that happened. But she'd need to replace what Skeeter took. She silently cursed him again.

Jinxi turned over, bunching the pillow under her head. If she left now, she'd never find out what happened with Hannah. She sighed. What did it matter, anyway. Hannah was a kid. She wouldn't notice Jinxi's absence.

Would she?

What about Dean—would he miss her? Or would he shake it off and move on?

Definitely that.

She scrunched the pillow tighter, rejecting the urge to grab her knife. She pictured herself plunging it into her heart, forever ending the constant pain of her life. Sweat broke out on her face despite the breeze. She was in a tug-of-war, pulling against the darkness trying to destroy her.

The words she'd read in Janice's Bible came to mind.

O Lord you have searched me and you know me. You know when I sit and when I rise; you perceive my thoughts from afar.

He knew her thoughts. He knew she sometimes wanted it all to end. At times, the pull was almost irresistible.

"God. If you're there, make it stop. Please."

CHAPTER 30

Jinxi rubbed the sleep out of her eyes as she made her way down the stairs.

Janice waved toward the pot as Jinxi slid into the kitchen on bare feet.

"There's fresh coffee made. I'm off to get ready for church." Janice busied herself at the sink, rinsing out her coffee cup and placing it in the drying rack on the counter.

Jinxi opened her mouth in a jaw-cracking yawn as she reached for her mug. "Why so early?"

"I'm helping greet today." Janice's voice was brisk. "You're welcome to come with me."

Jinxi inhaled the steam that radiated from her mug before taking a tentative sip of the hot liquid. "No, thanks. I'm kind of tired today."

"What did you do yesterday?"

Jinxi hesitated. Did she detect any suspicion in Janice's question? "I spent the day at Connie's, my friend from work. She's teaching me to cook." Jinxi leaned against the stove, sipping her coffee, watching for a sign.

"That's nice. Cooking is a good skill to have."

Dean pushed through the back door. He wore athletic shorts and a T-shirt. Dang, he looked good.

"You off work today?" Janice asked.

He shook his head. "No, I work tonight. I came by to see what the latest is about Hannah." He reached for a mug from the cupboard over the coffee pot, brushing Jinxi's shoulder. She moved to the table and sat. "And to get some coffee before I crash for a few hours."

"She's home from the hospital. She seems to be fine, other than being tired."

Dean rubbed the back of his neck. "Has the doctor said *anything* about what it might be?"

Janice shook her head. "She didn't even want to speculate."

"Hmmm. Well, I know you've been praying for Hannah, so everything should be okay."

Janice's face fell. "What about you, Dean? Haven't *you* been praying for her?"

Dean shook his head and enveloped his mom in a hug.

"Now, Mom, you know how I feel about all this God stuff. I'll leave the praying up to you and your friends."

"Dean—" Janice began, but Dean shushed her.

"Mom, don't worry. Go to church and pray for my niece, okay?" He held her at arm's length and smiled into her eyes. "You have enough on your plate to worry about without worrying about me."

Janice's mouth turned down. Jinxi watched their interplay. Were they always so kissy-kissy?

Janice turned away and started toward the narrow hall leading to the bedrooms. She favored one of her legs and used the walls for support. Dean called after her.

"As soon as this thing with Hannah is taken care of, you need to get that knee replacement done."

Janice waved her hand as if to say, "Leave me alone."

Dean shook his head and turned toward Jinxi. "She's so stubborn." With an impish grin, he said, "Reminds me of someone else."

Jinxi scowled at him and stood to refill her mug.

"You gonna save any of that for me?"

"Don't you usually go to bed about now?"

"Have you been keeping track of my schedule?" Dean's eyes sparkled with humor.

When she didn't respond, he said, "As a matter of fact, I usually work out after I get home. After *that*, I go to bed. You might want to write that down somewhere."

"You are so lame." Jinxi sat at the table and poured a bowl of cereal. Aware that all she wore was a pair of boxers and a T-shirt, she hunched over the table, keeping her gaze down. Dean scooped several spoons of sugar into his coffee and added milk. She made a gagging sound.

"What?" he asked, mid-pour.

"You're ruining your coffee."

"No, I'm improving it." He took a big sip and said, "Ahhhhh, that's wonderful." He smiled at her. "Want a sip?"

"I don't think so."

"That's right. You drink yours black."

"You remember that?" He was way too observant. She'd have to be more careful.

Dean sat back in the chair and stretched out his legs. He brought his two fingers up to his eyes, turned them around, and pointed at her. "I'm a trained observer. I see all."

Jinxi grunted and moved the box of cereal so it sat between them. How weird he remembered that detail. She pretended to read the box, intent on ignoring him. He seemed content to drink his coffee in silence. For once.

A few minutes later, Janice appeared in the kitchen doorway. "I'm off now. After church I'm going to Robin's. I'll call you later, Dean, and leave a message on your cell phone if there's anything new on Hannah, okay?"

"Thanks, Mom. Love you." He stood up and kissed her on the cheek. Jinxi watched out of the corner of her eye as Janice gave him a quick hug before she left.

"Bye, Jinxi. See you later tonight." Janice's voice was breezy, with no hint of suspicion. Jinxi's stomach relaxed.

Dean set his cup in the sink. "I'll see you later," he said, flexing his bicep. "Time for my workout."

Jinxi rolled her eyes. "Whatever."

After Dean left, she quickly washed and dried the dishes and went upstairs to shower. She was on a mission. There was something she had to do today. Something that would ease the knife thrust of Skeeter's appearance and theft of her cash.

An hour later, she locked the front door and bounded down the steps. After twenty minutes, she reached the strip mall opposite Walmart.

Her destination sat between a nail salon and a bar. Blacked-out windows and gothic red lettering announced its purpose. She pushed through the door and strode to the counter, where a dreadlocked girl sat with her head hunched over her cell phone.

"Help you?" she asked, not looking up.

Jinxi reached into her pocket and pulled out a wad of cash. She slapped it down on the counter. "I want a tattoo."

The walk home took longer. Jinxi stopped every few minutes to rub her calf. Although the artist had only done the outline of the tattoo, it itched. She stopped when she got to Janice's front porch. She sat down in one of the Adirondack chairs and pulled up her pant leg to admire the work. A rose superimposed over an anchor. Strength and beauty, the tattoo artist had told her. That was cool.

The sharp needle had brought a rush of endorphins similar to that of cutting her arm. She basked in the feeling, until she remembered the money she'd spent. The tattoo had cost more than she'd expected. She replayed the conversation in the kitchen that morning, examining every word, searching for any nuance to hint Janice had discovered the withdrawal. For sure, Janice hadn't told Dean. He would have arrested her. Probably not too gently, either. It was his mom, after all.

Satisfied there was no way Janice could have found out, Jinxi unlocked the front door and headed straight to the kitchen. From the window, she could see Dean's truck was gone. Good. Janice's car was gone too, which meant Janice wouldn't be home for hours.

Jinxi sat down at the computer and logged on to Janice's account. The second time was easier.

CHAPTER 31

Dean balanced the fast-food bag and soda in one hand, keys in the other. He pushed through the door to his apartment, anxious to dig into his meal. The smell had driven him crazy on the ride home.

During his growing-up years, his family rarely ate out. With his mom being a stay-at-home, money was tight. In college, Dean couldn't get enough of McDonald's, Taco Bell, Panda Express. These days, he justified his weakness by the fact he worked out regularly. Ever vigilant about his weight, the two seemed to balance each other out.

He couldn't help glancing at his mom's house. *Wonder if Jinxi's home.* Might be a good idea to check on her later, what with his mom gone.

Jinxi logged off the computer, leaned back in the chair, and stretched her arms over her head. She got up and went into the kitchen, searching for something to eat. As usual, the refrigerator yielded a bounty of snacks. As she pulled out a package of cheese and some lunchmeat, the back door opened and Dean stepped in. "Hey."

She jumped. "You scared me."

He grinned. "Sorry," he said, not looking sorry at all. "Were you doing something you weren't supposed to?"

"Of course not." She turned back to the fridge so he wouldn't see the runaway pulse throbbing in her neck. *Good thing he didn't come ten minutes ago.*

"Making a sandwich?" He pulled a chair out from under the table and turned it around, straddling it.

Well, duh.

"Uh-huh."

"Think I could talk you into making me one?"

Jinxi turned to face him. Why did he have to smile like that? She found herself smiling back. "I guess." She shrugged.

"My workout burned off all the calories from the hamburger I had earlier," Dean said, rubbing his stomach.

Geez, did he ever stop thinking about food? She set about making two sandwiches, aware of his eyes on her. She kept her back turned, working at the counter next to the stove. When she finished, she pulled two plates from the cupboard and retrieved a bag of chips from the pantry.

"Looks like you've made yourself at home in my mom's kitchen."

Jinxi froze. What was he getting at? Her hand shook as she set his plate down on the table. "I ... uh ... I guess so."

He chuckled. "I'm just saying."

"Your mom said it was okay," Jinxi explained, talking fast. "She said to help myself to whatever was in the fridge." She locked her eyes on his while she sat across from him. "Why? Did she say something to you about it?"

Dean reached over and laid his hand over hers. "Calm down. I was making an observation. It's fine."

Jinxi swallowed, her mouth dry. She swung around and went back to the refrigerator. "Want something to drink?" She pulled out two cans of soda and handed one to Dean before sitting.

"Great sandwich," Dean said around the food. He swallowed, then asked, "So what's your plan?"

"Plan?"

"Yeah, what're you going to do when you finish community service?"

She had a plan. Keep Janice on her side. Withdraw some more cash. Another thousand, plus her paychecks, might be enough to get her started someplace else.

She shouldn't have gotten the tattoo.

On the other hand, there was Dean. She wasn't sure what to do about him. He didn't get on her nerves as much these days. He was sort of okay. Maybe ....

"I'm not sure," she said.

The muscles in his jaw clenched as he chewed. The day-old stubble increased his appeal. "You need a plan. My dad always said you plan to fail if you fail to plan."

Now *that* was annoying.

After Dean returned to his apartment, Jinxi sat in the living room, channel surfing. Janice needed to up her cable package. She settled on *Young Frankenstein*, a movie she'd seen at least five times before. When the monster started to climb the wall to the castle, a motorcycle's roar drowned out the sound of the television.

Jinxi sprang to her feet and dashed to the window. A bike slowed to a stop in front of the house. A booted leg swung over the bike. Even before he turned, she recognized him from his leather-clad back. The helmet came off, and he shook his shaggy hair loose.

Skeeter.

She bolted to the door, fumbled with the knob, and stepped outside.

"What are you doing here?" she demanded, stomping down the steps toward him.

"Is that any way to greet your boyfriend?"

Jinxi's stomach lurched.

He was too quick, grabbing her by the back of the neck, pulling her toward him. "Got any more cash? You need to hook me up, J."

"No. I don't have any more money." Jinxi spoke through gritted teeth. Her eyes teared up as he squeezed harder.

"You better not be messin' with me." He shook her.

"There isn't any more," she said, and pulled away.

Skeeter put his hands on his hips, looking relaxed. She knew better.

"Tell you what," he said. "I'll come back by in a while. You get some more cash, and we'll share." His lips turned up in a smirk. "Sharing is caring."

"Go to—"

Before she could finish, his hand whipped out and connected with her face. Jinxi bent over, tears spilling over her stinging cheek.

When she straightened, Skeeter was on his bike, and seconds later, he was gone.

The empty house welcomed her. Jinxi stood for a moment in the living room and let its now-familiar smells comfort her sore face and bruised heart. When would she be rid of that scum? He was like some evil phantom, always a few steps away.

She'd have to revise her plan. But how?

Mentally shaking herself, she changed gears. Part of the plan was to keep Janice on her side.

The refrigerator yielded a carton of eggs and a package of shredded cheese. There was a container of Connie's special salsa and corn tortillas. A search of the cabinets revealed the bowls and pans she'd need. She beat two of the eggs into a frothy mix and dropped in slices of a corn tortilla. To this, she added a handful of the cheese and poured the mixture into a frying pan, setting it on the lowest heat.

Next, she pulled out Janice's TV tray and set it with a plate, fork, and knife. She found a cloth napkin in one of the drawers and folded it under the silverware, adding an icy glass of tea to the tray. She set the tray on the coffee table and went back to check on the egg mixture. She smiled when Janice's car door slammed outside.

"Something smells great," Janice said as she came through the door, her voice heavy with weariness. "What's this?" She eyed the TV tray.

"I thought you might be exhausted, so I made you some dinner." Jinxi opened her eyes wide with what she hoped was a look of innocence.

Janice dropped into her favorite chair and slipped off her shoes. "Really?" Her eyes lit up. "What is it?"

"Some eggs and stuff. It's almost done."

"What happened to your cheek?"

Jinxi's hand shot to her face, covering the red splotch left by Skeeter's violence.

"Oh, I, uh, tripped." Was that the best she could do? She cursed her pale skin.

Janice closed her eyes and leaned her head against the back of the chair. "You should be more careful."

Yeah, careful to avoid guys with a hefty backhand.

Jinxi retreated to the kitchen. The eggs needed one more stir before she scraped them off onto a plate. Perfect.

"Here you go," she said, setting the plate on the TV tray.

Janice's head snapped up, and her eyes flew open. As she reached for the plate, she inhaled deeply. "This looks delicious. Thanks."

Jinxi waited until Janice had eaten a few bites before she struck. "Your daughter doesn't like me."

Janice's eyes widened as she swallowed. "Of course she ..." Her hand shook as she took a sip of tea. She set the glass down and wiped off the condensation with the cloth napkin.

"She doesn't want me to see Hannah," Jinxi continued. "She booted me out of the hospital room last week."

Janice's hand went to her throat. "Oh, I'm so sorry. I don't know what's gotten into Robin lately." She picked up her fork and toyed with a piece of tortilla.

Jinxi pressed in, sensing the older woman's weakness. "Do *you* mind if I see Hannah?"

Janice's answer came quickly. "Of course I don't mind. Hannah adores you."

Jinxi turned away to hide her smile of satisfaction. "I'll go clean up the kitchen."

She got as far as the dining room when Janice called out, "By the way, Hannah's home from the hospital."

Jinxi's heart jumped as she turned around. "Did they find out what's wrong with her?"

"Dr. Bell wouldn't say. She's going to meet with Carlos and Robin tomorrow. Her fever is down, but there's this strange rash." She shrugged. "I don't know what to think."

Jinxi chewed her lip as Janice got up and started down the hall, calling over her shoulder that she would take a shower.

Fever, rash—what was wrong with Hannah? Jinxi thought back to the times she had interacted with the little girl. Had she transmitted some rare disease to Hannah? Jinxi hadn't lived the best lifestyle. Could she be carrying something that the child caught? Maybe God was punishing her through Hannah.

No. Ridiculous. Jinxi didn't even believe in God.

Well, not unless she needed help.

CHAPTER 32

The phone rang as Janice prepared for her shower.

"Jan, dear, I'm calling to check up on you and your granddaughter."

"Hi, Emma." Janice sank onto the stool in front of her makeup table.

"I've been praying all day."

Janice pictured her friend on her knees, even at her advanced age. "I'm so grateful for your prayers. What would I do without you?" She fiddled with the jars on the makeup table, arranging them in height order.

"Has there been any improvement?"

"Well, her fever is down, but she has a rash. But there's good news. She's home."

"Oh, my, that is good news." Emma's voice crackled with joy. "I'll keep her in my prayers until she's completely healed."

They agreed to talk the next day.

Oh, bother. She'd forgotten to tell Emma about what Dean said after he'd taken Jinxi to the lake. She made a mental note to tell her tomorrow.

In the meantime, she'd have to do something if there was any indication Dean was interested in the girl. Including asking Jinxi to leave. She'd have to have a good, long talk with the Lord about that

Jinxi fingered her cell phone, composing a text to Savannah.

JINXI: Skeeter showed up here. What's the 411?

The answer came two minutes later.

SAVANNAH: He said he had some big score up there.

Jinxi huffed a humorless laugh. Yeah, he scored all right. Stole her money.

JINXI: He's getting on my last nerve.

Jinxi chewed at her lip stud, waiting.

SAVANNAH: Sorry, girlfriend. Got my own drama here.

Well, thanks a lot, *girlfriend.*

Jinxi stared into the open refrigerator, letting the frigid air cool her heated face. What could she eat? She needed fuel after the day she'd had. She and Connie had done double duty, preparing for Connie's absence. They had not only cooked lunch for today but had premade the sauce for tomorrow.

A yellow sticky note on the fridge, bearing Janice's neat printing, said she'd be home around six.

Jinxi pulled a couple of hard-boiled eggs from the fridge, cracked off the shells, and chopped them in a bowl. She experimented with some spices the way Connie had taught her, adding some paprika and cumin to the eggs and mayonnaise. The egg salad needed more kick, so she searched around until she found some Dijon mustard in the far back of the refrigerator. She added a little, tasted, added more. Perfect. She spread the mixture between two pieces of toasted bread. This cooking thing was awesome.

After eating, she rummaged through the cupboards. She pulled out several cans of tomato sauce, various spices, tomato paste, and some stewed tomatoes. She located the cooking pot and the can opener and made a batch of spaghetti sauce for Janice to have for dinner. As the sauce bubbled and cooked, she added seasonings a little at a time and tasted between each addition.

A jolt of panic shot through her when she glanced at the clock on the microwave. Six-thirty already, and Janice wasn't home yet. What if something terrible had happened to her? She wasn't that young. Several scenarios flashed through her mind, all ending in disaster. Car accident, heart attack, mugging. Another crack opened in her crusty heart. Was she starting to care for Janice?

Jinxi shook off the unaccustomed feeling and busied herself straightening the kitchen. She rinsed out the cans and tossed them in the recycle bin. She grabbed a rag and scrubbed the red splashes of sauce on the stove and counter. When the kitchen was presentable, she slumped down on one of the wooden chairs with a glass of water. And worried.

The side door from the carport opened. "Hello? Anyone home?" Janice called.

Jinxi sprang up and stood in the kitchen door, releasing a pent-up breath. She squashed the urge to demand Janice's whereabouts. She wanted to grab the older woman and shake her.

"Whatever you're cooking smells delicious," Janice exclaimed with a smile.

"Spaghetti sauce."

"Is it for dinner? I'm famished."

Jinxi shrugged, teeth gritted. "Sure."

Soon as you tell me where you've been.

"Let me put my purse down and take off my shoes, and I'll tell you all about Hannah," Janice said over her shoulder as she headed for the bedroom.

They met back in the kitchen. Janice filled up a glass from the water dispenser on the fridge and settled down on the other chair.

"Mercy, I'm tired. You have no idea how difficult one little girl can be. If she wasn't my granddaughter ..." Janice took a big gulp of water. She sighed and looked at Jinxi directly as if she were about to share serious news. "The doctor says Hannah has juvenile rheumatoid arthritis."

"Juvenile what?" Okay, so she'd been babysitting. Why didn't she say so?

"It's an autoimmune disease, common in young children."

Tension knotted Jinxi's stomach. "Is she going to die?"

Janice turned her glass in circles on the table. "No, not at all. It's treatable. RA causes swelling and inflammation in the joints, and intermittent fevers. They're going to give her some steroids for a couple of weeks and monitor her. She'll likely be under treatment for a long time unless she outgrows it. The doctor is referring her to a rheumatologist who works with children."

"So she's going to be okay?" Jinxi chewed on the stud in her lip. Thank God she didn't have anything to do with Hannah's pain.

Janice sighed. "It's tough, her being so young, but she should be able to lead a normal life. She'll have flare-ups where she'll be tired and achy, but she should be okay."

How unfair was that? A little kid like Hannah, having to live with a disease. Why would God allow that? Jinxi turned toward the stove and lifted the lid. Satisfied the sauce wasn't cooking too fast, she replaced the lid and sat down across the table.

Janice indicated the pot. "So, you're making spaghetti sauce."

Jinxi picked at a splinter of wood on the edge of the table. "Yeah. Connie taught me how to make it, because she'll be gone tomorrow."

"Gone?"

"I have to cook the meal tomorrow at the food bank," she said in a rush. "Connie is going to see her attorney, and they asked me to be in charge. I hope it's okay that I used a bunch of your stuff."

"Goodness, you can use anything you want, if it turns into something that smells that good."

Jinxi's mouth turned up despite herself. "It does smell good, doesn't it?"

"Can we eat some?" Janice asked, a hopeful look on her face. "I've got spaghetti noodles in there," she added, motioning toward the pantry. "There's some hamburger in the fridge, too, if you want to add meat."

Jinxi chewed on a fingernail. "Hmm. Maybe that would be good." She got up and opened the refrigerator and rummaged around until she found a package of ground beef. "Is this it?" She held the package toward Janice, who nodded and shoved her chair back from the table.

"I'm going to lie down for a few minutes until dinner's done. How can one small child tire me out so much?" She shuffled toward the hall. "Don't let me sleep through dinner."

Jinxi found the spaghetti noodles in the pantry, along with an unopened package of Oreos. She held them for a moment before ripping them open and grabbing a handful. She poured herself a glass of milk and carried the milk and cookies into the front room.

A few minutes later, the back door opened. "Something smells awesome," Dean exclaimed, coming into the front room.

Geez, was he going to show up every ten minutes?

"Shhhhh. Your mom is sleeping," Jinxi said in a loud whisper.

"My bad," he whispered. "But whatever is cooking smells great."

"It's spaghetti sauce."

"Did you make it?"

She nodded.

"Why does it smell so good?"

"Shut up. Just because you said that, I'm not saving you any."

"Did you save me any Oreos?" Dean said as he turned back toward the kitchen. He returned a few minutes later with a handful of cookies and a glass of milk.

She eyed his cookies. "If you eat all those, you won't want dinner."

His mouth was full as he answered. "Ha. Try me." He held up a glass of milk in a mock salute. "What about you?"

She gave him a disgusted look as he shoved an entire cookie in his mouth. "Never mind me. Besides, they'll make you fat."

Dean's face turned bright red.

Score.

Grinning, she turned back to the television.

"What happened to your face?" He leaned close to examine her cheek.

Heat rose from Jinxi's neck up to her hairline. "Back off, dude. I did a face plant into a door." She kept her eyes glued to the television. Anything to keep from being pinned by his cop eyes.

"Looks more like a hand plant than a face plant."

Janice shuffled up the hall and into the living room, rubbing her eyes. Saved from having to respond by Betty White.

"Whew. I needed that power nap. Hi, Dean. Did you get my message?"

He nodded. "Yeah. That's some news about Hannah, isn't it? I thought only old people got arthritis."

"You mean like me?" Janice asked, ruefully indicating her knees.

"Naw, Mom, you're not that old. Yet." He sent her a lopsided grin.

"Well, anyway, Hannah's home, and Robin and Carlos are spoiling her rotten. She's a miniature dictator. 'Bring me some juice. I want fruit snacks.' They feel so bad for her. They're letting her have anything she wants." Janice shook her head. "Hope this doesn't last too long."

Dean got up and patted her shoulder as she sat down. "C'mon, you know you do the same thing when you're babysitting."

"I do not."

Dean rolled his eyes toward Jinxi. "Okay, whatever you say. I'm going to get ready for work." He glanced back at Jinxi and added with a boyish smile, "Any chance that spaghetti will be done by the time I get ready to leave?" He batted his eyes and folded his hands together in supplication.

Jinxi heaved a fake sigh. "Maybe." She got up to go to the kitchen.

Janice asked, "Anything I can do to help?"

"Nope. I'm going to boil some water for the noodles.

Jinxi added the browned meat to the sauce and stirred until everything was thoroughly mixed. She took a spoon, tasted, and smiled to herself. Perfect. She took two plates from the cupboard and stacked two sets of silverware on top. She carried them into the dining room and set their places at the table. When she returned to the kitchen, she stood undecided for a moment before grabbing another set of silverware and another plate. After transferring the spaghetti to a serving bowl, she put everything on the table. "It's ready."

"I'll be right there. I'm going to get a Motrin from the bathroom."

Jinxi filled two glasses with water and set them on the table.

When Janice sat at the table, she said, "My, this is lovely. Now I feel spoiled. I don't ever have someone cook for me in my own home."

Jinxi basked in the warm glow of Janice's approval.

"What's this?" Dean clomped through the door, protesting. "You didn't wait for me?"

"Calm down, Son. Sit. We just started."

Jinxi shifted in her seat. Why did she think he was scary in his uniform? He looked good. The dark blue of his shirt contrasted with his tan. The short sleeves clung to his muscular biceps. Maybe skinny, shaggy guys weren't her type anymore. She'd have to think on that some more. When she was alone. Away from his overwhelming maleness.

"You're not wearing your gun, are you?" Janice asked. "You know how I feel about guns at the dinner table."

"No, Mom, I'm not," Dean answered with exaggerated patience. He pulled out the chair across from Jinxi and sat.

"Dean, would you say grace?" Janice asked, extending her hands to both young people.

"Mom—"

"Don't 'Mom' me. You remember how to say grace." As she closed her eyes, she took his hand and indicated that Jinxi should take her hand as well. Jinxi tentatively touched her. Janice's hand closed firmly around hers. Dean's hand engulfed Jinxi's other hand, its strength passing from him to her. She shivered despite his warmth.

Dean cleared his throat, mumbled a hasty prayer of thanks for the food, and grabbed his fork.

"This is so nice," Janice said with a smile. "We're having dinner together."

Both Dean and Janice took servings of spaghetti after letting Jinxi help herself. She waited for them to eat, stomach tight.

"This is great," Dean exclaimed around the mouthful of food.

"Mmmm," echoed Janice. "Very good, Jinxi."

Jinxi took a tentative bite and chewed thoughtfully. She examined the flavors and tried to identify the individual seasonings as Connie had taught her. She swallowed and decided, yes, it was good. Surprised at herself, she dug in.

"To what do we owe this awesome treat?" Dean asked, helping himself to another portion.

Jinxi shrugged. "I needed to practice."

"Well, you can practice on me anytime, if your food turns out this good."

"Didn't you say something about having to cook tomorrow at the food bank?" Janice asked.

She nodded. *Thanks for reminding me.*

Janice turned toward her son. "Padish asked her to take over the cooking while Connie, the regular cook, goes to see her attorney about the immigration mess. Remember when Padish told me about Connie's husband, Natividad?"

"Yeah, right." Dean twirled more noodles around his fork with a grin. "Looks like I'll have to pay a visit to the food bank this week."

"Only on Tuesday," Jinxi corrected him.

The conversation turned to other subjects.

"Mom, remember how I said I wanted to get a dog to help guard the place? Well, Jinxi gave me a great idea."

Jinxi snapped her head up, waiting to hear what he'd say. When did they talk about this?

"When we were coming home from the lake, she suggested letting Hannah pick out the dog. What do you think, Mom?"

"I think that's a wonderful idea. If Hannah gets to help choose, maybe she won't be scared of it."

Oh, yeah. Dean had said something when they were in the car. How did he remember that?

"I was thinking of taking her with me to the pound. We can go tomorrow if she's up and around. Otherwise, I'll wait a week or two until she's able."

"Perfect." His mother smiled and patted his arm.

Jinxi watched the casual display of affection with an ache. She couldn't remember ever having a sit-down meal with her mom. If her mom occasionally fixed something, she stuck with Hamburger Helper, eaten in front of the television. Jinxi sucked in her lip, letting the stud rub against her bottom teeth. Had her mom ever touched her like that? Maybe when she was a baby. Human contact came to her in the form of grabbing, pulling, and sometimes a slap. No tender "I love you." No comforting hugs.

Dean's hug in the hospital had been nice. When he wrapped his arms around her, she had melted against him. Even his uniform hadn't gotten in the way. She remembered the way he had stroked her head. The ache spread through her like a vine, twining around her heart.

"I'm going back over to Robin's tomorrow to see if I can do anything to help." Janice twirled the last of her spaghetti onto her fork. "Too bad you have to work so late on Saturday nights."

Jinxi frowned. Where was Janice going with this?

Dean took a deep breath, but before he could respond, Janice continued. "I know, I know. It's simply that your father would be disappointed to know you've stopped going to church."

"Don't go bringing Dad into this conversation."

"But, honey—"

Dean's voice was firm. "No. Don't. All Dad's religion and faith or whatever you want to call it doesn't change the fact that he died, and he shouldn't have." His voice rose. "Where was God when the load of steel crushed him?"

Janice gasped. "You know better than to ask that question. We can't question God. His ways are not our ways."

That's for darn sure. Jinxi shuddered.

"Well, his ways pretty much s—"

Janice put her hands over her ears. "Stop it, Dean. Stop."

"How can you say God is good when he took Dad from us? Did you even love Dad?"

Snap. This was getting heavy. Jinxi's grip tightened on her fork.

"How dare you ask that?" Janice pointed the fork toward him. "Of course I loved your dad. Why would you say that?" Her voice shook.

"How come you never talk about him? All you spout is religious cr—stuff about God's plan. Really, Mom. It was God's plan to kill Dad?"

Jinxi pulled the stud against her bottom teeth and bit down on her lip, wishing for a crack in the floor to open and let her drop through. When would this end?

Janice's eyes filled with tears. "God didn't kill your father—"

"Oh, yeah? Well, he's dead, isn't he? Nothing can change that." Dean stabbed his fork into the spaghetti, twirling the noodles around and around.

Jinxi stood, slamming both hands on the table.

"*Stop!*"

Dean and Janice looked at her in shocked silence.

"Stop." Jinxi's legs barely supported her. She was even shocked at herself.

Janice touched her arm. "What is it? What's wrong?"

Dean stared with his mouth open.

Jinxi covered her face with her hands and spoke through her fingers.

"Stop fighting." Images from her past assaulted her. She squeezed her eyes closed and willed them back into the dark place inside her.

Janice stood and put her hand on the girl's shoulder.

"Jinxi," she said, her voice calm, "this is an argument we've had many, many times. It doesn't mean we don't love each other, or we're mad at each other. Sometimes people argue. It's okay."

Hands still over her face, Jinxi shook her head. As her fingers rested on the tender place on her cheek, she realized she'd chosen to hook up with a man exactly like her mother's boyfriends. Next, someone would take a swing, and police would show up, crowding the small spaces where she could hide.

As if reading her mind, Janice said, "It's okay. We're not going to hit each other. We may get mad and even stomp out of the room, but we will never use violence to get our point across." She squeezed her affectionately. "Okay?"

Jinxi nodded and dropped her hands to her sides. What would they do if she ran from the room and out the door? Adrenaline surged and receded. Her legs shook from the effort of standing.

"Now sit down, and let's finish this nice meal that you prepared." Janice patted her shoulder.

Jinxi took a shaky breath and sat. Her old friend fear settled in her stomach. Like a movie loop, replays of fights between her mom and the parade of men passed through her mind. How many times had she landed in the children's receiving home? Seven? That didn't even take into account the soul-sucking foster homes.

Dean cleared his throat. "So, um, Jinxi ..."

She startled at the sound of her name.

"Maybe you could go to the pound with Hannah and me to look at dogs?"

"What a great idea," Janice said, a cheerful note in her voice. "I'm sure she's getting bored hanging around the house with this old lady for company." She gave a short laugh. Mother and son resumed eating, but Jinxi only moved the food around on her plate, her appetite gone.

They probably thought she was crazy. Maybe that's why she cut herself. Perhaps they'd have her committed to the state hospital or something. After her little outburst, they'd probably throw her out of the house, and she wouldn't blame them.

Jinxi didn't want to leave. The chains that had bound her for so long had gradually loosened. Her stomach didn't clench like it used to at the sound of someone coming through the door.

What if she lost everything she'd gained? If Janice's family found out about the money, they'd convince the old lady to kick her to the curb. What did she need to do to make Janice let her stay?

Dean dropped his napkin, stood, and patted his stomach. "I'd better get a move on if I'm going to get to work on time. Thanks for dinner." He dropped a kiss on his mother's cheek and headed through the kitchen and out the door.

Janice smiled at Jinxi, indicating Dean's plate left on the table.

"I guess I've still got some training to do. C'mon, let's get this mess cleared off." She stood and piled her plate and utensils on top of his and moved toward the kitchen. "I'll wash dishes since you cooked."

"No. I'll do dishes."

"No you won't. You cooked. I'll wash up."

"But your knees," Jinxi began, carrying her plate and the serving bowl into the kitchen.

"I'm much better. That Motrin finally kicked in. Besides, I can't let you do all the work."

"Well, how about you wash, and I'll dry?"

Whatever it took to stay on Janice's good side.

"Deal," said Janice with a smile as she added soap to the water.

Later that evening, Jinxi sat on the windowsill in her room, smoking her last cigarette of the day. She'd pushed out the screen, resting it against the side of the house. Janice would kill her if she smelled the smoke. As the wisps curled toward the sky, she replayed the conversation at the dinner table. How could she be so stupid? Her outburst had shocked Janice and Dean, and even herself. The tenuous peace she'd experienced in Janice's home had unraveled with their argument. What if their family was the same as hers? Maybe all families were alike. Maybe some were better at hiding their dysfunction.

Jinxi stubbed out the cigarette and crawled into bed, falling into an uneasy sleep. Her dreams were filled with images of the food bank on fire while she kept trying to cook. She was jarred awake by a noise outside the bedroom window. Heart pounding, she waited breathlessly for a hint of the source. Was someone trying to get in? Had she forgotten to replace the screen?

Tears gathered in the corners of her eyes as she squeezed them shut. Barely breathing, she tuned her ears to the slightest sound. In her mind, the sound of a man's heavy tread outside the open door froze her on the bed. She should have kept it closed, with the nightstand pushed in front. She squeezed her eyes tighter. *Make it go away. Make it go away.*

A few minutes later, she opened her eyes and glanced toward the door, then the window. Nothing there. She sat up in bed and hugged her knees. Whatever or whoever had made the noise was gone.

Or had she dreamed it?

Worry tugged at her already-frayed nerves. How would she cope with the responsibility of tomorrow's lunch? She should have gathered up her stuff and headed down the road before she could fail. But not until after Janice's money arrived. Three to five days before the funds would be waiting at the money kiosk in Walmart.

She shoved down the sudden slam of guilt. What if she *could* stay here in this pink cocoon? Maybe even happily ever after. But the money ...

She'd scraped and scratched and clawed her whole life. Didn't she deserve a break? Why was everything so complicated?

CHAPTER 33

Tuesday morning. Stomach aching, hands shaking, do-or-die time. Hank stood at the door of the food bank kitchen as Jinxi strode in.

"M-m-miss Jinxi, I c-c-cleaned the k-k-kitchen real g-good for you today." His head bobbed on his tall frame as he sent her a shy smile.

"Thanks, Hank." Distracted by the stove burner's unwillingness to light on the first try, she didn't look up.

"Finally," she exclaimed, as the excess fumes around the burner ignited with a whoosh. Jinxi looked out toward the dining room and saw Hank staring at her. She raised her hand with a wave, which he enthusiastically returned. Seemingly satisfied, he went back to his sweeping with renewed vigor.

She shook her head and began to prepare a meal for a hundred hungry people.

By the end of lunch, all staff, and even some volunteers, had stopped by the kitchen to offer a helping hand. Jinxi barked orders to everyone, Padish and Aneesa included. By two-thirty, the food was gone, the kitchen gleamed, and Jinxi was ready to sit down and finally relax.

"Amazing," Padish exclaimed, standing in front of her with joy radiating from him like the heat from the cooling stove. "What did I tell you, yes? Everything is perfect today."

Jinxi looked up at him with droopy eyes. She barely had the strength to raise her arm to wipe her forehead.

"I tell you what," he said. "You go home now. We will mark on your papers that you were here all day. Okay?"

"Really?" Jinxi couldn't believe it. Finally, the break she deserved.

"Really." He clapped his hands together. "Right now. Before I change my mind."

Jinxi leaped up with renewed energy, grabbed her backpack from under one of the counters, and stampeded out the door. She could hear his laughter echoing as she dashed for the bus that had pulled up to the stop.

Jinxi stepped off the air-conditioned bus into the afternoon heat and began the short walk to the house. As she neared the gate, childish laughter and frantic barking sounded from Janice's yard. She passed through the gate and was almost knocked off her feet by Hannah, who was being chased by an exuberant medium-sized mutt.

As Hannah skidded to a stop, she greeted Jinxi with enthusiasm. "Unca Dean got a dog. And I got to pick him out." The dog in question approached Jinxi and began to sniff her ankles.

Dean had said he'd take her with them to pick out the dog. Guess he didn't mean it. Figured.

Smaller than a German shepherd but bigger than a wiener dog, his coat was a mixture of black, brown, and white. She lost her heart when he looked up at her with glistening brown eyes, the same color as Dean's.

"And I want to name him Ted, but Unca Dean said no." Hannah crouched down to pat his head. The dog nosed her chest until she fell backward, laughing.

Dean came around the corner of the house, huffing and puffing dramatically. "I can't keep up with you two." Seeing

Jinxi, he greeted her the same way as Hannah. "We got a dog."

"No kidding. Hannah says his name is Ted." One quick jab.

Dean put his hands on his hips. "Uh-uh, no way. He is not going to be named Ted. He needs a strong name. You know, Brutus or King or something."

Figured. What a jock.

Hannah had gotten to her feet and tried to get the dog to sit. Jinxi knelt to Hannah's level and patted the dog's back.

"Why do you want to name him Ted?"

Hannah put one hand on her hip and held out the other hand, palm up. She looked exactly like her mother. Poor kid.

"Well, in my book, *Big Dog Little Dog*, the big dog is named Fred, and the little dog is named Ted." As if that explained everything.

Jinxi stood. "I think Ted is a great name for him." As she said this, Ted sat and wagged his corkscrew tail.

"See, Unca Dean? He knows his name." In a sing-song voice, Hannah said, "Good boy, Ted, good boy." She took off running again, the dog at her heels.

Jinxi turned to look at Dean before mounting the porch steps. "Don't stand there glowering at me."

"Glower? Did you say *glower?*" His eyebrows almost met his hairline.

"Yeah, what about it?"

"That's a—"

"A what?" she demanded, one hand on the rail and one hand on her hip.

"Well, it's a fifty-cent word."

"What, and I'm a twenty-five-cent person? Is that what you're saying?" She frowned at him, eyes narrowed.

"I didn't mean that, exactly," he began, taking a step backward.

"For your information, I do know how to read."

Jinxi stomped up the steps toward the front door and paused. "And I know how to use a dictionary." The screen door slammed behind her. She spoke through the screen. "And you were supposed to let me help Hannah pick out the dog."

Dean stood rooted in place, wondering if his foot would fit any further into his mouth, or if he should just exchange feet. Hannah walked around the side of the house and put her arms up.

"Unca Dean, will you carry me into the house? I'm hot."

"Sure, Princess," he answered, scooping her up in his arms. He took Hannah into the house and returned outside a moment later to fill up a bowl with water for the dog. When he reentered the coolness inside, Hannah sat on the sofa watching a cartoon, with Jinxi nowhere in sight. He sat next to Hannah and sipped on a Coke. Maybe he should arm himself for whatever revenge Jinxi had planned. Would his Kevlar vest be enough protection for female wrath?

A few minutes later, Jinxi appeared around the corner from his mom's office. She strode to him with a book in her hand and dumped it in his lap, barely missing his important male parts.

"Ow! *Watch* it!"

"This is a dictionary," she said, sarcasm dripping from every word. "I think you'll find 'glower' in it." As she turned away, she added, "Unless you need help spelling it." She returned to the kitchen, a satisfied look on her face.

He smiled to himself and shook his head. Putting an arm around Hannah, he said, loud enough to carry into the kitchen, "I think we'll name him Ted."

"What's all the commotion?" his mom said, appearing in the hall from her bedroom. She settled into her chair.

"We're discussing what to name our new addition to the family. He squeezed his niece's shoulder. "Hannah wants to name him Ted."

"Yeah, Grammy, after *Big Dog Little Dog*." She ran over to his mom and pulled herself up in her lap. "Don't you like that name?"

Looking down at the child in her lap, Janice said, "Princess, I think Ted is a great name for him. He looks like a Ted."

Jinxi ambled into the front room with a smirk on her face. Figured. She sank onto the chair across from Janice, legs splayed out in front. She rolled a cold can of soda across her forehead.

"You're home early," his mom commented. "How did it go today?

Jinxi took a big drink of her soda. "I'm glad it's over."

"But how did you do?" Janice persisted.

"I guess okay. Padish let me off early. Probably to recuperate."

"Nothing got burned, and no one went hungry?"

Jinxi shook her head.

"That's a miracle," Dean muttered under his breath.

"I think we should go out to dinner to celebrate," his mom said.

"Really?" he and Jinxi spoke at the same time.

"Really. Robin should be here in the next half hour or so to pick Hannah up, so we can go after that."

Dean stood and stretched his arms over his head. "If we're going out to eat, I guess I'd better go get my workout in." He stooped down to kiss the top of Hannah's head. "Bye, Princess. Thanks for helping me pick Ted out." After closing the back door behind him, Dean stood on the top step and whistled for the dog.

Ted trotted behind him as they crossed the back lawn to Dean's workout room. He opened the big garage door to catch whatever slight cross breeze he could capture in the late afternoon heat. Ted dropped to the concrete floor out of reach of the sun, already at home.

Dean climbed on the treadmill and set the machine for a twenty-minute run. As his feet pounded, his mind leaped to the dinner ahead. What should he wear? Jeans or Dockers. Polo or button-down. He shook his head. Did his clothes matter?

With a jolt, he realized it did. He wanted to look good for Jinxi.

Jinxi followed him with her eyes as he leaped off the porch, skipping the concrete steps. Through the lace curtains, she watched him trot around the side of the house, Ted at his heels.

"You're welcome, Unca Dean," Hannah said sleepily, pillowing her head against Janice's chest. "Grammy, can I watch a movie?"

"Sure, Princess." Janice rose to her feet with the child in her arms. She almost fell back as one of her knees buckled, but she caught herself with a painful grimace.

"You're getting to be such a big girl," Janice said. "Grammy won't be able to carry you too much longer." She set Hannah down on the sofa and reached for the box of children's DVDs on the shelf of the end table. "Pick which one you want."

Hannah looked at each one before pulling out a Dora video. "This one."

After starting the movie, Janice said, "I'm going to go take a shower and change clothes. How about we leave in an hour or so?"

"That works."

"Can you stay here with Hannah for a while? If Robin doesn't show up before I finish, send Hannah into my bedroom when you need to get ready."

Jinxi frowned. "I don't think Robin wants me anywhere near Hannah."

Janice stopped, her back to Jinxi. She slowly turned. "I think it'll be all right. Let me know if she says anything."

Jinxi formed her face into a mask of worry. "Okay."

Hannah watched her grandmother leave and patted the sofa next to her. "Come sit by me," she commanded. "You can watch the movie with me."

Jinxi moved over to the couch and sat. Hannah molded herself to Jinxi's side and snuggled in. She pulled Jinxi's arm across her and began to pat it as she put her thumb in her mouth. Jinxi's pale skin contrasted to Hannah's darker coloring.

After a few moments, Hannah pulled her thumb out with a moist sound. "Why do you have marks on your arm?"

Jinxi started to pull away, but Hannah lightly rubbed her hand over the bumpy scars. Hannah's touch brought back the feeling of a hundred butterfly wings gently stroking her, soothing, healing.

"Sometimes I cut myself." Did she admit that? To a four-year-old?

"You mean with a knife?"

Jinxi nodded.

"My mom says I'm not allowed to play with knives. Did you play with a knife?"

"Sort of."

"You should be more careful." Hannah snuggled back to her side.

Yeah, I should.

Jinxi put her hand over Hannah's and let her thoughts drift back to school when her PE teacher had sent her to the office to talk to the nurse about her cutting. As if the nurse was equipped to counsel her. All she received was a tube of antiseptic ointment and a bandage, plus a lecture about the dangers of unprotected sex. A lot of good that did. The next time she was sent to the office, the counselor, who was at the school two days a week, asked about her plans after graduation. He was a guidance counselor, after all, not some sort of emotional advisor.

Jinxi remembered Aneesa and their confrontation in the bathroom at the food bank. She recalled Aneesa's scarred arms and her expression when she'd said, "Let me know when you want to stop." She looked down at Hannah's chubby child arms, smooth and brown, and wondered if she had ever been that innocent. Or had she been marked since birth, scarred and broken, not even significant enough for her own mother to notice?

The Psalm she had read in the Bible said God knew her even before she was born. If that was so, why was she this way? Did God make her flawed? Could she do something to make herself worthy, so that maybe someone would notice her, maybe even love her?

The front door opened. Hannah flew off the couch with renewed energy. "Mommy!"

Robin opened her arms and scooped up the child. "Hi, sweet girl. Did you miss me?"

"Uh-huh. Unca Dean got a dog. And I got to help pick him out. And his name is Ted. Unca Dean wanted to name him something else, but I got to pick out his name. Like in *Big Dog Little Dog*. And before that, Grammy and me played secret treasure. We had fun."

Robin laughed as Janice appeared around the corner from her bedroom. "Whoa, slow down." Over Hannah's head, she said to her mom, "What's this about a dog?"

Janice smiled ruefully. "Dean finally did what he's been threatening to do for months."

As they chatted, Jinxi watched for an opportunity. She didn't need to wait long. Robin glanced her way with a scowl.

Jinxi addressed her question to the child. "Hannah, should I turn off the movie we've been watching?"

"Go ahead and turn off the TV," Janice answered. She followed Jinxi with her eyes as the girl disappeared up the stairs.

Robin's mouth was set in a line as she put Hannah down. "Dinner?"

Janice started to gather up Hannah's things. "We're going out to dinner tonight to celebrate Jinxi's successful day of cooking on her own at the food bank."

"And Dean also?"

Without making eye contact with her daughter, Janice answered, "Yes. Dean too."

"Anything going on that I should know about?"

Janice paused in her folding of Hannah's extra clothes. "No."

"Mom," Robin exclaimed. "Please tell me nothing is going on. I mean, that would be a total train wreck."

"Don't go blowing anything out of proportion." Janice sighed. "I do think there's a fascination on Dean's part. You know how some nice girls are attracted to bad boys." She resumed the task of putting Hannah's things into her bag. "But with the way they banter, they're more like brother and sister than anything." At least she hoped so.

Robin planted her hands on her hips. "I'd keep an eye on her if I were you."

Janice handed her the bag. "Honey, I'm praying about her daily. How about if we leave things in God's hands?"

If Robin knew about the missing money, she'd be furious. Better leave some things unsaid.

Undeterred, Robin gathered up her child and retorted, "Fine. But you'd better keep your eyes open, too." Robin turned to Hannah. "What's this about a game of secret treasure?"

Janice walked them to the door as Hannah told her mother more about her day with Grammy. Janice leaned down and kissed the child's soft cheek.

"Bye, Princess. See you soon."

"Bye, Grammy." Hannah gave her a sloppy kiss on the cheek and a quick hug. "Tell Ted bye for me. And Jinxi too." She took her mother's hand as they walked out the door. Turning back, she said, "I love you, Grammy."

"Love you too, Princess." Janice watched them from the door as they drove away. She heard the water running upstairs. Jinxi had pulled her disappearing act again. Janice sighed with relief. Perhaps the two should be kept separate, like cats. If Robin knew what the girl had done, the fur would fly.

Janice pushed the door until it shut with a click.

God, am I doing the right thing, keeping things from my family?

Now, what to do about Dean?

CHAPTER 34

Dean's cell phone vibrated on the bathroom counter as he shaved. He recognized the number.

"Li'l D."

"Big D. What's up?"

"Hold on, let me put you on speaker. I've got shaving cream on my face."

"What you doing with a razor in your hand at this time of day?" Damaris's voice held a note of surprise. "Wait ... unless you've got a date."

Dean cleared his throat. "Uh ... no, I'm going to dinner with my mom."

"Riiight. You always shave for dinner with your mom." His friend's voice dripped with sarcasm.

"What do you want, anyway."

"I want to know who you're going to dinner with."

"I told you. My mom."

"*And*?" Damaris was relentless.

"And none of your business." Dean finished the last stroke of his razor and rinsed off the blade.

"Aha. I knew it. It's that girl, isn't it?"

"What girl?" Dean asked, feigning innocence.

"The girl with the weird name. The one you brought to the lake."

What could he say? He could lie, or he could tell the truth and forever be teased about it. Or he could not answer.

"Why'd you call?"

Damaris laughed triumphantly. "I called because Patrice said you're getting moved to patrol."

"It's not final yet."

"Oh yeah, it is. I saw the transfer request on Sarge's desk. Signed *and* approved."

Damaris had an uncanny ability to read upside down. "What were you doing in Sarge's office?"

"I was delivering a phone message, and I happened to see the paperwork sitting on his blotter. Sarge didn't make any attempt to cover it. We need to go out and celebrate. You up for some pool?"

"Can we make it later? After dinner."

"Sure. Whatever. Don't blow off dinner with your *girlfriend*."

Dean spoke through gritted teeth. "She's. Not. My. Girlfriend."

"But you're going out to dinner with her. Must be special if she's staying with your mommy *and* you're shaving for her."

If Damaris only knew.

They made their plans, and Dean disconnected. He reached for his shirt and was shrugging into the sleeves when the phone vibrated again. This time Patrice's number flashed on its face. Would Damaris have already called her to gossip?

"Hey, Patrice. What's up?" He held the phone between his ear and shoulder as he buttoned his shirt.

"Dean, I'm telling you this because I care about you, okay?"

Uh-oh. This couldn't be good. "Okaaaay. What is it?"

Patrice inhaled sharply. "There's a rumor going around about you. I thought you should know."

Dean's temper rose quick and hot. "Did D call you?"

"I haven't talked to Damaris. This is about that girl you brought to the lake. Jinxi."

Why couldn't people stay out of his business? "Look, Patrice—"

"No, Dean, hear me out. Someone saw you at the courthouse with her. They said she was arrested for prostitution. You took her to court, and after her appearance, she got into your truck. They're saying some awful things."

Dean muttered a curse. "People should mind their own business." His shirt was suddenly too tight. He unbuttoned a button and pulled the shirt away from his chest.

"So it's not true?" Patrice's voice held concern.

Dean swallowed. "It's complicated." What could he say? That he'd had a lapse in judgment, and now Jinxi was staying with his mom? That he was getting ready to go out to dinner to celebrate her success at her community service project?

"Look, Patrice, I can't talk about this right now. I'm supposed to be over at my mom's." Well, at least that much was true.

There was silence on the other end for at least ten seconds. "Fine." Patrice's voice sounded hurt. "When you're ready to talk to your *friends*, call me." Dean stared in disbelief at his phone. Did she hang up on him?

Janice watched in amusement as Jinxi read the menu like a novel. The aroma of wood-smoked meat wafted over the dining room. Janice's stomach growled. Lunch had been hours ago, a quick PB & J with Hannah.

"What's *beurre blanc* sauce?" Jinxi asked.

Janice and Dean both shrugged.

With a sly smile, Dean answered, "You could always look it up in the *dictionary*."

Jinxi narrowed her eyes at him over the top of the menu and flared her nostrils but didn't answer. Janice glanced back and forth at them with a flutter of concern. What had Robin said about the undercurrent between the two of them? Also, there was Dean's admission about his attraction to the girl. Janice shook off her worry, determined to enjoy the meal.

Dean ordered pork chops with garlic mashed potatoes. Jinxi asked for soft shell crab tacos. Janice settled on the Southwestern chicken salad.

After the waiter topped off their water glasses, no one spoke for a moment.

Janice ran a finger through the condensation on the outside of her glass. "You're quiet tonight, Dean."

He shrugged and pulled his gaze away from the window. "Tired."

Janice reached across the table and patted his arm. "I would imagine so. Your job is so demanding."

He drew himself up and rested his elbows on the table. "How was your day, Mom?"

Janice laughed. "Talk about tired. Hannah and I played a game she made up called secret treasure. That child has such an imagination." Her heart swelled with pride.

"What's the gist of it?" Dean asked.

"We went through some of my old jewelry. Hannah said it was like a pirate treasure. We took turns hiding rings and necklaces around the house. But each time it was Hannah's turn, she used the same spot."

Dean chuckled. "Sounds as if she kept you hopping."

"My goodness, yes."

Their meals arrived. Dean and Jinxi started to eat. Janice bowed her head for a moment, praying quietly. She looked up to find both of them staring at her.

"Let's eat and celebrate Jinxi's success."

After a few minutes of quiet eating, Janice asked, "Jinxi, how are you enjoying your meal?"

Jinxi chewed in concentration. "Good. Different."

"Different how?"

Jinxi's face was serious. "More flavors. Like fireworks in my mouth."

Janice laughed. "I've never heard food described that way." She turned to Dean. "Everything okay, son?"

"Uh, yeah. Fine." He shifted on his chair. "By the way, I'm going out with some of the guys later to play pool."

"That nice young man, Damaris?"

Dean nodded. Cleared his throat. "I know you won't like this, Mom, but I'll be transferred to patrol pretty soon."

Janice's mouth turned down. "Oh, dear." Fear rippled through her.

Dean leaned back in his chair. "Mom, it'll be fine. Nothing's gonna happen to me."

Maybe so, but life had taught her they were only words.

Jinxi sat in the back of Janice's Prius, resisting the urge to burp. Dinner had been amazing. She'd kill to be able to cook like that. She'd eat a gourmet meal every single day.

When they got back to the house, Ted greeted them with enthusiastic barking. He'd found a shady spot under one of the trees in the yard, and after a good stretch, he ran to the car, curly tail wagging. Dean had left a tennis ball on the side porch.

"Watch this," he said. He threw the ball across the yard, and Ted raced to get it before it could bounce twice. He brought the ball back and dropped it at Dean's feet, tongue hanging out as he panted.

"I can't believe someone would abandon such a well-trained dog." Dean shook his head. As the women mounted the steps to go into the house, he threw the ball again, turning to Janice. "When are you going to the doctor, Mom? Are your knees are bothering you?"

Janice nodded, wincing as she took the last step. "They are. I have an appointment on Friday for another MRI, and they'll probably set a date. I can't say I'm looking forward to two knee replacements, but I'll sure be glad to be in less pain."

"Let me know if you need a ride," he answered as she and Jinxi went inside. "Oh, and thanks for dinner."

"Yeah," Jinxi added. "Thanks for dinner. It was good."

"You are welcome," Janice responded, with a light touch on Jinxi's shoulder. "I'm glad we could celebrate the fact that no one died as a result of your cooking today."

Jinxi huffed out a breath with a tiny smile. She sat on the sofa and turned on the television, muting the sound. Janice returned from the bedroom without her purse. She had exchanged her shoes for a pair of slippers. She sat in her chair and picked up a book, opening to a bookmark.

Jinxi fiddled with her earrings. "I think Dean kind of likes me."

Janice tensed, her knuckles white as she gripped the book.

"He kind of, you know, flirts with me. But I don't really like him. Not that way, anyway."

Janice sagged against the back of her chair.

"Do you want me to say something to him?" Janice asked.

Jinxi worked the stud back and forth against her teeth. "No, it's okay." She shrugged as if it weren't important. "I wanted you to know."

She got up from the sofa and stretched. "I'm going upstairs. Thanks again for dinner."

Janice acknowledged her with a nod. Jinxi trudged up the steps. In her room, she sank on the bed and bent over to unlace her boots.

She'd intended to see if Janice had noticed the interplay between her and Dean. She hadn't imagined the unintended consequence. Her heart hurt to see Janice's relief when she'd said she wasn't interested in Dean. Did the woman think she wasn't good enough for her son?

Of course, you're not.

Jinxi rubbed her hand across her chest, above her heart, waiting for it to harden. She wasn't good enough to be around Hannah, and she surely wasn't good enough for Dean.

Jinxi's thoughts turned dark. Janice deserved to have her money stolen. Who did she think she was, anyway? Janice had more than enough to spare. Jinxi had none, and she *needed* the money. Janice didn't. With her Christian piety, she should be offering some to Jinxi. Even more than what Jinxi had taken. So there.

I deserve it. And I'm going to get my fair share.

CHAPTER 35

Jinxi stared up at the ceiling. The moon cast eerie shadows on the walls through the lace curtains. After an hour and a half, she threw the covers off with a curse and stomped downstairs to get a snack. When she got to the kitchen, snuffling at the back door froze her in midstride. Her breath caught in her throat. Someone was trying to break in.

Jinxi remembered the dog and silently mocked herself. With shaky hands, Jinxi opened the back door and let Ted in. He nudged her leg, and she squatted down and scratched his head, running her hand along the wiry fur on his back. He snuffled in her ear, tickling it. She glanced down the hall toward Janice's room. There was no light coming from beneath her door, so she started for the stairs. Ted looked at her with his head cocked for a moment before following her. When they reached her room, he settled down on the throw rug by the side of her bed with a sigh. Jinxi climbed into bed and looked over the edge of the mattress at him.

"G'night, Ted." She turned on her side and was asleep in minutes.

As Jinxi got ready the following day, Dean's voice boomed from downstairs.

She moved to the top of the stairs to better catch what he said. Something about Ted. She descended, taking the steps quickly, the dog following her.

She headed straight for the coffee pot. "What are you yelling about?" She looked around the room for Janice but didn't see her. *Who* had he been bellowing at?

"Someone's stolen Ted."

"He doesn't look stolen." Jinxi turned to the dog who remained in the doorway.

"What have you done?" Dean exploded. "He's supposed to be a guard dog. You know, *guard* the house, not sleep *in* it."

"He was lonely."

Dean's face visibly reddened as he struggled for control. "Lonely." He paused to take a breath.

Ted barked and twirled in a circle.

"Sheesh. Calm down."

"I got him to be a guard dog while I work nights," Dean said, teeth gritted. A vein pulsed in his forehead.

Jinxi crossed her arms and tapped her foot. "He can guard as well inside the house as outside. Besides, if someone tries to break in, he can alert us quicker if he's inside." She opened the cupboard above the coffee pot, reaching for the star mug.

"C'mon, Ted, time to go outside." Dean grabbed the dog food from the back porch on his way out the back door.

Talk about overreacting. What a tool.

"What was all that about?" Janice asked, stepping into the kitchen.

Jinxi reached for the coffee. "That was your son. Yelling."

Janice looked as if she wanted to say more but held back. She reached for the phone with one hand and poured herself a cup of coffee with the other. She carried the cup to the table and set it on the edge of a placemat, then punched in some numbers.

"Hi, Robin."

Jinxi sat at the table and pulled the newspaper toward her, pretending to read the morning headlines.

"Did I leave a pair of earrings at your house this weekend? The ones your dad gave me? Uh-huh. The gold hoops with the diamonds."

Jinxi's senses went on full alert as Robin responded.

Janice continued, "I didn't think I wore them, but I can't seem to locate them. They're not in my jewelry box. Yes, I've looked in my car, but I can't think of where I put them."

Jinxi wracked her brain to come up with a reasonable explanation for Janice's misplaced earrings. She didn't remember seeing them when she'd searched Janice's bedroom.

Janice concluded her call and returned the phone to its charger. She leaned her back against the counter and sipped her coffee with a doleful look on her face.

Jinxi's voice was tentative. She'd have to proceed with caution. "You can't find your earrings?"

"No, I can't. They're very special to me. Tom gave them to me for my birthday, a month or so before he died."

Jinxi looked at her with what she hoped was pure innocence. "I'm not sure I've ever seen you wear them." She tried to remember if she'd seen the earrings Janice described. "When was the last time you saw them?"

Janice didn't answer. She pushed away from the counter and headed down the hall toward her bedroom.

Jinxi exhaled the breath she'd been holding. Did Janice suspect her of taking the earrings? Taking her money had been one thing. But jewelry? No way, lady. Too easily missed and too hard to get rid of.

Later that week, Jinxi stood at the money transfer kiosk. "Do you have some money for Jeanette Lansing?" she asked the clerk.

This time a blue-haired older woman waited on her.

"Yes, right here. Sign this, and you'll be good to go." Jinxi signed her name and initialed the appropriate places. "Someone is quite generous to you," the woman commented

Jinxi answered without making eye contact. "Yeah, my grandma is helping me out." The lie slipped out of her mouth like silk.

Jinxi pocketed the money and hurried toward the exit. She relaxed after a glance around the parking lot. No motorcycle.

With this money and her paychecks, she should have enough for her own place. *Wonder what an apartment costs.* Spotting a "For Rent" magazine in the free publications rack, she pulled one out and scanned as she walked. The magazine was broken down into neighborhoods. Easy enough, but she was unfamiliar with Sacramento. As she thumbed through it, she was dismayed to see that most places were at least a thousand dollars a month and required a security deposit. At this rate, it would take her forever to be on her own.

Unless she could somehow get away with more of Janice's money.

The pounding of Dean's shoes on the treadmill matched the music pumping through his earbuds. He'd hoped the loud volume would drown out the remnants of his conversation with Patrice. It wasn't working.

She'd pulled him aside after their shift at the jail.

"I'm worried about you, Dean. Your career could be at stake." She'd told him the PD took a dim view of cops dating former inmates. The rumor mill was worse than a high school boy's locker room. Talk regarding who slept with whom, who was being investigated by Internal Affairs, who got promoted. Anything that could be gossiped about, was.

Dean couldn't lie to her. He'd dragged her into a corner and told her everything, from meeting Jinxi outside the jail to having dinner with her the previous evening. Disappointment had filled Patrice's face.

"You've got to be kidding, Dean." She glared at him, hands on hips. "A *hooker*."

Dean's armpits tingled. "She isn't a prostitute. She got into a little trouble, that's all."

Patrice smirked. "Right. A little trouble."

"C'mon, Pat. Gimme a break here."

"So now you think you're Richard Gere in *Pretty Woman*?" Patrice waved her hand, dismissing his words. "She's not Julia Roberts."

Dean rolled his eyes. "Look, you don't know her like I do. She's good for my mom. Keeps her company. You know□"

"I know one thing. You're playing with fire. And you know what happens." Patrice had shot him a look of concern before she strode away with a squeak of her police-issue shoes.

Dean's stride slowed, and he jumped off the treadmill. He picked up a towel and wiped his face and neck. He grabbed the water bottle off the holder on the treadmill and guzzled half of it, pouring the rest over his head. Some of the water splashed on the cement floor in small puddles.

Dean slumped onto the weight bench and hung his head. He'd set something in motion, like tossing a pebble into a pond. Unintended consequences. Something his dad once said teased the back of his mind. He pulled out the earpieces to concentrate.

"Dean-o, God tells us that when we're kind to someone, it's like lending to God, and he'll reward us." There was some sort of Bible verse, but Dean couldn't remember it. Dad loved his Proverbs.

Dean huffed out a humorless laugh. Would his reward be getting fired? He couldn't conjure up a happily-ever-after scenario. What if his one action of inviting Jinxi to have breakfast had created a chain reaction of chaos?

I am not a God of chaos.

Dean's head snapped up. Where did *that* come from? A chill swept over him despite the heat of the garage. With jerky movements, he shoved the buds back in his ears, hoping the thumping beat of the music would drown out that still, small voice.

CHAPTER 36

Jinxi rested her head on her arms, lying still on the hard tattoo table. The relentless whine of the needle lulled her into lethargy, despite the pain on the calf. Her mind drifted to Hannah, diagnosed with that horrible disease. Talk about unfair. Such a sweet kid. No one should have to go through that at such a young age. At least Hannah had two parents who loved her.

"Not much longer." The tattoo artist spoke, startling her. "A little more color to fill, and you'll be good to go."

Good to go. The phrase echoed in Jinxi's ears. Where had she heard that phrase before? The money kiosk lady. She'd said the same thing.

Good to go. When had she ever been good? Even as a child, she'd done what she'd needed to do to survive. What had begun as pilfering from her mother had grown into something she couldn't control.

"Okay, all set."

Jinxi sat up, turning her calf as far as she could to view the artwork. "Beautiful," she said with a smile. Beauty and strength. That would be her new mantra.

She gathered her things, thanked the tattoo artist, and walked the distance back to Janice's house. She increased her pace as she passed the convenience store where she had stolen the pack of cigarettes. Two men lounged outside the store. They glanced at each other, hustling to fall into step with her.

"Whoa, girl, where you rushing off to?" asked one with a leer. His tank top revealed some wicked-looking tattoos on his arms and shoulders.

The other one added, "Yeah, slow down. Let's talk, *chica*." His shaved head gleamed in the heat. A teardrop-shaped tattoo sat at the corner of one of his eyes. Had he killed someone? Or lost a homie to a rival gang?

Jinxi's heart thundered in her chest as they tried to engage her. A few more houses and she'd be home. Her pace increased, even as her feet protested inside the heavy boots. She reached Janice's front gate with them on her heels. Ted rushed at the chain-link fence, barking at the strangers.

Dean appeared in the doorway and stepped out onto the porch. "Is there a problem here?" he asked, coming down the steps. He looked huge and scary in his uniform. For once, Jinxi didn't mind.

"Uh, no. No problem," said one of the young men, backing away. Jinxi grabbed the gate latch and hurriedly closed it behind her with a clang.

"Hey, *ese*, no harm, no foul," the other man said. "Right?"

Dean rested his hand on his weapon. "Just so you know, she's staying here, and I don't want her bothered. Got it?"

"Sure, man. We didn't know she was staying with Miss Janice." They nudged each other and jogged across the street, heading back the way they came.

Jinxi's heart beat a staccato rhythm as she mounted the steps. She threw herself down in one of the porch chairs, exhaling loudly. Ted bumped her hand with his nose, tail wagging.

Dean sank into another chair. "What happened?"

Jinxi shook her head. "They started following me, but I didn't talk to them." She pulled her backpack on her lap and unzipped it.

"Don't worry. Word will get around the neighborhood you're to be left alone."

Jinxi shrugged and rummaged around in her backpack and answered without looking at him. "Good." It was bad enough to have Skeeter on her tail. How much worse if she was robbed.

"Probably not a good idea to carry around much cash. Even though you're safe now."

"What makes you think I'm safe? Because you're a cop?" She pulled things out of the backpack one by one and placed them on the small table between the two chairs. Ted sniffed her stuff. She shoved his nose away. "When this happened before with some of Skeeter's friends, we took care of it."

"Skeeter?" Dean asked, a blank look on his face.

"Yeah. Skeeter. My boyfriend."

"Boyfriend?"

She finished emptying the backpack, leaving the money tucked in the outside pocket, and turned it upside down and shook it. "Yeah. This one time when we were doing this drug deal. Well, a couple of his friends were like, hey, you cheated us, so they grabbed me and tried to threaten us."

"Drug deal?"

Something dropped out of the backpack. "There it is." Her pepper spray pen. She held it up in victory. "*This* is what I should have used."

"Drug deal?"

"Why are you repeating everything I say?"

Dean squinted and leaned forward. "You have a boyfriend who's a drug dealer?"

She felt the blood drain from her face. "Well, ex-boyfriend."

He shook his head. "I didn't see that coming."

Jinxi looked away and picked up each item, carefully placing them in the backpack. She felt his eyes on her but didn't dare look up. Jinxi stood to leave, but Dean restrained her with a touch on her arm.

"Wait."

She shook off his hand. "Could we, like, not talk about this? It's none of your business."

"Sit down," he barked. "It *is* my business if your drug-dealing boyfriend shows up at my mom's house."

"*Ex*-boyfriend."

"Look, if he shows up and I'm here, he'd better not expect to be invited in, okay? Just so we're clear."

"Fine. Whatever." Like she'd invite Skeeter to pizza night or something. She started to get up again, but he stopped her.

"Don't let him hang around." Dean's hand gripped the arm of the chair. "My mom lives here, too."

"I said fine." Sheesh. Move on.

But his eyes pinned her, granite-hard and unblinking. She held his stare until his eyes softened. He stared out at the street. "Last year, there was this incident."

Jinxi sat on the edge of the chair. "Go on." And make it snappy, Captain America.

"Let's just say my mom intervened in something that could have gone down badly. She intervened, and now she's a kind of neighborhood icon."

Not to mention she has a cop for a son living in her backyard. "So because of that, no one will hassle me anymore?" Right. And I'm Princess Elsa.

"That's right." Dean slapped his hands on his thighs and stood. He leaned over and patted Ted's head. "I'm off to work. Later."

Jinxi sat back in the chair, thinking about what happened. Janice was a serial do-gooder. Did she get some sort of God points for helping people? *She's probably working on getting into heaven or something.* Good luck with that.

Dean paused at the bottom of the stairs from his apartment. Ted ran to him and nudged his leg.

"Good boy, good boy." Dean patted Ted on the head, scratching him on the spot between his ears. "Keep an eye on things, okay, buddy?" Ted woofed as Dean opened the gate leading to the side street where he parked his truck. Sweat trickled down the back of his neck, itching under his Kevlar vest. *Probably should have waited to put it on.* His stomach quivered with anticipation as he hoped today he'd hear when he'd be transferred to patrol. His buddy, Damaris, had begun patrol duty a few weeks prior. Li'l D lost no opportunity to rub it in.

What about those two men who'd followed Jinxi? Although he was sure word would get around, she was still vulnerable. Why his sudden need to protect her? Hadn't she made it clear she could take care of herself?

If her drug-dealing ex-boyfriend showed up—what kind of name was Skeeter, anyway—what if there was a confrontation? What if he had to use his weapon? A cop shooting a civilian—probably a felon—on his property while protecting a girl doing community service for prostitution. Wouldn't that look great in his file?

Was Jinxi doing drugs? No. he hadn't seen any evidence of her using.

She'd said *ex-boyfriend*.

Dean's thoughts turned to the day they'd spent at the lake. He'd had a good time with her. She was different than any of his friends or the women they tried to hook him up with. Underneath all that black stuff on her eyes was a heart that cried for his little niece.

It had been nice to hold her briefly in the hospital. He'd felt a stirring inside, something he hadn't felt for a long time. What would his friends say if they knew he liked her? He shook his head. Who dates someone who's been arrested for prostitution? He sure hoped Patrice could keep a secret.

CHAPTER 37

"I'm going to pick some squash for our supper," Janice announced as Jinxi came through the front door, dragging her backpack behind her. Her day could not have been worse. Connie had overcooked the vegetables, Jinxi had cut her finger while slicing tomatoes, and they discovered a mouse had gotten into a ten-pound bag of rice. Aneesa had jumped all over her for not reporting her finger. Sheesh. You'd think she was going to sue them or something.

"Sure. Whatever." Jinxi dropped her backpack at the foot of the stairs and headed straight for the fridge, pulling out a cold soda. As she popped the top, fizz shot up and overflowed onto the floor. She shouted a curse, thankful Janice was already out of earshot. She wet some paper towels, mopped up the floor, and walked to the sink to wash her hands.

Jinxi idly watched through the kitchen window as Janice swung open the shed door—a decrepit square of rotting wood—and disappeared inside. Jinxi finished drying her hands, tossing the towel onto the counter. She glanced out the window again just as Janice staggered out of the shed, crumpled to the ground, and lay still.

Jinxi dashed for the back door and flew down the back steps.

"Janice," she shouted as she approached the prone woman. Ted appeared from his shady spot under the trees and danced around, barking. She ran to Janice, kneeling to touch her arm. "Janice. Answer me." She shook Janice's arm. Good, she was still breathing. Janice's eyes fluttered.

"Oh, God. Oh, God. What do I do?"

Jinxi stood, making a sudden decision. She ran across the lawn to Dean's apartment. She raced up the stairs, screaming, "Dean! Dean! Help!"

Jinxi raised her fist to pound, but he was already pulling the door open. "What's going on?"

"It's—hurry—your mom—I—" She grabbed the front of his T-shirt and pulled him behind her, back down the stairs. They ran together toward Janice, who hadn't moved from where she had fallen on the hot concrete.

Dean quickly assessed the situation. "Go inside. Call nine-one-one. Take Ted with you. Bring me a towel and plastic bag filled with ice. And grab your cell phone."

"What is it?" Jinxi asked, panicked.

"Look at her hand. Spider bite."

Jinxi stood frozen in place.

"*Go*. Now."

Propelled into action, Jinxi sprinted to the back steps, calling to Ted. Once in the house, she picked up her phone with clumsy fingers. She punched out the emergency number, holding the phone between her ear and shoulder as she fumbled for a plastic bag.

What if Janice died? What would her family do without her? Janice was the glue holding them together. What would *she* do? Where would she go? Questions circled in her brain.

"9-1-1. What's your emergency?"

Jinxi opened her mouth to speak, but only a squeak came out. She already had the police right there in her backyard. Clearly, Dean knew how to do some medical stuff.

"Hold on," she managed. Grabbing the towel off the counter, she hurried back outside, carrying the bag of ice and the phone.

"Dean," she called out. "It's 9-1-1." She jutted the phone toward him.

Dean took the ice and the phone from her. "This is Officer Dean Rafferty," he told the dispatcher. "Badge number BR09472J. I believe a spider bit my mother. On her hand. She's breathing but nonresponsive."

Jinxi chewed her nails as Dean relayed the rest of the information. He disconnected, fumbling with the bag of ice.

"Here, hold this."

Jinxi held the bag on Janice's hand. Dean turned his mother's head to the side.

"She's got a lump on her head where she fell. Run in the house and get another bag of ice." His brown eyes glistened with tears.

Jinxi couldn't move. The same eyes that turned hard when he warned her about Skeeter were now filled with concern. Would anyone ever look at her the same way? Tears prickled the back of her throat. What was this feeling? More than sympathy, the feeling was deep terror for both Janice and Dean.

"Please, Jinxi. Listen to me. Go in the house and get more ice." Dean spoke with calm authority.

"I'm sorry." Jinxi let go of the bag, straightened, and jogged into the house. She returned a minute later and handed the ice to Dean.

"Thanks. Hold the bag on Mom's arm, and I'll hold the other on her head."

"She was going out to get some squash or something for dinner. I didn't know what to do. She came out of the shed and fell. I thought she tripped. But she didn't move." She squeezed her lips together to stop babbling.

"Mom. Mom." Dean pried open one of his mom's eyes.

"I shouldn't have let her—"

"Stop. This isn't your fault." Dean shifted his position to bump her shoulder with his.

She closed her eyes to savor the moment. How weird to bond with him over his mom's prone body. But no more bizarre than the rest of her life.

Jinxi yearned for time to slow down, at the same time anxious to hear the sound of approaching sirens.

Janice groaned and stirred.

"Sh, Mom. Hold tight. Help's on the way."

Jinxi watched his hand smooth Janice's hair back. She wondered how his hand would feel on her face. Dean's touch looked gentle as he stroked his mom's face.

The sound of approaching sirens ruined the moment.

The ambulance bounced over the curb at the end of Janice's driveway and screeched to a halt. A moment later, a full-sized fire truck pulled in behind it. The siren wound down, but the lights continued to spin, flashing red and white across the front of the shed. Blood drained from Jinxi's head, leaving her light-headed. She hated fire trucks, firefighters, and anything to do with fire. Dean shot her a questioning look as she took a couple of deep breaths.

Two burly paramedics jumped out of the ambulance's cab, followed by a third from the rear. They ran toward Jinxi and Dean, who still hovered over Janice.

Dean removed the bag of ice from his mother's arm. "Looks like a spider bite. Maybe two."

One of the paramedics glanced Jinxi's way. "What about her head?"

"She passed out and hit her head." Dean pulled the bag of ice away to show an egg-sized lump on Janice's head.

Two firemen approached, their leather belts creaking. Jinxi kept her eyes glued to Janice. No way the firemen would recognize her here. All that happened in Bakersfield six years ago.

I'm going to be sick.

"We've got this." The shorter paramedic shouldered Jinxi aside. She fell backward onto her bottom from her squat position. Dean stood and extended his hand to help her up.

They stepped away, letting the paramedics do their work. Dean kept his hand clasped around hers.

"What's going to happen to her?" Jinxi pulled the stud against her teeth, clicking it back and forth.

"You know that drives me nuts, right?" He yanked on her hand.

"What?"

"That clicking. Makes me crazy."

One of the paramedics approached before Jinxi could respond. "We're taking her to Sac Gen. You can follow us."

Dean nodded and turned toward Jinxi. "You coming?"

Duh. Absolutely, she was coming.

Dean and Jinxi followed the ambulance in Dean's truck.

"Do you think she'll be all right?" Jinxi clamped her lips together to keep from chewing on the lip stud.

Dean's knuckles whitened as he gripped the steering wheel. "Sure. They'll probably pump her full of antivenin."

"I thought they only did that with rattlesnake bites."

Dean didn't answer. He seemed intent on racing through every signal, whether green or yellow. Jinxi clamped one hand on the armrest and gripped the seat belt with the other.

Buildings sped by in a blur. Jinxi gasped when Dean swerved into the opposite lane to pass a slow-moving delivery truck.

They arrived at the emergency entrance a few minutes later. Jinxi released a pent-up breath.

Dean dashed in ahead of her and strode to the reception desk.

"Janice Rafferty. She was brought in by ambulance a few minutes ago."

The guy in scrubs behind the counter seemed unimpressed. "Sign in here." He pointed to a clipboard. Waves of frustration undulated off Dean.

"When can we see her?" He signed his name and leaned forward as he slammed the pen down on the counter.

The scrub guy took his time flipping the clipboard around. "You family?"

Dean looked ready to explode. "Yes, we're family. When can we see her?"

Jinxi touched his arm, hoping to calm him down. He drew in a deep breath. "She's my mom. She was transported here not more than ten minutes ago."

Scrub guy reached for a phone on his desk. "I'll check and let you know. Have a seat and wait until I call your name."

"C'mon, Dean. Let's find a place to sit." Jinxi tugged on his arm. He sighed and turned toward her.

"Fine."

They sat in the emergency room with squalling babies and sick adults. A television blared the evening news, adding to the noise.

"I gotta call work." Dean stood and reached into his shirt pocket for his cell. "Be right back. If they call my name, come get me."

As if she wouldn't. Her phone buzzed in her back pocket. Another text from Skeeter.

[Text block begin]

SKEETER: You gonna hook me up with some cash again?

[Text block end]

Jinxi bit her lip, trying to decide if she should respond. She whipped her head up when the scrub guy called out, "Rafferty family."

She jumped to her feet. "Uh, one minute." She dashed for the door as Dean was entering. They collided with an *oof.*

Dean put his arms around her to steady her. "We gotta stop doing this hospital dance."

"They called us. You." She panted as if she'd run a fifty-yard dash.

Dean strode to the reception counter, Jinxi at his heels. "I'm Rafferty."

Scrub guy pointed to a door at the end of a short hall. "Stand by that door, and a nurse will be out in a minute to take you back."

They hustled down the hall. At least no one had asked if she was family. Yet.

A nurse in pink scrubs opened the door. Jinxi gaped up at her. She must have been at least six feet tall. Even Dean had to look up.

"Y'all Ms. Rafferty's folks?" Her drawl said Texas, or maybe Louisiana.

She and Dean nodded in unison.

"Well, c'mon back. Your mama's gonna be jus' fine. No little spider bite is gonna take her down. No, sir." She led them to a glass-walled cubicle. Janice sat in the bed in a semi-reclined position.

"Dean. Jinxi." She reached out her good hand toward them. A clear bag of liquid hung from a pole with a tube connected to Janice's other hand. Jinxi shuddered. She hated needles. The medical kind, anyway. Tattoos were different.

"How're you feeling, Mom?" Dean took her hand.

The nurse answered for her. "Your mama's a mite woozy. We'll keep her a little longer until this bag is empty." She rested her large hand on the pole as if she had all the time in the world to spend with them. "She's gettin' a cocktail of muscle relaxants, antivenin, and pain meds. Oh, and some antibiotics. Isn't that right, sugar?" She looked down at Janice, whose eyes had closed.

"I'm Sam, by the way. Y'all can mosey over to the family waiting room across the hall."

Jinxi and Dean trooped to a waiting room no bigger than a cubby hole. Three stiff chairs sat against the walls. Jinxi took the one closest to the door. The room was so small, their knees bumped when Dean took the chair to her left.

"Sorry." They both spoke at the same time.

"Do you think she'll be okay?"

Dean exhaled, rubbing the back of his neck. "Sure. The nurse—Sam—didn't look worried." He sounded as if he was trying to convince himself as much as her.

They lapsed into silence. Dean pulled out his cell phone. "One bar. Wonder if my text will go through?"

Jinxi's phone buzzed with a new text. "Apparently so." She glared at her phone. Another text from Skeeter.

SKEETER: We ain't done. Don't think u can ignor me

"Everything okay?" Dean leaned toward her.

Jinxi tilted the phone away from him and slipped it under her thigh. "Yeah. It's all good."

"My sergeant said not to come into work."

"Right on." Jinxi shifted on the stiff seat. How long would they have to wait? Her stomach rumbled. Lunch was a light-year away, and she'd kill for a cup of coffee.

As if in answer to her unspoken question, a dark-skinned man wearing a lab coat over blue scrubs appeared in the doorway. His white shoes had rust-colored stains across the top. Jinxi blanched.

"Rafferty family?" The doctor didn't look up from the metal clipboard in his hand.

Dean rose to his feet. "I'm Dean Rafferty."

The doctor made brief eye contact before focusing his attention on the papers on the clipboard.

"It looks like your mother was bitten twice by a spider, probably a black widow. Do you know her whereabouts prior to her passing out?"

Jinxi cleared her throat. "She, uh, went into her shed. She was going to get some squash or something for dinner." Jinxi bit down hard on her bottom lip.

The doctor glanced up again. "She's responding well to the antivenin. We'll send her home with some oral antibiotics and something to help with the muscle spasms."

Dean stopped the doctor before he could leave. "How much longer will she be here?"

The doctor shrugged. "An hour, maybe more. You can look in on her."

"Thanks."

Jinxi followed Dean back to the cubicle where Janice lay, eyes closed. Sam appeared at the entrance.

"She's restin' easy. Why don't y'all head down to the cafeteria? She's gonna be here a while longer."

Four excruciating hours later, Janice was released from the hospital, bearing a bandage that stretched from fingers to elbow. Jinxi and Dean loaded her into the truck.

"How you feeling?" Dean leaned forward to glance across Jinxi to his mom.

Janice rested her head against the headrest, eyes closed. "I'm all right. I want to go to bed."

"You gave us quite a scare, you know." Dean's hands held a death grip on the steering wheel.

"I know. I'm sorry."

"Mom, you don't have to apologize. I'm just saying, you scared the ..." Jinxi waited for Dean to utter a curse word. "... you scared us, that's all. I thought we'd lost you." He chuckled. "And I've never seen Jinxi run so fast."

The corners of Jinxi's mouth turned up as she glanced over at Janice's pale face.

"We're going to get you home and put you to bed. The doctor said to take things easy for a few days. I'll call in sick and take care of you," Dean said.

Janice sighed. "You don't have to do that. I'll be fine."

"No, Mom–"

"I'll be there," Jinxi interrupted. Dean shot her a doubtful look as she continued. "Hear me out. I'll stay downstairs on the couch tonight. When you get home from work in the morning, you can sleep on the couch all day in case she needs something." Why was she offering to do this? Janice wasn't *her* mom, after all.

"I don't know ..."

"Don't be stupid. It makes perfect sense." Jinxi turned to Janice for validation.

Janice nodded wearily, eyes closed. "You two work it out. I can't think about it right now."

"Mom." Dean's voice rose. "Jinxi needs to get her sleep so she can work. Besides, I've got sick time available. My sergeant said to take the night off."

Dean's voice pounded at her like a hammer, but Jinxi held her ground, stomach quivering. "Why should you take time off work if you don't have to? I'm at the house at night, anyway, so it's no big deal." Jinxi didn't know why it was so important to her to win this argument. Was she starting to care for the woman? Or did she only want to show Dean she wasn't the loser he thought she was?

Janice's eyes opened.

"You two stop. Dean, listen to Jinxi. She'll be with me tonight, and you can be there tomorrow. After that, we'll see how it goes. The doctor said I'd be fine in a few days." Janice slumped back against the seat as if the effort of speaking had exhausted her.

Jinxi turned to Dean with a smug smile. She'd won. For now.

She savored the small victory.

Why was he so bothered by what his mom had said? It wasn't as if Jinxi didn't sleep there every night, under his mom's roof. Why should it make a difference to him if Jinxi slept on the couch, within calling distance of Mom's bedroom?

Maybe he wanted to be the only one his mother relied on. Jinxi was an interloper, an outsider. Her presence disrupted their comfortable family dynamic. Robin had pitched a nonstop fit over Jinxi being there. Then again, Robin pitched a fit about most things. In Dean's conversation with his brother Brian, he'd promised to keep an eye on Mom and let Brian know if he noticed anything hinky. Brian had told him stories about elder financial abuse he'd seen in his CPA practice.

Dean resolved to have a frank conversation with his mom about her finances as soon as he could get her alone. Maybe tomorrow after Jinxi left for work.

Jinxi seemed genuinely concerned about his mom, which pleased him. Still, they should be careful. He wouldn't fully trust her yet.

CHAPTER 38

"Look, Ted's waiting for us," Jinxi said as Dean pulled the truck up to the front of the house. No lights welcomed them. Dean opened the passenger door and helped his mom out, while Jinxi swept her eyes up and down the street, searching for a nonexistent motorcycle.

Ted stood at the fence, curly tail wagging. He gently nudged Janice's bandaged hand as they went through the gate.

"No, Ted," Dean said sharply.

Jinxi shot him a look. *Leave him alone.*

Jinxi supported Janice on one side, Dean on the other as they walked up the front steps and crossed the porch to the door. Dean unlocked the door and pushed through to the dark living room. Jinxi switched on a light.

"Jinxi, could you help me get into my nightgown?"

"Sure." She took Janice's elbow and guided her down the hall.

"You can go now," Janice said to Dean over her shoulder.

"You sure you're all right?"

"I'm sure. You better get to work."

"I told you, I don't have to go in tonight. It's too late, anyway."

Janice's voice was sharp. "Go home and get some sleep."

Jinxi shot him a quizzical look. Dean hesitated, sighed, scrubbed a hand across his face. "Okay, Mom. See you tomorrow."

Jinxi watched him turn and head down the hall. The back door shut with a bang.

Janice sank onto the bed with a weary sigh.

"What an ordeal," she murmured. "I never even saw that darn spider."

Did she say *darn*? Jinxi chewed on the stud in her lip. She'd never heard Janice utter a word resembling a curse. *Darn, shoot, heck*. They weren't part of her vocabulary. She must really be upset.

"Where's your nightgown?" Jinxi knew the nightgown hung on a hook in Janice's closet but didn't want Janice to realize she knew.

"Would you get a clean one out for me? Bottom drawer of the bureau." Janice kicked off her shoes and began to unbutton her blouse, using her left hand.

"Here, let me get that." Jinxi tossed the gown on the bed and leaned over to work the buttons. Janice shrugged out of the blouse. Jinxi pressed her hands together. "Um, do you want me to undo your bra?"

"That would be great." Janice turned her back. Jinxi quickly unhooked the older woman's bra, averting her eyes as she lifted the gown over her head. "Can you give me a hand?" Janice's muffled voice sounded through the fabric.

With hands that shook, she pulled the nightgown over Janice's head, guiding her right arm through the sleeve as gently as she could. Janice winced.

"I'm sorry."

"Don't apologize," the older woman said wearily. "My arm hurts whenever I move it." She stood so Jinxi could pull back the covers, and then collapsed onto the bed with a grateful sigh.

Jinxi stood by the side of the bed, shifting from one foot to the other. "Can I get you anything?"

"How about a glass of ice water? All those drugs have made me parched."

Jinxi went into the kitchen and filled a glass with ice and water. She rooted around in the pantry for the package of straws kept on hand for Hannah. Placing the glass on the nightstand, Jinxi stood back. Janice had fallen asleep.

She watched her for a moment, her insides shaking. What happened to Janice? She'd been strong and constant, like a ship pushing through the ocean waves. Jinxi chewed on a fingernail. What if Janice died? Only in the last few days had Jinxi discovered that she had something too important to risk losing.

Jinxi rummaged in the linen closet and pulled out a set of sheets and a blanket to make up the downstairs sofa. After smoothing out the last wrinkles from the sheets, she trudged to the bathroom and braced her arms on the counter for a long moment, head hanging in weariness. Finally she washed her face and prepared for bed.

Before turning in for the night, she checked on Janice, who slept peacefully. Her splinted arm lay outside the covers. Jinxi shuddered, thinking about the red welts where the spider had bitten. Jinxi didn't think she'd ever been as scared as when she watched Janice drop to the ground outside the shed.

Jinxi realized with a start that she'd only thought once about what would happen to *her*. She'd thought Janice was dead, and her first concern was for Dean and the rest of their family.

"What's your plan?" Dean had asked. She had planned to get enough money to start over somewhere. Now that was all messed up. A new plan was needed. A plan to make sure Janice was okay.

Jinxi's brain swirled as she shifted on the sofa, searching for a comfortable position. The old house creaked and groaned, keeping her awake and making her nerves jump. Light from outside filtered through the lace curtains, turning the furniture into macabre shapes. Like she'd done as a child, she pulled the covers over her head, eyes squeezed shut.

Think about something else. Jinxi rubbed her hand on her chest, trying to massage away the soreness. Her heart had recently expanded to fit in Hannah, Janice, Ted, and even Dean. Never had she been forced to make so much room for others. A Dr. Seuss story about the Grinch—the one her mother had read to her when she was a little girl before all the madness set in—said that his heart was "two sizes too small."

Was she like the Grinch? Would there be a happy ending, like in the Dr. Seuss book? *Could* there be?

Familiar scratching at the back door reminded her that she'd left Ted out. She threw back the covers and padded through the kitchen to let him in. Once inside, he cocked his head as if to ask, "Is everything okay?"

She sat down on the kitchen floor, hugging Ted's neck. "Hey, Teddy-boy. It's going to be all right. Everything's cool." Were her reassurances for him? Or were they to herself?

Janice woke, arm throbbing. She sat up, carefully lowering her legs over the side of the bed. She waited for the dizziness to pass before standing. The clock read two a.m. She padded into the living room and spied Jinxi, asleep on the couch, one hand holding a stuffed rabbit. Her heart melted. Jinxi might be nearly grown, but there was still a scared little girl down in there somewhere.

Light from the street spilled through the front windows, silver and white. The smell of damp fur tickled her nose. She gasped when a lump under the coffee table moved. Ted raised his head, eyes glowing from the outside reflection.

She shook her head and turned back toward the bedroom. She hadn't remembered permitting Ted to be in the house.

Janice shook out a pain pill from the prescription bottle and washed it down with a sip of water before returning to bed. Her bandaged arm lay outside the covers. Even their light weight hurt. *What a thing to happen. What next?*

Her fears, usually under careful control, grew into a tangled ball of barbed wire. What if she didn't regain use of her hand? How would she maintain her independence? What if something happened to Dean when he was on patrol and couldn't help take care of her? Because he was born ten years after Brian, she'd coddled him more. Made it easier for him to remain dependent on her by letting him stay in the apartment over the garage. He had been her miracle surprise. After Brian, she was told she'd never be able to have more children. Then Robin arrived practically on their doorstep two years later. She and Tom had meant to tell Robin she was adopted, but the circumstances of her conception were so horrific, they'd never done it.

What if Robin discovered the truth about her birth? Would she prohibit Janice from seeing Hannah? What if Hannah became disfigured because of arthritis?

And why hadn't Brian called lately? He used to phone her at least once a week. He'd been distant lately. Less attentive. Questions bounced back and forth in her head like a ping pong ball.

Janice had done more than her share of wrestling with God lately. Since Tom's death, life had settled into a comfortable routine. Now everything was changing, and she didn't like it one bit.

Jinxi woke with a start, the acrid smell of smoke lingering in her nose from the recurring nightmare. She sat up, forgetting for a moment where she was. As she rubbed the sleep from her eyes, she realized the smell was not smoke but coffee.

Heavy footfalls clomped through the kitchen and into the dining room. Dean appeared, carrying a cup of coffee, a smile on his face. Jinxi shoved the bunny under her pillow.

"Good morning, sleepy head. How was the sofa?" He handed her the cup.

Jinxi closed her eyes and breathed in the aroma of fresh-brewed Starbucks. "I guess you'll find out soon enough. What time is it?"

"Eight-thirty."

"Oh—" She bit back a curse as she flew to her feet. "I'm late." She rushed toward the stairs.

"Want me to call the food bank and let them know why you're running late?"

Jinxi paused, foot on the bottom step. "Uh ... yeah, I guess." She turned back toward Dean. "Do you think they'll be ... ticked?"

Dean shrugged. "I'll find out."

Less than twenty minutes later, Jinxi burst into the kitchen, breathless from her haste. "Okay, I'm taking off. What did they say? Did you talk to Padish? Or Aneesa?" She grabbed an apple from the fridge.

Dean sat at the kitchen table. He stood as she entered. "They said no problem. C'mon, I'll drive you."

"But your mom—"

Janice padded up the hall toward them. "I'll be fine. I promise not to get into any trouble while you're gone." Her wan smile and pale face showed the strain of the past eighteen hours.

"Go back to bed, Mom, and stay there until I get back." Dean used his cop voice, the one that brooked no argument.

Jinxi and Janice exchanged a look that said, *See what he's like?*

Dean held the back door open as Jinxi swept by him. They hurried across the back lawn toward his truck.

"You sure she'll be okay?" Jinxi spoke over her shoulder to Dean, following on her heels.

"As long as she doesn't try to do anything."

Dean unlocked the truck, they climbed in, and he jammed the key into the starter. Before turning it, he glanced at Jinxi. "Thanks for staying downstairs last night and keeping an eye on my mom."

"Sure. No problem."

A stab of guilt pierced her. Once she'd finally fallen asleep, Jinxi hadn't heard a sound until Dean's heavy tread woke her. She'd promised herself to stay awake enough to listen for any movement from Janice's room. That didn't happen.

She was supposed to help take care of Janice, not figure out how to relieve her of her money. So much guilt. Her shoulders slumped with the weight of it.

"You okay?" Dean glanced in her direction as he pulled into the street.

"Yeah. Why wouldn't I be?"

"You seem less, I don't know, snarky this morning."

Irritated at his perceptiveness, she snapped, "Give me a minute."

"That's more like it." His grin ramped up her irritation.

Jinxi stifled an unflattering description of his personality. How could he be so charming one minute and get on her last nerve the next?

CHAPTER 39

The apartment's stuffiness hit Dean head-on as he pushed open the door. He had one goal—to dump his uniform and change into shorts and a T-shirt. Afterward, he'd head over to Mom's and try to catch some z's. He'd disobeyed his sergeant's order and gone to work. Even after only a few hours, the jail stench clung to his clothes. He looked longingly toward the bathroom, but a shower would have to wait. Maybe a quick douse of his head under the bathroom faucet.

Ten minutes later, he unlocked his mom's back door. Ted rushed to him from inside the house and bolted into the yard, relieving himself noisily against the closest tree.

"I'm gonna have to deal with that," Dean grumbled.

He retraced his steps, picked up Ted's water bowl, and refilled the bowl with fresh water. "Sorry, boy. You're outside the rest of the day."

Ted cocked his head as if to say, "We'll see."

The house was silent, except for the ticking of the grandfather clock. Dean crept down the hall to his mom's bedroom. He found her sitting on the edge of the bed, head down.

"Mom."

Janice swiveled her head to face him. "Oh, hi, honey. I'm glad you're here. I'm going to take a bath."

"Are you sure that's wise?"

"I'm not an invalid." Her voice was sharp with irritation. "I feel smelly, and I need a bath since a shower is out of the question because of this." She raised her bandaged right arm, wincing.

Dean shrugged. "Fine. I'll get the water started for you."

After starting the bath, Dean closed his mother's bedroom door and headed into the living room. A few hours of sleep would help rejuvenate him. The sofa didn't look too inviting, though it was still made up with sheets and a light blanket. He sank down, stretching out.

Jinxi's scent remained on the pillow beneath his head. He breathed in the flowery fragrance of her shampoo, surprised by its fruitiness. What was he expecting? Some dark, musty smell more in keeping with her persona? He scrunched up the pillow. Why was the sofa so lumpy? His hand searched until he found what caused the lump. A stuffed rabbit. Jinxi slept with a bunny rabbit.

He held it, flipping it back and forth. He tossed the stuffed bunny on top of the sofa pillows piled on the coffee table. A smile worked its way up to his mouth. He grabbed the bunny, got to his feet, and headed up the stairs to Jinxi's bedroom.

He stopped in front of the closed door, wondering what he'd find. The door opened easily. Dean took one step in. The room was spotless. Bed made, closet door closed, nothing sitting on the surface of the dresser. Except ... He crept closer to inspect the photo propped against the lamp. Her parents? They looked normal enough.

He tossed the bunny on the bed and retreated downstairs.

More disturbed than he cared to admit, he turned onto his back, arching and pushing on the plushy sofa. He forced thoughts of Jinxi out of his mind, concentrating on the phone conversation he'd had with his brother Brian on his way home that morning.

"What's going on over there?" his brother had demanded. As if Mom's spider bite was Dean's fault. "Ever since you brought that girl to Mom's, stuff's been happening."

"You can't blame me for this. Or her." Why did Brian always put him on the defensive?

"You're the one who's supposed to be watching out for Mom. I mean, you live there."

Was there a tone of jealousy in Brian's voice?

"Look, Brian, I can't watch Mom twenty-four seven. And there's no way Jinxi had anything to do with Mom getting bit by the black widow. That's crazy."

Brian hadn't backed down. "But what about all the stuff with Hannah? Her hands swollen. What kind of a person did you let into Mom's house? What do you know about her, anyway?"

Dean's anger had risen to a level he wasn't sure he could control. "First of all, Hannah has juvenile rheumatoid arthritis. That *also* has nothing to do with Jinxi. Second, maybe if you'd spend a little more time visiting Mom, or at least calling her, you'd find out firsthand how she's doing."

That had shut Brian up. At least for a moment. He thought he was so much better than the rest of them.

"I gotta go," Dean had said. "I'm pulling up to Mom's house now." He'd hung up, tossed the phone onto the seat, and slammed his fist on the dashboard.

Their relationship used to be different. Though ten years separated them, Brian used to reach out every few weeks. They'd meet for dinner or a game of pool. Since Dad died, the phone calls had dwindled to nothing. The only time he saw Brian was at their family pizza nights.

I guess the phone works both ways.

Dean had dozed off when a rasping sound awakened him. Someone was moving furniture. He jerked to his feet and strode down the hall to his mom's bedroom, his bare feet loud on the wood floor.

The door was open. Dean found her standing next to the dresser, which she'd moved six inches away from the wall.

"What do you think you're doing?"

Janice turned her head to squint up at him. "I'm looking for my earrings."

Had she lost her mind? The pain meds must be making her hallucinate. Dean touched her good arm. "C'mon, Mom. Let's get you back to bed."

"Not till I see if they've fallen under the bureau."

Dean's voice took on the slow, patient tone he used when confronting a recalcitrant prisoner. "Mom, I'll look for them as soon as we get you back into bed, okay? I'll pull the dresser out."

Janice sighed. "Okay." Once she was settled in the bed, back propped up against the pillows, Dean returned to the dresser.

"What am I looking for?"

"Remember the earrings Dad gave me for my birthday? The last gift I got from him before he ... died." She hiccupped back a sob.

"What did they look like?" Dean asked, already on the floor, sweeping an outstretched arm under the dresser.

"The gold hoops with the diamonds."

Dean scooted over to give himself more room to move. His arm swept gray balls of dust bunnies out from under the dresser. "What makes you think they're under here?"

"I've misplaced them somewhere. I hoped maybe they'd fallen behind the bureau."

He remembered his conversation with Brian.

"Did you ask Jinxi?"

Ten seconds passed before Janice answered. "She said she hadn't seen them."

Dean froze. Something in his gut rose and squeezed his lungs. "And you believe her."

Another ten seconds. "Yes."

He closed his eyes against the vision of Jinxi taking his mom's jewelry. She wouldn't. Would she? After everything they'd done for her?

Innocent until proven guilty. He'd have to ask her.

That'll be a fun conversation.

Dean stood and brushed his hands on his shorts.

"Well, they're not here." He shoved the dresser back against the wall and shrugged. "I don't know what to tell you."

The bed creaked under his weight as he sat. "Mom, Brian called me this morning." He held his mom's gaze, uncertain how to proceed. Maybe throw his brother under the bus. "He's upset about the whole Jinxi thing."

Janice exhaled a weary sigh. "I can't talk to you about it right now."

"But—"

"No, Dean, don't press me."

Dean rubbed the back of his neck. "He thinks Jinxi had something to do with your spider bite—"

"That's nonsense."

"—and Hannah's illness."

"Oh, bother. As if I don't have enough to worry about. Tell Brian if he wants to talk to me directly, he knows the phone number." Janice closed her eyes and slumped back against the pillows. "I'm tired."

Dean watched her for a moment before standing. "I'm gonna go try to catch some more z's."

Janice didn't open her eyes. "You do that."

Dean returned to the living room and eyed the sofa. Sleep was out of the question. He wandered into the kitchen, opening and closing cupboards, looking for something, he didn't know what.

Confident his mom was resting, he headed out the back door and grabbed the rubber ball off the shelf above the washer.

"Here, Ted," he called. Ted jumped up from his shady spot against the house, tail wagging in anticipation. Dean threw the ball again and again until both were panting from exertion and the heat.

Dean plopped down on the bottom step, Ted at his feet, tongue lolling. Dean idly stroked the dog's fur. His family was falling apart. Everyone wanted to blame Jinxi—

and blame him for bringing her home. What had he been thinking? He smacked the rubber ball against his forehead, oblivious to the dog drool coating it.

His cell phone vibrated in his pocket. He pulled it out, shoulders tightening as he recognized his sergeant's number. "Rafferty."

Sarge's voice was clipped and hurried. "Did I wake you?"

"No, sir ..." Was Sarge ticked because he went to work last night?

"Got some news for you. You'll be transferred to patrol next week. You'll work four twelve-hour shifts, three days off, then four more."

Dean inhaled sharply.

"You'll have two day shifts, two swing, and two graveyard."

"What about the last twelve?"

"I don't know yet. You'll be working with seasoned officers. Any questions?"

Dean had a thousand questions, but they stayed in his mouth unasked.

"Uh, no, thank you, sir." Either the rumors about him and Jinxi flying around the station hadn't reached his sergeant, or the dish wasn't as big a thing as Patrice had made it.

"Report for duty a week from today. Enjoy your time off." Sarge hung up before Dean could respond.

A grin stretched across his face. Finally. He'd get to be a real beat cop. He couldn't wait to tell Jinxi.

Whoa.

Where had that come from?

CHAPTER 40

A slight breeze stirred the canopy of trees hanging over the street. Grateful for the respite from the sun, Jinxi quickened her steps as she neared Janice's house. An errant sprinkler from a neighboring yard splashed onto the sidewalk. She did a quick side-step to avoid the spray.

Before she opened the gate, she looked up and down the street. No motorcycle. No Skeeter. Not today, anyway. But he would be back. If she knew anything at all, she knew that much. But when would he be back, demanding more money? And what if Dean was home when he showed up?

Nerves tingled in her fingertips as she considered several potential disasters.

The gate rattled as she stepped into the yard. Ted looked up from his shady spot, tail thumping twice. Jinxi leaned down to give him a quick scratch between his ears before striding up the concrete steps and into the house.

She dropped her backpack on the floor with a loud thump. Dean slouched on the sofa, watching TV. He looked up as she entered and muted the TV.

"Hey. How was your day?"

She shrugged. "Busy. Tiring. How's your mom?"

Dean straightened. "You'll never believe this. I was trying to sleep on this lumpy sofa when I heard her moving furniture."

"What?" Jinxi sank on the opposite end of the couch, her eyes wide.

"Yeah. Mom was trying to push the dresser away from the wall." He held out a hand, palm up as if to say, *Can you believe that?*

"Did her meds make her hallucinate?" She'd seen people do stranger things while high.

Dean shook his head and rubbed the back of his neck. "Nope. She said she was looking for a pair of earrings." His gaze held hers.

Jinxi rolled her eyes. "Oh, yeah, the ones your dad gave her."

"You wouldn't happen to know anything about them, would you?"

He did not just say that.

Dean's gaze pinned her as the air was sucked from the room.

"You think I had something to do with them disappearing."

Dean's silence was answer enough. Jinxi shot to her feet. "She asked me if I'd seen them, and I told her no. She believed me." She turned on her heel and headed for the doorway, boots clomping like thunder on the stairs. When she reached her bedroom, she grabbed the door and slammed it hard.

Sinking onto the bed, she unlaced her boots and tossed them in a corner. She stood and paced around the room, pulling back the lace curtain, running her hand along the top of the dresser. Her eyes flicked to the bed. Her stuffed rabbit lay face down against the pillows. Had Dean been in her room? Warmth spread from her stomach up to her cheeks. How embarrassing. She grabbed the stuffed bunny, hugging him to her chest.

Dean was still a total jerk. Why would she steal something that meant so much to his mom? Money was one thing. Cash had no sentimental value. Money was merely a way to survive in this world of razor-sharp edges.

Guilt cut her like a knife. She'd let her guard down, opened her heart to Janice, and was now under scrutiny for something she didn't do, rather than something she'd actually done. Go figure.

She couldn't sulk in her room for the rest of the day. Hunger motivated her to set the bunny back on the bed and slip on a pair of flip-flops. She briefly considered changing into a pair of shorts, but decided she'd rather not answer any questions about the bright tattoo on her calf.

Before leaving the bedroom, she opened the dresser's bottom drawer to check on her stash of food. She'd covered the various packages with a sweatshirt. Still there.

She crept down the stairs and soundlessly reached the bottom, but instead of turning left into the living room, she detoured through the kitchen and down the back hall to Janice's bedroom.

Janice sat on the edge of the bed, pulling on a pair of slacks.

"Need some help?"

Janice jumped at Jinxi's voice, her good hand flying to her throat.

"You startled me." She stood to pull the slacks up, one-handed, under her gown. "Maybe you could help me find something to wear on top. I'm tired of wearing a nightgown. I feel like an invalid."

Jinxi went to the closet. "You must be feeling better." She sorted through Janice's clothes with a feeling of déjà vu.

"Yes, I am. My arm still hurts, but I don't feel like I've been run over by a freight train anymore." Janice shifted around so she could see Jinxi. "Can you find anything that doesn't button?"

Jinxi shook her head no.

"Check the bureau," Janice suggested. "I think I have a T-shirt the kids gave me for Christmas somewhere."

Jinxi hesitated in front of the dresser, stomach clenched. What if Janice asked for the money sock?

"Look in the bottom drawer."

Jinxi let out the breath she'd been holding. She dug through the drawer and found a pink T-shirt that said *World's Best Grandma*. "Is this the one?"

Janice smiled. "I've never worn it. I'm not really a T-shirt kind of person." Her smile faded. "I guess I'll have to go braless. I won't be able to fasten it with this." She raised her bandaged arm.

"I could help you." Jinxi crossed her arms over her chest, wishing she could take back the words. This was getting too personal.

Janice smiled up at her. "Yes, please."

The two of them working together replaced the nightgown with the T-shirt.

"I'm going to go sit in the living room for a bit." Janice wobbled as she got to her feet. Jinxi held out an arm, offering support. Guiding Janice was different from helping her mother to bed after a drinking binge. Better. Jinxi's heart burned with unexpected warmth.

They staggered down the hall and into the living room. Dean still reclined on the couch, eyes closed. He appeared to be asleep. He startled as Jinxi deposited Janice in her favorite chair.

"Hey, Mom." He rubbed his eyes and yawned. "You're up."

Jinxi left them and went into the kitchen, calling over her shoulder, "I'll fix you something to eat."

Rummaging in the refrigerator, she found some tortillas, cheese, and eggs. Standing in the door, she said to Janice, "Quesadillas okay?"

"Yes, thank you."

Jinxi began the process of grating the cheese and cracking the eggs into a bowl. A few moments later, Dean appeared in the kitchen. He scooted over to get out of her way as she moved from counter to stove, back to the counter.

"I, um, wanted to say—"

Jinxi's voice was curt. "You don't have to say anything."

He held out an entreating hand. “No, really, let me say this. I’m sorry I didn’t believe you. About the earrings.”

Jinxi sniffed.

“If my mom believes you, that’s good enough for me.” When she didn’t answer, he continued. “I also want to tell you I got transferred to patrol. I start next week.”

Jinxi stirred the eggs with more force than was necessary.

“Great. Perfect. Now you’ll be able to shoot people.” She slammed down the bowl, spilling some of the egg mixture over the side.

Dean’s excitement wilted. He’d pictured things going differently. Jinxi would be enthusiastic over his promotion—maybe she’d even hug him. Boy, did he get it wrong. Then again, he *had* accused her of theft.

He slunk into the living room and sank onto the sofa. His mom had her Bible open on her lap. She glanced up at him. “Everything okay?”

“Yeah. Sure.” He picked up a magazine from the coffee table and flipped through it.

Janice placed a bookmark in the Bible. “Son, I know you well enough to know something’s bothering you.”

Dean rubbed the back of his neck, wondering how much he should reveal. “I guess I blew it. I kind of accused Jinxi of stealing your earrings. She’s upset with me.” He looked up to see Janice staring at him intently. He lowered his voice. “I should have believed you when you said she didn’t take them. It’s that …” He glanced toward the kitchen. “My gut tells me something is going on, but I don’t know what it is.”

Should he tell his mom he was thinking of asking Jinxi out? What was wrong with him? Part of him suspected she was up to no good, and part of him wanted to date her.

Janice gripped the Bible with her good hand, knuckles white. “Dean, stay out of this. Something is happening that is bigger than both of us. Trust me.”

Wheels turned in Dean's head. Were they still talking about earrings?

"Dinner's ready," Jinxi announced from the kitchen doorway.

CHAPTER 41

Jinxi yawned and stretched, savoring Saturday morning's extra time in bed. She'd head downstairs, start the coffee, and enjoy two unhurried cups. No running to the bus today for this girl.

She peeked in on Janice, and closed Janice's bedroom door with a gentle click. She'd poured her second cup when Dean appeared at the back door.

"You home from work already?" She moved to the table, aware that her boxers showed a considerable amount of leg, including the new tattoo. Maybe he hadn't noticed.

Dean pulled a mug from the cupboard. "I'm off for a week before I go on patrol." He fixed his coffee the way he liked it and joined her at the table.

Jinxi glared at him over the rim of her cup. "Don't you have coffee at your place?"

Dean grinned. "Yeah, but yours tastes better."

"Whatever."

She stood and walked to the refrigerator. Seeing its shelves stocked with food sent a satisfying shiver of reassurance through her.

"Nice tattoo." Dean's voice broke her concentration.

Jinxi swung the door closed and swiveled around to face him. "Uh, thanks." She busied herself putting a piece of bread in the toaster.

"Is it new?"

Jinxi kept her back to him, shoulders rigid. "More or less."

"Tell me about it."

Sheesh, so persistent. "What do you mean?"

"Why the rose, superimposed over the anchor? I'm no expert on tattoos, but don't most people have a story to go along with them?"

Jinxi ground her teeth in frustration. He talked too much, asked too many questions. Her toast popped, and she grabbed it with two fingers and slathered on peanut butter. "It's strength and beauty."

The room suddenly felt too small. Dean's presence seemed to expand to fill the space. Jinxi's breath quickened as she waited for his response.

Dean nodded. "It's good. I like it."

Jinxi crunched on her toast, no longer hungry. Why didn't he go home?

Dean set his cup down and moved it in small circles on the table. "What are you going to do today?"

"I dunno. Probably see if your mom needs me to do anything for her."

Dean rubbed the back of his neck. "I was wondering—" He was interrupted by the sound of Janice's footsteps coming up the hall toward the kitchen.

Jinxi breathed a sigh of relief. She didn't want to hear what Dean was going to ask. She smiled as Janice stepped into the kitchen.

"Is that coffee I smell?"

Jinxi and Dean nodded in unison.

"You look better today," Jinxi said.

"I feel better. More like myself." Janice filled a cup with her left hand, sloshing a bit onto the counter. "What are you two doing?"

Jinxi shot a look at Dean, who wore a strange expression. She filed that observation away to think about later.

"Not much. Just talking." Dean kept his eyes down.

Janice lifted her cup toward Jinxi. “Thanks for the coffee. I’m going to attempt to dress myself today.”

“Call if you need me,” Jinxi said to Janice’s retreating back.

Dean turned to watch Janice until she rounded the corner toward her bedroom and turned his attention back to Jinxi. “Where were we? Oh, yeah. I was wondering ...” Jinxi shot a quick look toward Dean as he spoke. “Do you think you’d want to, you know, maybe go out with me sometime?”

A tsunami of adrenaline engulfed her. Was he kidding?

“G-go out with you.” She glanced at Dean and caught the tremble in his hand as he lifted his cup to his lips.

“Well, yeah. Maybe go play pool or something.”

“Like a date.”

Dean exhaled loudly. “Yeah, like a date.”

Snap. Why did he have to go and ruin everything? What was she supposed to say? If she said no, would he make her life here difficult? Jinxi raised one shoulder to her ear. Before she could stop them, the words tumbled out of her mouth.

“Uh, yeah, I guess.” She was surprised at the sudden rush of relief at saying yes. Could be fun. Maybe.

Dean slapped both hands on his thighs and stood. “Great. I’ll let you know my schedule, and we’ll figure out a time.”

“I thought you were off for a week.”

He blushed, the red covering his ears. “Oh, yeah. I mean, well, I’ll get back with you.”

Jinxi watched him hustle to the back door and let himself out, the kitchen still warm from his presence.

What had she agreed to? A date, that’s what. An *actual* date, something she’d never had before.

Her relationships with the opposite sex had started at the tender age of twelve. The year of lost innocence. The son of one of her mother’s boyfriends had seduced her, softening her resistance with alcohol he’d sneaked from his dad. Not to mention that she'd enjoyed the attention from an older boy. When he'd gotten what he wanted—when he discarded her—she sought affirmation from other boys who professed their love but were only interested in one thing.

Then along came Skeeter, who controlled her with violence and threats.

But a man like Dean. What exactly did he want? Could this be another trap? Fear warred with the need for affection inside her.

What about Janice? What would she think if she knew Dean had asked her out? This was all kinds of bad. She had to keep Janice on her side at all costs.

CHAPTER 42

"Good morning, sleepyhead."

Janice's early morning cheeriness barely broke through Jinxi's fog. There should be some kind of law to prohibit speaking until after a person's first cup of coffee.

"That was fun last night, at least for me," Janice continued.

Jinxi filled her mug, determined to suck down a few gulps before answering.

They'd watched a chick flick the night before, sharing a monstrous bowl of buttered popcorn. At times, they'd mute the sound and mimic the characters, pretending more and more outrageous conversations.

She'd taken on the role of the male lead, lowering her voice. "Oh, darling, how I've longed for your embrace."

Janice had kept the nonsense going by raising her voice an octave. "Let's run away to Aruba. Let me pack twelve suitcases of cosmetics. Then I'll be ready."

Jinxi: "What about your boyfriend?"

Janice: "He'll never notice I'm gone. He doesn't love me like you do."

They'd practically fallen off the sofa laughing.

Jinxi smiled despite herself. "Yeah. Fun."

"You have a marvelous sense of humor."

Marvelous. Who uses words like that? Oh, yeah, this was Janice—Betty White—speaking.

"I've been accused of a lot of stuff, but never that." She'd let her guard down last night. Scary, but nice. She'd shown more of her real personality than with anyone other than Savannah. Speaking of, she should text her soon. Find out what was going on with one skanky ex-boyfriend and one sort-of friend.

Janice stared into her cup of coffee. "I forgot to ask you something. The doctor doesn't want me to drive until after my checkup. Do you mind taking me to church this morning?"

Seriously? "Uh ..."

"Never mind. I'll call one of my friends." Janice's voice was brisk. She reached for the phone.

"No, it's cool." Another opportunity to stay on Janice's good side. "I'll run upstairs and get ready. What time do you want to leave?"

"Nine?" Janice rubbed a hand along the bandage on her arm.

"Sure."

Jinxi showered and dressed in her usual—skinny jeans, Doc Martens, black long-sleeved tee. She added an extra layer of black around her eyes. Might as well keep it real for Jesus.

She waltzed into the kitchen twenty minutes later.

"You look nice," Janice commented.

Nice. Hmm. Jinxi ran a hand through the jagged ends of her hair. She desperately needed to touch up her blonde roots.

"Ready?"

Ready or not.

They pulled up to the church, a neat, square building surrounded by a wrought-iron fence. A bell tolled from the old-fashioned steeple, like that poem she'd been forced to read in school. *The bell tolls for thee*. She shivered.

Death bells. Yep, she was dead. Or would probably wish she was by the end of the morning.

As soon as they were out of the car, Janice's friends approached like pigeons, peppering her with questions.

"What happened?"

"Did you fall? I told you to be careful in your garden."

"I heard you were bit by a snake."

"A snake? Was it a rattler? They can kill you."

"Bless your heart, Janice."

"Thanks, ladies," Janice interrupted. "I'm fine. I want you to meet Jinxi. She's staying with me for a while."

"How sweet," someone commented. "Someone to take care of you."

"So this is Jinxi." An ancient woman, no taller than Jinxi, smiled into her eyes. "I've heard lots about you, dear."

Janice hugged the woman, awkward because of the arm sling. "Jinxi, meet Emma. She's been my best friend and spiritual mentor forever."

"Nice to meet you, Emma."

As they trundled into the church, Jinxi's stomached tightened into a nervous knot. She moved the stud back and forth against her teeth.

Click, click.

God wouldn't be happy to see her, she was sure of that. She'd broken most of the Ten Commandments—probably. Something about stealing, lying, coveting. What was coveting, anyway?

Her feet dragged as she followed Janice into the building where, at the very front, a stage with instruments perched like they were waiting for a rock concert to start.

Cool.

Janice moved toward the middle section of pews, and Jinxi feared she'd head straight for the front row. She released her breath when Janice sat neither too close to the front nor the back. An older couple slid in beside her, leaving a safe space between them. The man smiled at her, but his wife gave her a stink-eye. What's wrong, Grandma, never seen black eye makeup before?

All around her, people chatted. The church bell rang, and the crowd hushed. Janice settled in next to her as a small group of people came into the church from a side door, marched up to the stage, and picked up their instruments. A man standing center stage plucked at his guitar and shouted out for everyone to stand and praise the Lord with them.

And just like that, everyone stood—Jinxi a beat behind. She looked at Janice as heat rushed over her, but Janice only smiled.

Within half a minute, the upbeat music had everyone clapping. Words to the songs were projected on a big screen above the platform. Not that Jinxi sang along, at least not at first. But she clapped. She had to—the music had a cool country vibe. She'd expected some form of "Amazing Grace," but wasn't disappointed when the song didn't appear on the overhead. Too bad they didn't sing Carrie Underwood's "Church Bells." She'd sing along with that one.

The music changed to a slower beat. Jinxi glanced around. Many of the people had their hands raised and their eyes closed. What were they *doing*?

The congregation resembled Janice's neighborhood—a mix of blacks, whites, and Hispanics. She'd always thought blacks went to church with blacks and whites with whites and whatever. But at least at Janice's church no one cared about a person's skin color.

But would they care about the color of a person's heart?

When the singing finished, and the band stepped off the stage, a tall—really tall—black man took their place.

"Our pastor," Janice whispered to her.

"Let's pray," he said, his voice deep and booming. A flurry of motion around her made Jinxi's head turn left and right. All eyes closed, and everyone's chin tucked down toward their chest. But not Jinxi's. Instead, she kept her eyes on the pastor.

Fascinating.

When he prayed, he seemed to be talking directly to God as if they were friends. For a moment, Jinxi remembered being a little girl, lying in her bed at night, asking God for ... what *had* she asked God for? A better life. A mom like the ones on television. She couldn't remember. But she did remember talking to God. Not so much as a friend. More like a grandpa.

How could she fit in? That was the ongoing question. Jinxi looked down at her clothes and glanced around again. The younger ones dressed like her, but the blue-hairs looked a lot like Janice. That part of this church was a polyester palace.

When the offering plate passed her, she wondered if she could snatch a twenty before anyone saw her. A glance at Stink-Eye told her she'd better not. The woman was like the warden at the Girls' Ranch.

Janice settled in again as the pastor began to preach. He talked in simple terms and used situations from his own life that had the congregation laughing. The pastor spoke about his children and tried to show them they needed to plan but to consider God in the plans. Jinxi didn't understand much of what he said, but she'd never forget one of his lines.

"What do you plan to do with your life?"

Yeah, that caught her attention.

Jinxi loved having a plan.

"You know," Janice said, between bites of the sandwich Jinxi made her for lunch, "tonight there's a potluck at the church. I was thinking of stopping at the store and buying some cupcakes."

"Or I could, like, make something," Jinxi blurted. "Not that I want to go with you or anything. But I could maybe make something for you to take." She held her breath, waiting for the other woman's response.

"You'd do that? That would be wonderful. Are you sure?"

Jinxi gulped. "Yeah, it's okay."

"And maybe you could take me there?"

"Sure."

Janice finished her lunch and stood up to take her plate to the sink. She touched Jinxi lightly on the shoulder. "Thanks. And thank you for lunch. I'm a little tired. I think I'll take a short nap."

Jinxi sat for a moment, savoring the warm spot from Janice's touch. She stood, pulled her phone from her back pocket to dial Connie's number.

"It's me, Jinxi. I need your help. I told Janice I'd make a cake or cupcakes for her church potluck."

"Come over right now, *mija*. We will think of something."

Jinxi disconnected and dashed upstairs for her backpack. A short time later, the bus let her off at the stop near Connie's apartment. Rosa and Miguel greeted her from their bikes.

"Hi, Jinxi. You're coming to our house." The children's chatter surrounded her as they began the short walk to the apartment. The kids rode their bikes in circles around her as Jinxi tried to keep up.

At the apartment, Connie greeted her with an enthusiastic hug. "Good to see you, *amiga*." Connie grabbed Jinxi's arm and pulled her into the kitchen. "We will make a cake for your lady. Angel food."

Connie had already set out flour, sugar, eggs, and a mixer on the counter. "Come," Connie said, helping Jinxi tie an apron behind her back.

Connie showed her how to separate the egg yolks from the whites and instructed her on using the beater. As Jinxi held the mixer, Connie gradually added the sugar, handed her a rubber spatula, and told her to scrape the sides of the bowl as she mixed. Jinxi was clumsy at first, and the mixer sprayed bits of batter over the two of them. The children had come into the kitchen and shrieked with laughter. All four had batter freckles on their faces and hair.

Connie guided Jinxi's hands until she got the hang of it. After they sifted the flour, she showed how to fold the flour into the egg-and-sugar mixture, half at a time, until they were thoroughly blended. They poured the batter into the cake pan and slid it into the oven. The children good-naturedly squabbled over who got to lick the pan and who got the beaters and the spatula.

Connie started a fresh pot of coffee, and they sat at the table to wait for the cake to bake. As they sat, Jinxi told her about Janice's encounter with the spider.

"Poor lady," Connie said with a shudder. "Her family is very worried, yes?"

"I was scared to death," Jinxi admitted, remembering how Janice had collapsed on the driveway.

She stared down at her lap and pretended a nonchalance that she didn't feel. "Can I ask you something, Connie?"

"Of course. We are *amigas*."

"Did you go to cooking school?"

Connie laughed. "No, I did not. I learn from my mother, who learn from her mother."

"Oh." Jinxi picked at a loose thread in her jeans. "But what if you didn't learn from anyone? Would you go to a school to learn?"

Connie reached across the table and touched the hand that Jinxi had gripped around her coffee cup. "*Mija*, I think you can do anything you want to. Do what is in here." She touched her fist to her chest.

Connie made the frosting while the cake cooled. Jinxi handed her a wooden spoon.

"Can I pay you for all the stuff you've used in the cake?"

"Of course, no, *chica*. The landlord gave me two dozen eggs for free. His daughter owns chickens, and they were not able to sell these. He tell me to use them quickly before they go bad. So is fine."

"But what about all the other stuff, the flour—"

"No, no. You will someday do something for me. Friends do not expect payment for the help. Remember that."

Jinxi stared at her for a moment, surprising herself by throwing her arms around Connie.

When they'd frosted the cake with white, meringue-type icing, Connie handed her two Minneola tangerines. "Remove the peel and separate the pieces." Meanwhile, she pulled a package of strawberries out of the refrigerator, washed them, and sliced them in half. Once she had a pile of tangerine pieces, Connie showed her how to press them onto the cake. Jinxi stared in awe at the masterpiece.

"We did that."

Connie smiled with her hands on her hips. "*Sí*. We did it. How pretty."

Jinxi glanced at the clock. "Well, I'd better get this back so Janice can take it to her potluck." Her hands flew to her mouth.

"*Snap*. I can't take this on the bus. Oh, no, what am I going to do?" Agitated, she pounded her fists against her head. "Think, think."

Miguel and Rosa were playing a card game in the living room. Miguel called out to her, "Why don't you call and see if the lady can pick you up? Doesn't she have a car?"

Connie smiled at him, "Good idea, Miguelito." She turned to Jinxi. "Do you know the number?"

"Yes, but Janice can't drive yet."

She should never have offered to make something. Why was she always messing up? She couldn't do anything right.

A sudden thought hit her. What if she called Dean. Would that be too awkward? "Maybe I could call Dean?"

Connie had the phone in her hand and motioned for Jinxi to take it.

With fumbling hands, Jinxi dialed the number, hoping he wouldn't answer, hoping he would.

"Hello." The deep timbre of his voice warmed her insides.

"H-hello, it's me. Jinxi." She ran her hand down the leg of her jeans.

"What is it? Is everything okay?"

She glanced at Connie, who smiled and nodded reassuringly.

"Yes, I'm fine. It's that ... well, I made this cake."

There was silence on Dean's end.

"What I mean is, I made this cake for your mom to take to her church thing tonight. I'm scared to carry it on the bus."

"I'm not sure I follow you."

"Well, the thing is, I was, you know, wondering if you could maybe, you know, pick me up." Jinxi chewed on a fingernail, waiting for his answer.

"Where are you?" His voice was noncommittal.

"I'm at Connie's house."

"Who's Connie?"

Why was he making this so difficult?

"She's somebody I work with." For someone so eager to ask her out, he didn't sound all that excited about giving her a ride.

"I'll come get you. What's the address?"

With clenched teeth, she relayed Connie's address to him. He promised to be there within the next half hour. Jinxi's finger jabbed the OFF button. *Snap.* He was such a tool.

She and Connie sat in the living room, watching the children play and occasionally joining in.

"I have the meet with the attorney," Connie said. "*Mi marido* come home in two months." Connie crossed herself and kissed her thumb.

"Right on," Jinxi answered. "Will you stay here?" How awkward to permanently sleep on the hide-a-bed.

"No. The family of Natividad, my husband, have room for us at their house."

"Cool." Did that mean Connie would move? Would she stay at the food bank? She'd miss her cooking *amiga*. Sheesh, first Hannah, and Janice, now Connie. All had managed to needle their way into her heart. Now they were a part of her, etched into her skin like a tattoo.

Thirty minutes later, there was a knock at the door. The children rushed to let Dean in.

Jinxi introduced everyone.

When Dean saw the cake, his mouth dropped open. "*You* made this?"

Jinxi shook her head in exasperation. "Such a tool," she muttered, stepping around him.

CHAPTER 43

Sunday evening yawned. Jinxi roamed through the downstairs, restless and bored. Dean had taken his mom to her church potluck, leaving Jinxi to her own devices. She rummaged around in the refrigerator, not looking for anything in particular. She dug through the pantry, finally closing the door with a thump.

Her cell phone vibrated to life. A text from Savannah.

SAVANNAH: What'd you get into, grl? Skeeter is all up in my business about your business.

Jinxi tapped out a response.

JINXI: Found some money, S wanted half. Said he'd be back. Keep him away from me!!!!

SAVANNAH: Not happening. He's on his way back to NorCal. Sorry.

Not as sorry as she was. Her nest egg was growing, although the pressure to leave had lessened in intensity. It was too easy to stay here. But easy wasn't what she wanted. Freedom, yes. Control of her life, double yes.

Jinxi wandered into the living room and sank onto the sofa. The television offered sports recaps and movies she'd seen. Spying Janice's Bible on the coffee table, Jinxi remembered the pastor had printed an outline of his sermon on the back of the paper Janice placed in her Bible. She opened the book where the bulletin was stuck and was surprised to see the Bible open to the same spot she'd read a couple of weeks ago. Psalm 139.

Where can I go from Your Spirit? Or where can I flee from Your presence?

How could something be scary and comforting at the same time?

Even before there is a word on my tongue, O Lord, You know it.

Now that was scary. Jinxi had uttered her share of swear words. But maybe if God knew she was going to swear, it was okay. Or maybe not. If she couldn't get away from God—since he knew everything—what hope did she have? She was doomed. She closed the book, pulled out the bulletin, and carried it into the office.

The message was titled "What Do You Plan to Do with Your Life?"

She had planned to gather enough cash to start over somewhere. Now that her plan was closer to reality, the attraction of leaving had faded. Difficult to leave all these people who seemed to like her.

She picked up a pen, tapped it against her teeth, and pulled out a yellow pad of lined paper.

Things I'm Good At

1. cooking
2. reading
3. reading cookbooks

She snorted at the last line, crossed it out.

"What are you doing?"

Jinxi jumped at Dean's voice. "Holy cats. You scared the you-know-what out of me."

He grinned. "I know. You jumped at least a foot."

"Snap." She put her hand on her chest, willing her heart to return to normal.

"What are you doing?"

"Nothing." She looked down, subtly covering the paper with her arm.

Jinxi glanced up when Dean was silent for a moment. "What?"

He leaned against the doorframe and crossed his arms. "You look sneaky." His gaze searched her face.

Her face grew hot. "Don't you have anything to do?"

"Nope. All my friends are busy tonight. Plus I have to pick my mom up in a couple of hours. And I'm off work for a week." He shrugged. "Basically, I'm bored."

He wore his usual tank shirt and gym shorts, and Jinxi couldn't help but notice his tattoo-free arms, a stark contrast to the guys she'd known. Her gaze traveled down his body, past his shorts, to his legs and feet.

Dean crossed one leg over the other. "Don't look at my legs."

Jinxi's eyes snapped back to Dean's. "What?"

His face turned red. "Don't look at my legs. They're ugly."

Giggles started somewhere in Jinxi's stomach and worked their way up her throat. She covered her mouth with her hand, but the laughter was intent on escaping.

"I'm serious," Dean protested. "My calves are too big."

Jinxi leaned out of her chair to get a closer look. "I don't think so. They look fine to me." She smiled up at him. Was she flirting? With Dean? The notion sobered her up.

"You think so?" Dean looked down at his legs and over at Jinxi. His expression reminded her of Ted when he begged to be petted. She giggled again and shook her head.

"Well, I guess I'll leave you to do nothing."

Jinxi threw a pen at his retreating back. "Don't forget to pick up your mom from church."

He was so annoying. Shaking her head, Jinxi turned back to the paper. Could she write the words, *I want to go to cooking school*? No, it was impossible. Writing that down would hurt when it didn't happen. That dream hung too far out of the realm of possibility. Still, she went online and typed in a Google search for "cooking schools." She found two that looked interesting, one in Sacramento and one in San Francisco. Taking a deep breath, she filled out the online request for information and pressed SEND before she could change her mind.

Before heading upstairs, Jinxi raided the pantry again for snacks easily carried and stashed away.

The opened windows in both bedrooms ruffled the lace curtains and allowed fresh air to blow through the upstairs, pushing out the stuffiness. Jinxi was almost used to the abundance of lace at Janice's house. But the overwhelming pink of the bedroom still made her gag. If this were her room, she'd do black-and-white stripes. Or maybe ...

She dropped onto the bed, hugging her knees to her chest. No use going down that road. As soon as she got her plan together, she was history as far as this house and all its lace was concerned. Maybe she'd get a job as a cook somewhere. Like on a cruise ship. Yeah, that'd be cool. Eyes closed, she allowed herself a moment to dream.

The curtains billowed in a sudden guest of wind. A breeze—warm and cold at the same time—feathered over her skin. Goosebumps prickled her arms and raised the hair on the back of her neck.

Calm engulfed her, and she heard a whisper.

Peace, be still.

Biting back a sob, Jinxi covered her face with her hands. She should be frightened, but the quietness in her spirit was like a drug, intoxicating with its sweetness. The white noise, the self-incriminating words, all fell silent. Her hands dropped. The curtain hung from the rod without so much as a flutter. Ted snored from his place on the bedside rug, oblivious to any voice, real or imagined.

Jinxi lay back on the bed and stared at the ceiling, savoring the serenity inside, the absence of accusation.

What just happened? She didn't know, except the urge—the compulsion—to take up the knife had left her.

Could God have said, "Peace, be still"?

But why would God take the time to speak to her? Even if Janice's Bible said he knew everything. Did he know she wanted to cut herself? If so, why hadn't he stopped her before this?

Janice leaned back against the headrest of Dean's pickup, eyes closed, relieved he'd offered to pick her up from the church potluck.

"You okay, Mom?"

"Yes. Tired." Tired of the throbbing in her arm. Tired of worrying about Hannah. Tired of waiting for some evidence of change in Jinxi's life. Yes, even tired of her kids. Angry at Dean for continuing to pursue Jinxi, ignoring her warning to stay away. Mad at Brian for talking to Dean and not to her. Annoyed at Robin for not trusting her judgment. Furious at Jinxi for stealing from her one day, helping her get dressed the next.

She sighed. The only thing she wanted right now was to crawl into bed. After taking a pain pill.

Dean helped her out of his truck and into the house. "Thanks, Son. I'll be fine."

Hands on his hips, his face full of concern. "You sure, Mom?"

"I'm sure." Her voice sounded weary to her own ears. She straightened her spine. "You go on home now. I'm going to bed."

She followed him through the kitchen, locking the back door behind him. He glanced back once before bounding down the concrete steps and across the lawn.

Janice turned back to the kitchen and poured herself a glass of water. Instead of walking down the dark hall to her bedroom, she went through the door leading to the dining room. The door at the bottom of the stairs was open, but no light or sound came from upstairs. She'd wanted to tell Jinxi her cake was a huge hit at the potluck.

On the other hand, perhaps she'd take herself to bed. Oh, bother. She'd have to struggle out of her clothes by herself. One more glance up the dark stairs before she shuffled through the living room and down the hall to her bedroom.

First, the pain pill to ease the throbbing which radiated from her fingertips to her shoulder. Sleep didn't come easily.

Why is all this happening to me, Lord? What are you doing?

Janice rehearsed her grievances like a petulant child. When would she see some fruit from her prayers for Jinxi? How much more money would Jinxi take before the girl came to her senses?

Do not grow weary in well-doing, for in due time you will reap a harvest if you do not give up.

The verse from Galatians dropped into her spirit, a bolt of lightning. Repentance followed swiftly. "Oh, Lord," Janice prayed. "I will be patient for as long as it takes."

Dean strode across his mother's lawn toward his apartment, whistling for Ted. No response. He stopped, turned back to the house, and walked around to the driveway. He stepped back to the fence separating the driveway from the next-door neighbor's and raised his eyes to Jinxi's room. No light shone from the window. He'd bet anything Ted was up there with her. The corners of his mouth turned down. Was he jealous of a dog?

The famous Delta breeze had risen earlier in the evening, blowing away the day's heat. He headed back toward his house and stopped at the rocker under the oak tree. Plopping down on the seat, he stared up at the sky. He caught a glimpse of the full moon through the leaves.

He smiled with satisfaction, remembering Jinxi's comment about his legs. He knew he'd never have the good looks of Damaris, with his ebony skin and green eyes. He'd always be stocky, a bit on the heavy side.

But maybe she liked him a little bit. He'd definitely have to make plans before she changed her mind.

As soon as he helped his mom find those earrings.

CHAPTER 44

Hunched over her cereal bowl, Jinxi acknowledged Janice with a glance as she entered the kitchen.

"I hate to ask, but would you mind driving me to church again tonight?" Janice filled her cup with the morning coffee, sloshing a little over the side. "I'll be glad to get this thing off." She motioned toward Jinxi with her right hand.

Jinxi frowned. "This isn't Sunday."

"I know. We have a special service again tonight, with a different speaker."

Jinxi weighed her options. If she said no, maybe Dean would take his mom, and she'd be able to transfer some more money from Janice's account. But if she said yes, she'd stay in Janice's good graces. The stud clicked back and forth across her teeth.

"Yeah, I guess I could."

"Oh, thank you. That would be wonderful."

Janice's gratitude grated on her nerves. In the light of day, what she'd heard last night seemed a silly dream. Why would God talk to her? She blamed Janice and her constant talking about God. So okay. She'd take Janice to church one more time and be done with it.

Soon her community service would end, and she'd have a little nest egg to use to start over. She'd slipped into a comfortable routine, work, home, practicing cooking, playing with Ted. Plus Janice still needed her to cook, clean, and sometimes help her with personal needs.

Jinxi frowned. She'd become soft.

Not good.

When they arrived at church later that evening, Janice's friends greeted them with enthusiastic hugs. Janice hugged right back, but Jinxi kept her arms by her sides.

"You're such a good cook," one of Janice's friends gushed. "That cake was amazing."

"Young lady, you should open a bakery," another said.

Jinxi responded with what she hoped were appropriate noises.

The evening's music was especially spirited. Everyone sat when the singing ended. The pews creaked and groaned from the weight of a hundred bodies.

"We have a special song from our choir," the pastor announced.

Peachy. Maybe it'll be a country song.

Janice leaned toward her. "Our choir is quite good," she said.

Not knowing what to say, Jinxi nodded.

The choir stood, smiles planted on their faces, mouths open and ready to serenade. Jinxi cocked her head to one side as if, in doing so, she would hear better.

With every scar I've inflicted, with every wound by others,
When worry cuts deep into my soul,
I stand beside the Healer, healed.

Jinxi's breath caught in her throat. *With every scar ... worry cuts ...*

When I am broken, and in the lonely moments,
When my heart is full of pain,
I stand beside the Healer, healed.

Jinxi blinked back tears that threatened to spill over. She bit down hard on her bottom lip.

When life despairs, when no one seems to care,
When the shadows of the night fill me with fear,
I stand beside the Healer, healed.

Or did he stand by her? Did he whisper from a window, across a room, *Peace, be still*?

He soothes the wounds
He sheds light so courage is found
His love embraces me, no more tears
I stand beside Jesus, the One, the Healer.

The song faded. The only sound in the church was the muted rustling of the choir as they filed off the platform.

Jinxi flushed warm, cold, and warm again. Her heart swelled, pressing against her lungs until she couldn't breathe. Everything around her dissolved until nothing existed except the words of the song, beating ruthlessly on her chest. Jinxi rubbed her arms as new tears welled up, unshed, in her aching throat. Instances from her life passed through her mind. Things she had done that shamed her now. She was glass—brittle and hard—and all her sins were visible.

Like a pebble hitting a windshield, a tiny hole formed at first, fanning out into a spider web of cracks until her hard shell disintegrated into a pile of broken pieces. Jinxi looked down at her arms, remembering the cuts and scars. The lyrics returned, touching her in the depths of hurt and anger.

God felt her pain. He'd carried her wounds, her scars, to the cross. At once she knew. Fighting back the tears, she glanced down at the bulletin to the title of the message.

My Strength Is Made Perfect in Your Weakness.

Jinxi didn't hear a word of the sermon. A battle raged inside her. A fight for her life. A voice told her God would surely never accept one such as she. A loser, morally weak, a cutter. She was broken, beyond redemption.

Janice shifted next to her. Could Janice hear the voice shouting inside her?

Another voice, softer but no less firm, said, *I have carried your sins in my body. Your sin is no longer the issue. Bring your scars to me and let me heal you.*

Jinxi was unable to stand when the service was over.

"Are you okay?" Janice asked.

Jinxi nodded as she stood on legs made of cooked spaghetti. Desperate to be alone, she drove to the house in silence. For once, Janice didn't try to engage her.

When they got to the house, Janice unlocked the door and went inside, but Jinxi made a beeline for the swing seat that had become her favorite outdoor perch. The trees filtered the fading light, turning the backyard into muted tones of gold and gray.

There, in the quiet of the yard, seat gently swaying, Jinxi surrendered. Her voice was barely a whisper.

"I don't know what to say. I've made a mess of my life. But God, you already know that." A sob rose from her throat. "If you want my life, you can have it. Please help me."

Ted rose from a shady spot under the tree and crept toward her. He nuzzled her leg. Jinxi collapsed onto the ground, arms around Ted's neck. Tears poured from her eyes as she recounted all her sins one by one and released them, washed away and gone forever. She sobbed as Ted licked her face. But they weren't sobs of grief. Hers was the cry of gratefulness.

Janice watched from the kitchen window, forehead knotted. Jinxi clutched Ted as if in physical pain.

Janice gripped the edge of the ancient tile counter and prayed.

After answering some emails, Dean got up from his desk to get a glass of water and spied Jinxi from the window overlooking the yard. She was crying. That was a surprise. The only other time she had shown any emotion other than sarcasm and anger was in the hospital outside Hannah's room.

What was going on?

He turned up the AC, which had been nearly impotent against the incessant heat outside, and sat on his futon, thoughts crowding his head. He remembered the time at the hospital and how good it had felt to hold Jinxi as she cried. He also enjoyed their bantering. Like joking around with his sister, only better. He and Robin used to have that kind of relationship. They joked and teased and fought, but beneath the joking, they were committed to each other.

He scrubbed his face with one hand. He was acting like a crushing teenager. How could he want to take Jinxi on a date, yet protect his mother from her? And what about those earrings that had disappeared?

Jinxi crept into the house, anxious to escape to the sanctuary of her bedroom. Ted followed, bumping her leg. His nails clicked on the linoleum, alerting Janice to their presence.

"Everything okay?" she called from the living room.

Jinxi walked through the kitchen, stomach jumping. What could she say to the woman from whom she'd stolen over two thousand dollars? She saw Janice in a new light, one not tainted by her own need for survival. Janice had become a friend and an adoptive mom.

Jinxi clutched the door jamb. "Uh, yeah. Fine." Her eyes filled with tears again, and she blinked them back.

"Are *you* okay?" Janice's voice floated across the room, soft and encouraging.

"I can't stop crying."

"Why not?"

She shrugged. "I don't know." The tears flowed faster now.

Janice set her Bible on the coffee table. "Did something happen to you in church?"

"Yes. No. I feel—I don't know—the song, the scars." Jinxi sobbed, incoherent.

Janice stood and wrapped Jinxi in a motherly hug, rubbing her back and making soothing noises.

Jinxi relaxed into the embrace, feeling herself melt, as if her spirit exhaled a long sigh.

After a few moments, she pulled back and looked Janice in the eye. "I feel different. I *am* different. All the stuff in the past"—she paused to wipe her eyes and nose on her sleeve—"bad stuff that I've done is all gone. Like nothing happened. Does that make sense?"

"You mean it's forgiven."

Comprehension dawned. "Yeah. Forgiven."

"It has been. That's the wonder, the beauty of salvation. Jesus carried all that and bore our sins on the cross so we don't have to. Amazing, isn't it? Wait here, and I'll be right back." Janice returned and handed Jinxi a box. Inside was a red leather Bible. Jinxi caressed the soft cover.

Janice smiled. "I bought this some time ago. I hoped you'd need it someday."

"Thanks," Jinxi mumbled, taking note of the price tag on the box. "It's heavy."

Janice looked way too pleased with herself. Somehow it wasn't quite as annoying as usual.

"I marked a couple of places where you can start reading," Janice said, taking the book out of Jinxi's hands. "See? There are two little ribbons to mark your place. The first one is the Gospel of John."

Janice flipped open the Bible, the pages sticking together from the gold along the edge. "Right here," Janice said, pointing to a part with red type. "The red indicates Jesus speaking."

Was she expected to read this? It weighed a ton. Like Janice's. Oh, snap. She was going to become like Janice.

Maybe that wouldn't be so bad. Maybe. But she would never, ever, wear polyester. Bible or no Bible.

CHAPTER 45

When Jinxi arrived at work the following day, she bounced into the office to fill out her timecard. She greeted Aneesa with a cheery, "Hi."

Jinxi felt Aneesa's eyes on her as she put her pack down and leaned over the table to pull out her timecard. When Jinxi straightened up, Aneesa scowled.

"You look different."

"You mean my hair?" Jinxi touched her head self-consciously. The trim she'd done with Janice's craft scissors wasn't her best effort.

"No. Something else. Show me your arms."

Jinxi obliged by pushing up her sleeves and stretching out both arms for Aneesa's appraisal.

"No new scars. What's going on?"

Jinxi gave her a close-mouthed smile and shook her head as she walked out the door.

"Padish wants to talk to you," Aneesa said to her retreating back.

Jinxi whirled around. "What?"

"He asked me to tell you he wants to talk to you sometime today."

Jinxi mumbled a response, heading to the storeroom to begin working. What could he want? There must be a problem with her community service. The coffee she'd drunk that morning rose burning in her throat. What if someone discovered she'd taken money from Janice? She'd totally broken one of the Ten Commandments. The one about stealing. She put the heels of her hands against the side of her head and pressed. What would happen to her when they found out?

Jinxi clutched at one of the metal shelves, head spinning from a swoop of vertigo. Forcing herself to breathe deeply, she uttered, "Jesus." As the name slipped from her lips, the dizziness passed, and peace poured over her. Relieved for the moment, she worked in the storeroom until the time came to help Connie in the kitchen.

"More people today," Connie observed as she scooped coleslaw onto plates.

"End of the month," Jinxi said. Close to the end of the month, more people showed up. They'd had to make sandwiches for the last few stragglers who showed up too late for the hot meal.

When Padish approached, the afternoon had waned.

Jinxi jumped when he spoke to her in his lilting voice, "You will come with me to the office?"

Jinxi exchanged a glance with Connie, who gave an encouraging smile and a quick hug. Her feet dragged as she followed Padish out of the kitchen. Aneesa sat at her desk in the office. She looked up as they entered, but her expression gave away nothing. Jinxi made eye contact for a second before focusing on a state labor poster on the wall.

Padish waved toward one of the scarred wooden chairs facing his desk. He opened a file folder labeled with her name. She held her breath as he looked through the file.

Hurry up ...

After what seemed like twenty minutes, he looked over the desk at her.

"You have almost completed your eighty hours of community service, yes?"

Jinxi nodded.

"There is paperwork for you to sign. You have the choice to mail the papers back to the court or deliver them in person, or we can fax from here."

She licked her lips with a tongue as dry as sand.

"My suggestion is to let us fax. Faxing is much quicker and less chance to get lost."

"Okay," she choked out.

Padish regarded her for a moment, finger tapping on the papers piled in front of him. "I must tell you that very few of our workers complete their time here. Many disappear after a few days." He looked over at Aneesa.

"That's right," Aneesa added. "Some people don't want to do the work. Or can't." She mimed someone sticking a needle in their arm.

What did this have to do with her?

Aneesa gave her a stern look. "To be truthful, I didn't think you'd make it either."

Jinxi shifted in her chair. Padish really needed to buy some new chairs. Ones with padding. Maybe a recliner.

"But here you are, all finished and getting paid for being here too. The question is, what happens now?"

"What do you mean?" Jinxi glanced from Aneesa to Padish. This was it. They were firing her. She could collect her last paycheck and finally be free.

She was terrified.

"What Aneesa means is, do you want to continue here?"

Jinxi's eyes widened as she exhaled the breath she'd been holding. "You mean I have a choice?"

Padish's eyes crinkled as he smiled even wider. "Of course. What did you think?"

Her heart pounded in her chest, certain they could hear the thumping through her T-shirt. "I—I guess I thought you'd say goodbye."

Padish chuckled as Aneesa took pity on her. "No, baby, we want to offer you a full-time job. If you're interested, that is."

Jinxi tried to swallow. "But-but what about Norma?"

Padish's face clouded over. "Norma has returned to the drugs." He shook his head slowly. "She will not be back."

The bell sounded as someone came through the front door. Padish excused himself to see who was there. Aneesa stood and walked over to his desk, taking his place.

She and Aneesa were alone. Jinxi's heart raced. She waited for Aneesa to bring up their confrontation.

"So," Aneesa began. "Let's talk about this. We've been paying you ten dollars an hour for four hours of work a day. Your job would stay unchanged. You'd be helping Hank in the storeroom in the mornings and afternoons and working with Connie as well. We can't afford to pay you any more money per hour. As a non-profit, we have to watch every penny, and we set our budget at the beginning of the year. We've budgeted this position for ten dollars an hour, and you'll be full time. If we get any other people assigned by the court to do community service, I expect you to show them the ropes, okay?" Aneesa looked sternly at Jinxi. "Okay?"

"Okay."

"Do you have any office experience?"

Jinxi shook her head.

"Can you use a computer? File stuff alphabetically? You did graduate from high school, right?"

"Yeah." She wasn't stupid. "I use the computer at home. I could probably figure out the filing thing."

"Good. Sometimes I need help in the office." Aneesa indicated the piles of papers on every surface. Jinxi's stomach clenched at the thought of working in the same room with her. Being around Aneesa turned her stomach upside down. Their shared secret hung between them, unspoken.

Aneesa took another twenty minutes to go over the employee manual and all the papers she needed to sign to complete her community service and become a full-time food bank employee. Her head spun by the time they finished.

"We're done. Go talk to Connie. I'm sure she's waiting anxiously. When you're done, go home."

Jinxi got up to leave. As she put her hand on the door, Aneesa said, "Wait."

Oh, God, she's changed her mind.

"Padish said you could have a couple of days off. We still need you this week, but how do next Monday and Tuesday sound? Before you start full-time on Wednesday."

Biting her lip to hold back a smile, Jinxi turned to go. She resisted the urge to do a happy dance and a fist pump in the hallway.

Pots and pans clattered as Connie finished washing up after the noon meal. Hank hovered near the door, sweeping and re-sweeping. Both looked at her with an expression that read, "Well?"

Jinxi closed her eyes for a moment and grinned. Connie let out a whoop. Hank dropped the broom with a clatter. They rushed to her and grabbed her in a hard embrace. Hank dwarfed both Connie and Jinxi and leaned down from his height. Connie held her at arm's length, hands on Jinxi's shoulders.

"I am so happy," she exclaimed. "We will work together."

Hank added, "M-m-miss Jinxi, I sure g-gonna l-l-like w-w-working w-w-with y-y-you." His stutter was more pronounced as he wiped a tear from the corner of one eye.

Jinxi turned away so Hank and Connie couldn't see her face.

"Is there anything else I can help you with?" She grabbed a rag and wiped the already-spotless counter.

At their negative responses, Jinxi said, "Well, I guess I'll see you tomorrow." She gathered her backpack and headed for the door. Padish was in the hallway. She paused and fought to express what was in her heart. How could she explain the feeling of being wanted for the first time in her life? "Thank you" seemed inadequate. She didn't know if Padish understood, but he put his hand out and shook hers vigorously.

"We will see you tomorrow, yes?"

"Yes." Slinging the backpack over her shoulder, she hurried out to catch the bus.

For once, things were going her way. Janice hadn't discovered the stolen money, Dean wasn't as scary as she once thought, and he seemed to like her. She had a place to stay, friends, and a job.

What could go wrong?

CHAPTER 46

Dean sat at the kitchen table, munching on potato chips. He'd come early to his mom's house for pizza night, hoping to catch Jinxi alone for a few minutes. Everything felt out of synch. Being off work, pizza night on Tuesday instead of Sunday, and Jinxi nowhere to be seen. The last glimpse he'd caught of her was when she'd been hunched over Ted in the back yard, crying. He shrugged off unease that had settled in his gut.

"Pizza's here," Brian's announcement brought him out of the kitchen.

Robin, Carlos, and Hannah were right behind Brian and Courtney.

Hannah jumped up and down with excitement. "Where's Ted? Where's Ted?" she demanded. "Uncle Brian, did you get to meet Ted?"

As if on cue, Ted trotted down the stairs, his toenails clicking on the bare wood. He barked a greeting and rushed to Hannah to sniff her.

She giggled. "See? He knows me. Don't you, Teddy boy?" She scratched his head and patted his back.

"When did you get a dog?" Brian demanded. "Whose idea was that?"

"My idea, that's who. Got a problem with that, bro?" Dean grabbed Brian's arm and pretend-punched him. Brian swung his arm around Dean's neck, and they began to wrestle.

"Just because you're getting a promotion doesn't mean I can't beat up my little brother," Brian said.

"As if there's not enough chaos here," Janice said. "You two knock it off or take it outside."

Ted danced around, barking, unsure if he should protect his master or enter into the fray. Hannah had wrapped herself around Dean's leg and tried to hold him back. The noise level had risen considerably.

When things settled down, the family took their places at the table as Robin pulled sodas and iced tea from the refrigerator and took them to the dining room. Courtney helped fill the cups with ice, and Robin's husband, Carlos, settled Hannah into her seat at the piano bench Dean had brought in from the living room.

"We're going to say grace," Janice said as she sat. She looked down the table at Carlos. "Will you do the honor for us, Carlos?"

Dean tried not to roll his eyes.

Carlos nodded. "Lord, thank you that we could have this special night of celebration. We give you thanks for Dean's promotion. We ask your protection on him as he goes out on patrol. We thank you for Janice's recovery from her spider bite and that she'll have no lasting effects. Thank you now for the food. Amen."

Every family has its own unique language, its own rhythm. Jinxi watched from the bottom of the stairs, a stranger in a strange land. She needed a translator, especially while Carlos prayed. He'd made praying look simple, a conversation. Since her experience at church, she'd tried to pray but had felt stilted and awkward. She'd never get it right.

After the "Amen," Hannah opened her eyes. She squealed when she saw Jinxi. "Come sit by me. Come sit by me."

Janice turned in her chair. "Yes, come join us."

Hannah scooted over and patted the space next to her. "What kind of pizza do you like, Jinxi? My favorite is cheese. Uncle Brian buyed half cheese for me." She giggled. "But I can't eat a whole half. Can I have my pizza now, Mommy? Can Jinxi have some of my cheese half? I want to share with Jinxi."

Hannah chattered on and on as her dad placed a piece of pizza on her plate. "Be careful. It's hot," Carlos warned.

"Blow on it, Daddy. No, you blow on it, Jinxi." Carlos took her plate and blew on her pizza to cool it. "No. I want Jinxi to blow on it."

Carlos lowered the plate and warned, "Stop whining, or you will be dismissed from the table."

"Please, Daddy, can Jinxi blow on it?"

Robin huffed. "Why doesn't she obey me like that?" she inquired of the table at large.

Jinxi took the plate from Carlos's outstretched hand. She blew on the pizza, observing the family, wishing she were invisible.

"How's Hannah doing?" Courtney asked.

Robin talked around the piece of pizza she'd bitten. "She has her good days and bad. Like, today you'd never know she was sick. But sometimes, she cries from being in pain." Robin shrugged, her face showing the strain of the past few weeks. "The doctor said she'll grow out of it. I hope it's soon."

"Mom, how are you doing?" Brian asked, sending Dean a sidelong glance.

Janice's face brightened. "Much better. I'll be glad to get this thing off my arm." She waved her bandaged right arm. "Imagine not being able to use your right hand."

"How are you getting along? Do you need anything?" Courtney asked.

"Oh, no. Jinxi has been a big help."

Jinxi's eyes flew to Janice and down to her plate. Her face grew hot as the conversation around the table stopped. So much for hoping to be invisible.

"Grammy, did you get bit by a spider?" Hannah's voice broke the silence.

As Janice turned her attention toward Hannah, Jinxi raised her eyes to see Robin whisper something to Brian. He nodded, glancing her way. Jinxi quickly averted her eyes.

The conversation gained momentum as they got caught up on each other's lives. Dean expressed his excitement about the upcoming transfer to patrol duty. Courtney talked about her work designing clothing catalogs, and Janice told the family that she was going to ask about knee surgery at her next doctor's appointment.

"You're going to need someone here to help you for a few days after surgery." Robin said as she reached for more pizza.

"I can help," Dean offered.

Robin snorted derisively, and everyone chuckled. "Ha. That's like saying your dog Ted could take care of Mom."

Dean faked indignation. "Are you comparing me to a dog?"

"I'm just saying that as a caretaker, you are woefully inadequate." Robin glanced around the table for agreement.

"We could take turns," Courtney suggested.

"I'll be fine," Janice insisted. "If someone can check on me during the day, and with Jinxi here to help at night, we'll make it work."

After dinner, as the family prepared to leave, Jinxi escaped to the backyard to her favorite spot on the swing.

Ted nuzzled her hand with his wet nose, begging for attention. After a few minutes of petting, he trotted off and returned with a tennis ball. He stood in front of her, quivering with anticipation. When she didn't respond immediately, he gave a quick bark.

"You are spoiled, little dog," she told him with a smile. She heaved herself to her feet and picked up the ball. "Is this what you want? Is this it?" She waved the ball in front of him a few times as he paced back and forth, eyes never leaving the prize. She threw the ball toward the back fence. He raced to get it before it could bounce more than once.

Dean's voice startled her. "Did anyone ever tell you that you throw like a girl?"

She jumped. "Stop doing that."

"Doing what?"

"Sneaking up on me." She fanned herself with her hand, trying to cool her hot face.

Dean carried two bottles of juice. "I wondered if you wanted something cold to drink." He started to back up. "But if you're going to be crabby, I'll drink them both."

Ted brought the ball back to her. Seeing her chance to get even, Jinxi threw the ball as hard as she could toward Dean's chest, making a smacking sound as the ball, wet from the dog's saliva, connected with his T-shirt. Before he could react, Ted was on him, teeth grabbing the ball before it could hit the ground. He dropped both bottles and stumbled backward, reaching for the tree before he fell. Jinxi trotted up to where he had dropped the juice, snatched up both bottles, and ran back to safety behind the swing.

"Hey," Dean yelled. "That was gross." He looked down at the gooey spot on his shirt front. "Yuck."

His look of disgust was so comical, Jinxi laughed. Within a second, Dean joined in. Ted pranced back and forth between them as they both doubled over with mirth. Weak and breathless, Jinxi collapsed onto the swing seat, dropping the juice beside her.

"I think one of those is mine," Dean said, approaching cautiously. "You're not armed or anything, are you?" Jinxi shook her head as he lowered himself next to her, causing the swing to gyrate crazily. He opened one of the bottles and handed it to her.

"Thanks." She guzzled several gulps, pausing to wipe her mouth with the back of her hand.

They sat side by side, the swing gently moving as Dean tossed the ball again and again for Ted to fetch.

"He's a good dog," Dean said. "Hannah made a good choice."

Jinxi nodded in agreement.

"But it still irks me that you let him sleep in your room."

"Are you saying I stole your dog?"

"Pretty much," Dean said with a sigh.

Jinxi grinned. "Sounds like the beginning of a country song."

Dean rolled his eyes. "That's wrong on so many levels."

"I think Ted's lonely. Besides, he keeps me company."

"Are you lonely too?"

Was she? She'd always been on her own, even when she was with Skeeter. Personal survival ruled her world, dictated her actions. Her so-called friends had never given her the kind of love and affection she'd received from Janice these past few weeks.

What she'd experienced the night before in church made her head spin. Jinxi had no idea what it would mean going forward. All she knew was she was different.

"What are you thinking about?" Dean's voice interrupted her musing.

Shrugging, she twirled one of her earrings.

"My sister is having a hard time with you being here." Dean's voice was matter-of-fact. "Maybe you haven't noticed."

"Oh, I've noticed, all right."

"Why do you suppose that is?"

Jinxi shrugged. "I dunno. Maybe she's jealous." She jiggled her leg back and forth, watching her flip-flop slap against the sole of her foot.

Dean seemed to consider this. He abruptly changed the subject. "How's work going?"

"Okay, I guess." She gave him a sidelong look. "Why?"

"Wondering what work's like at the food bank. You know, making food for all those homeless people." Dean leaned back and stretched his arm across the back of the seat, accidentally brushing her shoulder.

His touch jolted through her like emotional lightning.

Jinxi hoped the shaking in her voice didn't betray her. "It's nice."

Dean made a disgusted sound. "Nice? Is that all you can say? Aren't you the girl who knows all the big words?" His smile took the sting out of his comment.

Despite herself, Jinxi's face creased in a grin. "It's immensely, rapturously, satisfying and convivial."

Dean gently smacked the back of her head with the flat of his hand.

"Hey, knock it off," Jinxi warned. "Were you this mean to your sister?"

He gave a bark of laughter. "You haven't seen anything. I was the quintessential bratty little brother."

"I can believe that." They sat for a few minutes in silence.

"So," they both began at the same time, then, "You first," they said together.

Dean made a motion across his lips, zipping them closed. He pointed at her.

"I have a couple of days off next week, so I'm thinking about going down to Bakersfield to visit my mom." Her hands twisted together in her lap, knuckles white.

"Bakersfield. Is that where you're from?"

She nodded. "Yeah. I kinda feel I should tell her what's been going on."

"Going on? What do you mean?"

Jinxi's eyes focused on the house, several yards away. "Well, you know, the arrest thing, community service, God." She held her breath.

"God?"

Jinxi shrugged again. "Yeah, God. I went to church with your mom last night."

"So?"

"So there was this song." She stopped, unable to put her experience into words.

Dean's hand brushed her shoulder once more. There was that feeling again, a zap, like sticking a fork into a toaster. Had he felt it too?

"You seem different."

Jinxi turned so her eyes could meet his. "I do?"

Dean leaned closer and lowered his head toward her, eyes closed. He smelled like an intoxicating combination of pizza and aftershave.

Jinxi stopped breathing. Was he going to kiss her? Panic skittered up her spine.

At that moment, Dean's cell phone erupted in the latest Walker Hayes song. They jerked apart as Dean dug in his pocket to silence the incoming call. Jinxi leaned back against the swing and released her breath.

"Sorry," Dean said as the phone went silent.

"I should probably go back in the house. See if your mom needs anything." Jinxi stood, her back toward Dean.

"What about what you were going to tell me? What God thing?"

"I'll tell you later." The pizza she'd eaten rose to meet the juice Dean had given her. Had she *wanted* him to kiss her? Dismayed at her response, Jinxi strode toward the house, Ted trailing behind her. She halted on the top step.

He'd changed his ring tone to a country song.

Interesting.

CHAPTER 47

Dean mentally kicked himself as he watched Jinxi stride toward the house. What had he been thinking, trying to kiss her? He was acting lame. Like a college student obsessed with some other guy's girlfriend.

Like a slingshot, his mind jumped to a night he'd tried to forget. There'd been a party, lots of alcohol, and a girl. Dean had seen her around campus. He'd been too intimidated by her beauty to talk to her. She'd shown up at the frat party, crying about being dumped by her boyfriend

After more than a few drinks, Dean offered her the comfort of his arms and his bed. So easy. She'd been too drunk to know what she was doing. How could he have been so stupid and so selfish to take advantage of her? He'd wanted to be one of the guys. To belong.

Dean's father's words echoed in his ears. "Son, treat women like you would your sister or your mother. With respect. Do that, and it will serve you well."

Well, Dad, I sure blew that. Glad I never told you about it.

Shame covered him, sticky and impossible to remove. He wasn't sure the girl even remembered what happened. Or maybe she did. After that night, he'd seen her around campus a few times, always with the same guy. She'd gone back to her old boyfriend, and she seemed to avoid Dean. From that night, he'd made a vow never to drink again. And to remain celibate until he married. His dad had taught him well. His dad had only been with one woman, his mother. Dean would never have that.

He remembered the first time his dad had taken him fishing. At ten, he'd felt grown-up, rising before dawn, dressing in the cold darkness, riding through the sleepy fog to a quiet place beside a river. As he grew older, his dad took him out of school for a few days every October to spend time fishing together along the Klamath River.

Brian, ten years older, was already in college. He'd never connected to the outdoors the way Dean had with his father. To Dean's delight, Robin had squealed in disgust when he'd described slipping a worm onto a hook.

Dean's dream of going into law enforcement was born during one of their many camping trips. He remembered his dad's encouragement to pursue his dream.

"Law enforcement will give you the structure you need, Dean-o, and will allow you to fulfill your need to save the world."

His father had taught him many life lessons while waiting for fish to bite, including to be thankful even when they went home empty-handed.

The sun dipped low in the sky. Dean shifted on the wooden seat, putting the swing in motion. He needed some of his dad's wisdom now. A day didn't go by that Dean didn't think about his dad. About how he lived. And how he'd died.

Dean shook his head. So much for God's care.

Jinxi bounded up the back stairs and into the house. She found Janice sitting in her chair, head back and eyes closed.

"What time is it?" Janice asked, opening her eyes and rubbing them with her good hand.

"It's eight-thirty."

"My heavens, I must have fallen asleep after everyone left." She ran a hand over her hair, smoothing it back.

"Guess I'm not back to a hundred percent yet. I'm going to have a bath and go to bed." She struggled to her feet. "You've been quiet."

"Yeah, I was outside, playing with Ted and"—Jinxi swallowed hard—"talking to Dean."

Janice froze. "Oh?"

That one word held a thousand questions. Jinxi grew hot as the silence lengthened.

Janice resumed her course toward the bedroom without another word. Jinxi breathed a sigh of relief and slumped onto the sofa. She hadn't done anything wrong. It wasn't as if Dean had *actually* kissed her. So why did she feel so guilty?

Jinxi needed a new plan. Some way to pay Janice back before she discovered the missing money. So many things to make right, starting with the money.

The sound of the faucet filling the tub drowned out the voices shouting in Janice's ears. She sank into the warm water with a contented sigh, careful to keep her bandaged arm on the side of the tub. In the quiet of the bathroom, doubts assailed her again.

She'd told Dean to leave Jinxi alone. Why was he pursuing her? Especially now that she had made a profession of Christ.

Torn between the love for her son and her need to protect Jinxi's new faith, Janice tried to pray, but her prayers seemed to bounce off the ceiling and drop into the bathwater.

What about the money? Should she confront Jinxi? Angry at herself, Janice sank deeper into the water. She'd resolved this before the Lord. Why did these doubts keep coming back?

Do not grow weary in well doing, for in due time you will reap a harvest if you do not give up.

There was that verse again. Bother. She hadn't had any rest since Dean had shown up on her doorstep with Jinxi.

What was wrong with her? She should be praising God that Jinxi had turned her heart toward the Lord. Instead, she focused on herself. She breathed yet another prayer of repentance.

Cross-legged on her bed, Bible in her lap, Jinxi turned to the Gospel of John. As she read, she remembered the conversation with Dean. She'd been on the brink of telling him what had happened after church to her the night before. She wasn't sure she could even put the experience into words. How could she describe the feeling of being clean to someone who'd never been dirty?

Her heart quickened as she remembered his face, so close to hers. Had she wanted him to kiss her? Would God want her to kiss him?

She exhaled, fanning the thin pages of the Bible. Her gaze fell on a verse.

And this is the judgment, that the light is come into the world, and men loved the darkness rather than the light; for their deeds were evil.

"That pretty much describes me," she said aloud. Ted raised his head from his spot on the floor. Jinxi slipped off the bed and crouched next to him. Grabbing him around the neck, she buried her head in his wiry fur.

"Teddy, what am I going to do? I've made such a mess of my life. How can I ever clean it up?" Tears welled up. Unchecked, they wet Ted's coat.

The dream came forcefully that night. Fire crackled around her, exploding the walls of the house in a kaleidoscope of red and gold. Someone screamed for help. Running down the hall, looking into every room, she couldn't find the source of the screams. One by one, room by room, the fire grew hotter with every step down the endless hall. Throat burning, lungs aching, she reached the last room. The screams grew louder and more frantic. She lunged across the threshold, skidding to a stop.

The person screaming for help was herself.

Jinxi woke with a gasp, T-shirt wet with sweat. Hysteria bubbled in her throat. Choking back sobs, she wiped her damp forehead with the back of one hand.

She got out of bed on shaky legs and stumbled to the bathroom for a drink of water. Bracing her arms on either side of the sink, she let her head drop. The dream hadn't been that bad for a long time.

She returned to the bedroom and sat with her back against the headboard, knees drawn up under her chin. The verse she'd read earlier returned to her mind, relentless. Their deeds were evil. *My deeds are evil.* There was one thing she was sure God couldn't forgive. She'd killed a child.

CHAPTER 48

The aromatic smell of coffee wafted up the stairs, drawing Jinxi like an addict in need of a fix. She rolled out of bed and stumbled downstairs, Ted on her heels. After letting him outside, she stood with one foot on top of the other, waiting for the coffee to finish brewing.

"I see you're up. I thought the smell might wake you." Janice smiled.

Jinxi's mouth curved into a close-lipped smile. "I'm addicted. I admit it." The coffeemaker beeped and sighed. Mug in hand, Jinxi poured the first cup, handing it to Janice. She reached up into the cupboard for another mug, her favorite. The one with the gold star.

"Did I tell you Padish asked me to stay on at the food bank after I finish community service?"

"No, you didn't. That's wonderful. He must think you're a good worker."

Jinxi raised one shoulder in a shrug. "I guess. Anyway, he's giving me a couple of days off next week." She took a tentative sip of the hot beverage. "I'm thinking of visiting my mom." She kept her eyes on the floor, waiting for Janice's response.

"That's a great idea. When will you leave?"

"I thought maybe I'd go to church with you if that's okay." Her eyes shot to Janice and back to the floor. "I'll leave Sunday afternoon."

"I think that sounds fine."

Jinxi gestured toward the stairs with the hand that held the mug. "Well, I guess I'd better get ready for work. Wouldn't want to get fired for being late." She dashed up the stairs, holding the mug away from her to keep from spilling.

Janice sat at the kitchen table sipping her coffee. So Jinxi had a full-time job. What was her plan? Would she want to stay here?

Do I want her here?

Maybe Jinxi would take the stolen money and set herself up someplace nice and cozy.

Janice fought against the bitterness that threatened to invade her soul. She'd had it out with God more than once and was determined to stay in the place of peace.

The phone rang. Janice glanced at the clock. Nobody called this early. Her stomach clenched. Had something happened to Hannah?

"Jan, it's me. Emma."

Janice exhaled with a whoosh as she slumped onto the wooden kitchen chair. "Hi. Is everything all right?"

Emma chuckled. "Of course, dear. I was praying for you and had the urge to call you. Hope you were up."

"Oh, yes, of course I'm up. I was talking with Jinxi. She was offered a full-time job at the food bank."

"Well, isn't that nice. Perhaps a celebration is in order. Maybe a few presents or something. Especially after what you told me about her salvation experience."

Janice smiled into the phone. "Aren't you sweet for suggesting it. I'm trying to stay peaceful about the"—Janice looked around the corner toward the stairs and lowered her voice—"money."

Emma clicked her tongue. "God will guide you, Jan, dear."

"I'm struggling with giving her something, knowing she's stolen from me. Oh, Emma, sometimes I wonder what I'm doing."

"You may not know what you're doing, but God knows what he's doing. Rest assured in that."

Janice set the phone on the table and sat with her chin resting in her hand. She'd always celebrated milestones in her children's lives with special gifts. Could she do the same for this girl who'd been dumped into her life? God had asked her to do the impossible, to love Jinxi unconditionally. So far, she'd done a poor job. Maybe it was time to let God do the impossible through her.

The rank smell of unwashed bodies overwhelmed the fragrance of meatloaf fresh out of the oven. As the end of August neared, the number of people lining up for the free food bank meal increased by at least a third. Glad for the distraction, Jinxi heaped mashed potatoes on dozens of plates. Her mind returned again and again to her upcoming trip to Bakersfield, Dean's almost-kiss, Janice's money. Each time, she forced the images into the back of her mind, intending to deal with them later. The temptation to escape into the bathroom, to draw blood, brought sweat to her overheated face.

Able at last to take a break, she headed to the vending machine for a soda. Leaning her head against the glass front, she waited for the can to clunk to the bottom. She jumped when Aneesa touched her shoulder.

"Are you okay? You look a little pale. Well, paler than usual."

Jinxi's mouth curved up slightly as she turned. "I'm okay, I guess. Hot. Tired." She shrugged. "Got a lot on my mind."

"Planning anything special for your days off next week?"

Jinxi popped the top of the soda and waited for the fizz to stop. "Yeah, I'm thinking of visiting my mom in Bakersfield."

"How long since you've seen her?"

"Since I got here, to Sacramento. A lot has happened, and I kinda want to tell her about it. Does that make sense?" Confusion clouded her eyes as she looked at Aneesa.

Aneesa nodded. "Child, sounds like a nudge from God. Maybe he wants you to go. Be careful, okay?"

What was there to be careful about? She'd take the bus down, spend a day with her mom, come home. As long as her mom's boyfriend—and Skeeter—stayed out of her way, everything would be cool.

Knowing she had a few days off after the weekend quickened Jinxi's steps as she neared Janice's house. She was tempted to skip, but the weight of her boots held her to the ground.

"Hey, Teddy, how's my boy?" Ted waited at the front gate, tail wagging and tongue lolling. "Let's get inside where it's cool." Jinxi mounted the front steps and unlocked the door. She started toward the kitchen, but Janice's voice stopped her.

"Hello, I'm in the office," Janice called. "Come in here for a moment."

Jinxi's stomach dropped. If Janice was in her office, that could only mean one thing. She'd been on the computer and had discovered the missing cash. All thoughts of prayer disappeared as fight or flight kicked in.

Jinxi's feet dragged as she let herself be pulled down the hall toward certain doom.

The sight of Janice's smiling face brought her to a halt in the doorway. A sliver of hope shot through her, like the first sip of coffee in the morning. A brightly colored gift bag on Janice's work table grabbed Jinxi's attention.

"I know I should wait until Dean gets here, but I'm too excited." Janice stood and retrieved the bag, extending it toward her. "He drove me to the store and helped me pick it out, so it's from both of us."

Jinxi reached for the bag. Was this a present? Or a trap ...?

"Go on, open it."

"But ... what's it for?"

Janice sat back in her chair, a satisfied smile on her face. "We always celebrate milestones in this family. This is a celebration, because you were offered a job at the food bank."

Jinxi sank onto the other chair. This couldn't be happening. She'd done nothing to deserve a gift. Exactly the opposite. She'd lied, cheated, stolen, and manipulated this woman, and here she was, offering Jinxi a present.

"Open it," Janice urged.

Jinxi pulled the tissue paper from the bag, revealing its contents. The first thing she pulled out was a cookbook.

"It's a cookbook," Janice exclaimed.

Jinxi held the book in her hands, examining the title. "Betty Crocker's Cooking for Beginners."

Janice leaned toward her, pointing. "Look, it's got all sorts of tips and information, and recipes from simple to more complex."

Speechless, Jinxi stared at the cover. She couldn't imagine anyone putting so much time and effort into a gift. She recounted the endless birthdays where her mom had handed her some money and said, "Go get yourself something nice, honey." Jinxi had ended up squandering the money on video games or fast food. She'd never received a gift so perfect. Jinxi hugged the cookbook to her chest.

"Thanks."

"Go on, there's more," Janice said.

Jinxi pulled out a tissue-wrapped bundle and slowly opened it. As she shook it out, she saw it was a cook's apron, black, with a white skull and crossbones dead center. *Eat or Die!* it exclaimed in white letters.

"One more thing," Janice said, taking the apron from her.

There, on the bottom of the bag, was a three-ring binder. Janice had decorated the front with her scrapbooking stuff with the words, "Jinxi's Favorite Recipes." Inside were several plastic sheet protectors.

"It's so that if you find recipes on the internet, or somewhere in a magazine or something, you can save them and have a place to keep them," Janice explained.

"Wow." Jinxi's throat ached with unshed tears while she wondered where in the world Janice had found the perfect apron.

"It's from Dean, too," she added. "We both chipped in." Janice laid a warm hand on Jinxi's shoulder. "I'm so glad you like it. I must admit, I'm a little selfish. I'm looking forward to being a guinea pig for all the new recipes you have to try."

Jinxi sniffed once, trying to hold back her emotions. "Uh, thanks." She stood, gathered the gifts back into the bag, turned on her heel, and ran out the door and up the stairs. Ted followed, his nails clicking on the wood stairs.

By the time she reached the bedroom, tears leaked out of her eyes and dripped off her chin. She sat on the edge, covering her face with her hands.

Why was Janice so nice to her? Things were so much easier when she was someone to be used. Janice had ruined everything.

CHAPTER 49

Dean's treadmill rolled under his feet, comforting him with the familiar sound of his shoes pounding out the five miles he'd promised himself. He'd thrown open the big garage door, pulling in fresh air on this beautiful Saturday morning in August. One more mile to go before he'd start on the weights. He didn't want to become lazy on these days off work. He'd begin patrol in prime condition, ready to take on the bad guys.

Drops of sweat flew as he shook his head to clear his vision. He grabbed a towel and swept it over his face. His cell phone, cradled in the drink holder of the treadmill, chirped to life, the familiar rap song bringing a smile to his face.

"Li'l D. 'S up?"

"Big D. You running? I can hear you panting."

"Yup. A little less than a mile to go."

"You're outta control, dude. This is your vacation."

Dean smiled. "Gotta keep up with you, bro."

"In your dreams. Hey, listen, Sommer and I and some of the guys are going out tonight. We'll celebrate your move into the line of fire. First beer's on me."

Dean shook his head. "You know I don't drink."

"Fine. I'll buy you a Coke, lightweight."

"What time?"

"Five. We'll grab some burgers and shoot some pool. You owe me a game."

"Whatever. You're a sore winner. Sounds good."

"Awesome. Oh, and bring your girlfriend."

Dean jumped off the treadmill. "Huh?"

"You know, the freaky one."

Dean's stomach dropped. "Uh, okay." He punched the END button and dropped the phone back into the drink holder. Stepping to his weight bench, he dropped down with a loud exhale. Wasn't that what he wanted? To ask Jinxi out on a date. Perfect opportunity to do that. So why were nerves tingling in his palms?

Dean remembered his mother's words.

Leave her alone, she'd said. *You don't know what you're getting yourself into.*

Shrugging off her warning, he lay back on the weight bench and grabbed the barbell.

Jinxi's fingers flew over the keyboard as she tapped out an email to her mom, letting her know what time she'd arrive on Monday afternoon. Janice leaned against the door frame, watching her, concern etched on her face.

"You need to do this," Janice said. "You need to not only clear the air but also let your mother know you're doing well. I know *I'd* want to know—if you were my daughter."

Jinxi paused, eyes glued to the keyboard. She wasn't doing this for her mom's peace of mind, but for hers. Even so, part of her resisted the urge. What could she possibly tell her mom about what she'd been through? She was setting herself up for disappointment. Again.

Jinxi hit SEND. She raised her eyes to Janice's. "I know it's been a couple of days, but I wanted to say thanks for the present."

Janice smiled and waved her hand. "You're welcome. I'm glad you liked it."

Jinxi watched as Janice turned and headed into the living room. She bit her lip, wondering how and when she should say something about the money. The secret sat inside her, dark and festering. She longed to be free from the shame. She tried to conjure up the feeling of peace after her experience Monday night, but it was like trying to hold on to smoke.

Maybe something to eat would quench the gnawing in her stomach. She poured herself a bowl of cereal and wandered outside to eat under the trees. Ted followed, watchful for dropped morsels. The sound of grunting lured her toward the garage. Surprised to see the door open, she peeked around and spied Dean on the weight bench, lifting a barbell over his head.

Jinxi took a moment to admire the muscles rippling in his arms before clearing her throat.

"Hey," he greeted her, setting the weight back on the rack. "I was gonna come see you when I'm done." He sat up, scrubbing his face with a towel.

Jinxi leaned against the doorframe, bowl in hand. "You were?"

"Yeah." He paused to use the towel on the back of his neck. "Damaris, Sommer, and some of the guys ... and ladies ... are going out for burgers and pool tonight." Dean's eyes focused somewhere over Jinxi's shoulder.

Jinxi couldn't help it. She was enjoying his discomfort. "Sounds like you'll have a good time." She took another bite of cereal.

Dean snapped the towel back and forth. "Well, yeah, we always have fun. You might enjoy it too."

"Ya think?" She smirked at him over the rim as she raised the bowl to her lips and drained the last of the milk.

Dean stood and lightly snapped her leg with the towel. "Yeah, I think. Why don't you go with me and find out?"

"Hey. That hurt."

"Did not. I barely tapped you." He threaded the towel through his hands. "What do you think? Burgers. A game of pool. Might be fun."

Jinxi raised one shoulder. "Okay."

"Okay?" He broke into a grin. "I'll come get you around five." As Jinxi turned to go, he added, "Oh, and don't say anything to my mom."

Jinxi's face stiffened as she backed out of the door and headed for the house. Why did he have to go and ruin it?

Ted dogged her heels as she trudged back to the house. What was she supposed to do, leave the house with Dean and not say anything to Janice? What a hot mess.

After dumping her cereal bowl in the sink, she headed upstairs. In her room, she yanked open the dresser drawers and pulled out her limited wardrobe. Long-sleeved black T-shirt, short-sleeved black T-shirt. Long-sleeved white T-shirt, short-sleeved white T-shirt. Gray sweatshirt. A couple more nondescript tees. What would be appropriate to wear on a date? Her limited knowledge on the subject rose up and smacked her on the face.

She needed to go to the store and buy something new. Maybe Janice would let her use the car, so she didn't have to wait for the bus, especially if she complained about how hot it was outside.

Janice sat at her computer in the office, typing one-handed. Her bandaged right hand lay in her lap. Jinxi's stomach fluttered at the sight of the red welts. Janice glanced up with a rueful look. "This is such a bother."

"I'm heading to the store to get a couple of things. Do you need anything?"

"Well, I think we're about out of milk, so you could pick up another half-gallon? Oh, and I'm craving chocolate chip cookies. Could you pick up a package of them?" Janice stood and brushed past Jinxi, who stood in the door. "Let me get you some money."

Jinxi closed her eyes for a moment. "I could make some cookies from scratch," she offered.

Janice stopped in the hall. "That'd be wonderful. I haven't had homemade cookies in a month of Sundays." She hastened toward her purse, which lay open on the bed. She pulled out some bills and handed them to Jinxi.

Jinxi took the money from Janice's hand with a twinge of guilt.

"Will that be enough?" At Jinxi's nod, Janice turned back to her purse. "Let me get my keys. You better take the car. I think we're out of eggs, too. You won't be able to carry everything back on the bus." Janice handed her the keys with a smile.

That was too easy. She didn't even have to play on Janice's sympathy. She took the keys and turned away, hiding a smile. "I'll be back in a bit."

Jinxi pulled into the Walmart parking lot. Jerking to a stop, she spied a clothing store in the strip mall next to the superstore. Susie's Styles. Perfect. Better than looking for something in Wally World.

After trying on more than a dozen tops, Jinxi decided on a turquoise one that shimmered when she moved. The neck and hem were stitched with black thread, and the sleeves were black lace, covering her arms to the wrists. Perfect. She paid for the top and headed to Walmart to buy ingredients for chocolate chip cookies.

The smell of baking permeated the house. Jinxi slid the second dozen onto a cutting board to cool.

"It smells heavenly in here," Janice announced, entering the kitchen. She poured herself a glass of milk and snitched a cookie before sitting at the table. "Mmmm, these are delicious. Exactly what I've been craving."

Dean appeared at the back door. Swinging it open, he sniffed the air. "Do I smell cookies?" he asked with a hopeful expression.

Janice chuckled. "Throw something in the oven, and you never know who'll turn up at your door."

A shimmer of pride shot through Jinxi. "Help yourself." Sharing really was caring.

Geez, she was starting to think like Janice.

Dean didn't hesitate a second before grabbing three. "Great idea, Mom. Milk and cookies." He poured himself a glass and sat across from Janice.

Jinxi busied herself with scooping out spoonfuls of dough for the next batch.

"Mom, I'm going out with a bunch of the guys tonight. And ladies. We're gonna grab some burgers and play pool."

Jinxi kept her back turned toward them, concentrating on the dough.

"That's nice." Janice stood and walked to the counter to take another cookie.

"Yeah, D and Sommer want to celebrate the whole patrol thing."

Jinxi's stomach tightened. Would he tell his mom he'd asked her to go too? Awkward.

"Anyway, I asked Jinxi to go, too. You know, let her get out, meet some people. Other than the people she meets at the food bank."

Dean's words poured out in a rush. Jinxi glanced at him. He seemed to be panting. Her gaze intersected a warning glance from Janice to Dean.

"I'll be over about five o'clock to pick her up. You'll be okay, right?"

Janice's voice held a tone of either disappointment or weariness. "I'll be fine. I've been on my own before."

Dean slapped his hands on his thighs and stood. "Great. See ya later." He snagged three more cookies before heading out the door.

Jinxi kept her eyes on her task as Janice spoke. "You're going out with Dean and his friends tonight?"

"It's not like it's a date or anything." Jinxi closed the oven door with a bang and wiped her hands on the black apron Janice had given her.

"I see." Janice drained her glass and stood and carried the glass to the sink. She walked by Jinxi into the living room without another word.

She was on a collision course with either Dean or Janice. And neither one would have a happily-ever-after ending.

CHAPTER 50

"No, I'm telling you that strawberry shakes should be outlawed. It's unnatural." Dean gestured with a French fry before shoving the fry in his mouth. "I mean, who wants to drink something pink?"

"That's where you're wrong. Nothing says summer like the creamy goodness of a real strawberry milkshake." Damaris proved his point by taking a gulp of his shake.

Jinxi watched the interplay between Dean and his friends with mild irritation. Sommer caught her eye and gave her a conspiratorial smile. They'd gone to the local In-N-Out Burger for dinner before heading to the pool hall. Jinxi had watched in amazement as Dean ordered two double-double hamburgers and two orders of fries. Plus a vanilla shake. Her hamburger and Coke looked tiny next to his.

Now he and Damaris continued their ongoing argument about the best flavor of milkshake.

"Do you want to take this outside?" Dean threatened.

Damaris laughed scornfully. "I could take you."

"I'm gonna shoot both of you if you don't shut up," Sommer interrupted. "Can't we have a civilized conversation among four adults?"

Dean's eyebrows shot up. "Sure, Sugar. Whatever you say."

Sommer glared at him for using her nickname. She glanced at her watch and did a double-take. "We'd better hustle. Patrice and the rest are meeting us in ten minutes."

After throwing away the remains of their meal, Jinxi and Dean jumped back into Dean's truck for the drive to the pool hall.

"Sorry about that," Dean said.

"Sorry about what?"

"Acting stupid."

"You're very good at it." *That* shut him up.

Patrice, Sanjay, and the others from the day at the lake were already at the pool place, along with a few Jinxi didn't know. The group broke into foursomes to play after everyone was introduced.

"Do you know how to play pool?" Dean asked, coming up behind her. He rubbed the chalk over the top of the cue.

Jinxi shrugged. "I've played a little."

"That could mean one of two things. Either you've really played a little, or you're a sleeper."

Jinxi smiled and shrugged again. "Guess you're about to find out."

The games began with good-natured sparring and trash talk. Jinxi easily won the first game against Patrice. She and Dean paired up for the next. Midway through, a woman approached the table. Her tube top perched dangerously low on her chest, the bottom resting above the waistline of her low-slung skinny jeans. Knee-high stiletto boots completed the ensemble. Several uncomplimentary words formed in Jinxi's head as the woman sauntered up to Dean.

"Hey, Mr. Clean Dean. I didn't expect to see you hanging out here." Her talon-like nail tapped Dean on the chest.

Dean moved away to set up for his shot. "Hi, Misty."

Misty shadowed him. "How've you been? I haven't seen you at the station for a few days."

Sommer rolled her eyes at Jinxi and whispered, "She's a new officer. Transferred in from Riverside. Damaris can't stand her."

Jinxi watched as Dean's shot went wild. She moved around the table to make her shot. As she pulled back the pool cue, Misty said with a loud voice, "Is that your girlfriend?"

Jinxi gritted her teeth and steadied her hands before shooting. The ball hit the side, missing the pocket by a wide margin. Straightening, she narrowed her eyes, hoping they sent enough sparks to melt Misty's smug look.

"We're here to hang out, play some pool." Dean set himself up for the next shot.

Misty stared back at Jinxi with a glint of malice. "Is this the one who was arrested for prostitution?"

The urge to attack rose up hard. Adrenaline shot through Jinxi, sucking the blood from her brain. She imagined herself smacking the girl across the face, grabbing her hair, and throwing her to the floor. She'd done it before. She could do it again.

"Go ahead, hit me," Misty taunted. "You want to go back to jail, don't you? Assaulting a police officer will guarantee that."

Damaris stepped between them, putting up a hand. "We've got enough players here, Misty. Go on back to wherever you came from."

Misty put a hand on her hip and tossed her hair back and flounced to the bar. Everyone heaved a collective sigh of relief. Adrenaline flowed out of Jinxi, leaving her limp as a wet towel. She turned and dashed to the restroom, into the first stall she came to.

Jinxi leaned against one wall, head in her hands. This was a bad idea. Dean would never hear the end of it. Even cleaned up, even saved, she would always be the hooker he took to breakfast one morning and home to his mother afterward. As much as Jinxi was starting to like him, some things weren't meant to be. She would always be on the outside.

Jinxi felt the subtle shift in the air when that girl outed her. She straightened her spine, determined to finish out the evening, clean up at pool, and never, ever, go on another so-called date with Dean.

As she exited the stall, Patrice came through the restroom door. "You okay?"

Jinxi turned the water on to wash her hands. "Not really."

Patrice leaned against the other sink. "Don't pay any attention to Misty. She loves to stir up trouble."

"Does everyone know I was arrested?" Jinxi watched herself in the mirror rather than make eye contact with Patrice.

"Not everyone. Dean told me, but that's it. But you know how gossip is. Once some juicy bit gets dropped, people are like dogs fighting over who gets it."

"Did *you* tell her?"

Patrice shook her head. "Nope. I promised Dean I wouldn't say anything." Patrice laid a hand on Jinxi's arm. "Hey, don't worry about it. Everyone in our group is cool."

Jinxi didn't answer. What could she say? She'd embarrassed Dean in front of his friends. Wait till he found out she'd stolen from his mom. That's when stuff would really hit the fan. She sighed, dried her hands, and squared her shoulders as she pulled open the restroom door.

Dean leaned against the wall outside the bathroom. He straightened as she came out. "You okay?"

"Why does everyone keep asking me that? I'm fine." She swept past him and back to the pool table. "Let's finish the game. I think you're about to lose."

The spicy smell of his aftershave wafted toward her from behind. He smelled good.

"Lose? I don't think so."

They finished the game, and Jinxi accepted the group's congratulations.

Damaris addressed Dean as he lifted his hand to high-five her. "Big D, didn't think I'd see you get taken down by a *girl*."

Dean rubbed the back of his neck. "Let's see how you do, broseph." Dean handed his pool cue to Damaris with a grin. He winked at Jinxi. "Don't be too hard on him. He has a fragile ego."

Jinxi grinned despite herself. "Not to worry. I have skills. Mad skills."

Patrice hooted a laugh. "I've got to see this."

"Name your game." Jinxi chalked the end of her cue as Damaris flexed his shoulders.

"One Pocket."

Jinxi raised her eyebrows. She'd seen Damaris play. He was good, but he wasn't that good. One Pocket required more defense than offense. Damaris played similar to Dean, all strength and little finesse. "Okay. Choose your pocket."

The others moved closer to the table to watch the drama better.

"Who's betting on Jinxi?" Sanjay asked. He waved a five-dollar bill above his head.

"I'm in." Patrice pulled a five from her jeans pocket.

Damaris shot a look toward Sommer. "Baby?"

Sommer shook her head. "Sorry, guys, gotta go with my man." She handed five ones to Sanjay.

"So that leaves you, Dean." Sanjay's grin was white against his dark skin. Jinxi watched in amusement as red crept up Dean's neck to his cheeks. Hilarious.

Damaris tapped Dean on the shoulder with his cue. "Yeah, Big D. What's it gonna be?"

Dean's gaze swept from her to Damaris. He heaved a fake sigh. "Can I abstain?"

The rest of the group howled in protest.

"Okay, fine." He slapped a five into Sanjay's outstretched palm. "My money's on Jinxi."

Damaris groaned and clutched his chest. "You're killing me, bro."

Warmth spread through Jinxi's middle. Dean believed she could win. So did the others.

"I'll let you go first," she said.

Damaris broke the rack. His first shot banked squarely into his chosen pocket. He grinned. "You may not know that One Pocket requires great shot-making skills, excellence, planning, and patience." He shot again, continuing with his patter. "Minnesota Fats allegedly said One Pocket is like the game of chess." His ball bounced off the side, narrowly missing the middle hole.

"Keep up the chatter, dude. You're going down." Jinxi took her time walking the perimeter of the table, sizing up the ball placement. Once she'd memorized the table, she set to work.

Damaris howled each time her ball landed with a clunk into her chosen pocket. Within minutes, she'd swept all her balls in. She stood, arched her back, and stretched.

"Go again?" Jinxi asked, widening her eyes in innocence.

"No, I'm good." Damaris rested his head on Sommer's shoulder. "Sorry, baby."

Everyone gathered around her, congratulating her on the win.

"You've got some mad skills for sure."

"Holy moly. I've never seen anything like that before."

"Where'd you learn to play like that?"

"Can you teach me?"

Their words were balm to her bruised spirit.

Later, as they pulled up to the house, Dean stopped the truck on the side street, outside his garage apartment. Jinxi jumped out before he could get around to open her door. As he pushed the passenger door closed, he said, "Let me walk you to the house."

"Don't." She strode across the back lawn toward the house, Ted at her heels. She needed to get away from him. No more almost-kisses. No more embarrassment by having her around.

Jinxi climbed into bed and thought over the evening and the confrontation with that girl. *Misty*. Jinxi sat with her back against the headboard, knees hugged to her chest. Something had held her back, an unseen hand restraining her from moving. She'd wanted to take that girl down, hurt her. Make her pay for telling the world she'd been arrested. She'd had the feeling her feet were glued to the floor. After delving into the book of Acts, she started to believe maybe God could do some amazing things. Even protecting her from doing something stupid.

The door of his pickup supported Dean as he sagged against it, watching Jinxi walk away from him. What just happened? He reviewed every moment of the evening, trying to find where he'd gone wrong. He'd complimented her on the blouse she wore. He hadn't gotten drawn into Misty's drama. He hadn't tried to make a move on Jinxi. Heck, he'd even let her win at pool. Maybe she hadn't wanted to go out with him at all. He'd heard the term "pity date" used by some of the women on the force. Maybe that's what this was. Maybe she'd said yes to him because saying no would be awkward since she lived with his mom.

Or maybe it was him.

Dean fisted his hands and pounded behind him on the door of the truck. Shaking his head at the fickleness of the opposite sex, he trudged up the stairs to his apartment.

"She even stole my dog," he muttered. His mind shot to his mom's earrings. What else had Jinxi stolen? He put his hand on his chest, rubbing the place where his heart beat.

CHAPTER 51

Birds in the maple trees outside Janice's bedroom window created a cacophony of sound. Janice reached her arm across the bed, feeling the empty space. *Tom must already be up. Hope he's put the coffee pot on.*

With a start, she remembered. She rolled over, shielding her eyes from the morning light seeping through the blinds. The smell of coffee roused her to full wakefulness. Jinxi must be up.

Before she could complete the thought, Janice remembered Dean and Jinxi had gone to play pool the night before. Bother. Why wouldn't that boy let God do his work?

Perhaps things would come to a head soon. Keeping secrets was frustrating.

Maybe something in today's sermon would prompt Jinxi to be honest. That is, if Jinxi still wanted to drive her to church today. The doctor promised she'd be able to drive Monday or Tuesday. Groaning with frustration, Janice swung her feet over the side of the bed. After pulling on a robe, she headed for the kitchen and the first coffee of the day.

Jinxi sat hunched over a bowl of cereal, Ted at her feet. He looked up and thumped his tail twice in greeting.

"Morning," Janice said with a note of cheerfulness she didn't feel. "Did you have a good time last night?"

Jinxi looked up briefly and back down, concentrating on her cereal. "I guess."

Trying to engage with Jinxi was worse than trying to talk to a teenager. She'd have to pry the details out of the girl.

"What did you end up doing?"

Jinxi shrugged. "Ate burgers and played pool."

Janice changed tactics. "Do you mind taking me to church again? Should be the last time."

"It's okay."

Good grief. Maybe Jinxi'd be more willing to talk after she'd had more coffee. "Fine. I'll be ready in an hour."

Should she tell Janice about the confrontation with the other girl last night? Jinxi still couldn't believe she hadn't smacked her down. The girl deserved it, too. Maybe better not to say anything.

How humiliating to have her arrest announced to the world. Dean was probably super embarrassed about last night. Not that she cared. She mentally shook herself as she sipped her coffee. At least he'd complimented her on the new top.

She'd had a good time playing pool. There'd been no drunken jostling and shoving that usually accompanied a night out with Skeeter and their friends. Jinxi had sharpened her pool-playing skills during her years with Skeeter, and she'd won a couple of games last night. She'd drunk in the high-fives and fist-bumping she'd received as congratulations. The final match with Damaris was epic.

They probably talked about her after she and Dean had left. They were probably wondering why Dean was with her. Still, it had been nice to feel accepted, even if only on the surface.

When the time came to go to church, Janice handed Jinxi the keys to the car as they walked out to the carport. "Nice top," she commented.

Jinxi glanced down at the new top she'd worn the night before. "Thanks," she murmured. They climbed into the Prius, and as she pushed the START button, she saw Dean running across the lawn toward them. Today he wore a pair of pressed khakis and a white button-up shirt. Dress shoes instead of tennies. Nice. Janice rolled down the passenger window.

"I thought I'd go with you to church today," he said, slightly out of breath.

The two ladies exchanged a look. Jinxi clicked the stud back and forth against her teeth. Dean had a sudden interest in church. Well, well. She leaned across Janice.

"Okay, but I'm driving. You'll have to sit in the back."

Conversation stuttered and stopped. No one wanted to address the elephant in the car. After several years, why was Dean going to church?

The pastor began his sermon with, "Brothers and sisters, please turn to Ephesians, chapter one, verses one through seven."

Jinxi squirmed on the wooden pew and tried to inch away from Dean, whose thigh jammed against hers. He reached over and grabbed the Bible off her lap, turning the pages rapidly until he located the passage. Setting the Bible back into her lap, he crossed his arms with a smug smile.

Why did he have to smell so good? She resisted the urge to lean toward him and sniff. Instead, she pressed her back against the pew. Janice sat on one side of her and Dean on the other, like they were a family. Doing something ordinary people do on a Sunday morning. Something she'd never known.

"I want to focus our attention this morning on verse seven. 'In him, we have redemption through his blood, the forgiveness of our trespasses, according to the riches of his grace.'" The pastor read the definition of the word "redeem" from the dictionary. As he spoke, Jinxi understood, and comprehension dawned. Everything she'd ever done and would do in the future was dealt with. She was forgiven.

The feeling she'd experienced after Wednesday night service returned, only to be replaced with doubt. It couldn't be that easy. Believe in Jesus, and every evil thing was wiped away. What about Janice? When she found out about the money, things wouldn't be easily forgiven. Especially with Dean. The tiny seedlings of doubt grew.

After the service, Jinxi stood in the courtyard of the church while Janice chatted with her friends. She watched as Janice and Emma embraced and began a spirited conversation about the message. At the door, Dean talked with one of the pastors. He raised his hand to rub the back of his neck, a familiar gesture. He must be uptight about something the pastor was saying.

As Janice concluded her conversation, the senior pastor approached them.

"Good morning," he said with a warm smile. Glancing at the sky, he chuckled and corrected himself. "I guess I should say 'good afternoon.' How are you ladies today? How's the arm, Janice?"

"It gets better every day. Thank you for asking."

Jinxi spied Dean leaning against the Prius, arms crossed. Jinxi held Janice's good arm as they made their way across the parking lot. Jinxi and Janice climbed into the car, with Dean again sitting behind Jinxi, who had pulled the driver seat as far forward as it could go. Janice, as tall as her son, had the passenger seat all the way back.

Janice broke the silence as they pulled out of the church parking lot. "Dean, why the sudden interest in going to church?"

Jinxi glanced at Dean in the rearview mirror. His hand crept up to the back of his neck and down to his lap. When he caught her eye, she sliced her gaze forward.

"Well ... uh ... I guess I thought I'd better see what I was missing. You know, now that Jinxi's going with you and all."

"What did you think about the message?"

"It was good."

"I noticed you talking with Pastor Mark."

Jinxi looked at the mirror again. Dean gazed out the window. He didn't answer, and Janice let the subject drop.

Yeah, Dean, why the sudden interest?

Was his intent to spy on her, or was it an excuse to be near her? Jinxi's stomach quivered, an equal mixture of fear and hope.

CHAPTER 52

The bedroom door was open, a habit she'd gotten used to since Ted had come to stay. He'd stop any bogeyman, real or imagined. She crouched down to rub the soft fur between his ears. She'd miss him. With a sigh, she pulled on jeans and a T-shirt.

Ted snoozed on his spot on the floor as she pulled out her backpack and laid out her clothes for the trip. Where had she put her cigarettes? The craving for nicotine had almost disappeared since her experience the previous Wednesday evening. Still, she didn't want to take the chance she'd need them during the potentially stressful visit with her mom.

As Jinxi searched through the dresser, her ears registered the sound of Dean's heavy tread on the stairs. She pulled open the drawer of the nightstand. Maybe she'd thrown the cigarettes in there by mistake.

No, it couldn't be. There in the drawer lay a pair of gold hoop earrings encrusted with tiny diamonds. Jinxi pulled them out and held them up, watching the light sparkle off the jewels.

"Jinxi, my mom wanted to know if you—" Dean skidded to a stop inside the bedroom door. "What the—"

For the first time since she'd known him, Dean was speechless.

Blood rushed from her head, leaving her light-headed. "I don't know how they got here."

Dean's face hardened into an angry mask.

"I can't believe you stole my mom's earrings. After everything she's done for you."

"I swear. I opened the nightstand, and there they were."

"Sure they were." He crossed his arms and leaned forward. "How convenient. Take the earrings, disappear down to Bakersfield, if that's where you're really going."

Dean's words exploded against her like shrapnel.

"It's not like that …."

His face settled inches from hers. "You better tell my mom, or I will. She can decide whether or not to press charges against you."

Jinxi held out a hand in supplication. "Here, you take them. I'll talk to her when I get back from Bakersfield, okay?"

"No. Leave them right where they were. In *your* bedroom. You have until the day you get back to tell her." Dean shook his finger in her face. "If you don't come back, I'll make sure to find you, and my mom *will* press charges. Understood?"

Jinxi nodded mutely. Dean's footsteps clomped down the stairs. She sank onto the bed, nausea clawing up her throat.

Oh God.

Oh, God.

Dean stomped down the stairs, through the kitchen, and out the back door of his mom's house, slamming the door behind him. Fists clenched, he fought the urge to punch something.

After everything his mom had done for Jinxi, she'd turned around and taken the earrings. What else had she stolen? After Jinxi left would be a good time for his mom to do an inventory.

He should have known better than to let her stay. He should have realized what kind of person she was. He should never have fallen for her.

Dean's phone chirped an incoming text. It was from Patrice.

PATRICE: Sorry about Sat nite and the Misty thing

He tapped out an answer.

DEAN: Not your fault

She sent another text.

PATRICE: Can u talk?

Dean blinked slowly before his thumb pads hit the keys.

DEAN: No

He shoved the phone back in his pocket. Time for a workout on the speed bag. Punching something would feel good right about now. Until he figured out what to do about Jinxi.

Her betrayal hurt on so many levels. Had she been playing him all along?

The air conditioner barely kept the heat at bay as the bus traveled Interstate 5 South through California's Central Valley. Jinxi stared blankly out the window at the passing groves of fruit trees. Each orchard had a sign nailed to the surrounding fence, indicating the type of fruit grown. Apricots. Peaches. Cherries.

After an hour on the road, beads of sweat ran down the sides of her face. At the first rest stop, she departed the bus, intent on buying something to drink. She'd filled her backpack with snacks, courtesy of Janice's abundant pantry, but after the confrontation with Dean, her appetite had disappeared.

After using the restroom, Jinxi shoved some bills into the vending machine. The soda can dropped with a *clunk*. A few feet away, a young Mexican boy drew her attention, who watched her with liquid brown eyes. He reminded her of Connie's son, Miguel.

"Hi." Jinxi smiled down at him and took a long gulp of the soda. When she lowered the can, the boy was still looking at her. He licked his lips.

"You want a soda?" Jinxi asked. He nodded.

The boy's mother spoke sharply to him in Spanish. Jinxi caught enough of her words to know she told him to "leave the lady alone."

She pulled some more bills from her pocket and fed them into the machine, glancing at the mother who stared at her with suspicion.

"*No te preocupes*," Jinxi told the mother. *Don't worry, little mama*. "Which one?"

The boy pointed to a Coke, so Jinxi pushed the button. They watched the can drop. After handing the can to the boy, she asked, "*Tienes hambre*?" Because she'd seen that look in her own eyes. That kind of thirst came with hunger.

Again he nodded. Jinxi walked him to the snack machine and asked what he wanted. Jinxi bought two of everything he pointed to and handed the snacks to the boy's mother, who thanked Jinxi effusively. Jinxi understood less than half of what was said, but enough to know they were grateful for the small favor.

The bus coughed to a halt inside the Greyhound station in Bakersfield. The late afternoon heat hit her full blast as she stepped off the bus. She trudged across the concrete and into the slightly cooler reception area. Her mom wasn't inside. Big surprise. She'd probably forgotten what time Jinxi would arrive.

People jostled past her, eager to greet friends and family, each one leaving the station until she stood alone. She slung the backpack over her shoulder and pulled her cell phone from the back pocket of her jeans.

Her mother answered on the fourth ring.

"Mom, it's me. I'm at the bus station."

"Hi, Jinxi-girl. Ron and I will be there in a jiffy." Her voice was slurred.

Seriously, Mom. It's four in the afternoon.

"Ron says you better be waiting on the curb."

Thanks, Ron. Make me wait in the heat.

The heat assaulted her again, and she struggled to catch her breath. Was the heat always this bad? The sky was a hazy brown, and her lips curled with disgust. If this is how Hell felt, she thanked God one more time for his salvation.

With her back against the outside wall of the bus station, she slid down to sit and wait.

She'd had hours on the bus to review every word of her conversation with Dean. What was she going to do? Would anyone believe she hadn't taken the earrings? Especially after the money. Good thing she hadn't left the note behind. Jinxi pulled open the outside pocket of the backpack to check. Yup. Still there.

She'd written the note to Janice, confessing everything, even the earrings found in the nightstand. Promising to pay back every last dollar. The big question was, could she go back and face Janice? Perhaps there was a way to stay in Bakersfield, get a job, and send money when she could.

Yesterday, the preacher had said she was forgiven of every sin ever committed. But that was from God. Could she expect the same forgiveness from Janice? And Dean. What would happen to her if she returned? She whispered something like a prayer as she waited for her mother.

An hour later, Ron's car slowed in front of the station, and she jumped in, grateful to escape the heat. The air conditioner in the vehicle cooled her body but did nothing for the turmoil inside her.

Her mother turned in her seat and reached for Jinxi, laying a weak hand on her arm. “Baby, I missed you so much.” The smell of stale cigarettes and alcohol fumes filled the car. Jinxi held her breath against it. Still, it was good to see her mom again. Her ice-blond hair, the same as Jinxi’s actual color, showed streaks of gray. There were more wrinkles around her mouth, as if her face had shrunk. But the blue eyes that stared back at her were as familiar as her own.

“Tell her the truth, Susan,” Ron demanded. “Tell her how mad you were that she took off without saying anything. Tell her how much money she owes you.” His words beat against her. Jinxi flinched.

Her mother turned back. “It’s okay. For right now, my baby’s home.”

Jinxi looked out the side window of the car. Coming here had been a bad idea. Nothing had changed.

They arrived at the house. Her mother swung open the passenger door, using the door to leverage herself to a standing position.

“Go on in, Susan. I want to have a word with Jinxi.”

Jinxi watched her mother sway and take a faltering step toward the house. Before she could open her door, Ron turned in his seat to face her.

“Don’t think you’ve heard the last of this.” He leaned toward her, his breath hot against her already flushed cheek.

An icy shiver crept up her back as she gathered her things. “I’m going to help my mom.”

Jinxi climbed out of the car and hurried to her mom’s side. Her mother leaned against her, and Jinxi could feel the bones in her mom’s back.

In the house, her mother poured a generous serving of bourbon into a fingerprint-smudged glass. Newspapers littered the floor, and the smell of stale pizza wrinkled

Jinxi's nose. She could see into the kitchen where dirty dishes covered the counter, along with open cereal boxes and a carton of milk. Cigarette smoke clung to the walls.

Ron sank in his stained recliner. "So, how long are you staying?"

Avoiding his narrowed eyes, she addressed her mother. "Only for a day or so, if that's okay."

Susan used her arm to sweep off a spot to sit on the sofa. "Only a day. You got a job or something that you have to go back?"

Still standing, Jinxi shifted her backpack to the opposite shoulder. "Yeah, Mom. I do. I have a job. I'm working—"

"Ron still doesn't have a job, do you, baby?" Susan sent Ron a look. "They don't recognize his potential."

Jinxi glanced over at Ron and saw him looking at her appraisingly. The hair on the back of her neck bristled. His flat features shaped into an ugly smile.

"Get me a beer, Jinxi."

She stared back at him silently before setting her backpack down on the dirty carpet.

In the kitchen, she leaned her forehead against the front of the refrigerator. "God, what am I doing here?" She longed for the neat kitchen back at Janice's house and the well-scrubbed linoleum floors, rooms free of clutter.

Jinxi caught a glimpse of a carving knife on the butcher block counter. So tempting. A glance into the living room showed Ron, his eyes glued to the TV. Mom was biting her fingernails. She reached for the knife and jumped when Ron shouted.

"Where's that beer?"

The fridge held two six-packs of beer, half a carton of orange juice, and some unidentifiable green stuff that might have been a salad. Maybe. What a contrast to Janice's fridge. There was nothing edible here. Her stomach rumbled in protest as she shut the door with a grimace. She'd think about food later.

Jinxi returned to the living room and handed the can of beer to Ron before escaping to her old room. Nothing had changed in the last two and a half months, except a thicker layer of dust coated the furniture.

She startled when Ron appeared in the doorway. His dark T-shirt stretched over his beer belly. He gripped the beer in a massive fist. Black hair sprung from his knuckles. Jinxi focused her gaze on his receding hairline and willed her pulse to return to normal. She wouldn't let this troll get to her.

Gesturing with his beer, he said, "Getting all settled, I see."

Jinxi didn't answer.

"Your mom was upset when you left."

Under her breath, she muttered, "Yeah, for about ten seconds."

"Don't be sassy or I'll smack your smart mouth."

She glared at him.

"You took some money. I want it back." His voice held a hint of a threat.

"It's not your money."

"Doesn't matter. You stole it, and you give it back." He took a swig of his beer. "Or I'll call the police."

A surge of adrenaline left her breathless. Ron must have seen the terror in her eyes. He took a step toward her. "You better have the money before you leave here, or else." With a nasty chuckle, he turned on his heel and stomped down the hall.

Jinxi collapsed onto the bed. A cloud of dust choked her already dry throat. What had Janice said to her about praying? Like talking to a friend.

"I hate him. I mean, dear God, I really hate him. He creeps me out. Help me get some time alone with Mom."

Jinxi leaned over, dragged her pack onto the bed, and pulled out her wallet, counting out a hundred dollars. She couldn't remember how much she had taken from her mom, but she didn't think it was more than that. Counting the rest of the cash, she had the forty dollars she'd taken from Janice's sock, plus the second withdrawal. She'd left the money from her paycheck behind. She shoved her wallet down to the bottom of the bag and pushed it under the bed. Not a great hiding place, but it would have to do for now.

Jinxi walked back into the living room with a set mouth, where her mother and Ron had started to bicker.

Mom scrubbed her hands over her face. "It's your turn to get dinner."

"Nuh-uh. I got the pizza last night. Get off yer behind and order something. I'm starved."

Her mother looked up at her with red-rimmed eyes. "You okay, baby?"

Nodding, Jinxi approached her, money in hand. "Mom, this should take care of what I took when I left. I'm sorry I stole from you."

Her mom reached out, but before she could take the money, Ron grabbed the bills from Jinxi's hand. He counted out the twenties with a look of satisfaction.

"That's a good little girl." Mom didn't argue as Ron stuffed the cash into the pocket of his jeans.

Jinxi glared, helpless to fight him. He could still call the cops. She shivered despite the heat that pressed against the house and radiated through the windows.

"I'm going to take a shower." She stomped into the bedroom, grabbed some clean clothes, and double-checked the lock on the door was secure. There wouldn't be a repeat of the last time she'd stayed here.

The muffled sound of the doorbell and a man's voice came through the bathroom door. Skeeter's? She shook her head to clear it. No way could he have followed her here. No way.

CHAPTER 53

After another restless night of half-sleep, Jinxi woke the following day determined to talk to her mother alone. Her chance finally came late in the morning when Ron announced he was going out on some errands. Jinxi made coffee, hoping a bracing cup would clear the cobwebs from her mom's brain. The aromatic roast filled the kitchen, driving the stench of old food away, if only for a while.

She poured two cups, adding cream and sugar to her mom's. The memory of how Dean liked his coffee tugged at the corner of her brain. Hopefully, by the time she got back, he wouldn't be ticked off. If she went back.

"Here, Mom." Jinxi set the steaming mug on the old wood table. "Just the way you like it."

The sunlight filtered through the opened blinds. Mom's gray skin took Jinxi's breath away. Even at her worst after the spider bite, Janice hadn't looked this bad. Dark circles under her mom's eyes made her look haggard, older than her thirty-nine years.

"You okay, Mom?" The words slipped out before she had a chance to preface them.

"Sure, baby. Thanks for the java."

"No, I mean, are you feeling all right?" She took a sip of coffee, unable to tear her eyes away from her mom's face. Had she always looked this bad? Maybe when she was on the tail-end of a binge?

"Sure. Maybe a little tired." Her mom lifted one thin shoulder. "Work keeps me busy, and, you know."

Jinxi didn't know. From the house's condition, it was pretty obvious her mom wasn't knocking herself out cooking and cleaning.

Susan wrapped her bony fingers around the mug and took a sip of the coffee. Her fingernails were slightly yellow. "It's been a little stressful since Ron lost his job."

Jinxi grimaced. She hated to offer with Ron in the picture, but this was her mom. "Do you need some money?" She gritted her teeth, waiting for the answer.

"Maybe. Sometimes. I'll let you know."

Jinxi exhaled. "You've got my cell number, right? You can always call me."

Her mom set the mug on the table and folded her arms across her stomach. "Sure, baby. But you have your own life now, and I have Ron."

"Do you love him?" Jinxi wished she could grab the words and stuff them back into her mouth.

Her mother barked out a laugh. "What does love have to do with anything? He keeps me company."

I think I threw up in my mouth. Time to change the subject before her mom's creep of a boyfriend came back.

"Mom, I'm living in Sacramento. I'm staying at the home of a nice lady. Her name is Janice. I have a job at the food bank, and I'm learning to cook. I think I'm good at it too." She chewed on a fingernail, looking to see if her mother was focusing on her. "I got into some trouble, but I got it all worked out."

Her mother's eyes snapped up.

"I wanted you to know."

"Okay, Jinxi. That's good," her mom said. She took a sip of her coffee. "I hope you do something with your life."

Emboldened, Jinxi continued, "There's something else." She took a deep breath, stomach in a ball of flames. "I found God."

Susan struggled to her feet and grabbed both mugs off the table. She tottered to the counter and poured more coffee for both of them.

"Well, good for you. I hope he does more for you than he ever did for me."

Jinxi opened her mouth to respond and closed it again. What would Janice say to that? Probably something spiritual, or she'd quote some verse from the Bible. Jinxi couldn't remember a single thing she'd read except for the one Psalm about how God knew her before she was born, and somehow that didn't apply here.

"Yeah," Jinxi finally breathed out. "Me, too."

Her mom set the mugs on the table and resumed her seat.

"It's good to see you, Jinxi girl." Her mom eyed her with a look Jinxi couldn't decipher. "You can cook, huh?"

Jinxi sat up straighter. "Yes. This lady, Consuelo, or Connie, teaches me to cook, and I'm helping her learn to speak English. I mean, she speaks English, but not great. And you should see her kids. They're so cute. Janice is the lady I'm living with. She's super old but totally cool. She lets me cook all the time." Jinxi slowed to catch her breath and take a gulp of coffee. It hit her stomach like lighter fluid on an open flame. She clicked the stud back and forth across her teeth. "Maybe I could, you know, cook something for you tonight?" Waiting for her mom's answer took every ounce of Jinxi's patience.

"I guess that would be okay. You'll have to ask Ron."

Always Ron. Geez. She smiled despite the mention of Ron's name. "I'll start making a grocery list." Jinxi shoved the chair back, scraping it across the graying linoleum.

"Wait. I almost forgot. Your friend Skeeter stopped by last night while you were in the shower."

Jinxi's stomach dropped. "What did he want?"

Her mom shrugged. "He said he had something for you. I don't remember. He said he'd put it in your room."

Jinxi sat back in the chair. She hadn't noticed anything unusual in her backpack or the bedroom. An icy shiver crept up the back of her neck. What was he up to?

Ron returned with a rattle of keys and noisy footsteps into the house.

"Hey, guess what," Susan called out. As Ron came into the kitchen, she announced, "Jinxi found God. What do you think about that?"

Her mom's words stabbed her with their sarcasm.

Ron poured himself a cup of coffee and turned one of the kitchen chairs around backward so he could straddle it. "No kidding. So now you're a Jesus freak."

Jinxi stood, bumping the table in her haste. Coffee sloshed over the side of her mug. "No, it's not like that." She turned to find a rag to clean up the spilled coffee.

As she wiped the table, Ron grabbed her wrist in a tight squeeze. "You haven't been upsetting your mom, have you?"

She shook her head and tried to pull away.

"Good. You better not." He released her with a snort. He indicated her scarred arm. "You and your nasty little habit. You disgust me."

Jinxi looked at her mother, who stared down into her coffee cup.

Jinxi jerked herself free, rushed into her bedroom, and slammed the door. She should never have come. Why did she think it was necessary to talk to her mom? Why did her mom continue to live with that beast?

She sank onto the unmade bed, whispering a prayer.

"Why am I here? What do you want from me?" Tears gathered in the corners of her eyes. Her mom's careless dismissal of the most important decision she'd ever made stung. What did she expect, anyway? When had Mom ever really cared?

"God, why couldn't I have a mom like Janice?" Jinxi bent over at the waist as tears dripped off her chin, wetting her jeans.

"I can't do this, God." She wiped her face with the heels of her hands, then pawed through her backpack, searching for the knife that offered solace from the pain. The stuffed bunny was tossed carelessly onto the bed, followed by each article of clothing, and finally, her wallet. The knife lay nestled in a seam in the bottom of the backpack.

Frantic, she stuffed everything back into the pack, slinging it over her shoulder. Time to bounce. This trip had been an epic fail.

In the living room, Ron and her mom had started to argue.

Ron sat in the worn recliner. "When do you get paid? I need money."

Her mom looked even smaller than she had half hour ago. "I told you I won't get paid until Friday. When do you get your unemployment check?"

Ron snorted. "It's gone. I used the money to replace that tire on your car, remember?"

They looked up as Jinxi stomped into the living room.

"Where do you think you're going?" Ron demanded.

Jinxi focused only on her mother. "Mom, I'm leaving now."

Her mom looked up with watery eyes. "Leaving? Where you going? You just got here." Her forehead creased.

"I'm going back to Sacramento. Remember, it's where I live now, and I gotta get back to my job." Jinxi spied the open bottle of bourbon on the end table. Realization struck. Her mother drank more than coffee.

Ron laughed. "Good. You should leave. Go back to your God-loving friends. We don't need you here. You've always been a pain in the—"

"Bye, Mom." Jinxi walked to her mom and kissed her on the cheek. The words "I love you" stuck in her throat, and she left them there. Jinxi bit her lip to keep herself from responding to the man her mother had chosen over her.

Her mom grabbed Jinxi's arm. "Wait. Don't go, baby. Ron was kidding. Weren't you, Ron, honey?" She threw an imploring look at him. He shook his head and snickered.

Jinxi took a last look around the place she'd called home for most of her life. As the door closed behind her, a sense of peace settled on her. In walking out, she'd done the right thing.

Jinxi reached the Greyhound bus station after changing city buses twice and walking nearly two miles in the heat. The return ticket she'd purchased in Sacramento, tucked into the outer pouch, rested against the note to Janice. She pulled it out to read again while waiting for the bus.

"Bus 709 leaving for Sacramento in five minutes," came the announcement over the loudspeaker. Jinxi took the opportunity to use the restroom.

"Now boarding Bus 709 for Sacramento."

The blaring announcement over the speakers hustled her steps. Jinxi found a seat, plugged in earbuds, closed her eyes, and leaned back.

Her mind danced over the past twenty-four hours and the mistake of trying to reconnect with her mom. Why couldn't she have had a normal mom? With a grim smile, she wondered how it would have been to have Robin as a sister. Or Dean as a brother.

Dean. Her stomach twisted. What to do about his accusation?

Plan A. Go back to Janice's and tell her everything. Throw herself on Janice's mercy and pray for grace.

Plan B. Keep going past Sacramento to somewhere else. Use Janice's money to start over. Maybe even change her name so no one would find her. Not even Dean and his police connections. And definitely hide from Skeeter.

The rolling motion lulled her into an uneasy sleep. She startled awake when the bus jerked to a halt.

"Rest stop." The driver stood and stretched before opening the door.

Jinxi followed the other passengers down the aisle and out into the bright sunshine. A family had set up a table on the grass next to the restrooms to sell strawberries. Two months ago, she never would have considered buying fresh fruit. Now her mouth watered. A basket of strawberries would go down good in this heat.

"How much?" She dug into her backpack for her wallet.

"Four dollars for one basket. Twenty for a half flat." The plump mother rose to her feet and spread her hands over the fruit. "We grow them." Pride shown in her eyes and her gesture.

Jinxi knew the feeling. Creating food for someone else to enjoy filled her with satisfaction she'd never known before working at the food bank. Would she ever feel that again?

She dug around for her wallet and pulled it out. The backpack landed at her feet with a thud. She snapped open the wallet, intent on finding a five-dollar bill. Instead, her fingers came up empty. A swoop of vertigo hit. Her money was gone.

CHAPTER 54

Janice struggled into a short-sleeved blouse, preparing for her Widow's Club meeting. The radio tuned to a Christian station played softly in the background. The house was too quiet without Jinxi. The rooms sounded hollow. Though Jinxi left for work early each morning, the house had been full, until today. Even Ted was curled up at Dean's place, out of the heat.

A song by Michael W. Smith came on the radio, and she paused to listen to the lyrics about running blind on the wheels of faith.

Wonder how Jinxi's doing with her mom? As the chorus began, the urge to pray overcame her, an undeniable force. Words poured out of her like water. Before she knew it, twenty minutes had passed, and she sat back, exhausted as if she had fought a battle.

The cacophony of the police station assaulted Dean's ears as he pushed through the door. Someone had burned the coffee again. The sharp smell made his eyes water. He sighed with contentment to be back at work after a drama-filled week at home. His fists clenched as he remembered finding Jinxi holding his mother's earrings. He'd trusted her. That galled him more than anything. They'd given her a place to stay, food to eat, all without asking anything in return. For that, she'd betrayed them. Dean mentally kicked himself for the umpteenth time for taking her to meet his friends. He was an idiot. Where was his cop's sixth sense? Why hadn't he seen this coming? And to think he actually liked her. Had almost kissed her.

Filled with disgust, he shuddered.

"Hey, Dean, how was your time off?" a fellow officer asked. "Ready to start patrol?"

Dean chose to answer the second question. "I'm readier than ready. I was born ready." He grinned, shoving thoughts of Jinxi into a hidden inner vault that had no key.

The bus pulled up in front of the station with a jerk. Jinxi struggled down the steps, legs stiff. Hoisting the backpack over her shoulder, she studied the local bus schedule. At least she had a few dollars in her pocket. She wouldn't have to walk to Janice's.

On the bus, her thoughts hammered like a fist to her head. After removing everything from her backpack and searching every pocket, the only conclusion was her money had been stolen. By who? Ron? Totally possible. Then she remembered her mother's words.

Your friend Skeeter came by. Said he had something for you.

Right. Like he'd give her a gift. Why hadn't she taken her pack into the bathroom when she'd showered?

Why hadn't God protected her?

A few vagrants approached asking for spare change, but Jinxi dismissed them with a shake of her head. No money. Nothing but an empty wallet and an empty soul.

This God-Jesus-church thing didn't work. And why should it? Jinxi slumped down on a bench inside the bus station. The plan she'd made on the bus wasn't going to fly. It was one thing to tell Janice everything and hand her a wad of bills. It was another to expect Janice to believe her ex-boyfriend took the money.

Time for a new plan. First, she'd head back to Janice's, sneak in and grab the rest of her stuff before heading out of town.

She'd given everything to God, and what had she gotten in return? Accused by Dean. Robbed by Skeeter. Now Janice would probably hate her.

What was the saying about insanity? Doing the same thing over and over, expecting a different result. Why should she keep trying to do the right thing, when the result ended up broken. Her life was doomed from birth. *Suck it up, buttercup.*

Jinxi struggled to her feet. She'd use the restroom before heading out.

A woman and a little girl stood near one of the sinks. As she entered the stall, she couldn't help but overhear their conversation.

"Mommy, I'm scared. What if Grandpa doesn't like me?"

"Angel, he's going to love you. He promised. Let's pray."

Jinxi tried to close her ears to the words, but they pierced her heart. Words like grace, forgiveness, and hope wafted into her spirit. She finished her business and dashed from the restroom without slowing down to wash her hands.

The late afternoon temperature had dropped to bearable as she strode away from the station. A police cruiser slowed as it passed. Jinxi increased her speed, keeping tempo with her thumping heart. The cruiser kept pace with her. Head down, she turned the corner. The car followed.

The window of the car rolled down. A voice shouted, "Hey! Get in the car."

Weak with relief, Jinxi saw Dean's head hanging out of the passenger window.

She approached as Dean jumped out to open the back of the patrol car. “Of course, I’ll have to cuff you first.”

She froze mid-step. Was he serious? Probably. She deserved that and so much more.

The driver of the police car pulled his sunglasses down. Jinxi felt the intensity of his gaze, like a laser pointed at her heart. His black hair was buzzed short like Dean’s.

“Jinxi, this is my partner, Mike. Mike, this is Jinxi. She’s a ...” He waved his hand toward her without finishing the sentence. “I’m training in preparation for going on patrol duty. What are you doing down here? I thought you were at your mom’s.”

“Well, I’m back.”

He raised his eyebrows. “Quick trip. We’ll drop you off at the house.” He leaned toward her and whispered, his breath hot against her cheek. “You know what you have to do.”

Yeah, she knew what she had to do.

The squad car carrying Dean and his partner pulled away from the curb in front of Janice’s house. A hot blast of exhaust warmed Jinxi’s legs as she stood on the sidewalk, watching them drive off.

As she’d exited the car, Dean had taken the opportunity to lean toward her again. “Don’t forget. You’ve got something to tell my mom.”

Jinxi trudged up the front porch steps and unlocked the door. Janice’s car was gone.

The decision that had been brewing in the back of her mind on the long bus ride from Bakersfield came to fruition as she looked around the familiar living room. The faint smell of Janice’s lavender fabric softener wafted through the air as she mounted the stairs, steps slowing as she reached the top.

With a sigh of resignation, she dropped the backpack on the bed and pulled her meager belongings from the dresser drawers, stuffing them into the pack. The photo of her parents went into the side pocket. She left the cookbook, binder, and apron in the middle of the bed.

There was no room for the food cache she'd kept in the bottom drawer of the dresser. She ran downstairs, retrieved a grocery bag from the pantry, and jogged back up, panting from exertion. Once everything was packed, she looked around the room, remembering her time here. What had she been thinking? Staying here would never have worked out in the long run. The God thing wasn't for her. Bad things would continue to happen to her because she was, at her very core, broken.

Now that Janice's money was gone, she'd never be able to face her. She'd be better off hitting the road to someplace far away before Janice discovered the theft and booted her out. Or had her arrested. By Dean. Wouldn't he just love to put handcuffs on her and throw her in jail. This time, no fooling.

Tears gathered in the corners of her eyes, threatening to escape. Clamping her teeth together, she turned and headed downstairs, feet clomping on each step.

A new photo of Hannah sat on the top of the piano. She paused, touching the frame with her finger. Unshed tears closed her throat. *I love you, Jinxi.* The words echoed in her ears as she stumbled toward the front door.

Ted stood on the porch, tail wagging in anticipation of being let into the cool house.

"No, Ted. Not today." His tail drooped a few inches as he nosed her hand. His coarse fur tickled her cheek as she bent down to hug him one final time.

She stood, straightened her shoulders, and headed for the bus stop.

Janice stared unblinking at the black computer screen. She held a note in her hand, written on yellow tablet paper. The back door opened, and Dean's footsteps pounded in the kitchen.

"Hello? Anyone home?"

"In here." Janice choked out the words, her chest tight with grief.

Dean rounded the corner to her office and stopped. He wore a loose T-shirt and gym shorts. "What's going on? Where's Jinxi?" He bent over to straighten the laces on his sneakers.

Janice waved the note under his nose, unable to speak. He straightened, and she watched his face turn white, then red. "That ... that ... she can't—" He thrust the paper back to her.

Janice took a moment to reread the note. "Janice, I'm so sorry, but I can't stay here anymore. Thank you for everything. Jinxi."

"I knew it," Dean exploded. "She couldn't face you because she stole your earrings. Probably sold them for drugs or something." He crossed his arms over his chest, his look murderous.

Janice slumped in her chair as she looked up at him. "She didn't take my earrings."

"Of course she did. I caught her with them." Dean's voice shook with righteous indignation.

"No, son, you're wrong. Hannah took them. Hannah."

"What are you talking about?"

Janice put a hand to her throbbing head. "Robin and Hannah were here yesterday. Hannah wanted to play the Hidden Treasure game again. It's where we hide something for the other to find. The last time we played, I'd let her use some old costume jewelry." She rubbed her right arm, trying to massage away the pain from the spider bite.

"Yesterday Hannah asked me if I'd found the 'secret hidden treasure.' I didn't know what she was talking about. She ran upstairs, apparently to Jinxi's bedroom, and came down with the earrings."

Dean dropped his face into his hands, groaning. "Oh, no. This is all my fault."

"What do you mean?" Janice searched his face.

Dean lowered his hands, a look of dismay on his face. "I told Jinxi she had until today to confess to you that she'd stolen the earrings. Or else."

"Or else what?"

He shrugged. "I don't know. I swear I thought she'd tell you and be done with it. I didn't think through the rest." He rubbed the back of his neck. "What are we going to do?"

"We're not going to do anything. Jinxi is in God's hands, and he's not surprised by this. We need to stay out of the way and let him do what he needs to do."

Dean groaned again. "I've ruined everything. You told me to stay out of it, and I ignored you. I should have listened to you." He lowered himself onto the chair opposite her.

They stared at each other wordlessly. The grandfather clock in the hallway chimed eight long chords.

Janice pushed herself up from the chair. "God told me to love Jinxi unconditionally. I've endeavored to do so. I won't say it hasn't been difficult. Especially with ..." Her voice trailed off. Dean didn't yet know the fullness of it all. Of what she knew.

"With what?"

"There's more than the missing earrings." She returned to her seat. "Remember when your dad died."

Dean nodded, his look quizzical.

"You know he had life insurance, right?"

Dean nodded.

"I also got a sizeable settlement from the construction company after your father was killed in the accident."

"What does this have to do with Jinxi?"

Janice sighed. "I'm getting to that."

CHAPTER 55

The heavy backpack slid from Jinxi's fingers as she dropped it on the sidewalk at the bus stop. She set the grocery bag next to it. Rubbing her hands up and down her arms, she asked herself again if she was doing the right thing.

She tried bargaining with God.

If you give me a sign, I'll go back and confess. I'll spend the rest of my life paying Janice back.

A bus drove by on the opposite side of the street. The ad on the side read, "Fresh, organic beef. It's what's for dinner."

That wasn't helpful.

How did everything get so complicated? All she'd wanted was a place to belong. Someplace safe. She'd messed up big time. Her eyes took in the world around her. An old man, his face weathered but kind, stood near her. He slumped against a STOP sign. She blinked at it. Once. Twice.

Come on, God. Something. Anything. A sign, and I don't mean about beef. Or a stop—

A dog's bark jolted her concentration. She turned fully to see Ted racing up the street toward her. What the—? She must have left the gate open. She squatted as he approached and then reached her, nearly bowling her over with enthusiasm.

Tears began to fall as he eagerly licked her face. "Oh, Teddy, Teddy."

A chuckle from the old man brought her eyes to his. "When God can't be everywhere, he sends a dog," he said.

Jinxi buried her face in Ted's fur. "How could I leave you, Ted? And Hannah?"

Ted nuzzled her chin, lifting her head upward to where the old man had stood.

He was gone.

The doorbell rang, interrupting the silence that hung between her and Dean.

"Who could that be?" Janice asked, getting to her feet. She walked into the living room and opened the door, Dean on her heels.

Jinxi stood on the welcome mat, tears dripping off her chin. She held a paper grocery sack in one hand. The other clamped Ted's collar.

"I'm sorry," she sobbed.

Janice pulled her into an embrace, like a mother hen gathering a wayward chick. She backed up, closing the door with her foot. "Shhh, it's all right. Everything's all right."

"I—I didn't take your earrings." Jinxi looked over Janice's shoulder at Dean. "I really didn't."

"I know, I know," Janice soothed. "Hannah was playing a game. She hid them in your room." Janice glanced over her shoulder at Dean to see if he was going to say anything.

He tugged at the neck of his T-shirt. "I guess I owe you an apology." He stared at the floor.

Jinxi sobbed in earnest. "No." She pulled away from Janice. "There's something I have to tell you."

Janice put her hands on Jinxi's shoulders. "You don't have to say a thing."

"Yes, I do." She nodded, hair bouncing. Taking a deep breath, she continued, "I took some money—"

"I know."

Her mouth dropped open and snapped closed. "You *know?*" Jinxi's voice was incredulous.

Janice nodded.

"But—"

Janice's smile, sweetened by Christ's love, spread across her face. "I've known all along."

Jinxi took a step back and threw up her hands. "How can you ever forgive me? I can't repay all that money. My ex-boyfriend stole all of my—your—money while I was down there. All I have is a few dollars from my last paycheck."

Janice stepped toward her and grasped her arms. "I figure if God can forgive us for all the things we've done, I can forgive you. A very good friend once asked me, 'What is the price for a person's soul?'"

"You took money from my mom?" Dean's voice held disbelief. "Maybe I should take back that apology." A vein throbbed in his neck.

Janice looked over her shoulder toward him. "That's not important. What's important is Jinxi came back."

"But the money—" His cop eyes bore into Jinxi's.

Janice turned to answer.

"It's not about the money, Dean. I told you God was up to something greater." She put an arm around Jinxi. "Let's get something to eat while we explain everything to him, okay?"

Jinxi tucked her hair behind her ears. "Are you sure?"

Janice nodded.

Jinxi gazed at the room, at the abundance of lace, the worn sofa, the photos on the piano. The house wrapped itself around her, settling against her heart as warm as Janice's arm around her shoulders. The house breathed messages of comfort to her, whispering of safety and peace.

At last, she had come home.

Two weeks later

Jinxi glanced over to where Janice sat, eyes closed, in an Adirondack chair in the shade of the oak tree.

"Don't forget the extra napkins," Janice called.

Jinxi and Dean glanced at each other and grinned. They'd set up a folding table in the back yard for their monthly pizza night. Dean patted the two rolls of paper towels he'd brought from the house. "Got it covered, Mom."

Jinxi pulled her phone from the back pocket of her jeans and checked the time. "The pizzas should be here any minute. Your siblings better not be late."

Janice pushed herself out of the chair and padded toward them. "That's right. They better be on time. We have a lot to celebrate."

"Yeah, you got your cast off," Dean said.

"And you got your wish of being on patrol duty," Jinxi added.

"And Hannah is doing better," Dean said.

"And you have a permanent job." Janice smiled at Jinxi. "And Courtney is pregnant." The minute the words escaped her mouth, Janice slapped a palm to her forehead. "Mercy. I wasn't supposed to say anything."

"Our lips are sealed, right, Jinxi?"

Jinxi nodded. "Not a peep from me. Besides, I have an announcement to make."

Janice and Dean looked at her expectantly.

"I quit smoking." Jinxi grinned. Janice and Dean exploded with whoops and laughter.

"Good for you!" Janice grabbed her in a bear hug.

"Awesome!" Dean said.

The sound of car doors opening and slam-closing echoed across the grass. Janice strode toward the front of the house to greet the rest of her family.

Dean leaned in close and whispered in Jinxi's ear. "I'm glad you quit smoking. The next time I try to kiss you, I won't have to fight through a haze of smoke."

"Try?" Jinxi grinned up at him. "You better do better than *try*, Officer."

The moment was interrupted by Hannah's over-the-top joyous greeting and Ted's frantic barking.

Jinxi's heart warmed at the sounds of the family gathering around to celebrate some pretty cool stuff. For the first time, her future looked bright. Even the sound of a motorcycle revving in the distance couldn't diminish the peace she'd finally found. She was loved. She was accepted.

She was home.

ABOUT THE AUTHOR

After a career in banking, Jane Daly is living her dream of traveling the United States in her motor home. She's the author of two nonfiction books and one novel, The Girl in the Cardboard Box. She's written numerous articles and blogs, but her heart is in creating stories about women facing difficult and even impossible circumstances, emerging scarred but triumphant.

When she's not hunched over her computer, she can be found making new friends in whichever state she finds herself.

To everyone who has read and recommended this book—thank you! The best way to help me is to leave a review on Amazon, Goodreads, and Barnes and Noble.

You can sign up for my newsletter at

https://adept-trailblazer-1187.ck.page/bc6f6a4676 OR www.janeSdaly.com. Follow me on Facebook, Twitter, and Instagram.

If you've enjoyed *Broken*, you'll love *Broken Silence* … Chapter One follows for your reading pleasure.

CHAPTER 1

Jinxi Lansing stopped at the bottom of the stairs, listening to the silence. The old house seemed to be holding its breath. Even the normal creaking and groaning had ceased.

Goosebumps broke out on her arms. She jumped when Ted woofed from behind.

"Sorry, buddy, I know you need to go outside."

She dumped her backpack on the wooden kitchen table and opened the back door. Ted dashed out, making a beeline to his favorite tree. Rubbing her hands up and down her sweatshirt-clad arms, Jinxi couldn't shake the feeling something was wrong. Two-plus decades of vulnerability made her hyper-aware of the smallest change in the atmosphere.

Why wasn't Janice up yet? Jinxi's friend, mentor, and spiritual mom usually woke with the sun. A cursory glance around the kitchen indicated nothing had been disturbed, plus the fact that the coffee maker sat dark. Jinxi pushed the button to start the morning's brew, then headed down the short, dark hall to Janice's bedroom.

"Janice?" Jinxi's voice echoed in the silence. Sheets and blankets formed a messy wad at the end of Janice's bed. "Janice?"

The bathroom door was open, the room empty.

Nerves skittered up Jinxi's spine. She returned to the kitchen, then stomped into the living room. Fear and anger bartered for position. Janice never went anywhere without leaving a yellow sticky note.

Gone to WalMart—back soon

Coffee is ready to brew—just turn it on

Sandwiches in fridge—Help yourself

Janice's car was absent from the driveway. The Queen of Sticky Notes had left without letting Jinxi know. Of course, she did. Janice didn't owe Jinxi a thing.

Old feelings like knife jabs pierced Jinxi's heart. After six months of having Jinxi in her home, Janice probably tired of having to constantly let her know where she was. Maybe it was time to move on.

One thing Jinxi knew for sure, relationships were transactional. You do this for me, I do that for you. Maybe letting Jinxi know where Janice had gone wasn't part of the agreement.

Jinxi returned to the kitchen and poured a cup of coffee. As she sipped, she eyed the knife rack on the counter. Familiar craving crawled over her skin. One little slice and she'd feel better. Or would she?

Ted clawed at the back door. As Jinxi let him in, the sound of a car door slamming had her heading back to the living room.

"Where were you?" Jinxi demanded when Janice unlocked the door and stepped into the house.

"I, uh ..." Janice pushed the door closed with tear-filled eyes.

Alarm bells sounded in Jinxi's ears, drowning out everything except Janice's ragged breathing. Janice's short gray hair was a tangled mess, and her sweater was buttoned wrong.

"You should have left me a note." Jinxi's words fell into the empty space between them like shattered glass. She crossed her arms, determined to hold onto the hurt.

"Merciful heavens. I'm sorry." Janice set her purse on an end table, then shrugged out of her sweater, tossing it onto her favorite chair. "I got a call. I left in a hurry."

Leaves chattered against the living room windows, blown from the trees by a gust of wind. Jinxi watched them swirl. A rock of fear in her stomach pulled her down to slump onto one of the dining room chairs.

"What kind of a call?"

"Dean ..." Janice choked back a sob, one hand fisted to her trembling lips.

Jinxi's world tilted. Images flew through her mind. Scenes of Janice's son, Dean, teasing her, chasing Ted around the yard, throwing his niece, Hannah, into the air. She heard him yelling at her, their argument, trying to get him to forgive her. She bit her lip hard enough to draw blood. "Is he ... dead?"

Janice's breath caught. "Goodness, no. But he's in a coma. He fell and hit his head."

In her mind, Jinxi saw herself run to Janice and hug her, giving and receiving comfort. But her legs were wooden, body frozen to the seat. How could she extend comfort when she'd never received it?

"You should have left a note," Jinxi said, sniffing away the tears threatening to push their way past her burning eyes.

"I'm sorry," Janice repeated, her voice a monotone. "I have to call Brian. And Robin." Her hands dropped to her sides as she shuffled toward her bedroom.

"Wait." Jinxi stood, shoving the wooden chair back under the table. "Where is he? Can I see him?"

"Sacramento General, downtown. I don't know if they'll let anyone in who's not family."

Family. Which Jinxi was not. She heard the finality of Janice's bedroom door clicking shut.

The grandfather clock in the living room chimed, a sharp reminder she'd be late for work. She retreated to the kitchen for a drink of water to wash away the metallic taste of her blood. The coffee mug she'd used sat in the sink. After gulping some water, she slammed the cup down hard enough to crack it, then, not satisfied, she banged the cup down again and again. It shattered into jagged pieces, and the handle slipped off her fingers and clattered into the sink.

She rested her arms on the counter, gripping the edge of the sink with bloodless knuckles.

Enjoy Jane's novel, The Girl in the Cardboard Box.

Made in the USA
Middletown, DE
10 July 2022